TERRA

TRACY KORN

Cover Design Copyright © 2018 by James Korn
Photography by J.Korn Photographics
www.jkornphoto.com
ISBN 978-1-946202-69-7
www.TheElementsSeries.com
Library of Congress Control Number: 2016907714
Edited by Ryan Bachtel, Rachel Carpenter, and Michelle Phillips

Summary: Getting out of Gaia Sur was almost as hard as getting in, but there's no going back now. Jazwyn Ripley and her friends have no choice but to venture into the caves and tunnels underneath the ocean floor as the messages they've been receiving get stronger. Tensions rise and loyalties are tested when another of their crew is captured along the way, and one critical choice means following unlikely allies down a path most would never dare —across the seven biomes of the "Rush"—which, if they survive, will either lead to freedom or imprison them forever.
In the center, the only way out is through.

Second Trade Paperback Edition
Printed in the United States of America

Snowy Wings
PUBLISHING
Turner, OR

For my mom,
who always encouraged me to make my own path.

PORT OF ORIGIN: SEABOARD NORTH

NAME	CLASSIFICATION	CAREER TRACK
Jazwyn Ripley	Reader Empath/Coder	Diplomacy
Jaxon Ripley	Omnicoder	Molecular Encoding
Arco Hart	Navigator/Coder*	Astronavigation
Liddick Wright	Reader Empath/Coder	Diplomacy
Vox Dyer	Reader Empath/Nav	Diplomacy
Fraya Clearmore	Coder/Projector Empath	Biodesign Primary
Myra Toll	Projector Empath	Biodesign Auxiliary
Ellis Raj	Navigator/Coder	Astronavigation
Avis Ling	Navigator/Coder	Astronavigation
Joss Tether	Navigator	Astronavigation

*Latency: Receiver Empath

PORT OF ORIGIN: SKYBOARD NORTH

NAME	CLASSIFICATION	CAREER TRACK
Pitt Spaulding	Omnicoder	Molecular Encoding
Tieg Spaulding	Navigator/Coder	Astronavigation
Dez Spaulding	Rec. Empath/Coder	Biodesign Primary

PRIOR CADET CLASS

NAME	CLASSIFICATION	CAREER TRACK
Liam Wright	Coder/Navigator	Biodesign Primary
Lyden Wright	Reader Empath/Coder	Quantum Programming
Arwyn Hart	Coder/Receiver Empath	Biodesign Primary

VISHAN

Jove Singer	Veece Singer	Cal Shepherd
Flora Singer	Liv Singer	Kora Shepherd
Vita Dyer	Ada Spring	Myka Scribe
Carr Shepherd	Axel Fisher	Rav Dyer

BADLANDERS

Dell Marchand	Jesse Gavin	Zoe Frank
Kesh Foley	Azeris Frank	Calliope Wyld
Ty Archer	Ghost Archer	Alec Farr
"General"		

"I shall either find a way or make one."

~ Hannibal

CHAPTER 1
Surfacing

I hear the splash of my footfalls, but I can't see where they're landing as I force damp, heavy air into my lungs, then taste the tang of seawater on my lips. Wayward grains of sand scrape the inside of my cheek, and my chest tightens as the narrow stone walls of the tunnel seem to close in on me.

Stop tweaking…you have to stop tweaking, I tell myself, then crush the sand between my teeth as if this will prove that I can still control at least one thing between the flashes of what has happened over the last few hours.

I squeeze my eyes shut against the images, but they play too quickly backward to the beginning—to Pitt stepping into the zipper-like mouths of the undulating black creature that surfaced in the air bell…the lesions from the poisonous spores appearing on his neck after Tieg had to sever two of Pitt's fingers to free him from the Leviathan's docking gate just before that…just before the Leviathan self-destructed and launched us end over end toward the seafloor entry vent in the first place. Everything before then seems like a virtuo-cine—a role-play experience to escape everyday life—and maybe that's all the dream of getting into Gaia and making a future for ourselves ever really was.

I nearly fall as my boot slips on the slick tunnel floor, but Arco's arm tightens around my shoulder and steadies me. "We need to get to higher ground!" he shouts to Avis, who is at the front of our group. "Can you get a scan?"

"There's a system above this air bell!" Avis calls back to us. "We'll need to squeeze through up ahead where it's more stable, but then we're clear."

His voice seems far away, muffled somehow, and I wonder if this is what shock must feel like. The Leviathan *actually* imploded, which means Ms. Rheen and Mr. Styx had to figure out we were trying to escape from Gaia. Maybe even Dr. Denison and Mr. Tark too—maybe all the teachers just let us walk right into the trap like Liddick said. *They knew we'd try to leave, but did they know why? Do they know we survived?* I think, but when Liddick doesn't answer, I wonder if our telepathy still works out here.

The walls in this tunnel don't glow blue like the ones in the air bell. Instead, they're slippery like the ground and shiny in the light of our shoulder lamps, but this isn't because they're wet.

"These drips are *alive!*" Myra cries out a few feet in front of me as she sees the rivulets shifting directions and pulling away from the wall like they're reaching for us, each of them as if drawn by a magnet.

"Don't touch them! Just keep moving!" Ellis shouts back as he disappears through the opening ahead, and I can't bring myself to look at the slippery ground.

"Are you hurt?" Arco asks, pulling me away from the thousands of clear, gel-like worms trying to latch onto us. "You fell hard when Liddick shoved you through that crevice back there," he adds.

I try to focus on what's happening right now, but *crite,* an hour ago Arco was unconscious, and we were pulling him from the wreckage of the imploded Leviathan.

"I'm OK, are *you*? Are your nanites finished working?" I ask.

"Almost," he says with a cough, and my heart seizes.

"Arco…why did you cough? Pitt was coughing before the spores started to…" I trail off and grip the side of his dive suit as the panic swells in my chest, which only catapults when he winces in a whole body jerk and sucks in a sharp breath through his teeth. "Wh—? Is that your ribs?" I ask, my voice pitching. "Dez's scanner didn't pick up anything there when we brought you out of the Stingray…"

"*It's OK,*" he tries to laugh as we get ready to duck through the opening that appears like a rip in the dark walls, which are now mercifully free of the water tube animals. "I've had worse from wrestling your gorilla brother," he says, gesturing to his side with a half smile. "Come on, we need to go in sideways. Keep your head level."

I take off my supply bag and push it through the fissure, then maneuver through the opening with Arco right behind me. On the other side, Avis stands to the right of a running stream in the dim, blue light of a glow rod someone has thrown to the ground while Ellis aims another blue light from his Nav system over the walls.

Avis angles the equipment on his arm toward the wall at his side, then waves us in. "There's a tunnel that winds up through that hole where the water is coming in, and one that winds down through where it's flowing out," he says, flipping the blue edged wing of black hair out of his eyes. "There must be a source pushing this current from above. We'll have to sync the sweep map with the terrain to see which route to take. With any luck, we won't have to go upstream."

"Here," Arco says, handing Avis the rectangular silver panel, which is embedded with the sweep map Pitt was able to save. Avis inserts it into his Nav system. "We'll stop for a while and rest, then start out fresh in the morning. Is everyone all right?" Arco cracks another glow rod against his leg, and the added blue light illuminates the rest of our group against a curved dark wall that bows out to our right. The cave seems to be the same striated rock as the other side of the opening we've all just come through, and every surface is smooth like beach stones.

"That water must have run all the way through here at one point," I say, retracting my glove and reaching for the stone, but I stop abruptly when Ellis shouts.

"*Jazz!* Don't touch that!" he warns as he reads something on his Nav screen. I jerk my hand away, startled, and wait for the explanation that he takes his time delivering. "All right, it's clean. Sorry, I had to make sure there weren't any spor—" he stops himself and darts a look at Dez and Tieg, "…that there weren't any toxins in here," he adds, pressing his thin lips into a line, and my stomach sinks with the realization that he's rewording because he doesn't want to add any reference of what happened to Pitt in front of them.

"Looks like we're heading down," Avis says with a sigh of relief. "We have about 18 miles to hike to get to the source of the messages. It's a tight squeeze for about 25 yards, but then it opens into a wider channel. We caught a break…for now," he adds before shutting down his Nav system and finding a spot to curl into against the wall near Ellis and the others.

Ellis crosses his long arms under his head and lies on his back a few feet away, but as tired and rattled as we all are, there is too much unsaid and unsettled for anyone to drift off. Dez sits next to Tieg in the blue light of the glow rods, tears streaming down her pale cheeks as she turns into her brother. He puts his arm around her, closing his eyes under a furrowed brow, and the sight of them in so much pain reaches into my chest and squeezes.

I look away from them only to see Myra standing just a dozen feet away, still hopefully watching the fissure for Pitt until Joss puts his hands on her shoulders and starts talking to her, his light eyebrows raised and his expression gentle. She starts shaking her head slowly after a second, then adamantly as he draws her against his chest, despite her pushing at him in denial of what he's evidently just told her: Pitt isn't coming back.

I start to go to her, but stop myself when Jax crosses behind Arco and me and takes a seat against the wall. He props his elbows on his knees, then clasps his hands behind his neck as he looks at the ground, and my stomach sinks.

"*Jax…*" I say, the weight of everyone's combined grief getting progressively heavier as we all start gathering in the same small space. I have to say something to alleviate it. "You did everything you could," I add, kneeling next to him and threading my arm through his.

"It should have been me," he says under his breath. "I should have gone back for the sweep map instead of him."

"That wouldn't have stopped him from getting his hand caught in the hydraulics," I whisper, careful not to let Dez or Tieg hear the details of their brother's accident recounted. "No one could have known when they would lock out during the self-destruct." I close my eyes against the memory of Pitt's scream over our helmet comms and the vision of him struggling to free his hand in the mouth of the Stingray gate as ribbons of blood wrapped all around him and Tieg, who finally ran out of options as the Leviathan's self-destruct counted down.

Arco moves behind me to clap a hand on Jax's shoulder. I feel his other hand slide over my back as Myra takes a step toward us with Joss, then sits down with him, her Empath projection abilities saturating everything with a suffocating grief. Liddick must feel it wash over too because he immediately tries to offset it.

"Myra...I'm so sorry," he nearly whispers, his expression wrenched as he takes a seat next to her against the charcoal colored stone wall, and for the briefest of seconds, I feel a flutter of relief.

"He said he was fine. He said he would be right behind us," Myra says, flashes of a still hopeful smile interrupting the quivering of her lips.

"He wanted to make sure you'd be safe," Joss says, angling his chin down to catch her wide blue eyes. When she looks up at him, he wraps his arms around her and pulls her close before leaning his head against the wall behind them. She looks so small and fragile sitting with him like this, especially when her tears begin spilling over her cheeks, and her nearly invisible brows draw in just before she tries to speak again.

"That's why he wouldn't kiss me—why he wouldn't even let me get close to him just before he sent us on?" she asks, almost to herself. Joss takes a deep breath and nods, pushing one hand through his nearly white blond hair, which seems to glow against the dark rock in the dim, blue light.

"He didn't want there to be any chance that you could get infected too," he says, looking down at her and wiping her tears away. She curls into him as both hers and Dez's sobs break free, and the already heavy air in the little cave begins reverberating in my teeth. I glance at Liddick, his eyebrows drawing together and the muscles in his jaw tightening against the *thrum*, as he said Ms. Reynolt called it—this static of everyone's emotions mixing all at once.

Liddick…I think as he scrubs his hands over his face, then meets my eyes. His are stormy and desperate as he presses his lips together into a hard line and swallows, then pulls in a deep breath like he's going to dive into the stream and swim as far away from here as he can.

In this minute, despite whatever I've decided about being more than friends with him, the relief that he can still hear my thoughts is so strong that it holds back the anxiety rushing at me from everywhere else. It makes me want to go to him because he's the only other person who can feel the chaos like I can, and I want to hold onto him through the storm of it just like when he kissed me after his port-carnate debacle—when it felt like we'd jumped off a cliff without fearing the fall because there's a comfort in knowing that however scary something is, at least there's always this connection…this one solid thing that reminds us we're not alone.

Instinctively feeling all this when things spin out is also infuriating, though, because I've already *made* the decision about being with him. It's not fair to Arco, it's not fair to anyone who cares about me, and *crite* it would be great if everything inside me would jack in with that.

I squeeze my eyes shut again and press my palms against them like I'm trying to hold this perspective in place long enough for it to stick, but I look up again when Jax stands abruptly. He walks to the little stream across from us to put a gloved hand in the water to refill his suit's desalinator. Arco's arm moves around my shoulders and pulls me toward him as Dez starts talking.

"He tried to flush Pitt's wounds when we first surfaced…when I was prepping the disinfectant," she says in an absent voice that cracks at the edges while she watches Jax. "He must have used all his water." Her head falls to Tieg's shoulder, and he closes his eyes in a long blink, then swallows hard.

"I should have looked for another way…found a tool or something to force his hand loose," Tieg says after a minute. "I'm so sorry, Dezzie."

She looks up at him and shakes her head as she opens, then closes her mouth, seemingly unable to gather the right words to let him know that she doesn't blame him for their brother's death.

"It was already too late by then," she manages, and I feel her frustration with herself rising in desperation to say *something* to help ease his guilt. Liddick must sense this too because he steadies himself and starts to lean in toward them.

"It was the only choice you had, Spaulding. He knew there was no other way out. But you gave him a chance to say goodbye. He wouldn't have had that without you," Liddick says. Tieg lowers his head at this, and a wave of grief pushes up through me like a geyser, then stops hard as my throat constricts and seals off the pressure like a hose suddenly bent in half. In the same second everything inside me shifts, and Tieg explodes onto his feet.

"We never should have helped you in the first place!" he growls, taking quick, purposeful strides toward Liddick, who doesn't have enough time to get completely to his feet before Tieg shoves him back into the stone wall. "None of this is our problem! We shouldn't even be here!" he shouts, taking advantage of his leverage and squeezing Liddick's throat with one hand, the other gripping the front of his dive suit and pinning him in place. Liddick struggles to push him off, but between the angle of the hold and Tieg's Skyboard select gene pool making him even more densely muscled than Jax and Joss, while Liddick, like Arco, is lean like a swimmer, he can't free himself.

"*No!*" I yell, but don't even realize it until I'm on my feet and rushing toward them.

"Tieg, stop!" Dez screams from somewhere in the distance, which is how everything sounds until my air is forced out of my lungs when an arm hooks around my stomach and pulls me off my feet, then puts me back on the ground. Arco flies in front of me with Jax quickly following, and together they pry Tieg away from Liddick. Tieg is so upset it takes both of them to hold him in place as Liddick coughs and gasps to regulate his airflow.

"Pitt's dead because of you!" Tieg shouts again, lunging against Jax and Arco, who have his arms pinned behind his back. "Because of *all of you!*"

"Tieg! It's not their fault! It's no one's fault. He wanted to help them find their family and their friends—*our* friends!—and so do I," Dez says, now at Liddick's side examining his throat. "Are you OK?" she asks, her voice cracking as she moves her long fingers over his face and neck. Liddick nods, leaning over to brace against his knees as he coughs again.

"It's all right. I'm all right," he whispers, straightening. Ellis and Avis have moved to help Arco and Jax, but Tieg doesn't stop struggling until Jax puts both his huge hands on Tieg's shoulders, locking him down on the wall.

"Listen to me! This isn't helping anything! Remember when you told me that after Fraya disappeared in the cave with Vox? I know how you feel, but this isn't helping. Blaming people just makes it worse," Jax says, looking him in the eyes as Tieg breathes through his teeth. "What happened to Pitt is no one's fault, do you hear me? No one's fault, all right?" Tieg clenches his jaw and looks away, but Jax shakes him and angles his head to line up their eyes again. "*All right?*"

Tieg finally nods in agreement, and I feel something break inside me. *He blames himself...they both blame themselves*, I think as a tear actually makes its way down the side of Tieg's face.

Too bad they can't seem to figure that out until after they tackle someone. Apes. At least we finally got a read on him, though, Liddick says in my head, having overheard my thoughts like he's been doing lately when I don't realize I'm transmitting them, as he calls it. When I look over, he's smiling to one side and rubbing his throat while leaning back into Dez's arms. I return his smile, but the sight of them like this causes a pinch in the hollow behind my jaw. I swallow to push it down because I'm not supposed to react to this—I've *already dealt* with it—but the feeling doesn't clear.

Jax grips the back of Tieg's neck, then slaps him on the shoulder a few times as they move back to their original places along the wall. They both spread out and close their eyes, giving over the rest of their anger, frustration, and guilt to the darkness as Arco crosses back over to me, his arm drawn tightly into his side.

CHAPTER 2
Recovery

"Are you OK?" Arco asks me quietly, then takes my arm and leads me around the bend of the wall to continue talking as everyone settles in. "Did I hurt you?"

"*Hurt me*?"

"When I pulled you back from jumping in the middle of them," he says, the corner of his mouth quirking up. "You know they both have at least forty pounds on you right? Tieg probably sixty," he answers, slipping his Nav system off his arm and putting it on the ground. I raise my chin to him.

"I would have held my own, thank you very much," I say, raising an eyebrow at him and setting down my supply bag from the Stingray, grateful to breathe easily again as the tension in the air dissipates with everyone now too exhausted to do anything but sleep. When I turn back to Arco, he's still smiling at me. "What?" I ask, but he just shakes his head and chuckles, then presses his arm into his side again. "Your ribs *do* hurt!" I say, brushing several loose hairs from my eyes. I try to stare straight through him, but instead of addressing my accusation, Arco lets his free arm slip around my waist and pull me into him as he leans back against the dark cave wall. I feel him wince when my hand moves over his ribs, and I immediately pull back.

"All right, take off your shirt," I say, and his eyes widen as a stupid grin spreads across his face.

"Well, I mean, I thought you'd never ask, but *here*?" he says, raising his brows as he angles his head at me. I roll my eyes.

"Oh, crite, show me your ribs." I pick up my bag again and fish through it for the medical scanner like Dez had —my kit should have one too, although I have no idea how to use it. I peer down the wall to see if Dez might still be awake so I can call her over, but she's fast asleep with her arms still wrapped around Liddick. I feel another sharp twinge when I see them like this again and force my eyes away to refocus on finding the white cylindrical medi-wand. Arco has managed to release the back panel of his dive suit and is just pulling his arms out of the sleeves when I find the wand and look up at him again, his face serious now. "How bad does it hurt?" I ask, but he just shakes his head and shrugs his right shoulder. "*Yeah*, sure," I nod. "Keep going." I angle my head at his jumpsuit, feeling the air suddenly shift as the rushing stream behind us seems to get louder in my ears.

Near the collar of his blue Gaia jumpsuit, he finds the zipper that only appears when he touches it, and I immediately remember being fascinated the first time I saw this happen when Vox showed me her tattoos in our dorm. My stomach sinks at the thought because it reminds me of our reality now—of having escaped the one place I've spent my whole life trying to get into because Gaia isn't what we thought it was. Worst of all, I remember that now our friends are missing, one of whom will never come back. I close my eyes in a long blink to force these thoughts out of my head because I just don't have the energy to work them through, not without some sleep. For now, I just need to find out what's wrong with Arco's ribs, and why his nanites aren't fixing them.

I open my eyes to find him pulling his arm out of his jumpsuit sleeve, then letting it fall to his waist with the other one just like he did with his dive suit. Both sets of sleeves hang at his sides as he pulls the hem of his dark base layer tank top to his collarbones, and I can't help but watch the fading blue light reflect dancing lines from the stream over his skin. My eyes dart to all his indentations: the notches of muscle over his hips, the grooves of his stomach, the curves of his broad chest and shoulders. I swallow and blink a few times to focus as my heart starts pounding, which I try to dismiss because it's not like I haven't seen him without his shirt at the beach or when playing gravity ball with Jax, but I suppose I've never seen him just inches from me like this...never felt the air spark and crackle all around us.

He lifts his arms to his sides just a little and bends them slightly at the elbow, his palms up like he's waiting to be searched. I suddenly remember that's exactly what I'm supposed to be doing with this wand, but when I see his biceps contract and the muscles in his shoulders pulling taut, I want to trace all the small places that weave in and out and curve and bend.

I move my fingertips up the long vertical line that starts above his navel, and he takes in a shallow breath, but doesn't flinch. I can feel his eyes on me, watching me study him, and as I trace the hard lines of his stomach, then press the palm of my hand over the narrow valley in the middle of his chest, I can feel his heart pounding too.

"Nothing hurts yet?" I ask looking up just enough to see him shake his head slowly. I meet his eyes and find something in them that I've never seen before—they're not kind or compassionate like they usually are, and they're not commanding like I've seen recently. He looks at me like he's hunting, like he's been gauging every move from a remote corner somewhere without me knowing, just waiting for the perfect moment to leap out —but I'm not afraid of him.

I watch my fingers move over the rounded edge of his chest, then along the interstices between each of his ribs on the left when I hear him start struggling to modulate his breath. *Is this because he's anticipating pain again? Or is he just responding to my touch?* I wonder, and try to look more closely for signs of injury in the dimming, refracting light. I don't see anything at first, but when he takes another breath, his chest expands and reveals the beginnings of two small purple bruises on his side. I touch them lightly, and he winces again.

"It's there?" I ask, pulling out of the spell I was just under, but he only answers with a slow, labored exhale. "Turn that way a little," I ask, gesturing to the right, and when he does, I see the rest of the nearly black bruising reaching around his left side. I gasp, then meet his eyes again. "Arco, crite. What happened? Dez's scanner would have detected this when we brought you out of the Stingray," I say, but he just clenches his jaw and looks away without answering me. "*Arco*, what happened to your ribs?" I repeat, more intensely this time as I wave the medi-wand over the damaged area. It immediately turns red, and I pull it back to read the diagnosis.

- **Internal hemorrhage and intercostal muscle tears between left ribs 4 and 5, left ribs 6 and 7.**
- **Calculated trauma lineage: 43 degrees at sternum point C, 61 degrees at sternum point D.**
- **Nano-restructuring reinitiated at 03:14. Current status: 12% complete. Estimated time remaining: six hours 23 minutes.**
- **Administer dopamine block and morphine surge for pain. Vein combination: 3, 7, arterial.**

"This says you have at least two torn muscles!" I try to whisper. "And the nanites had to reinitiate, so you made it worse when you stopped Tieg earlier. Give me your arm so I can figure out this vein combination to release the painkillers."

"No, I don't want that—I can't have them clouding my head," he answers, pulling his arm in.

"Arco, when did you first hurt your ribs? Dez didn't pick up *any* injuries like that after the Leviathan implosion," I insist.

"Coming through the crag then I guess, just before that black thing took Pitt. I tripped with the momentum or something, I don't know. I was still a little out of it from the concussion."

"But I saw Ellis and Avis on the other side waiting to help you. Didn't they catch you?" I ask.

"I remember them picking me up after things went black for a minute, but Tieg and Dez were the ones who caught me—or, I suppose didn't catch me," he tries to chuckle. "I don't know how I fell, Jazz, but it's nothing."

"I do, and it's obviously something," I say, showing him the scanner readout and biting back the urge to confront Tieg. Arco follows my eyes around the corner where Tieg is sleeping with his back to the wall a few feet down from Jax.

"Jazz, come on," Arco says, filling in the pieces. "He couldn't have done anything with the others standing right there."

"There's no way Dez could have caught you on her own. All he had to do was not take hold, and it would have looked like you fell by accident," I explain, suddenly wishing Liddick were awake so I could see what he thought.

"I don't know. You saw how upset he was about Pitt, and how he tried to help Dez through it. We have some friction, no doubt, but I can't see him taking cheap shots like that."

"That's *exactly* why he would have done it, Arco. He already had issues about seeing you kissing me by the moon pool, right? And there was nothing but tension between you two over piloting the Leviathan, plus, considering what happened to Pitt—you just heard him say that he blames us, and if you're the one leading us, he has to blame you most of all," I say, blood pounding in my ears as Arco's muscles tense, making him wince again. This pulls me back into the moment, and I know I need to shelve my accusations for now. "All right, so we just have to watch him. There's nothing we can do tonight," I say, looking around for the rest of the medical kit, then picking it up next to my feet. "You need to rest and let the nanites finish repairing everything—it's going to take them the rest of the night, so just be still a minute," I add, pulling the dark compression bandage from my supply bag to wrap around his ribs as methodically as I can in order to push back the urge to wake up Tieg with my boot.

Arco must sense my vehemence because he doesn't play down his injury anymore, especially not since he grimaces with almost every pass of the wrapping over his side. I press the bandage into itself at his sternum to seal it as he brings his hand over mine, then lowers his chin to catch my eyes.

"Thank you," he says quietly, then moves his hand into my hair and kisses me. I can feel his heartbeat quicken under my palms, his skin warm as one of his arms wraps around my waist, pulling me against him. I feel him wince again when he does this, and lean back. He makes a low growl from somewhere in his chest, but I raise an eyebrow at him.

"Go to sleep and let the nanites fix you," I say quietly. His eyebrows draw together as he opens his mouth to protest, but then thinks better of it and smiles to one side, resigned.

I help him put his suit layers back on before he stretches out carefully along the wall, then position the more cushioned part of the supply bag under his head and find another place for myself.

"Hey," he says, almost completely in shadows, save the dancing blue water lines reflecting over him. "Why are you all the way over there?" he asks, bracing his left side against the wall next to him and turning to me, his right hand outstretched along the ground.

"You're *hurt*. I don't want to accidentally—" I start to say, trying not to sound like I think he's a giant idiot for not putting this together himself, but he cuts me off.

"Come here," he says, waving me toward him, and I catch his smile in the fading light. "Next to me."

A warmth radiates through my chest when his arm tightens around me as I move to lie beside him. I turn toward him and take a deep breath, then close my eyes with the sound of his heartbeat echoing in my ear.

CHAPTER 3
Signals

The tunnel walls glow yellow and white, sending mottled light over the black, undulating mass in the distance, which turns just like it did in the cave from our Stingray practice run…just like when it took Vox and Fraya from the underwater cave. The high-pitched buzzing in my ears grows louder the closer it gets, and I look around for Arco—*he was just here, wasn't he?*—then for Jax, for Liddick, for anyone else from our group, but I'm alone as I cling to the sloping wall in this long, dark corridor.

I never saw it coming when I refused the stipend, but now I see that Denison's offer was targeted at those of us who turned Gaia down, my father's voice says from somewhere in the walls. My breath catches in my throat, but I still call out to him.

"Dad! Where are you?" My voice is muffled like it's underwater, and the buzzing grows louder as I move more deeply through the tunnel, straight toward the flipping black shadow creature and now…*Vox* in the distance? She's walking directly toward it with something in her hand that I can't make out. I call to her, and when she doesn't answer, I try telepathically, but she doesn't acknowledge me that way either.

*They needed us because we were capable of too much to be unaffiliated…to be unmonitored…*my father's voice echoes in the walls again. I bring my hands to my mouth like a megaphone to call for him more loudly this time, and feel the resistance of water against my arms.

What? I wave my hands back and forth, and hundreds of little bubbles appear in their wake. *I'm…underwater?*

I feel for my helmet, but it's not there. My heart hammers in my chest as my eyes dart to my torso, which should be covered by my black dive suit, but all I see is my pale woven shirt and pants from back home billowing around me. *How am I breathing? How can I still breathe down here?*

A tickle runs up the sides of my chest as Vox approaches the mass of shadows that now hovers against the stone wall, its high-pitched keening competing with the low, droning buzz in my ear. Vox extends her hand out to the creature like it's a skittish horse, and the sound starts to subside. As I get closer, the enormous black creature compresses against the rock wall like it's trying to cover something, its wings like a misshapen, much too large manta ray's. My blood freezes in my veins when I see the hundreds of differently sized mouths, some horizontal, some vertical, some with teeth, and some without running the length of its body. I nearly choke on a gasp when Vox starts *stepping* into the mouths… climbing them like stairs as she hoists herself all the way to the top, where she takes her pick knife out and actually leans down to *say* something to it.

Vox! What are you doing!? I shout to her in my head, then out loud when she doesn't answer me, but I'm too late to stop her from stabbing her knife between what I can now see are the creature's eyes. She slips off its back as it starts sliding downward along the rock, then she pounds her fists against the glowing tunnel wall as the manta ray monster slumps into a large, black heap that nearly blocks the rest of the corridor.

What gives you the right!? Vox screams into the rocks, her voice thick with tears. Her yellow eyes flash at me, and the glow of the walls surges in answer as another scream rips from her throat.

The tickle on the sides of my chest suddenly turns to an unbearable itch, and I pull at the buttons of my shirt until it falls open. The water that was just all around me vanishes, and my blood freezes in my veins when I see the skin over my ribs folding inward in long, red arcs that begin under my arms and disappear around my back. I reach around to feel for it on one side, and immediately choke when my fingers slip inside the fold. I yank them back, fear crawling up my spine as my eyes fall again on Vox.

"What are these!?" I scream at her, but instead of answering, she starts running toward me as fast as she can, gripping her pick knife in her hand.

Wake up, Jazz, she says in my mind. *Wake up and follow me.*

***

The dim, blue light of the glow rod has completely faded when my eyes fly open, and I hear the rushing sound of water against a dull buzzing in my ears. I don't know where I am at first as my heart crashes against my chest in the darkness, but immediately begin reaching around my side to feel for the indented sections of skin. When I don't feel anything but my dive suit fabric, I pull the cord release behind my shoulder. The back panel of my suit falls away as I pull my arms out, then fumble over the collar of my jumpsuit to find the invisible zipper. I startle when I hear a snap from behind me, which freezes me in place. Another dim light floods the ground just enough to catch the water about five feet in front of me, making the blue reflection dance over the stone walls.

"Rip?" Liddick whispers from around the corner, and the buzzing in my ears starts to get louder. I try to reply to him in my thoughts, but I can't seem to focus enough on the words to make the connection. He takes a few steps toward me. "What happened? What are you doing?" he whispers as loudly as he can without waking everyone up. I do the same, still scrambling to find the *stupid* collar zipper until I just give into frustration.

"Get this off! *Get it off*!" I stammer through my teeth.

"OK, whoa, hold still," he says, closing the distance between us and holding the blue glow rod he's just cracked under his arm so his hands are free to search my collar. "Get what off? Where?" he asks, confused.

"This! I can't find the zipper! Get this off me!"

"Your *jumpsuit*?"

"Liddick!"

"*All right*…calm down," he says, folding his hands around mine to still them, then he lowers his eyes to mine. "Stop panicking. Take a breath, OK? It was a dream. Rip, listen…"

"*Get this off me right now*!" I hiss as tears claw up the back of my throat and choke off the ends of my last few words. He presses his lips together into a hard line and takes a deep breath as he lowers my hands to my sides.

"All right, *all right...*" he says, then finds the zipper in an instant just under my chin. The second I feel it open, I start pulling my arms out of the sleeves and accidentally knock loose the glow rod he's returned to his hand. It rolls into the wall behind us as my hand rifles under my base layer and around to my side, groping for the long indentation I just felt, but I don't feel it now. I turn my back to Liddick, peeling my base layer tank top over my head and holding it to my chest.

"Do you see them? Are they there?" I ask, the buzz in my ears getting even louder.

"What? There's nothing there. Rip, it *was a dream...*"

"I had gills! Check."

"All right," he answers, pushing his hand over his face just before he walks away from me.

"Liddick!" I say through my teeth.

"I'm just getting the glow rod, *crite...*Rip, you have to calm—"

"Forget the glow rod! Check *right now.* Can you feel them?" I ask in a rush, turning my back to him and reaching as far as I can around my side.

"Riptide..."

"*Check!*" I say, now losing control of my voice with the droning buzz in my head and the crippling fear that some kind of mutation is happening to me. Liddick blows out a long breath and moves his hands over the small of my back slowly, then up over my ribs. His hands are warm and steady, and when I don't feel him jump away in horror, I start to think I might be OK. "Do you feel them?" I ask with the last of a breath.

"No," he says close to my ear now as his hands grip my shoulders reassuringly, and I can feel his warm breath on my neck. "I told you it was a dream. I had one too."

Relief washes over me and spills out in a deluge as I exhale, then turn to look at him over my shoulder.

"What the *hell*?" Arco's voice comes out of the darkness, and I jerk my head back, barely able to make out his face in the filtered blue light. "Jazz...wh—?" he starts, shaking his head. Suddenly, I realize how everything looks with my base layer shirt bunched in front of me and Liddick standing at my bared back with his hands still on my shoulders.

"Heh, no—*unfortunately*, no, this is not that, Hart, listen..." Liddick says, holding up one hand.

"Oh, I'm listening," Arco says, getting to his feet, his arm bracing against his side for an instant before he takes a motivated few steps toward us.

"Arco, stop. I had *gills*!" I blurt, and this stops him in his tracks. Others begin stirring now, and I quickly pull my base layer back over my head.

"*What*?" he says, his eyes narrowing and his brows crashing together as Liddick picks up the glow rod.

"And I caught on fire, but didn't burn..." Liddick adds, waving the glow rod in the air just before he makes his way back to the wall. I turn to face him.

"You were on fire? That was your dream? Do you still hear the buzzing?" I ramble at Liddick, noticing that the buzz has leveled off in the background of everything in my head. Liddick nods.

"OK, someone start talking to me," Arco insists, his hands moving to his hips.

"Liddick? Why are you—what happened?" Dez asks groggily from the other side of the cave. He closes his eyes in a long blink and sighs, then pinches the bridge of his nose before looking up at me, then back to Arco.

"Wake everyone up. We got a message last night."

CHAPTER 4
Bridging

Liddick tosses the glow rod into the center of the cave as everyone rouses. Tieg pushes his hands over his face and takes a swig from the desalinator tube in his sleeve as Jax makes his way in from the fissure on the far side of the cave. He looks very pleased with himself, considering everything, and I look at him wondering why he would ever go back down there after what it took to come through it the first time.

"What?" Jax says, his voice clipped as he passes me. "Did I miss the sign for the *designated* restrooms down here?" he asks, pressing his lips into a line like he's actually waiting for a response.

"But your suit can—never mind," Joss says, then holds up his hands in surrender. "Maybe *your* suit *can't*," he adds with a chuckle. I roll my eyes as Ellis nearly chokes on the water he's just swallowed, and even Tieg smirks as Avis starts to walk to the fissure with a tip of an imaginary hat to Jax.

"Truth. Just zone, Jazz," he says, flipping his blue bangs, and I gape at him.

"Did I say anything?" I ask, shaking my head and rolling my eyes, but he just shrugs as Jax leans back into his spot against the wall with a scowl.

"*So*, this message?" Arco puts his foot against the wall behind him and crosses his arms over his chest, angling his head at me, indignant.

What is this? I think as I raise an eyebrow at him, exhausted already and now confused, but also irritated when he just narrows his eyes at me like he's running out of patience. Is he *really* still bent about Liddick checking my back for gills? Heat radiates from under my collar, but as soon as I start to round on Arco, I hear Liddick.

Easy… he says in my head. *Just start at the beginning. He doesn't know what we know, and everyone is still on edge from yesterday. We need to get out of this cave.*

I don't risk a glance at him, but close my eyes to reset instead, then pull in a long breath to find my store of patience that's normally good for at least initial tolerance. Arco may not completely understand the *thrum*, but his latent receiver ability would definitely make him feel at least some of its effects…maybe he doesn't know why he's so clipped.

"The messages always start with buzzing," I say, opening my eyes again, but I try not to linger on anyone's expression too long, or I know I'll lose track of what I'm saying just because I'm worried about their reaction to it. "I first heard it with the marlin when we were still topside at the port-festival. Right after that I heard the *never saw it coming* message. It happened again when we went for our advisor meeting at Gaia, and that's also when I saw the lab with our dad and the others," I start.

"Some of the rest of you heard the same marlin message when we were in the cave during the Stingray practice run back at Gaia," Liddick adds, nodding at Arco. "And it happened again in the Boundaries room just before Vox reached out to Jazz. It's been the same for me for years, and Jazz and I are hearing it again now."

"So then what's the message from last night, and why are you still hearing the buzz if it's already come?" Joss asks as Avis hops back into his place between Myra and Ellis along the bend of the wall.

"I don't know why it's still here unless we're somehow still connected to the source of it," Liddick answers. "Maybe it's just like an open channel or something."

"I think it's supposed to help us find everyone because the buzzing in my dream last night led me back to Vox," I say, recounting everything I saw her do. I glance up at Arco, whose hazel eyes are still hard over the muscles working in his jaw. "She seemed to be talking to something in the walls—to someplace where our dad was because more of his message came through there at first."

"You heard him again?" Jax says, leaning in, and I nod.

"He said they targeted him because he turned Gaia down—that they couldn't risk people like him not being affiliated or monitored. Then his voice was gone, and the wall just glowed after Vox yelled at it."

"She was yelling at the *wall*?" Tieg raises an eyebrow. "Of course she was…" he trails off, closing his eyes and shaking his head and grinning as he leans back against the dark rock face.

"To whatever was *in* the wall. She blamed it for making her kill the creature we saw that first time in the cave—that same shadow thing that chased us in here. She did it out of pity, like she was putting it out of its misery," I say, trying to focus on the details before they fade. "Toward the end of the dream, my sides started feeling strange, and when I looked…when I felt with my hand, I had these long, wrapping…gills."

"*Gills*?" Myra asks, her voice pitching, and a cold blast of fear hits me. She's still so close to the edge of keeping it together. Liddick is right, we need to get out of this cave.

"So it was like Lyden in the transmission you saw in Plume's office back at Gaia?" Arco asks after another second, his hard expression finally relaxing.

"Right, and I tweaked. That's when you saw me with Liddick…I'd just woken up, and it still felt so real," I say, shaking my head as I remember the feeling of choking when my fingers slipped inside the long fold down my side. Arco's eyes lower as he takes in a breath, then sighs. "When I asked Vox for answers, the only thing she said was to wake up and follow her, and the buzzing in my ears hasn't stopped since." Everyone looks around at each other, and Arco nods as he comes off the wall to take a seat in the circle next to me.

"Follow her where?" Tieg asks, pulling a protein wafer from one of his dive suit pockets and opening the square package with his solid wedge of Skyboard engineered teeth, his surreal blue eyes enhanced by the glow rod light, which casts shadows along the sharp angles of his face.

"I don't know. Maybe follow the buzzing…go in the direction where it tends to get louder. That's what I felt compelled to do in the Boundaries room the last time I heard it," I answer.

"I got the same vibe from Liam in my dream," Liddick adds as he racks his forearms on his raised knees before ripping open his own wafer packet. "Only it didn't feel like a dream. It felt like ghost scripting in a virtuo-cine," he says, handing the first wafer to Dez. "We were walking down a long corridor in the beginning. Liam was wearing the lab coat like Rheen and Styx wore when Jazz saw them in her advising session with Plume. I kept trying to talk to him, but he couldn't see or hear me."

"You said you were on fire, but it didn't burn you. Like Arwyn..." Arco adds as Dez threads her arm with Liddick's. He nods, swallowing the bite he's chewing.

"That happened toward the end. Liam and I walked into this room with a bunch of metal console stations. He shut the door behind us and started telling me in a hurry that he was targeted because he said no to a program Rheen wanted to put him in when he got into Gaia. That's when I started smelling something burning. When I told him we needed to get out of there, I was suddenly in this big clear box like the ones Jazz saw holding Arwyn and Lyden," he says as his eyes scan the ground. "He couldn't get me out before flames started shooting up my arms and burning through my sleeves. Then he shifted—just got all serious and told me to wake up and follow him like Vox told Jazz in her dream."

Liddick's dark eyebrows dart together like he's contemplating something he can't figure out as Dez leans her head on his shoulder, her long blonde hair draping over his chest. She tightens her arm around his, and my teeth lock together in response. I make a conscious effort to stop as soon as I notice because this is ridiculous. *I shouldn't feel this way. How can everything he's just said be pushed to the side by…what, jealousy? It's just—*

It doesn't make it wrong just because it scares you, Liddick says in my thoughts, startling me, and once again I'm reminded that I need to figure out how to stop projecting every single thing I think. I meet his eyes, which he holds on me like a spotlight, making me feel seen, caught and held responsible for feelings that are too tangled to even begin untying, and the guilt this causes pulls down on me from the inside. *Just stop fighting it, Riptide. Stop fighting being with me...*he adds in my head, and I take a deep breath to refocus.

Arco's hand slips over mine, bringing me back. I clear my throat when I look up at him, the corner of his mouth tacking up with the start of a smile.

"So we should start getting out of here," I say abruptly, looking back out at the group. "The buzzing is almost gone now...we don't want to lose it if it's a beacon," I add, and just like that I've shut off having to process Liddick's comment.

Arco nods, squeezing my hand quickly before he gets to his feet. Liddick follows, then extends his hand to help Dez up. I watch her cling to him and feel the bottom fall out in my chest—her fear and instability again—and my own issues are eclipsed by hers...*the Leviathan imploding, then not being able to save Pitt, and now worrying about Tieg being so volatile,* I think, just as if she's dictated her worries to me. *Crite, the weight of it all is almost crippling.*

She'll be all right. I've got her, Liddick thinks, and again I'm reminded that I really need to get a lock on my thoughts down here. My eyes dart to his for just a second before he slides his arm around Dez's shoulder, and my throat tightens. Before I can process my reaction, a smile pulls at the corner of his mouth, and his eyes light. *Rip… you already know I couldn't want anything more than this with her. I told you what I was coming for.*

With one more nod and a piercing blue look that ignites a small explosion in my chest, he turns with her then and follows Avis and the others toward the tunnel path next to the stream. I don't know what to do with the sense of relief that washes over me when I hear this, or the anger at myself for feeling it, so I swallow hard to reclaim my composure as heat floods into my cheeks.

"Jazz?" Arco says, standing next to me and offering his hand as everyone starts moving toward the tunnel. I look up at him abruptly, then take his hand. He hoists me up, then takes a deep breath. "I'm sorry for the ice earlier," he whispers, angling his chin down to catch my eyes. "It was just easier to think you were *actually*—I mean, I guess it was easier to be angry than to think you didn't—" he stops again and looks at the ground, then blows out a breath. I feel him trying to rally, to chase after all the pieces of what he wants to say like they're so many marbles spilling from a jar. He can't do it, and I want to let him know he doesn't have to.

"Arco, you don't have to apologi—"

"It was just easier to be angry than to think you didn't want this…" he says quickly, then meets my eyes again. "That maybe you didn't want me." He smiles awkwardly, and it suddenly feels like the ceiling of this cave and the entire ocean above is crashing down on me.

"Arco," is all I can say as his anxiety squeezes my chest so tightly it's hard to take a breath. I wrap my arms around his neck and pull myself to him. "I do want you,"

I whisper against his ear, then feel his arms slip around my waist as his chin presses into my shoulder, and I can breathe again.

There isn't any chaos spinning around us—no raging ocean threatening to sweep us away, or some impossible depth we're about to fall. It's just the opposite. It's the second after the close call when everything is safe again…the one second when you see that everything you already have is actually what you've always wanted, and you're just grateful to have one more chance to hold onto it all.

CHAPTER 5
Breathe

The tunnel path is much narrower than the one we came through before, and the angle is also much steeper, especially shuffling upward and sideways. After about five minutes, the tops of my thighs start burning, and the pounding in my chest is so loud it almost drowns out the buzzing that is getting progressively stronger in my ears.

"How far do we have to be like this?" Myra's pinched voice wavers back to us.

"Ten more yards from up here. I can see the opening ahead!" Ellis answers from somewhere that sounds far away. I close my eyes against the ricochet of shoulder lamps along the damp, dark walls, which press against my back and cheek every few steps I take. The crushing mix of everyone's fear and anxiety is worse in the cramped space, especially when I try to take a deep breath to push down the panic tightening my throat.

"We're almost there," Arco says from behind me, his Latency Receiver ability no doubt picking up the same anxious feelings I am. "They made it up that far, so you know we can too. Just focus on something."

I answer him with the most positive sound I can make, unable to find any words as I try not to think about the walls narrowing any more than they are, or that in some places I can feel them pressing into my chest and shoulder blades at the same time. Instead, I count the bounces of the supply bag dangling from my wrist as it knocks against my outer hip, aligning the breaths I take that seem to get shallower in the thickening, heavy air that tastes metallic and gritty on my lips. *One...two...* Myra starts whimpering ahead of us, and I squeeze my eyes shut even more tightly to keep back the rising anxiety it stirs in me. *Three...I can't tweak in here. I have to hold it together. Four...*I think, but it's only a step ahead of the chilling terror pushing into my bones, just like the dampness making my hair heavy enough to stick to my face.

'Just hold it together until we get home...' I hear Liddick's voice in my head. *You know, I never told anyone else that story about Liam and me.*

Liddick! A warm rush of relief shoots through me at the sound of his voice in my mind, and the image of him as a kid walking home with his brother—both of them holding their slashed eyebrows closed after Liddick's fall and Liam's self-inflicted cut to console him—makes me forget about the cold and dense air for a second. *Are you out*? I think as my teeth start chattering against the permeating cold that's freezing my lungs. *Why aren't our suits...*I start again, but the buzzing in my ears is finally eclipsed by the pounding in my head as I try to get a full breath, and I abandon the question.

Remember how big the sky looked over the water? Remember the stars from up on that dune, and how the water reflected everything? Liddick thinks, his words measured and even. *Rip, tell me you remember that.*

I...remember, I answer after a second, and try to will my chattering teeth together so I don't bite my tongue.

When's the last time we'd seen stars? he asks. *The sky was never that clear.*

The realization that we really did see stars the night before we left for Gaia makes me open my eyes again. Shoulder lamps are still shooting white lights everywhere in the distance, but now I also see that sky. It was always hazy because of the port-cloud, but that night stars were everywhere, and the moonlight glinting off the water made it look like we were just floating in space.

How did we…not notice? I ask, dumbfounded as I finally get my teeth to lock together. *Were we that distracted by the marlin talking*? *By all of it that night*? I don't hear anything in response, so I reach out to him again. *Liddick*?

I was, he finally answers. *All I could see was you.*

Almost immediately after I hear this, the wall in front of me falls away, and I stumble forward into someone. I shut my eyes against the sudden, blinding light as strong arms close over me. *Liddick…*I think, relieved as I let my forehead fall against his chest.

I hold up my hand to shadow my eyes from the bright light that goes out a second later, and in the wake of the lamps up ahead, I see him.

"It's all right, I've got you," Tieg says, the solid bar of his Skyboard engineered teeth exposed in a knowing smile, which makes my blood turn to ice. His narrow, unnatural blue eyes seem to glow against the dirt smeared angles of his face, and his long arms tighten like a vice around my ribs as he looks down at me. "I knew you'd eventually see what a chutz Hart is," he says quietly, which sends a blanket of chills over my skin.

My teeth start chattering again before I can say anything in protest. I try pushing back from him, but the suffocating panic of not being able to get enough oxygen saps my efforts, then breaks my resolve altogether.

"I can't...breathe..." I manage, trying to focus my blurring vision. Tieg relaxes his hold, but still doesn't let me go.

"Sorry," he says through a laugh, then raises an eyebrow and tightens his arms around me again. "Come here...you're shivering," he says, his voice sounding far away even though he's just inches from me. *I need to get out of here...why am I so cold?*

"Spaulding—" Liddick says in a low, rigid voice that startles me as the blur of him comes into view off of Tieg's shoulder. "Help me with this so Dez can refill her water. I tripped...snagged it right out of her sleeve and can't connect it again. She's up ahead by the stream with the others," he adds, holding up something in his hand.

"Mollusk, that's talent. Those are secured in three places," Tieg growls, then turns back to me. "To be continued," he whispers before finally letting me go. The sudden lack of anything in front of me to brace against sends a jolt through my knees, and they almost buckle. Tieg snatches whatever Liddick is holding from his hand and shoves past him, knocking into his shoulder. Liddick stumbles back, then crosses to me.

"Are you all right? He's gone...just breathe, it's OK..." Liddick says, brushing away the damp hair clinging to my face, but before I can respond, a bright light shines in his eyes, and I hear Arco's voice.

"What happened? *Jazz?*"

"Damnit, Hart, kill the sun!" Liddick nearly yells. "She just got tripped up coming out of the squeeze. Everything is fine," he continues, dropping his hands from my face when Arco walks up behind us. "Everyone is up at the stream topping off their desalinators. Come on," Liddick adds, squeezing my hand before stepping back from me, but now his voice sounds far away too.

"Are you OK?" Arco asks, shining his light down over me, which hurts my eyes. He turns it off, and I shake my head to bring him into focus as his arm moves over my shoulder, drawing me into him.

*He's still coming down from worrying about **me** with you, so don't tell him yet about what Spaulding just pulled until I can figure out what that was all about,* Liddick thinks, but I can't find him when I look around. *Anyway, Hart is already paranoid, and he needs to get back to leading this thing. You know I've got your back, all right? Don't worry,* he adds. I hear him, but now his words sound muffled, and my head starts spinning as I try to put everything into perspective again. *Rip?* Liddick asks in my head again. I should say something in answer, but I can't seem to pull any words together.

Everything starts to feel like it's in slow motion...my heart has stopped hammering in my chest, and my teeth have even stopped chattering. Only the buzzing in my ears has picked up as I take a few steps toward the twinkling lights in the distance where Liddick was heading, but they're slowly going out. *Is this Azeris's signal...or Vox?* I think as the blur swallows everything and the room starts to spin.

"Dez!" Arco says from somewhere under the buzzing resonating in my ears, and suddenly, I feel weightless as the walls start glowing blue like in the air bell—like in my dream.

"Right here! Put her down!" Dez's voice is so much closer than Arco's. I look around for her, but can only see fuzzy shapes and mottled light. "Ellis! It's her nanites—help me sync her suit with the upgrade...I can't believe I forgot to do it before we left!"

"Hart, look out," Ellis says before everything goes completely dark. I start to feel like I'm floating again, but then I clearly see Vox sitting next to me, her wild yellow-green eyes narrowed as she shakes her head at me in mock reproach.

Sarin said you always had to be the center of attention. I'm starting to think she was right. Get up, sand dollar. Breathe.

Vox? Where are you? How are you messaging me? We're coming to find you and Fraya, I promise.

I know. Breathe, Jazz.

Is Fraya all right? I think as Vox starts to fade. *Wait!* I call to her in my mind, but she just keeps disappearing until finally, she's gone.

"Jazz!" Arco's voice is loud now and close to my ear.

"*Hart,* back the hell up!" Ellis shouts from somewhere just as close. "All right, it's sequenced, but it will time out in a few minutes without more oxygen," he adds.

"Then I'll lock the channel now. Myra, epinephrine sequence three, vein eight arterial on my mark. Ready?" Dez asks, and I feel someone pressing on the inside of my forearm.

"Ready!"

"Now!"

"Is it working?" Jax calls from somewhere high above me, his deep voice resonating like a bell, which makes my head hurt and my heart beat twice as fast.

"It's skipping…she needs to take in more breath for it to align. Myra, again…now!" Dez shouts.

Rip…I thought it was just claustrophobia back there, and then Spaulding all over you…crite…can you hear me? Liddick thinks, but his voice sounds the farthest away of all.

Liddick…

Yes! he laughs. *Listen to me, you have to breathe. You have to take a big breath, just one…in and out, all right? You need to do it right now, Rip.*

*It's too tight. The walls…*I answer as my heartbeat slows and merges into one low hum.

The walls are gone now…you made it through. We're on the dune and there's nothing but sky forever. Take a breath. Rip, damnit, take a breath!

"Dez, come on!" Arco shouts.

"I'm *trying*! Please, you have to back up!"

"Let me help you, Hart."

"Tieg, let him go! *Crite*, I can't do this now!"

"Joss, get his arm!" I hear Jax's voice again from farther away now. They're all getting farther away.

Rip! Remember that day you got stung by the jellyfish? Remember how I dared you to swim underwater with me? Take a deep breath and jump in with me now. Come on. Everyone else is a jelly.

Liddick…you said the fish glowed at night.

That's right. And nobody believed me, remember? But they wouldn't come find out. Don't be a jelly like them—come on, and I'll show you. Take a deep breath, and we'll jump, OK? We'll go together. One...two...take a deep breath now, Rip! Three!

And I do, but it hurts. It feels like I'm pulling water into my lungs instead of air, and it's sharp in my chest when I choke on it.

"OK, it's aligned! Sponge the epi', Myra, she can do it on her own now, just give her a second. Jazz, if you can hear me, you're going to feel a lot better in a minute."

"Dez?" I hear myself say—at least I think I do—but I can't see her.

"*Yes!* Yes, it's Dez! Just be still. Don't try to talk or move. I upgraded your nanites to your dive suit. They're syncing now so it can regulate your climatizer, OK? You went hypothermic because your old ones were too slow to keep up with your suit for this long."

"She's OK? Dez, is she OK?"

"Arco?" I ask, my voice sounding muffled. I try to open my eyes, but they're still too heavy. "Arco, it's all right. Don't be afraid," I say, but the words feel like gravel in my throat.

"Jazz...Crite..." he says at the end of a breath.

Riptide, Liddick thinks, and I outwardly hear him chuckle. *You're just brass.*

"She's all right, Dez? It worked?" I hear Jax again, closer now, and I know it's his hand closing over mine as I try to grip it to let him know I'm OK.

"Yes, she just needs a minute," Dez answers, and I hear Jax exhale just before my chest starts to ache again, but not like before. It's not the same kind of pain.

Liddick? I think.

Hart's right there, he answers. *Or I would—*

They did glow, Liddick. The fish. I saw them. I never told you, but I saw them, I interrupt, then open my eyes, and his face is the first I see. He's standing behind Dez with one arm wrapped around his stomach and his other hand extending up to cover his mouth and chin like he's some old philosopher pondering the universe. He blinks several times when he meets my eyes, and I see the smile escaping from the thumb and forefinger sentinels he has stationed at the corners of his mouth, keeping him back, keeping him unattached. He shakes his head almost imperceptibly as a laugh starts in his eyes.

Arco's arm slides under my shoulders and lifts me against him. He pushes the damp hairs off my cheeks, and my chest swells again, this time, with relief.

"I can breathe, and it's warmer," I say, noticing that the cold running through me is gone now.

"You'll be good as new in about ten minutes once everything finishes syncing," Dez says, smiling in front of me. "I'm so sorry, Jazz. I should have remembered that Dame Mahgi said your nanites needed to be upgraded…I should have remembered before we ever left," she adds, her blonde eyebrows darting together as tears glass her bioengineered crystal blue eyes, and I feel the stab of her guilt and anxiety low in my chest.

"I forgot too," I say, trying to nod. "A lot was going on, but I feel better now. Thank you," I say, trying to smile as wide as I can as I reach out for Dez and lean my head against Arco's chest. She takes my hand and squeezes it, and I can feel her guilt lifting.

Myra kneels next to me and pushes the rest of my hair out of my face, then brings my desalinator tube up to my mouth.

"Take a drink, OK?" she says, the smile crinkling the corners of her wide blue eyes. I take a sip, and the rest of the gravel in my throat washes away.

CHAPTER 6
Paths

The walls around us now have an eerie white and yellow glow just like the first cave we'd entered on our training run with the Stingrays back at Gaia, and all the rock formations look poured and set like something melted, then solidified. If I let my eyes fix on them too long, they almost look like they're moving as we walk by, and I wonder if there is still something wrong with my vision even after the nanite upgrade.

"Crite, you scared the hell out of me back there. Why didn't you tell me you were getting so cold?" Arco asks, shaking his head.

"I thought everyone was cold, and then things just, I don't know, fell out of focus I guess."

"Well, can you tell me next time if something is off?" he asks, and I raise an eyebrow at him. "What? Jazz, I'm your..." he says, trailing off with a smile.

"My what?"

"Your...team leader," he stumbles around a pause, then laughs it off as I raise my eyebrows and nod at him. "Of course. What did you think I meant?" he asks with a smirk.

"Right, no, of course," I nod again, closing my mouth in an enlightened smile. "And what about your ribs?"

"They're good as new, thanks to you."

"I didn't do anything. That was the nanites."

"You wrapped them. Made me sleep instead of what I would have rather—"

"*All right...*" I cut him off before he can finish the thought, then feel a warm flush hit my cheeks as I remember him pulling me against him in the small cave. "Everyone will hear you."

"Good," he says, chuckling, and I roll my eyes as Jax falls back and starts walking with us.

"You still OK?" he asks, throwing an arm around me. I nod and lean into him. "I'm sorry I was such a chutz earlier," he adds as a heavy feeling drapes over me. "I just can't believe Pitt is really gone."

"I know. I can still see it all, but it really was no one's fault, Jax, just like you told Tieg. You have to stop blaming yourself too."

He sighs. "I'll work on it," he answers after a beat, then raises an eyebrow as his mouth slowly pulls to one side. "That is, if you can manage to avoid having any more medical crises down here?"

"I'll work on it," I reply, and he grins.

Do the walls look like they're shifting to you? Liddick's voice registers in my head.

You see it too? I thought I was still fried, I answer, and he trots a few steps ahead to Ellis.

"Raj, what's with these walls?"

"What are you talking about?" Ellis asks, glancing down at the Nav system strapped to his arm.

"They're just limestone," Avis adds, crossing to them.

"You don't see them wavering? Like a heat mirage or something over them?" Liddick asks.

"Let me scan you," Dez says, rifling through her medical bag as she catches up to him.

"No, it's not just me. Jazz sees it too," he says, and Arco fires a shocked look at me as he holds out a hand.

I shrink into my shoulders and give him an innocent smile. "Sorry, I forgot about that," I mouth to him, and he rolls his eyes with a sigh.

"Nothing is coming up," Ellis adds, scanning the walls with his Nav system.

"Drink some water," Dez says, "maybe you're both getting dehydrated."

"I'm all right. It's not that," Liddick answers, shaking his head, then rubs his eyes with the heels of his hands.

"Do you even know where we're going?" Tieg barks back to Arco from somewhere up ahead.

"We're following the sweep map—Avis, how far are we loaded?" he answers, jogging a few steps to look at the extended readout Avis has been trying to pull up.

"In the overview, it looks like the destination ping came back about eighteen miles in and down. Our next three miles look a lot like this," he says, showing the screen on his arm to Arco, then looking back at everyone else. "Sorry, that's as far as I can get the ground feed to show at one time. But hey, at least we're out of that squeeze back there."

"Can you still hear the buzzing?" Arco calls back to me, and I nod.

"It's not as strong as it was before, but I can still hear it."

"And you?" he angles his head toward Liddick.

"It's the same."

"Then we just keep moving forward," Arco says, "if you're sure the sound is connected to the signals somehow."

"I know it is," I answer, then take a breath, trying to figure out how to bring up what I saw after I came out of the squeeze *without* dredging up the tension that accompanied it. After a second, I decide it's probably best just to say it. "I saw Vox again—when I was…under."

Arco's eyes dart to mine as everyone slows down to listen.

"Did she talk to you?" Ellis asks, turning to walk backward so he can see me.

"Not about where to go, but she tried to help me. I just don't know if I was imagining her, or if she was really there somehow. Port-call projected or something…it felt like that in my dream. Like she was actually there."

"Maybe it was a little bit of both—some kind of uplink like in Plume's office. You said the images fried when you lost focus, right?" Arco asks, starting to make his way back to my side.

"That's what I was starting to wonder too. But how could it have bypassed Plume? I was the only one who could see the lab with Rheen and Styx, and how they filled Lyden's containment box with water, and when the fire—" I stop myself, but not soon enough. The muscles in Arco's jaw jump as he clenches his teeth, and I feel like someone has punched me in the stomach. "I'm sorry. I didn't mean to bring that up."

"It's all right," he says, looking toward the limestone wall the way he looked out on the ocean when we were walking home from our Gaia interviews topside, and I know he's fighting again to understand what Rheen could have done to his sister to make her immune to flames shooting up her legs. Why does he think he always has to process the hard things by himself?

"We're going to find them," I say, but he just forces a smile when he crosses to close the gap between us.

"They might just find us," Liddick says, walking up from behind me and cutting Arco off. "I just realized something."

"*Wright!*" Arco growls after he almost runs into Liddick.

"Rip, the buzzing is still here because it's not the same buzzing. It's not as high-pitched. Have you noticed?" Liddick asks, and as I listen, I realize he's right.

"It is quieter," I agree, "but if it's not the same, where is it coming from?"

"Azeris. He opened a neural channel to us. I just got his signature confirmation."

"*Azeris*? How?" I ask as Arco crosses behind us and moves to my other side.

"He started working on it that night we heard the marlin—when I went to see him after I found out you heard it too. Hart, your piggyback code was the last piece he needed to trace enough of the ping to figure out how my brothers and Jazz's dad hacked into Gaia's mainframe —into my *particular* mainframe. Reader empaths, Rip— we're the same. That's why you heard the marlin message that night too."

"You said you'd been getting those messages for years. Why hasn't she heard them all along too if you're so much *alike*?" Arco balks.

"If she would have gone into any virtuo-cines, she'd have probably seen the others just like I did. That's the only time the messages ever showed up for me before Rheen put this bracelet on me. You said yourself they did something to us—kicked something on inside after they were clamped on in our interviews. How else did you know how to break into Gaia's mainframe that night and code that Lincoln program in the Records room...all before we ever left shore?" Liddick responds, and Arco's eyes narrow.

"Vox is a Reader too. Does that mean she heard the marlin?" I ask, my mind suddenly racing. That would explain why she seemed to be targeting me with her unblinking stares the rest of that night, and even after we arrived. She saw me tweak at the port-festival, and must have known why. Maybe she just wanted to find out how we were connected.

"I don't know if her Nav Hybrid classification instead of Coder Hybrid like us would have shut her out or not, but yeah, there's a good chance she heard it too, at least some of it," Liddick says.

"OK stop—so Azeris is talking to you right now?"Arco asks, shaking his head.

"In a way. The wavy walls, Rip. Look again," Liddick says, extending his arm and pointing at the lines in the rock face just ahead of us. I follow his trajectory, and as I focus my eyes, I see that the lines actually do morph into an *A* that repeats over and over again, shifting as we walk and spanning from the ground to the ceiling.

"They're letter *As*," I say, "all the way down the tunnel."

"It's him. Azeris. That's the signature we decided on in the Boundaries room after he helped us launch the automators...just before he closed his port-call. That would be how he'd let me know he'd successfully mapped the neural path my brothers and your dad used to deliver the messages we were getting from the marlin." Liddick says. "Do you know what this means, Rip? He traced the path back to them...he knows where they are —exactly where they are."

"So he can guide us," I add.

"Then you're our compass—whoa..." Arco says, then abruptly calls everyone to a stop.

"What is *that*!?" Myra shrieks, jerking our attention forward.

"Stay here," Joss's voice rises above everyone's gasps as his shoulder lamp clicks up two levels to flood the tunnel, illuminating a smooth, black mass that sits in the center of the light, contrasting passageway about 25 yards in the distance. Arco and Jax take several long strides toward it, and as we all get closer, a chill runs down my spine.

"Jax, wait!" I shout, suddenly overcome with fear just as Liddick darts in front of Jax and holds up a hand.

"You don't want to go over there," he says, apparently feeling the same sense of foreboding I do.

"Why not? Look out," Jax answers as Tieg pushes forward now too.

"Spaulding, stop!" Liddick shouts.

"Tieg, listen to him!" I echo, but it's no use.

"Why? What's the pr—" Tieg's words seize in his throat as he approaches the mass.

"That's a Nav kit! Why is there a Nav kit with that thing? *Pitt*?" Dez's voice quivers as she breaks away from the group and follows Tieg.

"Dez, no!" I call to her as she rushes up to the gear, then covers her mouth and the scream that would have otherwise come out.

"It's dead," Joss says, levering his boot to lift one side of the scarred surface of the creature, which looks like black dolphin skin, then leaps back. "Crite! Those are mouths! You saw all those mouths? Help me turn it," he says to Ellis, and they both deploy their gloves and grab the edge of the creature.

"It's that shadow thing from the cave and the air bell… it's the same thing that was in my dream," I say quietly, noticing the puncture wound in between its eyes and the shallow pool of red blood underneath it as Joss and Ellis try to flip it over. My breath stops in my chest. "It was real….I saw Vox kill this."

"She couldn't kill something this big by herself. You saw it take Pitt," Tieg says without looking at me as he jumps in to help Joss, Jax, and Ellis fold the thick, black mass over, and I can feel his anger and fear starting to boil again at the thought of his brother. I have to make him see.

"Because it wanted her to do it," I say, and everyone looks from the beast that must be fifteen feet in diameter to me. "It was suffering."

"Suffering…*pfff*," Tieg huffs out a breath, then moves in more closely, shouldering Liddick out of his way again. Panic squeezes my lungs as he also grips the side of the creature.

"No!" I call to him, but it's too late. His effort is the last needed to fold back the wing-like body nearly in half, which reveals Pitt's arm buried underneath.

"Pitt!" Tieg yells, then begins pulling again in earnest to completely flip over the blanketing black mass covering the arm. "Help me flip it!"

"Is he alive!? Dez!" Myra shouts, and Dez rushes forward.

Flipping the creature to its back reveals hundreds of small mouths of varying sizes, some with teeth, some without on the soot-colored underbelly. There's a foot-long gash running down the center of it, and at the end of the elongated sections near the bottom…*what is that*? The beginnings of two human feet?

"It's a *ray…*" Ellis says. "It's just a giant manta ray."

"Look at his face and neck," Jax says as Pitt is uncovered. "It's like he was never infected."

"Jax, get back!" I yell, and Dez darts in front of him with her medi-wand to kneel beside Pitt. It flashes black, and after several minutes of examination, she turns back to us shaking her head, her eyes glassy.

"He's gone, but there's no trace of the spore infection. He has the antibodies instead…he was almost cured before he—" she says in a broken, small voice that collapses on the last word. Liddick moves in quickly and pulls her in close to him.

"He's holding a cord knife…with blood on it," Avis notices, pointing to Pitt's good hand. "He must have fought the ray."

"Look at this," Ellis says in a low voice, deploying his glove to examine the mouths of the overturned ray just before he pulls out Pitt's little finger. I look again at Pitt's hand, which is only missing *one* finger.

"You said there were two—" I say to Jax, then turn to Tieg. "You had to sever *two*?" I ask carefully.

Tieg nods, his face blanching when he meets my eyes. "Back at the Stingray dock..." he says in a distant voice. Dez takes Pitt's hand in hers and examines it, then looks up at us with icy blue eyes that are almost electric with overflowing tears.

"It had almost finished healing before he..." she starts, then chokes on a sob again, "before he died."

"So that thing didn't kill him...it was trying to *help* him," Joss says, wrapping his arm around Myra, who covers her mouth as steady streams of tears run down her cheeks now too.

"He didn't know," Avis says widening his dark, narrow eyes as he gestures to the cord knife still held tightly in Pitt's other hand.

"He couldn't have known. Especially not when it looked like this," Ellis angles his head toward the underbelly of the manta ray. "What happened to it?" he asks, his tanned face contorted in a mix of sympathy and repulsion. "All those *mouths*..."

"Vox has to know—she was angry about having to kill it when she was pounding on the walls in my dream," I say. "We need to find her."

Arco nods at my side, then crosses to Jax and Joss.

"Help me bury him," he says to them.

"And the ray," Tieg adds after a second more, nodding solemnly before he follows the others.

CHAPTER 7
Seeing in the Dark

We spend the next hour gathering as many stones as we can, carrying them over to the enormous manta ray and Pitt, then stacking them up until each are appropriately covered. I'm not sure if everyone is just too exhausted to say anything when we are finished, or if it's just too hard, so we all stand still, eventually sit, and look at the enormous pile of white rocks sloping down the wall toward us like the bottom of an avalanche we've all barely escaped. Even with this feeling pressing on us, for what must be nearly another hour, none of us can bring ourselves to leave.

Yellow and white lights dot the shadowy walls and ceiling of the tunnel around us in the stillness, and just as soon as the question enters my head, Avis answers it.

"They're worms," he says in surprised realization, breaking the silence as he walks over to the wall nearest to him. "They're just like the clear ones from the other tunnel, but these aren't attached like those," he adds. I stand, then take two large steps away from the wall behind me. Avis holds one of the worms between his gloved fingers, and from where I am, it looks like he's just pulled a tiny star out of the early night sky. He puts the worm back on the wall as Arco steps forward.

"We should get moving again," he says with an edge in his voice. "According to the sweep map, we have at least 16 more miles before we get to the source of the messages. That's a lot of ground to cover, and our supplies will only last so long. Everyone with a Nav system should download the sweep map before we go any farther, though. We should have done that before we came through the squeeze." Arco holds out his hand for Avis's Nav system as he crosses to him, then enters a sequence into it. In another few seconds, one after another, each of the other systems lights up. "If you get separated, just follow the trajectory grid," he adds, taking my forearm and sliding on the silver Nav system he retrieved before we buried Pitt.

"And if we don't have one?" Jax speaks up, narrowing his eyes at Arco as he gestures to Dez and Myra, who don't have one either.

"Stay close to someone who does," Tieg answers, then nods to Jax as he puts his hand on Dez's shoulder. "Come with us."

I start to protest, but Arco replies before I can get the words out. "We're all staying together," he says, definitively. "I said just *in case* anyone gets separated." He looks directly at Tieg, and both of them standing off like this reminds me of two dogs with their hackles up.

"It'll be easier like this," Dez starts before her brother can protest, then turns to face him. "And Pitt would have wanted us to stay with the group."

Tieg exhales as he checks his Nav system. "So this overview says we're heading straight down at the end of the stretch we're on now. What kind of gear do we have for that, exactly? Some cords, some carabiners, but we don't have any rappelling kits, do we? What if it's too steep to descend?" Tieg stares down the sharp line of his nose at Arco.

"We can anchor each other and use slide knots if we have to. We'll figure it out."

"And for the last anchor? Then what?"

"I *said* we'll figure it out," Arco repeats, sharpening each word this time.

The air between them thickens with tension again, and I step into the space to break it up.

"Let's just get there first, all right? We can't do that standing here growling at each other."

It takes several more seconds for each of them to break eye contact, but Tieg eventually nods to me in acknowledgment, then smiles just a little before leaning in.

"See how easy getting everything you want can be?" he adds under his breath, leveling eyes with Arco just before crossing to Jax, and a chill runs down my spine at his surreal calm considering we've just buried his brother. Liddick is right, something is happening to him. "Shall we?" Tieg asks, clapping a hand on Jax's shoulder and throwing his other arm around Dez. I sigh when Jax looks back at me and shrugs, dismissing Tieg's drama. Arco's jaw is locked in place, and I feel a wall of ice between us when he meets my eyes.

"Oh, seriously? If you think I would—"

"I don't," Arco says, cutting me off as he turns to walk on with the others.

"Arco..." I say to his back, and he stops impatiently. I try to think of something to calm him down as we start moving again, but then hear Liddick in my head.

Don't even bother, Rip...he has to burn that off. Trust me, he says through a chuckle as he walks backward next to Dez and Ellis a few yards ahead of us, then faces forward.

They're both acting like idiots—what's happening? Is everyone coming apart down here? I think.

Not everyone, Liddick replies with a smirk over his shoulder to me. I roll my eyes and try to keep from getting caught up in his levity.

Liddick, this is serious, I think. *Something is wrong with Tieg and Arco.*

They're wrong with each other, Rip, Liddick adds. *But Spaulding is definitely the one on offense because—*

"I'll be right back," Arco says cooly, interrupting Liddick's thoughts in my head. He takes off the Nav system he borrowed as he jogs up to Avis, who immediately holds out his hands to shield his face from Arco's shoulder lamp.

"Crite, *why*? Why is this hard?" Avis says abruptly, then mumbles a long string of words in Chinese. "I am the only considerate person here. That is stretchless. *That is gospel*," he rants, throwing his hands into the air. After a second, he shields his eyes again and gapes at Arco, who now towers at his side. "Really? Are you confused? Do you think you're a lighthouse? Is this the problem?"

"*Wh..what?*" Arco asks, on the edge of a laugh.

"Kill the lamp! This is like, the eighteenth time one of you chutzes has tried to blind me. In fact, chutzes, can we *all* just kill the lamps? It's bright enough in here with the worms," Avis adds with an indignant huff as he snatches his Nav system from Arco, who finally gives in to a chuckle when Avis absently shoves him.

"Stop calling them worms," Myra says.

"That's what they *are*!" Avis's voice goes up an octave as he throws up his arms again, then turns around to mumble something else in Chinese.

"I know, I'm just trying to forget," she almost giggles as her face flushes, which opens the floodgate for everyone to release their stifled laughter, grateful for the break in mounting tension since we buried Pitt. In the dimming light as we turn off our shoulder lamps, I see Joss put his arm around Myra.

She's going to be all right, I think toward Liddick, who's walking on the other side of Dez a few steps in front of me. He turns to look at me over his shoulder again and nods.

We're all going to be all right, he replies, still chuckling.

I smile at him, and his eyes linger on mine a second more before he turns away. Just then, I believe him, and I forget about everything stacked against us. I forget about the four, or is it now five miles of water over our heads, which is only getting deeper the more we descend into this tunnel. I forget that we only have the supplies in our dive suits and in the bags that Avis and Ellis were able to snag from the Stingray vessels we used to escape the imploding Leviathan, and most of all, I forget that something terrible has been happening to the people we love…that it might be happening to Vox and Fraya now too.

I remember all of this when a cold burn starts in my stomach as Arco crosses back to me after returning Avis's

Nav system, his brief smile fading with the lines of muscle now locked in place under his cheekbones all over again.

***

We walk in silence for what must be another thirty minutes before I just can't take the tension anymore, and start to slow my pace.

"Arco, what else is wrong?" I ask, but he just shrugs and shakes his head. Liddick looks over his shoulder to meet my eyes again, then angles his head at Tieg and Jax.

Like I said, it's Spaulding…you see how he's trying to sidecar you and Jax, right? He's upping his game with Hart. Liddick thinks. I outwardly start to shake my head, but catch myself.

He's been jockeying for position with Arco since they met at Gaia, I answer.

Not like this. I thought the fear I was picking up just outside the squeeze was yours because he was all over you, but you were tweaking about your air and the cold too much to be that afraid of him, Liddick adds. *Some of the anxiety was Spaulding's—he's trying to outrun his guilt about Pitt.*

But what does Arco have to do with any of that? He was just the pilot when we took the Leviathan—Jax and I are more responsible for getting the Spauldings involved in this mess than Arco is, I say, remembering that the only reason Pitt helped us escape Gaia was because he wanted to help Jax, and Tieg only persuaded Dez to come along because I asked him to.

Only one king on the mountain, Riptide, and power heals most wounds, at least in the short term. If Spaulding can take you and Jax away from Hart, he's two steps closer to that crown.

I clench my jaw and remind myself that if Tieg is trying to sabotage Arco, he's doing it because he's in pain, but it doesn't really make me feel any better.

Well, he has to know there's no chance of that with me, and Arco and Jax have been best friends their entire lives. Tieg won't be able to get between them, I finally answer.

He doesn't have to. He just has to make it look like he is, and he's doing that pretty well. You saw how friendly he got with you in front of Hart back there.

*But Arco's not jealous like that...*I add, and in the soft yellow glow of the tunnel, Liddick nearly laughs out loud before he catches himself.

Rip, were you not in the cave this morning when he was ready to take my head off for making sure you weren't becoming a tuna? he asks, trying to hide a cocky smile. *He's been wound tight ever since the port-festival.*

"Are you talking to him right now? In your head again?" Arco asks impatiently, and it's like a window shattering right next to me. I jump, then look up at him. His hazel eyes are narrowed and his brows are drawn together as he looks quickly from me to Liddick.

I rest my case, Liddick thinks, the back of his head shaking from side to side before I answer Arco.

"Yes. We're both worried about you," I say, but the corner of his mouth just tacks into a hard smirk as his brows crash in even more.

"Yeah. All right, Jazz you know what, I can't—"

"That's what we were talking about, Arco—I'm not stretching. What's bothering you so much? Is it them?" I ask, gesturing to Tieg and Jax, who seem to be riveted in discussion now about the glowing walls they keep pointing to. Arco glances at them, then exhales and lets his eyes skim the ground. "You don't have anything to worry about," I say, sliding my hand into his. "I know my brother, and so do you. He's not going to turn on you."

Arco wraps his other hand around the back of his neck, then sighs and looks over at me, more softly this time. "Maybe it's just the pressure making me paranoid… I feel like even my skin is too tight."

"No matter what it is, you don't have to carry everything by yourself, you know? We're all good at different things for a reason…and you can talk to me about anything," I say, squeezing his hand.

He turns and looks at me for a long time, then slips his arm around my shoulders and kisses the top of my head, pulling me against him as he takes a deep breath and lets it out slowly. We walk like this for another several minutes before he leans down and whispers next to my ear.

"I love you," he says. "You know that?" I wrap my arm around his waist and rest my head against his chest as heat rushes up my throat and hits my cheeks, making it almost impossible to reply even if I did know what to say. We walk on like this in the dim, yellow light without saying anything else, but after a few minutes, some of that cold, knotted feeling I had returns. He's nervous again, afraid like he was in the cave just before we all left and he wasn't sure how I felt about him. But he can't feel like that now, can he? Aren't I standing right here next to him with my arm wrapped around him? Didn't I just tell him he could talk to me about anything? *How can he not be sure about my feelings?*

Because **you're** *not even sure about your feelings, Rip,* Liddick replies, and I curse at him under my breath for his eavesdropping.

"What did you say?" Arco asks, stifling a surprised laugh.

"Nothing," I answer, "I just…"

Stepped wrong… Liddick offers.

Stow it! Get out of my head!

"I just stepped wrong back there," I say before I realize it, then kick a shard of limestone from my path as Liddick's head dips in the dim light and his laughter echoes in my ears.

"Be careful," Arco answers, squeezing my shoulder, and Liddick brings his hand to his mouth to camouflage his idiotic chuckling with a pretend yawn.

Crite, you can't just barge into my thoughts whenever you want like that, I shout in my head, but he just keeps fighting his laughter.

You *have to learn to control what you're sending me. I'd be chum if you heard all my unfiltered thoughts,* he thinks again, finally pulling himself together.

How do I control them? I ask, and he just smiles and shakes his head again. *What? How do I do it?*

Sorry, Riptide. You're going to have to figure that one out on your own.

I try to think of something to say to him that will neutralize the anger I feel rising in me, but Arco's arm suddenly drops from my shoulder, and my frustration with Liddick gives way again to another wave of the same anxiety I felt from Arco before. *Now what? Ugh, this is exhausting!* I think, then close my eyes in a long blink when I hear Liddick again.

You know he doesn't understand what he's picking up from you, right? He thinks you're tolerating him because he can feel that gap you have for him...the one that I—

*Get **out** of my head! I'll handle it,* I say, cutting him off, and this time, he doesn't reply. I lace my fingers behind my neck as we move through the tunnel, which twinkles with white and yellow specks all around us, and I wonder, out of all the things we have to deal with right now, how Arco can be worried about the way I may or may not feel about him? Isn't he taking point on this entire trek, driving himself insane with responsibility? Aren't there much bigger issues at stake than if I love him or not? I mean, he's had all these years to decide how he feels, doesn't he understand that I should get more than a *few days*?

My heart starts to hammer in my chest as the pressure of this ridiculous expectation presses down on me. What does it mean, anyway? Is love that feeling of being safe like I thought at first? Maybe that's a start, but I can't believe that's all there is to it. Before I can stop myself, the words are out of my mouth.

"How do you know?" I ask abruptly, looking up at Arco and slowing down so there's more space between us and the others.

"What?" He startles, then slows his pace to match mine.

"How do you know you love me?"

His eyes soften in the warm glow around us as he looks at the ground for the answer, and the corner of his mouth pulls back just enough to make the dimple in his cheek appear.

"I've probably asked myself that same question a thousand times," he says, letting out a breath and taking my hand again before looking at the lights above us, and the cold knot in my stomach starts to thaw again. "The best answer I could come up with was that no matter if you ever found out or not...or if you felt the same way or not, I'd still feel like all I wanted to do was make sure you were happy and safe." He smiles quickly at me, then looks forward again and hooks his thumb in the dive suit rigging loop at his hip. "So I guess somewhere along the way I figured that must be what love is—just wanting to do everything you could for somebody even if you didn't get it back. I mean, if you do, that's perfect then, but it's not really about that." He pauses, then laughs under his breath. "Or, I don't know. That could just be what I've been telling myself..."

Just then I see who he is again, how brave he is just to admit all of this under a thin layer of nonchalance as he leaves the unfinished sentence hovering in the air between us.

"To make it easier? If you don't get it back, you mean?" I ask.

"Maybe..." he finds my eyes for just a second before continuing his explanation to the path at our feet. "What else could hang on like that except love, you know? Eventually, you have to stop holding out so you can get on with your life and all, and I guess it's the idea of actually having to cross that bridge that makes it…hard sometimes," he adds after a pause. "But telling myself hey, at least I'm capable of feeling like that for someone? I guess it's easier then because it wasn't all for nothing."

I can only respond with awe at the insight he seems to have about a question that is so baffling to me.

"Arco, how do you have this all figured out when I've had so much trouble even knowing where to start?" I ask after a second. The smile lights in his eyes before it shows on his lips as he grips my hand again, then winks.

"Years of practice."

CHAPTER 8
The Falls

"Hold up!" Ellis's voice filters back to us, but it sounds pressed and flat under the sound of the rushing stream, which after a few hours of walking, is louder than ever. Somehow a breeze has also kicked up, and the sweat on my upper lip begins to cool.

"Is that *thunder*?" Dez raises her voice over the low rumbling that shoots through the ground into my knees, which causes echoes all the way up my spine.

"Can't be thunder," Avis says, then stops walking altogether and looks over his shoulder at us, his expression blanched. "But waves can sound like thunder."

No one says anything else at first, and I wonder if he's trying to be funny. Finally, Joss starts to laugh.

"Waves? We're a little far south for surf, aren't we?"

Avis meets his eyes, presses his lips together, and nods slowly.

"All right, look, the drop is just ahead, so let's keep moving," Arco says as the roll we've just felt starts to dissipate.

The walls and ceiling around us seem to get brighter, denser with glow worms as we approach our checkpoint. After a minute, I start to feel a fine mist collecting on my face, which instantly chills in the growing breeze.

"Is it *raining*?" Ellis wipes his face with his hand and pulls it back to examine. Tieg clicks his shoulder lamp to its high beam, illuminating the rest of the cavern.

"It's a waterfall," Arco says, his words dropping to the bottom of my stomach like an anchor. Joss and Jax turn their lamps on the highest beam too, and in the increased light, the stream we've been following widens until it drops off like it has found the edge of the world.

"Is that where we have to go?" I ask as my stomach lurches.

"How do we get down there?" Myra's voice is too calm and too quiet, like she wants to stay perfectly still so the answer can't actually find her.

"Do we even *have* to go down there? What does the sweep map say?" Jax questions, crossing to Tieg to look at his Nav console.

"That's the route," Avis says, projecting the blue holographic image of the tunnel we've just come through and the drop ahead of us, which leads to another short tunnel at the bottom of the falls. Avis takes a big breath, then turns to examine the wall as another rumble pushes up under our feet, vibrating my bones. Arco closes his arms around me until the shaking passes.

"Avis! Structural?" he calls out over the growing roar, but Avis's answer is almost inaudible under the noise.

"It's stable! No cracks...at least not yet! We should move!" he answers, trying to pace his words so they fall in between the rumbles of the little earthquake. Arco releases me when it's over, then clicks on his shoulder lamp.

"Are you all right?" he asks, putting his hand on the small of my back as we walk toward the mist just ahead.

"Yeah…" I say, trailing off when I notice the waterfall isn't as big as I thought it would be given the echoing growl of it, which must be an effect of the cave wall acoustics. It's only about fifteen feet across, and when I click on my lamp, I can see the cascade bottom out into a small lake below us.

"That drop has to be at least a hundred feet!" Jax says, looking over the edge.

"Ripley, back up…" Liddick warns, and I hear the panic beneath his calm, even words. A cold spear stabs through me as I register his tone and look up, but I'm a second too late—one second too late to shout to Jax or to reach for him. His foot slips in slow motion, and then everything is in slow motion, especially my legs, my words, my whole trajectory is instantly suspended in this viscous, confining air. I'm screaming in my head, telling him to hold on, that I'm coming, but no words come out. In desperation, I look around for someone closer to him to help, and in the second I take my eyes from my brother, everything warps back to speed. I fall through the space between us, the thickened air now a luminescent, surreal haze as the ground rises up and knocks me back into the moment.

"Jax!" I scream, having tripped and fallen on the hard, stone ground now that my legs work again. I claw at it to pull myself forward until my feet catch up and move under me. Hands grip my arms and haul me up as howling crosswinds hit my ears and force my voice back down my throat, where it is muffled inside my head. I call to him again. "*Jax!*"

"Ripley!" Arco yells over the falls as he maneuvers me behind him, all of us scrambling to get as close as we can to the edge of the water.

"Back up! Stay out of the current!" Avis shouts, shining his high beam lamp in our faces.

"Jazz, back up!" Tieg's voice comes from my left as I push my way in front of Arco back to the edge. I can't tell where Jax is as I frantically scan the water below us, at least until I'm whipped around from behind.

"Listen, *listen...*" Arco says, looking straight into my eyes, but all I can do is shake my head at him.

"No. *No*...I have to get him. I have to go," I repeat as reality dawns on me. I hear my voice saying the words, but they can't be mine because I feel like I'm already halfway down the falls. I'm already landing in the water below and diving, surfacing and diving again until I find Jax.

"Jazz, *listen!*" Arco's fingers press into my upper arms, his grip tightening until I feel a twinge of pain when I start pushing against him in an effort to get free. This makes me see myself back here at the ledge instead of down in the water, held in place instead of swimming in search of my brother. Reality explodes inside me again, and there is only one thing I feel, one thing I see. I need to go after Jax.

"*Arco*! Let me go!" I finally yell, and before I realize what I'm doing, I drive my shoulder into his chest to break his hold. He stumbles back, loosening his grip just long enough for me to take two large steps in the opposite direction, then one more before the ground falls away and the orange light envelopes me.

The roar of the falls pours into my ears until I feel like I'm filled with sand under the weight of it, and in the pockets of clearing haze, the glow worms start to look like they're shooting stars—streaks of light against the darkness as the mist from the water rises in clouds all around me—and for a second, it's like I'm flying up instead of falling down.

When everything stops, it stops hard. There's no water anymore, no mist on my face, no rumbling—only rolling and tumbling until even that stops abruptly when I'm tossed against a *soft* wall and then land in a thud on the also *soft* ground. There is no sound of rushing falls in my ears, but in the broken, golden haze all around me, I can still see the water crashing.

"Jax!" I shout, my voice loud in my ears, bouncing back at me like I'm inside my closet at home playing hide-and-seek with him like when we were kids. I raise my hand to push the wet strands of hair from my eyes only to jam my fingers into my helmet, which has somehow deployed. I press the comms button on my collar, and the deluge of Arco yelling my name against a jumble of voices in the background floods in.

"I'm all right!" I shout over them all, and for a second, everything is still again. I turn on my shoulder lamp, which must have gone out in the jostle. It just ricochets off the haze in every direction, so I turn it off again and try to stand, but just fall to my knees again. Underneath my hands, I feel smooth, rubbery material. *What the...?*

"Jazz! We're looking for a way down to—" Arco's voice is ragged until Dez's slices through it in a sharp scream.

"*Liddick*!"

I look around wildly even though I know it's pointless in the blanket of opaque light. My heartbeat climbs into my throat one deep, heavy beat at a time when I hear him in my head, then realize why Dez screamed.

Do the fish glow down there, Rip? Liddick thinks, and my stomach falls.

Crite, you chutz...I reply with the ghost of a thought as a thick, cold dread spills over me, freezing me in place. He jumped.

Liddick doesn't say anything else, and I take a shallow breath because it's all I can manage as an ache spreads in the pit of my stomach. I close my eyes against the muted glow all around me, and everything inside begins swirling as I sit completely still, lost between the second of realizing that Liddick has really jumped from the ledge, and the second where I might confirm what I fear most. I shake my head against the pull that he's gone, that Jax is gone because I can't lose them...I *can't* lose them. The current of fear just widens under my sternum the more I resist, and my heart starts hammering a weighted toll that reaches up and wraps all around me, then drags me down.

CHAPTER 9
Descending

The distant buzzing starts building in my ears over everyone's combined voices, resonating until I feel it vibrating my skull. I squeeze my eyes shut against it, then force myself to take a long, slow breath, hoping if I can just stay calm and tune out everything else, she'll be there to show me what's going to happen again.

*Vox...*I think, though there's nothing except noise and the growing pressure of it inside my head in reply, even when I call to her again. *Vox!*

Panic rises in my chest because I don't understand. *Isn't that buzzing the sound of Azeris's open channel? Didn't we just figure this out?* I force my eyes open and squint through the orange, mottled light around me to scan for Jax and Liddick, then turn my shoulder lamp back on in the hopes it might help them see me. *I have to do something...I can't just sit here.*

"Can you hear me?" Jax's voice suddenly comes through my helmet comms and jolts me out of my paralysis. "Wh—! Get off!" he yells a second later over what sounds like a struggle, which cuts out just as quickly.

"Jax! What's happening? Where are you?" I scream, but he doesn't reply. "*Jax!*"

"Can you see him?" Arco says over the comms, his voice sounding boxed like it's coming through clenched teeth.

"No!" I answer, my eyes darting everywhere until I notice the white fabric casing from my suit's impact kit still attached to my toe caps. *Scraps of this are all that was left of Arco's kit when the Leviathan imploded on him*, I think, realizing now that mine must have triggered just before I hit the bottom of the falls. "My kit deployed! How do I get out of this bubble so I can go after him!? *Jax*! Can you hear me?" I call, pushing at the translucent, rubbery walls around me as my heart pounds in my ears. *Liddick*! I think, trying to keep back the wave of dread pushing over me again.

"There's a button on the inside left cuff of your dive suit sleeve, Jazz—push it twice," Ellis says, and I fumble for it. "How close are you to the fissure on our sweep map?"

"I don't know, I can't see anything from where I am. How are you getting down here?" I ask, remembering again that Arco's suit no longer has an impact kit.

"We'll find a way, just stay on comms so we don't lose track of you, all right?" His voice is still clipped and tight, and I press my teeth together against the guilt I feel welling up inside me for shoving him when all he was trying to do was keep me safe. I swallow hard, then sigh in relief when I finally find the impact kit button at my wrist and push it. The bottom of my bubble gives way immediately, and I fall into the water. The beam of my shoulder lamp shoots wildly in all directions, but I still can't see anything except opaque white channels of bubbles under the surface. *I need to get out of here*, I think as my heart pounds in my ears, muffling some of the increasing, high-pitched ringing as I swim toward a wall that seems to waver in the haze when I catch a glance. *Is that still Azeris's signal?*

"Jazz? What's happening?" I hear Arco's voice in my helmet. "Are you still all right? Did your kit retract?" I can't answer him at first because it's too hard to swim and talk, and by the time I get to the edge of the water, his voice is desperate. "*Jazz!*"

"I'm OK!" I finally answer, catching my breath, "I'm getting out near the fissure opening—can you see it? Can you see Jax? Something *took* him Arco!" I say, trying to get to my feet to raise my arms in a signal wave, but my breath is forced out in a whoosh as I'm grabbed from behind and pulled backward. My shoulder lamp clicks off when I start kicking, but it doesn't help loosen the grip. "Let me go!" I yell, forgetting that no one outside my helmet can hear me.

"*Jazz!* OK, that's it..." Arco says over the comms, immediately followed by Avis's shouting.

"Wait five seconds until I get the rest of the vertical terrain map! You don't have a kit!"

My heart jumps into my throat as I realize Arco might swan dive off the cliff without thinking, just like Liddick, and I can't get the words out fast enough.

"Arco, stop!" is all I manage to yell in reply before the grip tightens around my stomach again, squeezing off my words just before I stop hard against the rock wall.

"Are you OK!? What's happening!?" Arco shouts over the comms, but I can only get out the first syllable of a response before I'm cut off again.

Stow it! Liddick's words are loud in my head—louder than the squall of voices in my helmet yelling at Arco, and louder than the buzzing in my ears, which is now as strong as it was back in the cave after I saw Vox in my dream.

"Liddick!" I gasp, throwing my arms around his neck when I see him in the dim orange light. "It's all right, don't jump! It's Liddick!" I call back over the comms, hoping Arco hasn't done anything stupid yet. Liddick moves me back so I can see his face again, water dripping over his forehead as his eyebrows dart in. He brings a finger to his lips, and I narrow my eyes at him, confused about why he's wet if his kit and helmet deployed—which they had to do, or he wouldn't be standing here—and how can he hear me through my helmet without wearing his anymore?

"He's there? Is he OK?" Dez asks on the cusp of a sob. I try to answer her, but Liddick starts again before I can get the words out.

Finally, you hear me…just be quiet and still, he thinks scanning everything around us, but I only see the milky orange mist rising from the foot of the falls and the iridescent rock near us, which is speckled with glow worms whose brightness washes in and out in the haze.

Where's Jax? Why are you all wet? I think in reply, but he just shakes his head and squares himself in front of me, planting his hands on the wall at my shoulders as he cranes his neck toward the fissure opening about twenty feet to our side.

"Jazz!?" Dez calls through the comms again, her voice stretched and far away against the hum still reverberating in my ears.

"*Yeah*, Dez! He's OK!" I say too abruptly in my impatience, then catch myself. "Sorry, he's fine. I just need to cut out for a second," I respond, and Liddick's eyes shoot back to mine in a blaze of frustration as he knifes his finger against his lips again. I squint and shake my head at him.

What, I'm supposed to ignore her? How can you even hear me without your helmet? And where is Jax!? I think as I retract my helmet so I'm not tempted to respond to anything else, then gasp at the sudden brightness of the glow worms haloed in light. "Whoa…" I absently react out loud, and am cut off when Liddick presses into me, covering my mouth with his hand.

Crite! Stow it! We're not alone down here, he thinks, and my blood freezes as he looks at the fissure again. I follow his eyes, but don't see anyone or anything.

What are you talking about!? I ask, feeling like my chest is going to explode. *Let me go!*

*They took your brother when he tried **talking over the comms**!* he says, sticking the last several words in place.

Who took him? Where is he? I demand, shaking my head to dislodge his hand from my mouth.

Stop moving! Three of them pulled him through there, he adds, nodding at the fissure.

Was he in the water with you? Are the people from Gaia?

No, and I don't know if they're from Gaia. It happened after my kit retracted and wrapped around my legs—I bumped my helmet control trying to get free, but I saw that he'd made it to the ledge before I got pulled under.

Then get off me! We need to follow them! I think, struggling again, but he just pins me more firmly to the wall.

Not yet, stop! We don't know how many more there are, he thinks, pressing more of his weight onto me.

I don't care! Let me go! I say, trying to free my fists enough to hit his chest and shoulders.

Liddick's eyes flash as he seizes one of my wrists and blocks my other hand with his forearm, pinning it to my chest as he covers my mouth again, then flips wet hair from his eyes.

Rip, stop! he thinks, and when I don't stop struggling, he closes his eyes in a long blink and presses his chest hard into mine, which stops my breath for a second. He releases my wrist and interlaces our fingers. *Just read the scene. I know you want to fight, but just **read**,* he thinks.

The limestone scrapes the back of my knuckles as he grips my hand in his. He rests his forehead against mine, and after a few breaths, I can feel the itch in the back of my throat of something left undone—the need to check and make sure I locked the door behind me because somewhere in my mind, I know I didn't. It feels like someone is standing over my shoulder...just an awareness on another level, and I know they *are* watching us. Liddick's other hand finally drops from my mouth as he pulls back and meets my eyes again.

There...now you feel it, he says in my mind, and I nod slowly, finally registering the depth of his panic and fear.

I'm sorry, I think after a second more, and relief flushes his cheeks as he looks straight into me, the adrenaline igniting his blue eyes just like it did after I helped him recover from his botched port-carnate transfer. I want to turn away because it's too intense when he looks at me like this, but I can't seem to pull back this time.

I feel his heart pounding against my forearm now that I've stopped fighting him, and he loosens his grip on my hand, which he's still holding to the wall. His other hand slips into my hair as water drips onto his lips, and he leans in. *Action is always easy,* he thinks, the muscles in his jaw flexing as he angles his head, then takes a breath. *It's having to wait that's hard,* he adds, brushing my cheek.

It would be so easy to get lost in him right now with the roaring water, this buzzing I know he can hear too, and the uncertainty forcing us into each other where we can both disappear…where we can forget for now that no one is safe anymore, that Gaia must know we're gone, and that everything is falling apart.

Then I hear the word like an echo—falling—and the fantasy I slipped behind shatters, letting the rest of the world in again.

We have to warn them. They're going to come down here, and Arco doesn't have a kit, I think abruptly. Liddick exhales as he drops his hand from my face and straightens.

Tell them we're following the sweep map—but to wait for our all-clear before they try to catch up, he finally thinks, then lets go of my other hand and takes a step backward to look into the fissure. *Are you ready?*

I nod, then deploy my helmet again and turn the comms button in my collar back on as we move along the wall.

"Arco?" I say.

"*Jazz!* Crite! What happened!?" he asks under a rush of breath.

"They took him—they took Jax."

"Who? Are you all right? Where are you?" Arco asks again.

"Just outside the fissure—we're about to go through it. Liddick said there were three of them. They must be from Gaia—they must know we took the Leviathan," I answer as Liddick deploys his helmet, then starts inching toward the fissure opening.

"We're going to have to shut down comms for a while. What's your plan for catching up?" he asks.

"Why would you need to shut down comms?" Arco asks, the edge in his voice sharpening.

"They grabbed Ripley just after he tapped in, and it took all of them to do it. That's all I saw before my kit tried to drown me," Liddick says, then curses. "We need to move, and we need to stay invisible."

"Wait there. We're coming with you," Arco answers.

"We have to go before they get too far ahead, and you can't jump because your impact kit is blown," I say. There's a long pause before I hear him again, but when I do, it's more of a growl than anything intelligible. "Arco, listen, we *have to* follow them. Just catch up after you find a way down, all right?" I say.

"We'll have to rappel. Avis, check for an anchor rock," Arco adds after another beat, and I hear the rasp of air as he blows out a breath. "We're coming, all right? We're coming, so Jazz, please…" he pauses abruptly, then starts again. "Just keep your distance. Promise me you'll wait for us, and…just check back in when you can."

For a second it feels like there's more he wants to say, or there's something he wants *me* to say. I can hear the hollow of it lingering in the seconds after his voice stops, but it's overwritten when Liddick speaks up again.

"We'll be all right, Hart. Just get everyone down here in one piece."

Arco immediately bristles. "*You*—" he says, then stops himself. "Don't do anything stupid."

"Fine line between—" Liddick starts, but Arco cuts him off.

"Out."

Liddick stops inching toward the fissure and looks back at me, smirking under a quirked eyebrow.

"Liddick, are you hurt?" Dez's voice is more stable now, but still fragile. A cold wave washes over me as Liddick takes in a deep breath before he answers, and a dull ache presses into my chest.

"I'm all right, Dezzie…are you OK?" he asks as we move toward the fissure.

A small sob precedes her reply, and the ache pushes into my throat, closing it off. "Why did you jump like that?" Dez asks. Liddick stops for a second, then closes his eyes against the tension we can both feel. He's searching for the right words, but can't find them with everything spinning around us right now. "Liddick?" she asks.

"I'm here," he finally answers, gripping the stone behind us.

"You just…*jumped*," she says again like she's trying to convince herself it actually happened.

"I know," he says after a beat, and the weight of his expected explanation, which he can't seem to give, is suffocating.

"*Why*?" Dez asks so quietly I wonder if it was actually an echo of my own unasked question.

"I just..." Liddick starts, and for the first time in our lives, he really can't find the right answer. He doesn't have the charming comeback that will transform this awkward silence into levity, or the poignant turn of phrase that will offset the pain in her voice. He's just as surprised as I am as he slowly shakes his head, then suddenly stops searching himself. "I just had to," he says, looking up at me. Dez doesn't reply, which leaves Liddick's words hanging in the distance between the others, high on the cliff, and us, here at the edge of everything else. They're suspended over the roaring waters that neither of us can hear from inside our helmets, but know are strong, deep, and dangerous all the same.

CHAPTER 10
Through the Wall

We retract our helmets, and the rumbling of the falls fades in the distance as the buzzing gets more intense the closer we get to the opening in the wall. Liddick stops just before the fissure and peers down the dimly lit tunnel where they took Jax, then turns to me and nods.

It's clear, and it only goes one way. They're down there somewhere, he thinks.

I nod, and we walk about 10 steps when the buzz in my ears starts to crackle and the glow worms begin wavering into the letter *A* again.

Do you see that? I think toward Liddick. *Are the walls shifting for you too?*

Yeah, it's Azeris. It means we're going the right way.

Wait, I think, slowing down and finally having to stop when the buzzing in my head turns up another notch. It's so loud that my vision blotches until everything starts fading to white. I press the heels of my hands into my eyes, but it doesn't keep the stabbing feeling at bay. *Liddick! Something is happening!*

What's wrong? Liddick thinks. I feel his hands on my shoulders, but I can't see him anymore.

I can't see! Everything is just white, and it's getting louder!

Is it the same buzz from Azeris's channel feedback? Or if it's that loud, is it Vox? Rip!

Liddick's voice in my head fades away as colors start burning holes into the white landscape before my eyes until I see a fire shooting up from a dark, hollowed out boulder in the middle of a new cave. The walls are dark like the striated rock in the cave from last night. *Liddick!* I call to him in my thoughts, then again out loud, but he doesn't answer. *Where is this? How did I get in here?* I wonder, feeling the heat from the fire on my face as I walk past it toward another fissure in the wall, but when I hear Fraya screaming from somewhere just beyond it, I start running after the sound.

"Get back!" I hear her call, her voice high and urgent.

"Fraya!" I yell out loud, but only hear my own voice echoing back at me in a ripple. "Where are you?" I run toward the opening in the dark wall, but the fire from the middle of the cave reaches for me just before I'm completely past it, making me instinctively jump away. I inadvertently hit the stone at my side, crashing into it with my shoulder before the fire forces my back flat against it, singeing my throat. I raise my chin, turning my face to the side as far as I can until the flames recede. I start running again, then dive through the fissure opening as the fire licks out, faster this time, and scorches the back of my shoulder. It's like it can see where I am... like it's *alive*.

"Look out!" Fraya's voice is stronger now, so I must be getting closer to her.

"Fraya!" I call out, but she doesn't reply. I move along the wall slowly until I feel a tug at my hair, then reach back into something wet. When I yank my hand back in a panic and look down, the shiny, chunky gel is glowing blue, and I have no idea what it could be until I see the pieces gravitating back together, then trying to crawl up my sleeve. *The worms*! I think immediately, then shake them off before wringing my hair through my hands to make sure there are no more. I jump away from the wall, nearly swallowing my tongue as I suddenly hear Vox laughing, and the walls pulse blue like a heartbeat. "Vox! Where are you? Where are Jax and Fraya?" I yell into the air, then rush past the glow worms as I make my way down the tunnel, the orange light of the fire behind me somehow getting brighter even though I'm moving farther away.

"Get off me!" Jax says, but his voice is coming from inside the walls just like my father's in the dream I had.

"Jax!" I shout, then hear Fraya screaming again with the sound of cheering echoing down the tunnel. I scramble forward, nearly tripping in my hurry, but am frozen by the sudden flood of bright light when I come around the bend.

My eyes adjust after a few seconds, and I finally see Fraya—she's stumbling backward, then falling inside a roped off circle before she moves out of sight behind the rock wall threshold. Another girl draped in shadows advances in her direction, and after a second, I see why Fraya is so terrified. Flames reach around the girl's shoulders from the front. She's...*on fire*?

"Leave us alone!" Fraya shouts.

"Fraya!" I yell, no longer able to see her as the flaming girl suddenly turns to face me, and I recognize those yellow-green eyes, those burgundy eyebrows knitting together, and it feels like all the blood in my veins funnels straight into the ground...*Vox*!

***

"Rip! What's happening?" Liddick says from somewhere far away, and I feel too heavy to move—too heavy even to talk, but then his voice snaps like a rubber band in my head. *Jazz!*

I open my eyes and see him kneeling in front of me. He's blurry until his hands move up my neck and angle my head so I'm looking into his eyes, which start scanning my face. "Vox was…" I whisper, trying to find my voice again now that the paralyzing buzzing is gone.

"She was what? What happened? You just checked out," he says, brushing hair from my face. I blink to clear the fog lingering in my head, then grip his biceps as it all reconfigures in my mind.

"Vox brought me to some arena where Fraya was trying to get away from her. Vox was…*on fire*," I finally say, still unable to believe it myself. Liddick just stares at me for a second, then swallows hard and nods. "I don't understand it," I say, my voice cracking as the tears start to thicken in my throat, and I try to swallow them back before they choke me. Liddick pulls me in close, one of his arms slipping around my waist, and the other wrapping around my shoulders.

"It's all right. It's just a cine—just a virtuo-cine, Rip, just like before. It's all in our heads," he says, pulling me in so tightly I can feel the pulse in his neck hammering against my cheek, and I know he's trying to convince us both.

"But what if it's true? I saw Vox kill the manta ray because it was suffering in my dream, and then we found it with the same wound. What if they caught her like your brothers and my dad? What if these are her experiences right now, Liddick?"

"Stop…there has to be more to it. We just need to keep moving," he says in a quiet voice, brushing his hand over the back of my hair.

"But what if they have Vox and Fraya, and now Jax…*I can't…*" I start, but the tears come as promised and strangle the rest of my words. Liddick's fear and mine balloon in my stomach as he leans his head against mine, then takes a deep breath.

"We'll get them all back," he says, his arms tightening around me. I close my eyes and rest my cheek on his shoulder as the weight of the last few hours settles over us.

"What are we doing down here? How is this even happening…" I whisper. He moves back to study my face.

"Listen to me…we're going to get through this. We're going to find everyone. Just one step at a time, all right?" he says. "I've always got your back, Rip…" he adds, and I nod as he brushes hair behind my ear.

His blue eyes stand out in this strange yellow light, especially against the outline of his black lashes. His heavy, dark brows contrast with his wild blond hair, which is buzzed close and growing in dark on the sides. For just a second, it occurs to me that everything about him is a contradiction, and his lips quirk. In the next breath, the way he looks at me is arresting again, his eyes locking on mine so I can't look away as his thumb traces my jaw. He leans down, making sure I see, making sure I know what's coming, and for a second I don't move. For a second I think I'll let him kiss me because I want to feel something strong and solid again in the chaos all around me. But I can't, and I don't.

*Promise me you'll wait for us...*I hear Arco's words echo in the back of my mind, and I lower my chin.

"Liddick," I start just as he lets out a long, slow breath, then kisses my forehead as I try to find the right words. "I just...I'm sorry," is all I manage to say, feeling both a sense of relief and disappointment crest and fall like a wave before I look back up at him. He nods after a second, then strokes my cheek and smiles just enough that it touches his eyes.

"You don't ever have to be sorry with me, Riptide." A warmth spreads in my chest when he pulls me into a hug, and at least in this minute, it does feel like everything is going to be all right. "Ready to keep going?" he asks after another minute, then stands and extends his hand to me, backlit by the light at the end of the tunnel that seems brighter now than it did before. I take his hand, but a second later it's wrenched from mine as a shadow falls over us and he's jerked backward.

"Liddick!" I yell after him, then feel hands gripping my shoulders and pulling me forward in the same direction, the light darting in and out as we both struggle to get free. I can't see the faces of the people on either side of me, but they're tall and strong and smell like fire smoke. Liddick pulls free several feet ahead of me and swings at a man about his size before he's restrained, and another man raises something that looks like a club. "No!

Liddick!" I scream again, and a female voice rips through the air over us all.

"*Nicht! Fa na hols!*" it says, and the man lowers the club. I blow out the breath I didn't know I was holding as we move through the tunnel more quickly, almost too quickly for me to keep from tripping over my own feet.

"Where are we going?" I shout to the two marshaling me forward, but there's no answer. The men with Liddick turn around long enough in the growing light for me to see that they're actually our age, not teachers or security from Gaia. Two more younger men accompany them, their faces scarred in the same diamond and arrow pattern as Vox's, the same as the barbarians on the beach the other day in Tark's class. *Badlanders*? I think, but that makes no sense...*they were just virtuo-cine creations—they don't exist,* I think again, realizing their skin isn't as pale as the barbarians' from the cine, in fact, it's tan, and instead of dark hair, theirs is so blond it's nearly white.

"Who *are* you?" Liddick shouts as we catch up to them, but no one answers him either. The scarred boys go through the rock face opening first, followed by the two restraining Liddick's arms, each of his wrists held at an angle behind his back.

Inside, the new cave is so bright I can't see anything, but voices are everywhere when I land hard on the smooth, warm ground.

Liddick! I think, then feel him grip my hand.

I'm here! Are you OK? he answers, but before I can reply, a new female voice rises over all the others.

"Jesse, there you are...you and Ty lead out with us now. Jove wants another patrol of the swallow falls—

worms are stirred up clear to the reservoir. Those two ain't the last of their group, besides."

"A *third* run? Come on, it's time to eat!" one of the boys near me protests as another cheers from the other side of the room.

"About time we had some ruckus! Jesse, pass over that blade if you're staying behind for soup and cuddles," he adds.

"Yeah, come here…I'll pass you a blade," the one near me growls, then fades into the shuffle of dissipating voices. I shield my eyes enough to see the last of their group moving through the rock opening we've just come through, while the two blond, scarred boys walk along the wall. I turn and find Liddick right next to me, as well as two bigger boys standing about five feet behind him. They both have dark hair, one of them wearing it pulled back in a small ponytail while the other just lets it fall into his eyes. All four are wearing worn, woven shirts that range from tan to a reddish brown, and their dark canvas pants are tucked into riot guard boots just like Azeris's when he came to help us rig the port-call channel in the Boundaries room. They all seem to be about our age, but older somehow…wilder. They *can't* be from Gaia.

"I have to hand it to you," the female voice from the tunnel says behind us, and when I jerk around to face her, my damp hair whips against my cheek. She looks like Badlander Fringe, just like Vox, with her gray tank top and military green canvas pants. She's our age too with copper hair that skims her shoulders. Her freckles are marred by soot, but the sharp lines of her face, the scar that looks like a coiled snake running across her upper arm, and the clip of her tone cancel out anything innocent she may have once been. "Most people don't get past the word *cannibals*," she adds, adjusting the wide satchel strap that runs under her arms as she brings the blade of a huge machete to rest on her shoulder.

"Who *are* you?" Liddick demands again, but she just looks him up and down and grins.

"I'm Zoe. And you're a long way from home."

CHAPTER 11
The Beginning

Zoe takes a step toward us, and both Liddick and I get to our feet. We turn toward the opening in the rock we've just come through, but the two darker boys move in front of it and block our way.

We could break through if we took them by surprise? I think, glancing at Liddick.

Even if they weren't built like shuttle busses, they'd catch us. They probably know this place, and we don't, he answers without looking away from them.

They don't have dive suits...how are they even down here? I wonder, turning to scan for another opening on the far side of the cave where the blond boys are backlit by several green-tinted torches mounted to the dark rock walls. They are smaller than the other boys, but Liddick is right; even if we could get through, they'd catch us.

"There's nowhere to go," Zoe says, tossing her rusty hair off her shoulder and angling her head. She shifts her weight and sheaths her machete at her hip, then looks us up and down. "Nice suits."

"Where's my brother?" I ask, then round on the larger boys behind us. The long-haired one dabs a cut in the corner of his mouth with the cuff of his sleeve, and in the light, I can see a long vertical scar running down his cheek. "Where did you take him?" I add, but the boy with the ponytail just smirks in reply, then kisses the air in my direction. I recoil, and he moves his hand over his heart like he's suddenly in pain. "*Where is he*?" I insist.

"Feisty!" the boy laughs, his eyes widening when the other one stops dabbing at his mouth to backhand him in the chest. "What? I mean, dibs is all I'm saying, you know?" he adds as the boy with the cut rolls his eyes and shakes his head.

"Can we get on with it already?" he asks Zoe impatiently, then leans back against the wall to blot his lip again. Zoe sighs and slides her machete to her back.

"Look, we're not trying to hurt you, wise? Sorry about their manners and the rough escort, but you people were entirely too loud out there," she says with mock chastisement in her voice, then shakes her head at us. Liddick's eyes flash to mine, followed immediately by a tickle in my chest as he smirks at me. "Oh, it's all fun and games until someone gets eaten," Zoe says again, and Liddick's smirk disappears.

"Eaten?" he asks.

She said **cannibals** *Liddick.* **Canni**—I start to think, but Zoe's answer cuts me off.

"We could have let the worm or the tunnel sharks have you," she says, raising her rusty eyebrows in punctuation as she thins her lips into a matter-of-fact smile.

"The *what*?"

"But I promised Vox we'd make sure you made it here unkilled and in one piece, or thereabouts."

"Vox is here? Where? And Fraya? Where is *my brother*!?" I manage to say just before my throat closes against a new rush of adrenaline. Zoe's patronizing expression flattens into a hard, serious one as she pulls a knife from her boot and starts making it dance in her hand, flipping it end over end as the blade catches the green, glinting light of the torches on the wall in small, blinding flashes.

"First off, Fraya is fine, and your *brother* is as big as a walrus, not to mention about as graceful," Zoe says, locking her dark eyes with mine as she twirls, releases, and then catches her knife. "He took a swing at Dell there once we finally fished him out of the water. Lost his footing after he connected, though, and wound up kissing the rock face," she adds under a bubbling laugh. "But he made a pretty good dent in Dell's face first," she nods to the boy who is still dabbing his mouth.

"Is he all right? I want to see him," I say through my teeth, pushing forward until Liddick grips my shoulders.

Rip, just take a breath, he thinks, but I can barely keep myself from running at her as blood pounds in my ears.

"He's a little bit unconscious right now, but he's in good hands. I'll take you around when he wakes up, fair?" Zoe asks with that one-sided smile.

"There are more of you down here?" Liddick asks, taking a step forward so he's at my side again. "You said most people don't get past the word *cannibals*."

"That's right," she answers.

"So you're *Fringe*? Badlanders, this far down? How? And where is Vox?" I ask. Zoe grins, then puts her knife back into her boot.

"Most of us are Badlanders—we have a few Tinkerers from Seaboard, though how we're here is a story for later. Vox said you were a quick study," she answers with a wink. I look around like Vox is going to materialize on cue from inside the walls somehow, and one of the blond boys shakes his head.

"She's not here anymore. Left a few hours ago," the taller one says, his clear blue eyes catching the torches just off his shoulder. Now that there is more light, I can see that his scars aren't just similar, they're almost identical to Vox's tattoos.

"She knew we were coming. Why would she leave?" I press, heat rising in my cheeks all over again.

"You can thank Cal for that," the tall, ponytailed boy answers with a nod at the other blond boy, whose dimples tack his cheeks when he sighs and rolls his eyes.

"Look, for the *last time*, it's not my fault. How was I supposed to know what her people believe up there?" the blond boy who must be Cal asks, holding out his hand like he's waiting for one of us to put the answer in it. "She's gone, OK? She went to the Motherland that doesn't even exist in the mountain. Do you think I'm happy about that? *Vahg om*," he says, then closes his eyes and shakes his head at the ceiling as the boy with the long cheek scar and cut lip speaks up.

"It exists," he says from the other side of the cave, lowering the cuff of his shirtsleeve from his mouth. The temperature seems to drop twenty degrees as Cal and the taller blond boy both look away at this, and Zoe just clenches her jaw. Liddick must register the awkward tension too because he reroutes the conversation.

"You must be Dell," he says, nodding to the boy's bloodied shirt cuff. "Jax's handiwork? Bet that made your day," he adds, offering his hand. "Liddick Wright."

After a beat, the boy comes off the wall to take Liddick's hand with as much of a smile as he can manage, and I see several more scars on his hands and forearms.

"Dell Marchand," he says, then turns to me and winks, raising two fingers to his brow like a salute, and it seems like his round, hazel eyes belong to someone much older. "You're Jazz?" he asks, and flips his feathered brown hair back, revealing just for a second another long, white scar running just over his eyebrow. I nod, and he half smiles at me.

He's not quite as big as Jax after all, and not as intimidating as I thought at first. This close, I actually feel a sense of ease with him, but also a feeling of pity somehow. *Is it all the scars*? I wonder.

Bet he's got a story, Liddick thinks, evidently picking up on my feelings again.

"That's Alec," Dell says with a jerk of his head to the ponytailed boy still standing on the wall, who then pushes forward and offers his hand. Dell takes a few steps back, but still keeps his eyes on us.

"Alec Farr, welcome to our humble abode," he says, sweeping his arm out in a wide, exaggerated movement to present the room. He's much taller than everyone in the cave, and his long, thin nose and high cheekbones seem too refined for his tattered shirt and broad build. His long and graceful fingers wrap around my hand, and for a second I wonder if he's a lost *cloudy* from Skyboard.

"This is Cal Shepherd," Zoe adds, angling her head to the surly blond boy with the dimples who just told us about Vox. His diamond scars are also nearly identical to her tattoos, and so is his expression of relative disgust with everything. His ice blue eyes snap up at the sound of his name, and with another sigh, he bothers himself to come forward to offer us his hand.

"I would say it's a pleasure, but it's not. I had things to do today," he says before crossing back to the boulder he was sitting on. "That's Veece. He's a pain in the ass," Cal adds over his shoulder as he hooks a thumb at the taller blond boy who is already walking toward us.

"Veece Singer," he says under a raised eyebrow, which warps the edges of the diamond scar on his forehead. The collar of his shirt falls forward as he bends into the greeting, revealing scars that lead to the same maze pattern as Vox has on her chest.

You saw that? All their scars are like Vox's tattoos…like the Badlander barbarians' scars from Tark's virtuo-cine, I think, and Liddick nods cautiously as Zoe makes her way over to us and slips under Veece's arm, wrapping one hand around his waist and extending the other to us.

"Zoe Frank," she says, which makes Liddick flinch.

"*Frank*?" he asks too abruptly. She stiffens, raising an eyebrow at him and cocking her head to one side.

"Yeah. Problem?"

He freezes, and I have to nudge him after several seconds.

"There's no problem. You just reminded me of a friend of mine," he says, studying her face as a wash of anxiety floods from him. I start to ask what's wrong, but Zoe starts talking again.

"All right, well I suppose it's safe to introduce you around now that we're all finished being hostile—except for Cal, but he's always sore that way, so don't take it personal," she says with an air kiss to Cal when he rolls his eyes at her. "Keep in mind it won't be everybody because a good scoop went to lift the rest of your friends before they made bait out of themselves like you almost did," Zoe adds. "You saw they just lit out."

"They're going to bring the rest of our group here? Right now?" I ask.

"Well, yeah. Been awhile since the worm had anything live to eat as far as we know. Can't have hoolywallers rappelling down the rock falls and causing vibrations all over to draw it up. I swear it's like you never been in the middle of the world before," Zoe answers with a click from the side of her mouth, and I can only stare at her, dizzy with the swirl of her words. "When your walrus wakes up, we'll have you explain the happenings, wise? Dell sure wouldn't get two words into what was actual before he'd spring another leak," she continues, then angles her head at him and chuckles as he dabs the corner of his mouth again. He narrows his eyes at her. "Definitely going to be puffy for a spot, aren't you?" Zoe asks.

"I'm not going to be puffy," Dell answers, his heavy, dark brows knitting together, but his lip is clearly starting to swell.

"You're already puffy," Alec says, snickering.

"You want to see puffy?" Dell lowers his chin as he takes a step toward Alec, who raises his hands in surrender and laughs again.

"All right, so wait..." I start, trying to make sure I understand everything. "Jax hit his head on a *cave wall*, but he's fine, except for being *unconscious*. Vox was here, but she left for some homeland. She told you we were coming, so you're helping us not get eaten by the worm thing that hunts by *sound* at the bottom of the waterfall? And Fraya is fine here somewhere too. Is all that right?" I ask, shaking my head.

"Right, right, and right." Zoe says, her brown eyes sparkling in the torchlight as she fights the grin starting to tug at the corner of her mouth. "Next question?"

"You're *Fringe*—I mean, Badlanders, and you're going to tell us how you got down here later, OK," I say, looking from Zoe to Alec and Dell, "but who are *you*?" I glance at Veece, then at Cal, who grins, shaking his head.

"Noooo, thank you. The last time I answered that question, that *vig-rhova* with the yellow eyes lit out right now for purpose and conquest," Cal answers. "By all means, you tell it so everyone can blame *you* when they leave like Vox did," he adds, unfolding his hand palm up at Veece as if to introduce him on stage.

Veece smiles and closes his eyes in a long blink before taking a deep breath and letting it out with a sigh.

"We're called Vishan," he says, and I feel my eyes widen as I remember Vox's story about her ancestors.

"Vox said Vishan lived in the stars, and she didn't even believe that," I say as Liddick gives me a quizzical look. I guess I never told him about this.

"Legend says two of the original twelve—the twelve who started the six families—went to the stars, but we've lived in these caves and tunnels for almost two hundred years. I'll be happy to tell you the rest of the long story, but if it's no bother to you, I'd like to wait until we collect the rest of your friends so I can just tell it once," Veece says, his nearly invisible eyebrows raising slightly in question and wrinkling the arrow scars on his forehead again.

"But how are any of you down here at all with no protection against the heat? The pressure? We have these suits and nanites, and—" I stop abruptly when the look on Dell's face shifts from warm and curious to hard and withdrawn, the cold snap of the sudden change in his feelings stinging me like the whip of a tree limb pulled too far back. "What? What did I say?" I ask, confused, and wait for someone to start talking.

CHAPTER 12
Center Hall

What's wrong? What did I say? I ask Liddick in my mind.

I don't know. Dell must have an issue with nanites, he answers, then takes a step toward the others. "We got our nanites from Gaia Sur. Vox didn't tell you where we were coming from, or why?" he asks Zoe and the Vishan boys.

"Oh, she told us..." Cal answers, then takes a deep breath like he's going to continue, but Veece interrupts.

"We know you're looking for your family, and that you believe they're down here somewhere."

Liddick turns to him with a sudden adamance. "Right, and did she tell you about the experiments? About how Gaia just replaced people? We have a map to where we think they are, but we could use your help," he says.

Veece and Zoe exchange knowing glances, then look over at Dell, who pushes his hands over his face until he sucks in a breath through his teeth. He touches the corner of his mouth, then sighs at the fresh blood.

"I *said* don't ask me," Dell growls, walking purposefully toward the far wall. He pulls back a long, dark cloth, revealing another fissure, the glow from the other side spilling in as he goes through. Alec smiles at us sympathetically before following him as Veece thins his lips into a line, widening his eyes in question at Cal. Zoe opens her mouth to say something, but Cal's sudden guffaw stops her.

"Don't look at me!" he laughs, shaking his head. "I don't even believe that *sandy*, in case you're somehow squeezed for my position on the matter." Cal holds out his hands like he's presenting physical evidence right there in front of him. "There's nothing out there except the worms and the tunnel sharks pulling sandies through the ground—not *biodivers* or *molecuter combers*, or whatever Dell calls them—just the beasts, and I can tell you firsthand the only thing up in that mountain is hot and flowy."

"Will you just—" Veece starts.

"Not to mention, even if I wanted to go back there, which I don't, you saw what happened to Dell when his nanites wore off in the Rush. Without treatments, *these* sandies would make it exactly ten feet in-terra before—"

"Biodesigners," Liddick interrupts, which immediately and completely stops Cal's rant. "And Molecular Coders," he adds, taking a seat on a boulder near the wall behind us, then leaning over his knees and interlacing his fingers. "That's what Dell, the other *sandy*, actually called them, isn't it? We know about those too. They're real."

Cal's expression slips from adamance to surprise before he regroups, then exhales like he's exhausted.

"Look, no swipes intended, wise? But you're a little light on rainforests and swallow falls at your beachside city wrecks, right?" he asks, but doesn't wait for an answer before shaking his head and shrugging. "So, no, I'm not going back to that mountain," he insists to Zoe and Veece before making a move toward the cloth-covered doorway in the shadows, but then abruptly turns around after a few steps and holds up a finger.

"And I'm especially not going with new sandies in tow. I still can't believe you let Vox leave without more training," he says with a backhanded swat of the air, then finally pushes through the cloth that's covering the rock opening, temporarily flooding the cave with light again. After a few seconds of awkward silence, Zoe blows out a breath.

"So let's get to the introducing," she says, waving us forward. "Come on."

What was that? I think toward Liddick. *Dell thinks Biodesigners and Molecular Coders are taking people? And what's a tunnel shark*?

He shakes his head. *Cal said his nanites wore off too. He's from Gaia.*

We follow Zoe and Veece through the cloth covering and into a short tunnel that is brightly lit with more green-hued torches. They bounce light off the dark walls, which curve into a path that angles sharply upward, forcing us to brace against the rock as we climb. The stone is warm under my hands, and I wonder how it's possible that the temperature has gone from freezing to *this* in the span of what was only about ten miles from the seafloor vent we all first came through with the Stingrays. I remind myself to ask about the *Rush*, and what Cal meant by *rainforests*, *beasts*, and *tunnel sharks*, but I need to see Jax and Fraya first.

At the top of the climb, the tunnel opens into another cave, only this one is much bigger than the one we slept in last night, or even the one we just left. It's lined with more of the green torches and is almost as big as the

Leviathan hangar—nearly twenty feet from floor to ceiling, and probably almost a hundred feet long.

Bedding areas built up with the same kind of burlap cloth that covered the fissure we've just come through line the walls, and are separated by lines of piled stones. Some of the areas even have small, carved out shelves in the rock face that are stacked with more folded cloths and other things too small to make out from where I'm standing. More of the blond Vishan are standing around talking, and others close to our age look over at us warily. Zoe is right—most of them look like Badlander Fringe with their leather satchels and blade sheaths. *Are there any adults?* I think, and Liddick almost immediately responds to my stray thought.

There are more beds than there are people in here, so this can't be everyone. There was a group on its way out when we came in, right?

"This is Center Hall," Veece speaks up. "It's where we all sleep and eat. There's only one way in, so it's the safest place to be. Only way out is at the other end—you can't get in that way on account of the steep slide."

"Are my brother and Fraya in here?" I ask.

"I'll check on them," Veece answers, then nods to me with a smile. "Don't worry…I promise they are safe."

I scan the large cave again, the green light brighter in here along the dark walls, which reflect it somehow so that everyone looks like they're bathed in campfire light. As I let my eyes wander over the faces, I recognize Cal at the far end of the cave talking wildly with another Vishan girl, her nearly white hair pulled high off her neck as she holds up her hands to him like she's trying to calm him down, but apparently without much success. Dell is sitting on a flat rock about twenty feet from us leaning back on his hands. A girl in dark pants and a light shirt that is tied in a knot around her waist holds an old drill in front of his face…*she must have been a Tinkerer when she was topside. Did Cal say they were pulled through the sand*!? I think and Liddick glances over to her and winces.

I hope she was a dentist. Crite, is she going to…? Liddick starts, then trails off in horror as Dell curses when he sees the drill, then balls his hands into fists.

"So look, you can't move at all, or it won't fuse…wise?" the girl with the drill says, her mane of long, curly brown hair masking her face until she turns around to soak a cloth in a bowl before wringing it out with one hand. "*Wise*? Take this too in case I miss," she adds, shoving the cloth into his hand.

"Just do it," Dell answers, then opens his mouth as widely as he can.

"What is she actually going to do with that drill?" Liddick asks Zoe, each word on the heels of the last like they're racing to be the first out of his mouth.

"Calliope? She fixes things—fixes people sometimes too," Zoe answers as the girl picks up something from a little stone shelf in front of her and positions it inside the drill bit. "Looks like she's going to re-root the tooth your walrus knocked out," she adds. Liddick's eyes widen when he looks at me again, and I cover my mouth with my hand as Zoe pulls us toward the center of the large cave where a Vishan woman close to our parents' age is ladling soup into stone bowls. Several others start to funnel in behind us as Zoe completely dismisses the oral surgery taking place just over our shoulders and calls out to her. "Vita, we have two more, and maybe three if the walrus is awake."

The woman turns to us and smiles in response, her face marked in the same diamond pattern as the other Vishan, and her eyes flickering the same icy blue as Veece's and Cal's. She walks toward us with a younger blonde girl behind her, her wide blue eyes flashing too.

"Vita is my aunt, and that's my sister, Liv," Veece says, nodding, then moving forward to greet them. The girl is maybe twelve or thirteen, but her face isn't marked like the other Vishan. She throws her arms around Veece's waist as Vita sets down the bowl and ladle, then wipes her hands on the cloth tied around her hips.

"We have been expecting you. Are you hungry?" she asks us, her eyes darting to our dive suits before she settles on our faces.

"Yes, ma'am, thank you," Liddick says without hesitation, then looks at me over his shoulder and winks. *I am so done with protein packets,* he thinks, and I feel an instant, ridiculous wave of excitement radiating from him. What is it with boys and food?

Zoe takes a seat, and when we get closer, the girl slips behind Veece and peeks at us while we sit on the round, flat rocks that surround the huge stone cook pot, which looks like the hollowed out boulder from my dream. I squeeze my eyes shut as fast as I can to clear the image of the fire inside of it chasing after me, opening them to see Veece scrambling after his little sister.

"*Liv...*" he chuckles as he twists to bring her forward, but she won't come out from behind his back. "This is

Jazz and Liddick. Remember how Vox told us they were coming? Help them feel at home while I ask about the walrus and Fraya, all right?" he says, then nods to Vita before he walks away, but Liv just scans us with her wide, unblinking blue eyes.

"The sandies she wanted Dell and Cal to take to the Motherland?" another tall Vishan boy asks as he bounds up to the cook bowl. He's a little younger than we are, though older than Liv, with straight, shoulder length white-blond hair. Zoe shakes her head at him in warning when he looks over his shoulder, apparently trying to make sure Vita is distracted. When he's sure that she is, he plunges the side of a stone bowl into the soup, then maneuvers quickly under it to catch the stream of drips spilling down the side. He folds his long arms and legs in to sit next to us, beaming with his accomplishment as he brings the bowl to his lips, but spills the contents down his chin when Vita startles him.

"*Axel*! They're Seaboarders, and don't dip the bowl. Wait for the others." She frowns at the tall boy, then turns back to the line forming for bowls as Zoe sends him a thin smile and nods, pleased with herself. The boy reluctantly puts his bowl down in front of him, rolls his eyes at Zoe, and then fires a hand at Liddick.

"I'm Axel, obviously," he says with a grin, his face lighting with excitement as Liddick shakes his hand. "Are you Arco and Jazz?"

Liddick narrows his eyes at him, then gives me a flattened look that almost makes me laugh out loud.

"She's Jazz, but I am most definitely not Arco," he finally answers, and I knock my knee against his.

Don't be rude, I think.

If you think **that** *was rude, it's a good thing you didn't hear what I was about to say. Are we supposed to get in line here or what?* Liddick fidgets as several others gather around the cook pot, each of them taking a stacked bowl until two younger boys about Liv's age start jostling at the front of the line. One of them is blond, but he is also missing the Vishan markings, and one is darker like the Badlanders. Both of them are completely oblivious to us as Vita lets out a long sigh once she sees them.

"Were you in the Pinch again? What is that?" she asks the sandy haired Badlander boy who tucks the *glowing blue head* of something into his shirt pocket every time it pokes out. "All right, go—both of you go, and let that thing loose."

"But we just caught it! It's just a baby!" the toe-headed Vishan boy protests, and I crane my neck to get a better look.

"Then go take it back to its mother. She's probably spooning out their soup now too," Vita answers, and both the boys exchange guilty glances before heading to the far end of the cave, where they quickly disappear down an opening in the dark rock floor.

"Whoa," I say, watching them vanish.

"That's the *Swim,*" Axel says. "There's no water in there, so calling it the Swim doesn't really jive...well, unless you go down on your chest, and then I gather you could make out like you were swimming...maybe there was water gushing through once?" he asks the air as he sucks in his bottom lip in contemplation, then shakes loose of the thought. "Anyway, it'll take you to the river and the Pinch."

"What's the Pinch?" Liddick asks absently, stretching in his seat to gauge the growing line behind the cook pot.

"You can't go there," a small, stern voice from somewhere behind Axel says, and when he turns sideways, Liv is sitting there glaring at us while Vita helps ladle soup. Axel nods his head at her.

"*That* is what you say when you *want* people to go there," he looks over his shoulder at her, then turns back to us. "But nobody bigger than the littles who just went down the Swim can fit up there, so no matter. Nothing there but *luxes* anyway."

"*Ax-el!*" Liv enunciates his name with a hiss, and he whips back around to face her.

"Listen, why don't you go fret at Ghost and Rav about the *baby lux* Ghost was just poking down into his pocket, wise?" he says with an air of authority. Liv's face instantly flushes as she scrambles to her feet and runs to the opening in the floor after the boys, disappearing into it just like they did as Axel turns back to us shaking his head, exasperated. "*Littles!*"

CHAPTER 13
Reunion

The soup Vita passes us smells spicy like the stew my mother makes, and I recognize potatoes, carrots, and a white meat that I assume is a sort of fish.

"Thank you," Liddick sighs, inhaling the rising steam, and a laugh bubbles in my chest at how happy he is over soup. I nod and smile at Vita as Axel nearly drains his bowl, then looks back to us with a satisfied grin.

"I caught the fish in here," he beams. "From the *channel,* not the reservoir."

"What's the difference?" I ask, feeling his pride warm everything around us as I raise my bowl to my lips.

"About a mile that way," Axel answers, pointing at the ceiling. "Took Alec and me all day to hike there and back, but worth it, right?" he adds, tipping his bowl so far up it almost covers his face, but then he quickly pushes it to the side and rushes over to the girl with the drill who fixed Dell's tooth. I turn to see what has him so startled, and find Jax squinting against the light as he leans on Veece, a small Vishan girl with wavy blonde hair at his other side in the rock wall entryway.

"Jax!" I yell, and spill hot soup on my hand as I nearly drop the bowl on the ground in my scurry to get up.

"Jazz?" he says, squinting, then brings his hand to his head and lowers his eyes with a grimace.

"Are you OK? They said you passed out?" I bring my hand to his face to angle his head for a better look at the large knot that's still swollen over his left eye. "What is *that*?" I ask, seeing the clump of green mud smeared over his eyebrow.

"It's Avo paste," the small Vishan girl says, her soft features and round blue eyes making her look like a doll. "It's a disinfectant."

"It smells like dead fish. Do you smell it? Because that's not me," Jax assures, trying to widen his eyes, but he only manages to blink quickly.

"He hit his head on the rocks." The girl motions to the damage on his forehead. "His eyes flickering and shiny like that means it's swole on the inside too. I gave him a drink that will help."

"That also smelled like dead fish," Jax says, and both Veece and the girl stifle a laugh.

"So you have a *concussion*?" I ask him.

"You and Hart can trade war stories," Liddick says from behind me, offering his hand. Jax takes it and nods, smiling to one side.

"How can he still have a concussion this bad? The nanites had Arco's fixed in less than an hour, and a ship imploded on him," I ask Liddick, looking again at how glazed Jax's eyes still are.

"He has nanites?" the girl asks me under raised, invisible eyebrows. "Dell's don't work this close to the barrier," she adds. Veece clears his throat, and she presses her lips into a line before abruptly changing the subject. "Well, I'm Ada. You're Jazz, aren't you?"

Did you hear her? Nanites. Dell is from Gaia. Liddick thinks, but I can't respond to them both at the same time.

"Yes, and this is Liddick," I reply, ready to ask her to say more about Dell's nanites, plus whatever the barrier is, until I feel Veece standing guard over everything she says. "Thank you for helping my brother," I say instead.

"I didn't do much." She laughs too quickly, a flush rising in her cheeks as she looks back at Jax, evidently relieved that I'm not asking anything else about Dell.

"I will leave you in Ada's capable hands," Veece says with one last warning glance at Ada, then briefly lowers his eyes to the ground. "Zoe will check on you soon—we have a special event tonight," he adds with another nod, then walks back toward Vita as Ada smiles and nods.

"All right, well if you feel rush-ups starting, just send somebody after me, and I'll mix up more of the drink, wise?" She exhales, obviously grateful Veece has gone.

Jax looks at me puzzled, blinking several more times, and the look on his face is so clueless I nearly laugh.

"*Wise?*" he asks.

"I think it means *OK*, or *do you understand*?" I manage to say without losing my composure.

"Do I understand what?" Jax squints at me again, sincerely confused as he looks from me back to Ada. Liddick brings his hand to his mouth, clears his throat, and pulls the smile off the end of his chin.

"Should you feel the need to *roarf*, Ripley, if you would be so kind as to get word to Ada first, she'll bring you that fish drink so you don't cause an ecological disaster."

Ada starts giggling, and the sound of it combined with the sight of Jax's face scrunching as if Liddick just asked him for a kiss pushes me over the edge. A laugh bubbles up before I can swallow it, and Jax's eyes dart to mine.

"Sorry," I say. "You really should lie back down."

"Your brain is *swole*," Liddick echoes, wide-eyed as he nods and bites back a chuckle. I give him a fierce look, then glance at Ada to make sure she hasn't taken offense. I'm relieved when I see her nodding in full agreement.

"All right, then, I'll find you later if you don't find me first," Ada says with a big, bright smile at Jax before she turns toward the soup where Dell, Alec, and the other Badlanders are making their way toward it. Jax follows her with his eyes still narrowed against the light, but after a second, they open widely.

"What—?" he starts, taking in the room for the first time, and a wave of adrenaline crashes in my chest.

*He can't see Dell yet… If he just woke up, he won't know they were just trying to—*I start to think toward Liddick, but he's already talking.

"Ripley, you want some soup?" Liddick asks. Jax's heavy, dark brows flinch, and suddenly, Liddick has his full attention. "Just take it easy. Ecological disaster, remember? Jazz, why don't you take him somewhere quiet, and I'll bring it over?" he continues, lowering his chin and looking me right in the eyes. I glance over his shoulder to see Alec approaching and nod quickly.

"Jax, let's go sit down," I say, threading my arm through his, but the second we turn to go, I feel ice chase us down and run up my back.

"Walrus! You're awake!" Alec bellows to us, and my heart stops in my chest. I scramble to find the most readily available words to explain it all to Jax when I feel the jolt of his anger shoot through my stomach.

"OK, listen—*Jax*, listen…" I search his face until he makes eye contact with me. "He's just joking. It's not what you think. They only grabbed you because they were—" I start, but he jerks his head back to Alec and loses his balance as a result of the sudden movement.

"Whoa!" Alec says, taking two quick steps to help.

"I wouldn't—!" Liddick is just close enough to Alec to throw out a forearm to stop him from advancing, the jostle making Alec spill the soup he's holding all over his legs. He looks down at his pants and narrows his dark eyes at Liddick, who doesn't give him a chance to complain. "Listen, he doesn't know what really happened yet, so if you don't want him knocking your tooth out too, I'd give him a minute," Liddick explains, raising his eyebrows and then setting his jaw. Alec's eyes soften as realization sets in, and he nods before taking a few steps back. When I feel Jax's weight shift toward him, my words just start spilling out.

"Jax, wait—they pulled us back from the pool to get us away from something in the water. Vox was here already…she told them we were coming. They were just trying to help us, OK?" I try to put all the words in the same sentence before he stops listening, but his eyes just land on Dell in the distance.

"*That* one…" Jax growls, and I move in front of him to block his path. Dell notices the commotion and starts making his way to us, which puts an ice ball in my chest.

Stop him…I think toward Liddick, but he is already moving to intercept Dell. His cheek is bulging like he's holding a small plum in his mouth as he shakes his head and holds up a hand before Liddick can say anything.

"Don't get all shivery and proud...this is a poultice," Dell says to Jax as he points to his cheek. "It is *not* anything you broke or swoled," he adds, trying hard not to mumble. Jax tries to push forward, but I wrap my arms around his waist.

"Jax, stop!" I say through my teeth as Liddick crosses to us, and the girl with the drill from earlier leaves Axel's side to rush under Dell's arm. She snorts a laugh.

"Not broke anymore thanks to *me*," she says, nodding at us as she wraps both her arms around his waist too. "But it's definitely swole, and if it settles things any, I'll guarantee that poultice he's sucking on tastes just as rot as that Avo paste smells," she says to Jax, her green eyes darting to his eyebrow as she thins her lips and nods, and I can feel the anxiety behind her smile as the air heats up between Jax and Dell.

"Ripley, they were just trying to get us away from the worm. They were trying to help," Liddick says, turning in so his shoulder is in the middle of Jax's chest.

Everyone watches to see what will happen as Jax studies Dell, his dark eyes hard and his brows drawn in as he shoots a glance at Alec next, who nods.

"She had to dig up the poultice. *Dig it up*," Alec says, curling his lip and wrinkling his forehead.

After a second, Jax meets my eyes. I nod at him to confirm that everything really is OK, and finally, he lets a smile start in the corner of his mouth.

"Guess we're even, then," he says, and I see the green-eyed girl let out the breath she was apparently holding. I do the same, then nod to Liddick.

Jax offers a hand to Dell, who then takes a step toward him to receive it.

"Dell Marchand. That's Alec, and the instrument of my perpetual aid and torture here is Calliope," he says as the curly haired girl with the green eyes next to him touches two fingers to her forehead in a salute, then winks at me in shared relief. "Sorry about the hijack, but it was that or have you swallowed," Dell adds as Alec chuckles in agreement and offers his hand.

"Worm might just have choked on you, though," Alec says to Jax, and Dell closes his eyes in a long blink, trying his best to keep from smiling.

"Thank you," I say, then nudge Jax in the ribs. He looks at me sideways and exhales.

"Thanks," he says begrudgingly. "Happy not to be worm food I guess." I nudge him again, hard enough this time that he catches his breath and chuckles. "Hey, I'm injured." I roll my eyes, then smile and shake my head as Liddick clears his throat and raises his chin, his eyes darting over my shoulder. I turn and see Fraya standing in the doorway with another toe-headed Vishan girl, this one with huge brown eyes.

"Fraya…" I whisper, and Jax turns on his heel. Fraya brings her hands to her mouth, and I feel like my chest might explode. I look up at Jax, who is perfectly still like he's trying to gauge if he should trust what he's seeing.

"*Jax…?*" Fraya says in a quiet voice, and in the space of two steps, he is picking her up in a fluid rush, her long auburn hair swinging behind her in an arc as he holds her in the air, then puts her down quickly when he almost loses his balance again. She helps steady him, then wraps her arms around him. "I thought I'd never see you again," she says into his shoulder, her words giving way to a combination of scattered laughter and sobs as he kisses her forehead. My chest constricts, and my throat closes up so tightly I can't even swallow.

Liddick must feel the emotional weight of it too because he moves in behind me and wraps his arms over the front of my shoulders. I would have pushed him away back home, but there's more to it now…we're more, somehow. I lean back against him instead while I try to reset my composure.

"Isn't it funny…" Liddick asks after a few minutes, but leaves the sentence unfinished.

"What's funny?" I ask, and almost have to ask again when he doesn't reply right away.

"It's funny how you don't even realize you're in love with someone…" he finally says just behind my ear, trailing off as an ache spills into my chest. "How you don't even know what that feels like until you think it's too late," he adds, and I can feel my heart beating against his forearm.

Jax clears his throat and wraps his arms around Fraya again like she might drop into the floor any second. He leans down and whispers something in her ear that makes her draw back and swat him in the shoulder. She laughs, her eyebrows drawn up in surprise at Jax as the Vishan girl returns with two bowls of soup, then motions for them to sit in the circle with the others.

I watch them follow her as I lean my head back against Liddick's chest and let my breath come out in a few ragged exhales, overwhelmed with the deluge of happiness pooling around everyone.

They're really here, they're really safe again, I think, feeling the scruff of Liddick's jaw brush my temple.

"See? Everything is going to be OK," he whispers, and suddenly, the tension of what has happened in the last week seems to dissipate. I feel my throat start to close up again, but this time with gratitude that I'm standing here right now with the knowledge that the people I care about are safe and sound, but then I realize...it's only some of them.

As quickly as it comes, the warm, happy feeling I just had freezes in my chest as I hear echoes of Alec's words in my mind...*swallowed*...*worm*...and I pull away from Liddick, terrified all over again. I scan the faces around us for Zoe and Veece, and rush over when I see them ladling soup from the cook pot.

"Zoe, the people who went after the rest of our friends...they should be back by now."

CHAPTER 14
The Circle

Zoe's face blanches for a second until she forces a smile.

"Could be awhile before they're back. Ty and Jesse went along, so there's bound to be some extra adventuring involved," she says. "Could be a day or more."

"*A day* or more? The rest of our group was just down that tunnel!" I flare, pointing to the fissure we all came through.

"They're with Kesh." Veece holds up his hands, apparently to calm me down. "She'll bring everyone back."

"We need to warn them so they don't fight," I say, then try to deploy my helmet in the hopes that Arco might be listening to the comms, but Liddick stops my wrist.

"If they can hear your voice while they're still near the falls, whatever is in that water can too, remember?" he asks, and panic wells in my chest.

"We need to go back there," I say, turning toward the fissure, but he stops my shoulders.

"Hey, *hey*…just calm—"

"Liddick, get out of my way right now," I insist, but he only sets his jaw and takes a deep breath.

"You know I can't let you go back there, Rip."

"*You* know you can't stop me!" I answer.

"At least give them a chance to come back. It's only been a few hours. Getting everyone set to rappel those falls will take time," he says quickly, then calls after me when I turn toward the fissure again. "If they're not back by morning, I'll go with you, all right?" he adds, moving his hands to his hips as his dark eyebrows draw in.

My stomach churns with indecision, but then I meet Zoe's eyes, which are alert and worried. She looks away, and again I feel like she's hiding something.

"Cal said there were sharks pulling people down here. What are those?" I ask. She turns to face me, completely resetting her expression to carefree and casual.

"I'll tell you all about it after we—"

"Hybrids," Dell interrupts, sitting next to the cook pot. He drains the rest of his soup bowl, the poultice no longer bulging in his cheek as he flips his feathered hair off his forehead. Zoe closes her eyes in a long blink and shakes her head as Liddick narrows his eyes.

"Sorry, *what*?" he asks.

Dell sets his bowl down with the others and folds his hands when Zoe glares at him.

"Don't give me the hair eye—say it or don't, but quit dancing," he says to her. She looks to Veece, who just shrugs as if there's no other choice at this point.

"*This* again!" Cal says, walking up to the cook pot to ladle soup into his bowl, then takes a place in the circle next to Vita and the Vishan girl he was talking to when we first came in. He shakes his head at us before lifting the bowl to his mouth, and something about the petty tone in his voice hits me like a campfire spark. I react just as suddenly.

"Look, you promised Vox you'd help us, right? So help us. What are tunnel sharks? The *truth*."

Cal's eyes widen at Veece just before he laughs, holding his bowl in one hand as he jerks his thumb at me with the other. Dell clears his throat and pulls Cal's attention back.

"Go on. Tell her what happens if we try to go home. What happens if we hit daylight...*real* daylight," Dell says, trying to inhale the final few drops of soup from his bowl.

"You know that's just our genetics," Veece offers, but Dell only laughs.

"Right. *Genetics*...from the *Bestower*," he nods, narrowing his eyes and pressing his lips into a line.

"Why can't you let it go? We saved them, and you, *vig-rhovo!*" Cal says through his teeth as he sets his bowl next to him and gets to his feet.

Dell stands too, then suddenly pulls open his shirt. He holds his palms out to his sides, which stops Cal's advance. The muscles in his chest and stomach are silhouetted by the torchlight that has darkened from green to orange, but not enough to mask the scars and burns over his torso, including one the size of my palm over his hip. He holds out his hands, then points to a long vertical scar down his side. "This is from your *Bestower.* Tell them about *that,*" he adds.

"That's enough," a man's voice from behind us suddenly makes me jump and whip around. He's Vishan, and maybe ten years older than Vita with sharp, sculpted features like Tieg's. His clothes are the same light-colored shirt and dark canvas pants as the other Vishan, and his electric blue eyes fall hard on Dell, who stares right back at him. Veece pushes a hand through his white-blond hair and turns his eyes to the ground when a Vishan woman with the same tribal coloring and markings follows the man in from the fissure. "Dress yourself," the man says quietly, but firmly to Dell, who stands his ground for a second more, then buttons his shirt and stares fresh daggers at Cal.

"Tell them about what?" the woman asks Dell. Cal straightens his collar, then looks around at the handful of Badlanders and other Vishan staring at him.

"Scars…is how it started. We were talking about the Vishan map," Cal answers the woman after a pause, then gestures to his face before nodding to Veece, who sighs.

"These are Vox's friends. They have the same questions she did about our markings," Veece adds, trying not to disagree, but it's clear he's not happy about it. The woman's eyes narrow until Vita crosses in front of us with two bowls of soup, forcing the woman to acknowledge her.

That's not what—? I start to tell Liddick in my mind, then see that they're trying to hide what we were really talking about. Liddick meets my eyes and nods.

"I was just two steps from sending them to the Wall to read the Origin story, but now that you're here, you can explain the symbols to our guests. Come and sit; they've only just arrived," Vita says, directing the man and the woman to the circle behind her, then turning a warning eye on Cal and Dell while the man scans us.

"Yes, at the Gathering," he nods to Vita, then looks around the room. "Where is the rest of their group?" he asks, and my stomach falls at the thought that Arco and everyone else still haven't arrived.

"Kesh went with a group to the lip of the falls to collect them. These two, plus the one Ada was treating, had already made it down to the pool. Veece's scout party brought them back before there was…trouble," Vita explains, and the man's face relaxes as he smiles proudly at Veece.

"Welcome," the man says to us. "You have met my son, then." Our eyes dart to Veece, who smiles and lowers his eyes for a second before looking back up at us.

"This is Jove Singer, my brother-in-law, and our council leader," Vita says quickly, nodding to the woman with him and then to another man coming through the fissure. "This is my sister, Flora Singer, and that is Carr Shepherd—Cal's father. They are two of our council elders," she adds as the man moves to take a seat in the widening circle in front of us. I do my best to smile as he passes, but without hesitation, Liddick angles his head and then introduces us to the man and woman.

"Liddick Wright, sir…ma'am," he says, nodding to Flora. "This is Jazwyn Ripley. Ada treated her brother, Jax, and well, you've already met Fraya," he says, nodding across the enormous cave to her and Jax with his trademark charm, which is almost foreign to me after all we've been through lately—a relic of the life that seems so far in the past now. "Thank you for taking us in —it's definitely been a long day," he adds cooly. I try to keep the look of amazement off my face, then suddenly wonder where my bowl of soup went.

The woman smiles at Liddick—and of course she does —as Dell and Cal look around checking everyone's reactions.

"It is our way," Jove says in response to Liddick's *master of all occasions* commentary. "Your group will join us, and we'll celebrate their safe arrival. Kesh is our best tracker," he adds, holding his arm out for Flora before moving to sit by the other man at the far end of the circle.

"Please be comfortable," Flora nods to us, then touches her forehead to Veece's before she takes Jove's arm. When she moves out of earshot, Cal jerks his chin at Dell, and they both head to one of the far corners of the cave. Veece follows them, waving us along while Vita continues serving bowls of soup to the other Vishan adults who begin filtering through the fissure. When I gesture for Jax and Fraya to come with us, Alec notices and makes his way through the circle toward us.

"Well, it's plain there's more happening than can be sorted in the right now, so you'll just have to go easy with it for tonight and trust we'll catch you up, wise?" Zoe says to us under her breath, casually glancing over her shoulder to make sure the older Vishan aren't paying attention.

"Look, no offense, but your politics and whatever that scar thing was about is your business. I just want to know what's out there—what's *really* out there with our friends. Why aren't your people back yet, and why aren't Jax's nanites working?" I insist, trying to keep my voice low as we all come together near the far stone wall.

"*Vahg om,*" Cal says, then shakes his head at Veece. "So just say the *right now* version because as soon as the soup is gone, it'll be time to gather. We can tell the rest after that," he says, exasperated. Dell crosses his arms over his chest and sighs.

"It's more than the worm, but *there is* a worm, so don't get fancy ideas about going off to that pool when everyone tucks up tonight, wise?" he says with a nod.

"Fine, yes—what are tunnel sharks?" I press.

"Creations...from the mountain. They're people, but not all the way," Dell answers as Cal shakes his head. Fraya's eyes widen and my stomach lurches.

"Look," Zoe says, glancing at us, "it's hard to say this all on the quick, but when we told Vox about how we saw something that looked like a worm when it dragged us down through the sand—"

"Wait, *what*? Dragged you through the *sand*?" Jax interrupts, likely trying to reconcile this with the stories of the Badlands...*about the cannibal Badlanders who...*

*Who aren't actually cannibals...*Liddick thinks, jacking into my thoughts again. He covers his mouth as he studies Zoe—I have to find out what his problem is with her.

"Still interested?" Zoe says, jerking my attention back.

"Sorry...keep going."

"Right, so when we told Vox—more accurate, when Dell told her it was *Biodesigners* and *Molecular Coders* who made experiments like the tunnel sharks and let them loose, she had to go up there herself. Said she knew someone who got pulled through the sand too and—"

"And before you get all set to follow her as soon as everyone is asleep, understand that *most* people here think Dell is cooked on account of being out in the Rush so long. It's not a place to—" Cal stops abruptly when Dell lunges at him. Alec grabs Dell's shoulders, and Veece steps between them.

"Stop before you get a guard set on you tonight!" Veece says through his teeth, looking from Dell to Cal.

"You just remember that *I* told Vox not to go—the Rush is no place for a sandy, let alone the mountain," Cal continues. "There *is* no Motherland, or any *biodivers*, or related worm makers in that cooker," he adds to Dell, then pulls Veece's shoulder back so they face each other. "And because *your* father's council let her go without *at least* proving her blood with a treatment, she's probably already dead!"

Veece bristles and moves close enough to Cal to look straight down on him.

"Vox had one of their dive suits—and you know what would have happened if we had treated her," Veece says quietly with a quick glance at the older Vishan.

"Would that have been so bad? She didn't have anyone topside to—" Cal starts, but this time I cut him off before I realize it as the memory of Vox's tattoo story comes back to me from that first day Gaia paired us as roommates—of how each of her lines was part of the map of her travels.

"Wait, her dad…" I turn to Liddick, then to Jax and Fraya before addressing everyone. "She told me how her father took a group out to look for the people responsible for a trap she fell into one day in The Badlands, but none of them ever came back."

"You told her it was *Biodesigners* and *Molecular Coders* who made the worms and tunnel sharks?" Liddick asks Dell. "You used those words?"

Dell nods, and it all comes together.

"She thinks there's *another Gaia...*" I say, meeting Liddick's eyes. "She thinks it's in that mountain—that if our families are there, maybe her dad is too..."

"Why wouldn't she just wait for us, though? Why did she go ahead?" Jax asks, still squinting.

"Wouldn't you want to leave right now to help someone you loved?" Liddick asks, darting a glance at Fraya to remind him of his impatience to go after her the day she disappeared in the cave. Jax takes a deep breath and nods once, then pulls Fraya more tightly against him as Liddick turns back to Dell. "Is that what's in the mountain? Another Gaia?"

"Last I saw any advertising for Gaia was before I got pulled under a year ago, and this place didn't look like that."

"But you were there—you have nanites. Gaia gave us ours...how else could you have them, and why don't they work?" I ask as he tenses.

"That's not part of the *right now* version of things. It's for the catch up, wise?" Zoe says, glancing between Dell and Veece.

I bite back more questions about this for now because I don't want to worry Fraya or upset Jax, but my nanites worked when Dez reset them in the corridor, and Arco's worked in the cave when his ribs repaired over night. If they don't work now—*no....*the thought hits me before I can even put words to it. Liddick turns to me, his face blanched, but then he shakes his head.

Stop, you don't even know, so don't go there, he thinks, obviously having made the same realization I just did.

If Jax's nanites don't work here, ours don't work, Liddick. Our friends' don't work, and they're still out there with—

Just don't…that tracker will find them, all right? Thinking anything else won't help.

"Jazz, are you OK?" Fraya's voice saying my name pulls me back, and a sense of urgency washes over me. We must be just past the reach, or the signal, or whatever makes the nanites work.

"There's another cave about ten miles from here—the nanites work there," I start, and Liddick shakes his head at me.

*Rip…*he thinks, but I answer him out loud.

"Liddick, if they don't work, how are we not imploding right now? How are any of you not imploding? And Arco, the others…they don't even know their nanites won't—"

"Just *relax*," Liddick says, putting his hands on my shoulders.

"You see—it's already starting," Cal says to Veece. "I told you the suit wasn't enough. Treat them."

CHAPTER 15
Vishan

The torchlight has completely shifted from orange to red, and the whole cave looks like a sunset back home as Zoe starts rushing everyone around. Veece looks over at the older Vishan, who are assembling at the front of the cave while everyone else moves to their bedding areas.

"It's time for the Gathering. Come on and get set up," Veece says. "We'll find you later and explain the rest, wise?"

"You'll update us on our friends? And explain Jax's nanites? And what's in the Rush?" I ask as it all floods back in a deluge. Veece nods impatiently.

"*Yes*," he says, looking back at the older Vishan again. "Now go with Zoe, and don't say *a thing* else until you get to your stack." He nods to Zoe, then to Alec. "Show her brother and Fraya where to go."

Alec and Dell help steady Jax, then lead him and Fraya to the opposite end of the cave as Zoe is leading Liddick and me.

"Where are they—?" I start, but Zoe pinches my arm. "Ow!" I yelp, and she pinches me *again*. I hear Liddick laughing in my head and elbow him the best I can while she's dragging us close to the big hole in the floor that Axel called the Swim.

*Well, he said not to say **a thing else**...*

Stow it, that really hurt, I think, rubbing my arm. *Is she going to push us down that hole? Where are we going?*

As soon as I finish thinking it, Zoe stops at a stack of blankets like all the others, but there's nothing on the little shelves in this section, which I can barely make out in the dimming sunset light.

"Don't care if you lie down or sit, but you have to stay low in here until after the Gathering. I'll come back and collect you then, and we'll catch you up, wise?" Zoe says, holding her hands out in front of her as she takes a step backward, then another. "Just stay put," she adds just before turning completely around and disappearing into the shifting light.

"What the *hell*?" I say out loud.

"Let's just sit down…come on," Liddick says, lowering himself to the ground. I do the same, then turn to him ready to pull my hair out.

"This *whole place* is split, you know that, right?" I ask, looking around at everyone scrambling to get into a bunk area. "Do you see this *stupid* light, and do you know I lost my soup? Look at—are you *laughing* at me?" I stop immediately when I catch the look on Liddick's face, his pressed lip smile giving way to buckles of laughter that he can't control.

"Sorry… you're just so…" he answers, then is over come again.

"How are you *laughing* at me? Do you not see the complete split show happening here right now? Look at them, Liddick! They're running around like their bits are on fire all so Jove can tell everyone the bedtime story of *his people*? I mean what—*stop laughing*!" I hiss at him, but he collapses backward onto the blankets into silent guffaws that only get harder when I shove him. "I hate you," I say, which is not helpful *at all* because he just starts laughing so hard that he coughs and wheezes for air. I feel the corner of my mouth pulling to the side along with the bubble of a laugh starting in my stomach, but I refuse to let his stupidness infect me. I turn away from him and hug my knees, watching all these people hopping around like ants on a sinking log. *Ughhhh!*

*OK…OK…I'm done…crite…*he thinks, and I roll my eyes. "I'm sorry," he whispers, still choking on his idiotic laughter.

"I thought you were done?" I say without turning around, and he laughs a few more times before clearing his throat.

"I'm done—I'm done," he says, taking a deep breath and blowing it out. "Crite, I miss that."

"Miss what? Losing your mind?" I grumble.

"Absolutely," he says, a chuckle in his voice threatening to start the whole thing all over again. "The last time I laughed that hard was with you too."

"Well, I'm glad I can be so entertaining," I say, trying to hold onto my aggravation.

"So am I," he says, and I turn completely around to hit him in the arm. He's lower than I thought, leaning back on his elbows, and catches my wrist in his hand. With a quick jerk he pulls me off balance, and I land beside him where he springs off his elbows and pins me under him.

"Get off me," I say, squirming, though, unable to stop my own laughter now.

"Nope," he answers, starting to chuckle again too.

"You're going to make us miss…the story…*get off*…" I laugh, managing enough leeway from the squirming to jerk my hips up and create some space to roll out from under him, but instead of falling over at my side, he just holds onto my arms so I wind up rolling on top of him. As quick as I do, he wraps his arms around me so tightly that mine are pinned to my chest all over again.

"Liddick!" I say through muffled laughs.

"We are fortunate to have guests for this Gathering," a man's booming voice says, freezing us both in place. I try to swallow the rest of my laughter, but Liddick's widened, exaggerated eyes make it impossible. I press my lips hard into a line and bury my face in his shoulder to stifle it, and finally, he loosens his grip. My hips slide off him as he shifts his weight, and I feel his arm move down over my ribs, drawing me against him as my head moves from his shoulder to his chest, and neither one of us is laughing anymore. His heartbeat pounds against my cheek as he folds his hand over mine against his chest, and in this moment, I have the fleeting thought that this might be the most comfortable I've ever been in my entire life.

"Me too," Liddick whispers into my hair, which makes me smile until it occurs to me that this is just what is comfortable *now*—a break in the tension of this whole split reality—but it's not what I want. It's not what's best for anyone. I shake my head and press up to my elbow just as the voice starts again.

"They are like many of our former guests who have since become part of our society, and they will be welcome to stay as others have should this be their fate," the man's voice continues, and I feel my muscles tense.

"It's all right," Liddick says as he grips my hand. "We're not staying here."

"The Vishan began as twelve," the voice continues, "The twelve became six, and are now nearly two hundred. The Origin Wall shows twelve coming from the first great peak—the Motherland—reborn, untouchable by fire or pressure. The twelve saw this, and said that it was good."

Did you hear what he said? Untouchable by fire? I think, and Liddick's hand tightens around mine as I stretch to see the man who's talking.

"The twelve came down from the mountain and became six families who then took to the surface, but their gifts were not for the surface, so they took to the earth. In the earth, they found peace, except for one of these families who did not accept their gifts and wished to seek out The Bestower. They would return to the Motherland, where The Bestower would see fit to send them to the stars."

Isn't this what Vox told you? Liddick thinks.

Not about all the families, but about people living in the stars, yes, I answer, and he takes a deep breath.

"The five remaining families vowed to make maps for their earthbound lines that would chart the seven biomes from the Motherland to this, our terrestrial home. The sixth family left the five others a map from the Motherland to the ethereal home above the two skies. We carry these maps upon us, within us, as the Origin Wall instructs, and we will find our way to the stars to reunite the twelve who became six, and then became the Vishan."

I'm afraid to move when the man stops talking. The light doesn't change at first, but then it dims to a darker red until it is a deep purple, then blue, and then there is no light at all.

Is that it? That's the Gathering? I finally think, but before Liddick can answer me, the man starts talking again.

"Of the six families, the Singers of the ethereal line, who are born of the child, Sol, bearer of the ethereal map, are represented here at this Gathering by Liv Singer. Come forward now."

That's Veece's sister, I think. *She was the girl Axel sent after the two boys with the little animal.* I move to sit all the way up next to Liddick so I can see, but there's still no light.

Can you see them? he thinks.

Not yet.

"Of the six families, the Dyers, one of the five terrestrial lines, are represented at this Gathering by Rav Dyer. Come forward now," the man's voice continues.

Dyer? That's Vox's last name. And I think that's the Vishan boy who wanted to keep the little blue animal. What are they doing? I think.

I don't know. I can barely see them.

Almost in the same second that Liddick finishes his thought, a single green torch lights at the far end of the cave. Jove, Flora, and Veece are standing behind Liv, and Vita stands behind Rav with another Vishan woman.

That's him—that's one of the boys Liv was chasing, I think again, and in the ripple of light that reaches us, I catch Liddick's nod.

A second torch lights directly behind the people at the far end of the cave, this one yellow, revealing a wide stone platform with a shelf behind it, as well as the rest of the adult Vishan sitting directly in front of them in an arc from the far wall. Finally, a third torch lights to the left of those gathered in the front, and Jove starts talking again.

"This fire is the day, the transition, and the night. Our light cycle is a symbol of our life cycle. We combine the three fires to forge the mark of our people."

Flora and the woman next to Vita bring the green and the red torch off the wall while Jove and Vita take the yellow torch. They touch the flames together over the shelf as Veece takes the hands of Liv and the other boy and directs them to lie on the platform.

What are they doing? I think, feeling my heartbeat in my throat.

The three torches together nearly light the entire cave in a fiery glow as Liv and the boy take each other's hands and lie on the platform. Jove takes a long rod from the fire and holds it up to the ceiling.

They're going to brand them, Liddick thinks, but as soon as he does, I feel him trying to cover it up...he didn't want me to hear that thought. I scramble to get to my feet to stop them, but his hands clamp down over my shoulders.

Are you kidding? Let me go! They can't—

Listen! I don't know what they're doing, it just seems—

"Liv Singer, Rav Dyer, in your thirteenth year you are strong enough to carry the history of our culture forward, and we welcome your voice. You are Vishan," Jove says, then lowers the branding rod over Liv's face. The scream shoots up from my chest as I lunge forward and feel Liddick's hand covering my mouth before he pulls me back against him.

Stop, Rip, stop! he thinks as I struggle, bracing for her cries to shatter me, but they never come.

*What's happening…she's not screaming. Liddick, he just burned her **face** and she's not screaming*! I shout in my mind.

Vita sprinkles a yellow powder over Liv as Jove returns the rod to the fire for a second, then pulls it back out and lowers it over the boy. I feel all of my muscles tense against Liddick's arms, which tighten around me again, but the boy doesn't scream either. I shake my head, and Liddick's grip over my mouth loosens until he's sure I'm not going to yell out, then his hand drops to my other shoulder.

"Untouchable by fire," he whispers through my hair, his arms crossed over my chest holding me to him. My heart crashes against my ribs, and all I can do is stare in disbelief as Jove takes a shorter brand out of the fire and marks the kids' chins, then another to mark their throats and chests.

It doesn't hurt them. It doesn't burn…I think, and watch Vita's proud smile as she sprinkles the rest of the powder.

CHAPTER 16
Catching Up: Part One

I can't move, and I can barely decide what I'm thinking when Liv and Rav sit up to face everyone, their new burns already whitening. The whole room starts rubbing their hands together like they're trying to start a fire with a stick, and all of them doing this at once sounds like a strong wind echoing off the cave walls.

"You're shaking. They're not hurt, see? They're all right," Liddick says, and I try to swallow the shock so I can find my voice.

"How…?" is all I can manage to say in reply. I swallow again and shake my head to break free of the hypnotic wind sound swirling all around us, then feel Liddick's hands over my arms. "I'm OK. I just don't know what this…how this…" I start again, but as hard as I try to focus on putting one word after another, the sentence just won't come out.

"They could have warned us," Liddick says, and I feel an anger rising in him that helps me refocus. I lean my head back against his cheek and close my eyes. "There's more going on here than this Gathering—they're preoccupied," he adds.

"At least everyone is all right. I want to read this Origin Wall," I say, turning to look at him. His arms loosen around me just enough so I can turn my shoulders to face him, his eyes, his mouth just a few inches from mine.

Are you OK? You're not shaking anymore... he thinks, and I nod.

Are you? He nods in reply, and I see the spark of his smile light his eyes just as I nearly jump out of my skin.

"*Vahg om,* just unlock and come on for your catch up," Cal says, appearing from nowhere as his expression scrunches like his features are trying to run off his face. He shakes his head, then turns his back and heads for the hole in the ground just a dozen feet from us.

"Where's Zoe?" Liddick calls after him.

"Come find out!" Cal raises his voice just enough so we hear him before he disappears down the...what, the chute? Liddick and I both laugh, the adrenaline of Cal surprising us hitting my bloodstream, and we start to get to our feet. I clear my throat.

"Do you think it's just a slide like Axel described? We sit down and just...go?" I ask.

"Guess we'll find out." Liddick says, holding out his hand. I take it, and we both start walking to the edge of *the Swim.* "Ready to jump?"

"Do I have a choice?" I chuckle, looking into the darkness of the hole in the ground, but he doesn't respond. I look over to find him studying my face, and then the start of a smile pulls at the corner of his mouth.

"You always have a choice to jump, Riptide. It's only too late when you're falling." I stare at him, confused because he's addressing me, but it feels more like he's telling himself. I look at him closely and open my mouth to respond, but then realize I have no idea what to say. The rest of the smile spreads over his face just then, and the whole thing scatters in the air like the last of the powder Vita dusted from her hands. "So, I didn't hear any screams or squish sounds of what could only be a rather messy death down there…did you?"

"Ah, no," I answer with a laugh.

"All right, then. Shall we?" he asks, offering me his arm like some proper English gentleman from a nineteenth century story. I raise an eyebrow at him, then take his arm. He lays his other hand over mine and nods. "On three, then. One…two…"

The last thing I see before the total blackness of the chute is his wink, but by then it's too late to say anything about not being ready yet. It's always too late with him.

This is the only thought I have time to process in addition to *Crite! I'm going to die!* before we start to slow and then stop as light reappears in front of us. We crawl a few feet, and see Jax, Fraya, Veece, Zoe, Dell, Alec, and Cal at the bottom sitting on several differently sized boulders along the torchlit, limestone corridor. It looks almost exactly like the one we came nearly ten miles through, complete with white and yellow glow worms lighting the walls beyond the torches. There's a small stream across from us too, and the falls sound like they must be on the other side.

"Finally! Thought you might be face-locked again up there," Cal says, and Fraya and Jax's eyes widen at me.

"We were n—!" I start, but Liddick is already talking.

"Oh, yeah…almost had her half undressed in between averting her eyes and trying to keep her from rushing the altar to stop your show. Who knew child branding could be so romantic?" He scowls at Cal and shakes his head. Zoe's hands are on her hips as she looks from Liddick to me, then back again to Liddick before giving us both a knowing smile. I shake my head in protest at her, but she just smiles and bounces her eyebrows. I roll my eyes.

"Are we ready for the catch up, then?" Cal asks impatiently.

"Well, for starters," Zoe says, narrowing her eyes at Cal. "Sorry about all the hurry up without the heads up. Gatherings are only here and there—for when a little stops being a little—and since each of them only gets one, there's always a scramble to make it perfect," she explains.

"You could have mentioned something," Liddick says, starting to lean back on the wall until he sees the glow worms just a few feet away, then sits forward again.

"Wasn't enough time to explain anything until now. Trust me, I wanted to. If it weren't for Veece keeping me in my skin, I'd have one hundred-ten percent ruined Cal's Gathering," Zoe answers, and I immediately look over at Cal.

"You have to be at least eighteen, nineteen years old?" I ask, and he nods.

"Nineteen."

"So that means…" I turn back to Zoe, whose eyes shift from sharp and clever to soft for just a second. "You've been here…*six years*?"

Liddick gets to his feet and moves his hands through his hair, then laces his fingers behind his neck as he presses his lips into a line. What does he know about Zoe?

"Yep," she answers, all traces of that fleeting softness gone from her eyes now and replaced with her normal clip and sarcasm. "Pulled through that sand when I was twelve and stuck with these smelly wrecks ever since. Taught me to scrap, though my mom wasn't keen on that."

"*I* do not smell," Cal protests, then tosses a shard of limestone into the stream to our side.

"All boys smell," Zoe laughs, knocking shoulders with Dell, who is sitting next to her on another small boulder. He smirks and gives her a narrowed sideways look.

"Your mother knew you were down here?" Jax says just as the exact words form in my head.

"She disappeared with you, didn't she?" Liddick asks in the space between Jax's question and what would be Zoe's answer. She looks at him with a flash of those soft eyes again.

"So, what is it about you..." she says out loud, but to herself, and he quickly shakes his head.

"I mean, how else could she know, right? She had to be down here with you."

"She was. Long enough for us to make at least a dozen satchels like the one my dad made," Zoe adds, thumbing the strap of the one she's wearing. "Felt like he was with us for a while." Liddick closes his eyes and turns to face the mouth of the Swim chute, and I don't have enough time to ask him anything in my thoughts before Zoe continues. "Few months later she found out we could go back up at night, so she went to tell my dad we were fine, but...she never made it back. The supply-run parties looked for her some nights after. They found her." Zoe holds out her wrist to show us a gold bracelet with two letter *As* on it, one line crossing through them both.

"Brought me back what they could after the sun got her. She was just about a block away from her tunnel."

Zoe clears her throat after a second, and even though her voice, her posture, everything else about her snaps back to normal, her eyes take longer to harden and twinkle this time. The air seems to crack all around Liddick when I glance over and find him gripping his elbow with one hand while covering his mouth with his other fist.

Liddick? I think, but he just shakes his head without looking at me.

"That's why we can't go back after the Vishan treatments," Dell says. "The ones who got pulled through the sand before us were sure they could manage going back home at night, but they never came back here after trying. Eventually, the Council just stopped allowing it."

Liddick, they burn up…that's why all those bones were always in the Badlands…people were just trying to get back down here? But why do they let everyone think they're cannibals? I think, and when Liddick finally meets my eyes, he doesn't have to answer me. "The Badlanders have been letting everyone think they're cannibals to keep people out of the sand…to keep them safe," I say out loud to everyone as I look from Jax and Fraya to Zoe, Alec, and finally, to Dell. He nods, and we're all quiet for several seconds before he stands, then holds out his hands.

"All right, so let's have the other questions. We have to be back before curfew," he says, pulling a gold colored stone out of his pants pocket. "Which is in an hour."

"What's that?" Jax squints, then rubs his eyes.

"Cycle stone. It's synced with the torches. When it's red..." Dell starts.

"It's time for bed," they all say together, then join in a barrage of half smiles and eye-rolls.

"It's just not safe at night out here. Most everyone gets tucked up after gold, so any stray sounds stir up the water worms," Alec adds, and my eyes dart to the stream. "That's not deep enough, though. Worms can't shimmy quite this far in. Still, curfew helps keep people from wandering." He laughs, crossing his long arms over his chest.

"So there's more than one worm? And the sharks?" I ask.

"Never placed a bet, but for as many tunnel sharks as they have running from the barrier to the surface, figure there's bound to be more than one worm," Alec answers.

"The people in the mountain made them, you said... the Biodesigners and Molecular Coders? And the tunnel sharks gave you all nanites?" I ask.

"Not all of us—just those who got pulled through the sand. Those nanites only last a few hours, though," Zoe answers.

"Then why did they say Dell's don't work past the barrier?" I ask, but Zoe just looks at Veece as Cal closes his eyes and sighs.

CHAPTER 17
Catching Up: Part Two

Dell leans forward over his knees as he scans the ground, then takes a deep breath.

"I was crossing home one night. Kept to the outskirts of the sand, but not enough I guess. Once I got pulled through, the tunnel shark took me to the mountain...*into* the mountain," he says after a long pause, and I know he's telling the truth, or at least believes he is, when I feel the wave of suffocating anxiety flooding from him.

"But you escaped?" I ask, trying to help him wade through the memory. He nods again.

"Then found my way into the Rush—the seven biomes between here and the mountain."

"That's the rainforest you talked about before?" Liddick asks Cal, who looks up like it's a terrible effort.

"That's part of it," Cal nods slowly.

"*Rainforest*? Did I hear that because I hit my head? We're miles from the surface," Jax protests, then winces in pain with the effort. Fraya moves her hand over his arm as he covers his eyes with his hand.

"He needs to lie down," she says. "Where can I take him?"

"I'm fine," Jax argues, but his eyes are still narrowed against the torchlight.

"I'll show you back to Ada," Alec says, and Fraya nods before crossing to hug me.

"Thank you for coming for us," she whispers.

"*Of course* we came, Fraya."

She squeezes me more tightly, then returns to Jax's side. I wrap my arms around his waist and press my cheek into his chest as nearly losing him resurfaces. He leans down and chuckles.

"What's all this?" he whispers.

"I had to find you when you fell…when they took you," I say before my throat closes, and I have to swallow to keep the tears from choking me. We stand like this for a few seconds more before he takes a deep breath and leans down to whisper again.

"You jumped after me, didn't you?" he asks quietly, then tightens his arms around me. I choke on a sob. "We're going to be OK, Jazz. We're going to find dad, and this will all be OK." He kisses the top of my head, and I close my eyes against the tears flooding them, despite my efforts. I nod, and finally manage to take a deep enough breath to steady the convulsions in my chest.

"I love you," I say, then take another deep breath before wiping the tears from my face. Fraya is crying too when I look up, and I feel heat rush into my cheeks. "OK, go lie down," I say impulsively with a forced laugh as I take a step back from Jax, wishing desperately that everyone would talk, or at least stop staring at us with their wrinkled foreheads and watery eyes. I swallow hard to steady my voice, then wipe my face again as he moves his big hand from the back of my neck to my shoulder and squeezes. He smiles at me and nods, then disappears around the corner with Fraya and Alec.

"Isn't there any way to reactivate his nanites? The ones that will fix him?" I ask after Jax is gone, then turn back to Dell once I feel in control of myself again. "There's a cave about ten miles that way where they'll work," I add, but he just shakes his head.

"He needs help making it back to his bed stack. Not a chance he'll hang for ten miles in any direction yet," he answers.

"Where's the barrier? Is it closer? Your nanites worked until you crossed it, so maybe Jax's will work there too."

"Or, maybe they won't," Dell says, then stiffens. "Don't know if they're the same as yours...the only reason I had repair nanites at all was so I'd heal faster after they..." he trails off, then abandons the explanation altogether. "Anyway, it's suicide to gamble on nanites past the crop barrier. You need Vishan treatments."

"But Vox is out there," I say, and Cal lowers his eyes.

"Vox is Vishan," Veece answers, but is cut off by Cal's rebuttal.

"No, she's right. Vox might as well be like them because she hasn't been completely *trained*."

"Not now," Veece says, leveling a glare at Cal.

"Trained for what?" Liddick asks Zoe quietly.

"For using the gifts—the fire, the strength..."

"I don't understand...so none of the other people who were pulled through the sand ever had repair nanites like Dell's? Like ours? What kind were theirs then?" I ask.

"They were from the tunnel sharks, and weren't for keeps. They were only meant for making the trip to the mountain," Zoe answers.

"So they wore off?" I ask, and Zoe nods.

"The people the Vishan rescued from the tunnel sharks before us eventually started getting sick: paranoid, delirious, mean, and then…they died," she says, then takes in a breath. "The Vishan found a way to mix some of their DNA so it would fuse to theirs, so the sickness would stop, but the price of the fire, the strength, the price of being Vishan was that we couldn't go back to the surface, at least not into the daylight."

"But Vox is from the surface just like we are," I say. "If she's Vishan, she's lived her whole life in daylight."

"The Council thinks her gifts were dormant, but now that she's used the fire, she may not be able to go back," Veece answers.

"Does *she* know that? Does she know all the new abilities she has, but doesn't know how to control?" I ask, and Cal nods at the tail end of a long sigh.

"I *told* her not to leave before we could finish training her," he answers, then glances sideways at Veece. "The Council wouldn't stop her."

Veece starts to protest, but Liddick takes a step toward Cal, cutting off Veece's line of sight.

"Look, we need to get to that mountain. We need to follow her. Will you show us where she's going?" Liddick asks.

"You don't get it," Cal rounds on him. "There's nothing *in* that mountain except what will kill you five kinds of dead, and that's if you can even get through the Rush," he says, throwing a hand out to Dell. "Tell them. Take off your shirt again and tell the whole thing. It's because of your delusion that Vox left in the first place."

"Say that again." Dell's hazel eyes flash in the torchlight, and the muscles in his jaw tense as he takes a motivated step toward Cal, but Veece grabs his arm.

"No, let him come. He has no trouble preaching on how we're all mislead by the Origin Wall, but he won't lead anyone out to prove it. Well, you forget that I believed you, sandy. I went to the Motherland to see if it was nothing but labs and scientists like you said, but you know what I found? Nothing. No Motherland, no labs. It's just a volcano, and you're just another storyteller."

"*I'm* the storyteller because I won't go back out there to prove otherwise? Why do you think the tunnel sharks head for the mountain with people in the first place? But you're right about one thing—there is no Motherland out there…no people-gods, no great *Bestower*. What's in that volcano are people who *think* they're gods, and you simples run around here proud of being descended from their science experiments. Read your own wall!" Dell growls, and Cal lunges before Veece catches him with an arm in the chest.

"Enough!" Veece says, then turns back to Dell with the same warning glare. "*Most* of the Vishan believe the Origin Wall as it's written, but there are some who believe there's more," he says to us as he lets go of Cal. "But we can't destroy our entire culture to find out who is right."

"Why does knowing more mean it's destroyed? Why can't it just be changed? Evolved?" Dell presses.

"That's the problem the two who went to the stars had. Have *you* read the wall?" Veece returns his attention to Dell, then nods to Cal. "One of my distant grandfathers and one of his distant grandmothers refused the gifts of fire, strength, and pressure—they didn't want to change or to be advanced because it meant they could never go home to the surface again, so they *were lost*."

"To the stars? But Vox said all the Vishan were in the stars?" I ask.

"Her father's line is *Dyer*. Like Vita. There are legends of a terrestrial line of two brothers…one stayed on the surface, and one returned to the earth with the others. We never thought these were more than stories before Vox came here with most of the Vishan markings," Veece continues, his voice steady, but not calm. "Her people were lost to us, and we were lost to her people. *This* is what happens when we break from tradition."

There's a long silence before Liddick takes a step toward Veece.

"But if they didn't want to be changed, you should understand why we have to stop what they're doing in that mountain," Liddick says, looking from Veece to Cal.

"*We* understand, but the council won't believe mad scientists are trafficking sandies in there. The packs we send out for patrols, the ones like ours and Kesh's, they're sent because the Vishan believe we have to prove to the Bestower that we're still worthy of the gifts—the sandies are the chosen; the tunnel sharks are our tests," Veece explains.

Liddick looks from Veece to Dell, who tosses up a hand and shakes his head. Cal nods in reluctant agreement.

"Is he serious? People are dragged down here from the surface, and their council thinks it's because they're *chosen* for them? That these tunnel shark things are some kind of divine monster sent to test their—OK, I can't…"

Liddick closes his eyes and shakes his head, then pushes his hands through his hair.

"It's an old way," Veece says. "And it's a beam we can't shake, or we'll crash our whole culture."

"Truth doesn't matter...only tradition matters," Cal says. "Nothing new can replace it on account of it takes a long time to build. It would be like starting yourself over. How do you ask a whole culture to start itself over?"

"Maybe you don't. Maybe *you* just start over, and that eventually inspires others to do the same," I say, then immediately wonder where the thought comes from until I feel a tingle in the back of my neck just like I do when Vox is trying to push a thought into me. Everyone is quiet for a second as they look over at me. Liddick raises his eyebrows.

What is it? he thinks.

I don't know. Vox...somehow. I feel her.

"Well, Dell managed to inspire others to think he's cracked. Nothing out there is designed by scientists. It just *evolved*," he adds, and Dell narrows his eyes.

"Vox is still out there," I say. "I know she is, and I know she'll help us."

"She's going to have a hard enough time helping herself," Cal answers in a quieter voice, then blows out a labored breath. Liddick takes a few quick steps over to Veece and pulls up the sweep map on his forearm unit.

"Is this where she's heading? Is this the mountain?" he asks, pushing a button that doesn't do anything but make him swear. Finally, he pushes one that brings up a 3-D projection of the tunnels we're in, but he swears again when it cuts off after what looks like a grain field, and beyond that, dense...*trees*? "Crite, it only shows three miles at a time. Is she at least heading in that direction?" he asks, waving the map closed in frustration.

"Let's go to the Origin Wall," Zoe says to us all, and Cal launches a barrage of words in his language at her before switching back to ours.

"This is pointless!" he adds.

"No harm in them seeing what's between here and the mountain," Zoe says, then turns left of the chute we all just slid down.

CHAPTER 18
Origins

The white and yellow lights begin to haze near the top of the wide, limestone corridor until we reach a small cave that opens straight up into another narrowing passage, which is flooded with blue light trickling down. The walls in here are hard to see as a result, but they look like they have etchings all over them. As soon as we walk in, we can hear the blue lights above us *squeaking*—the closer we get, the louder it is. After a few seconds, the blue mass rushes down around us. I turn around directly into Liddick's chest, and he catches my arms so we don't fall with the momentum.

"What are those!?" I shout over their flapping, and just as quickly as they started moving, they're out of the cave. I look back over my shoulder to make sure they're all gone, then take a step back toward the middle of the room so I can look up into their narrow passageway again. "There were hundreds of—"

My words stop instantly in my throat when I feel something on my shoulder, then hear a high-pitched squealing close to my ear. I start swatting at the noise, making contact with something wet that then begins struggling in a tangle of my hair. I try to shake it loose, but it just starts squealing more.

"Hold still!" Cal says as the thing flaps and squeaks more violently.

"What is it!? Get it off!" I say through my teeth.

"You see?" I vaguely hear Cal's voice behind everything, then feel someone gripping my shoulder. When I look up, he's standing right in front of me with his other hand moving once, and then twice through my hair before he pulls it back and holds *a little, blue bat* in front of my face, caging it with one hand while holding his other underneath it like a saucer, which catches the glowing blue viscous liquid coming off it. "Can't deal with a lux, and you want to send them into the *Rush*?" he laughs over his shoulder at Zoe. Liddick takes a step forward and scratches the animal on the head, but the tiny, rounded blue ears and long, pointy blue nose instantly disappear into Cal's hand. He sucks in a quick, startled breath around a laugh and brings the creature into his chest to help catch *even more* of its pooling liquid. "Rav calls this *going goo*," he adds.

"Wh—? Did it just—? That's a *bat*! *Why is it—ugh*!" I shout, seeing nothing more of it except the blue, glowing liquid oozing through his fingers.

"Its insides are changeable like the other invertebrates down here, so it can actually break into pieces and move all its bits independent of itself before coming back together," Dell says, studying the animal as it starts to reform, "but mostly you'll just see them *going goo* like this. Stretched my head the first time I saw it happen too," he adds.

The viscous, blue fluid puddling in Cal's bottom hand pulls back into itself until it's nearly gone, and the same little ears and pointy nose begin peeking out from the top of his other hand again until the blue, glowing bat is caged again by his fingers.

"They only do it if they feel threatened, so if we can manage significantly less whaling around, it'll probably stay whole," Cal says, staring down his nose at me.

"See, it's harmless," Liddick says, reaching to carefully scratch the thing on the head again. "Touch it."

"No! I don't want to touch it! I've already touched it. Did you *miss* the part where I was *touching it*!?" I babble. Liddick's smile cracks into laughter, and I rake my fingers through my hair to make sure there are no more pieces of that animal entangled in it just like the gel worm was in the scene Vox showed me…and the second I realize what I'm doing, I feel the air rush at me all at once. *In the scene…it was wet just like this, and the pieces came back together…*I think, frozen where I stand as Liddick meets my eyes.

*Rip, this isn't a worm. It's not **exactly** like what you saw,* he thinks, but my heart still hammers in my chest. The vision is coming true, and now I'm terrified to remember that it also showed Fraya screaming…that Vox was on fire.

Cal releases the weird gelatinous bat into the mouth of the corridor, where it follows the others. He shakes his head, then wipes his hands on his pants as Zoe smiles, and I *swear* I see her open her fist to deposit a little red flame, which then lights a torch mounted in the wall. She reaches for it, then holds it to the etchings on the far left of the cave.

"Lots of things down here make their own light too, like those worms out there," she says.

"Did you just...was that fire in your *hand*?" I ask, stunned, but she just angles her head at me and raises an eyebrow.

"Well, yeah. The DNA treatment, remember? All of us can do it," Zoe says like it's as common as a weather update, and my heart drops to the bottom of my chest.

Liddick...Vox was on fire like this in the message she sent me in the corridor. It's all coming true! I think.

Maybe she was just trying to show us their abilities. Don't jump to conclusions, he replies, but I see the muscles in his jaw tense. He's not all right with this either.

"Everyone descended from the six lines, plus those we've treated has their gifts," Veece says, nodding to Dell and Zoe. "We're all untouchable by fire, heat, and we we're immune to the pressure this far below the surface."

"But you can *produce* fire too? It's not just a defense ability?" I ask, and just as I finish, a tiny red flame snaps to life in the center of Dell's hand. In seconds, it's a small collection of flames about the size of one of the wall torches. I raise my fingers to it, and can feel the heat several inches away. Dell studies my face, then his eyebrow quirks at the same time as the corner of his mouth. "That's amazing," I say, and he winks at me again like he did when he and Alec first pulled us through the corridor.

"Well, this probably won't be near as entertaining, but here's the Origin Wall," Zoe says, breaking my hypnosis with the fire. "You want to know which way Vox went, best just to see the whole thing spread out, wise?" she asks. Liddick nods in reply, then glances over at me with a new focus in his eyes.

"This is the map of everything out there? Everything on the way to the mountain?" I ask.

"More," Veece says, gesturing to the bottom of the wall. "All these words down here, that's what my father recited up at the Gathering," he adds, then points to the three dots hovering over each side of the upside down, stacked letter Vs, and then at a diamond shape just below that. "These six dots are stars—they're supposed to represent the six families. That's what the script down here says," he explains. I take a step closer to the wall and see that the diamonds and other etchings are almost the same as the marks Vox and the Vishan have.

I raise my hand to the wall and start to shake off the last of the random chills that stupid little bat gave me, then trace the diamond shaped maze at the bottom of the carving. Above it, seven inverted arrows are connected by a line up the middle like the veins of a leaf. A regular looking, open arrow with two dots over it and another diamond inside are above that.

"And this is where Vox went?" I ask.

"Yes, that's the Motherland, the first great peak Jove talked about," Cal answers. "And those two dots represent the two who went to the stars."

"It's here," Veece adds, pointing to his chin. "And the path to the stars…that's these two inverted arrows, the diamond, and the two skies here." He points to the pattern on the bridge of his nose and the diamond between his eyes, then to the arrows on his forehead with the three dots on each side.

"And this maze?" I say, pointing to the woven diamond pattern that both Vox and the Vishan have on their chest. "Vox said these were her lands?"

"The Vishan lands. In-terra," Cal says with a clip of aggravation in his voice. "Vox's tattoos aren't complete. These are the seven biomes, the templates for the climates on the surface. We call it the *Rush*—she's missing the line that connects them on her throat, see?" he adds, pointing to his neck, and then to his chin. "She's missing the Motherland diamond here too."

"So how will she know where to go?" I ask.

"Probably the same way she's always known. You saw the maps she tattooed on herself from all her other treks," Liddick says.

"But this isn't exactly Skyboard or even the Badlands. She has no point of reference here."

"Sure she does," Zoe says. "You can see the Motherland from here. It's the Rush in between that might complicate the whole endeavor some."

"Some," Cal and Dell both say at the same time, and Cal chuffs a laugh as they exchange glances. "Some is just the beginning."

"You said we could see it from here—the mountain. Will you show us?" I ask Zoe.

"Love to, but we're about out of time for tonight," she says, pulling her own nearly red cycle stone from her pocket. "They're going to sound curfew when this turns red, and we still need to walk back up to the Hall," she adds, putting the stone away and then returning the torch to the wall where she claps it out with both hands. It takes a second for my eyes to adjust to the relative brightness of the white and yellow light after the red torch.

"Tomorrow," Veece says as we turn back into the corridor. "We'll take you to the Lookout Pier. You'll need your sleep tonight." A feeling of hope washes over me as I nod at him, then turn to Liddick.

It's a good sign, don't you think...that they'll help us get through the Rush? Can't you feel it? I ask Liddick in my thoughts as we leave the cave, but he just keeps staring straight ahead, and then slows to a stop along with the others after a few more steps. *Did you hear me? Don't you feel it?* I add, compelled to giggle until I grip his sleeve and the ridiculous giddiness tempers.

"Jazz..." I hear my name in front of us, and immediately turn my head in the direction of it. All at once the flood of happiness crashes over me again, and before I realize I've taken one step, I've taken so many that I'm halfway down the corridor.

"Arco!"

Layers

Arco exhales like he's just thrown off a heavy pack, and the next time I blink, his arms are closing around me and lifting me off the ground. His skin is cool against my cheek and smells like the sea—the damp fabric of his dive suit pressing against my neck as he starts to laugh.

"It's all right," he repeats through my rambling apologies for pushing him away at the top of the waterfall, and I start laughing too once I finally unlock my arms from around his neck. I take a deep breath before I look up to see the same runaway smile he couldn't control when he first kissed me by the moon pool. Heat spreads over my cheeks at the memory of him rushing in without even thinking, of feeling his hands on my face, and the way his lips moved over mine.

"How did you get down the falls?" Liddick asks abruptly from behind me, which makes me refocus.

"Short version?" Avis starts. "We were rappelling, but then our new friends here came out of nowhere and tried pulling our lines back up. Tieg jerked one of them right off the edge!" he laughs as he cranes his neck, presumably to find either Tieg or the person who fell.

"Is he all right?" I automatically scan everyone until I see a tall Badlander boy narrowing his eyes at Avis as he bends to wring out his soaked shirt. He straightens to his full, imposing height, and I can see that his lean torso is bright with fresh scratches that run up his side.

"*I'm fine*," he snarls as Cal and Dell try not to laugh.

"We didn't know they were helping until we jumped the rest of the way down and landed in the pool. If it weren't for their sonar device..." Arco adds, taking a deep breath as he looks at me, then shakes his head and closes his eyes in a long blink. "I can't even think about you down there with that thing swimming right underneath..." he trails off again before looking over his shoulder at a Badlander girl behind him. Her skin is bronze in the hazy white and yellow light of the glow worm walls, and her short, black hair falls back from her forehead in choppy angles. "Thank you," he nods to her.

"Ty chased off the worm, I just kept Jesse from killing you after the all-clear," she shrugs, angling her head back to the scratched boy near the wall. He glares at her as he shakes water from his short, dark hair, then crosses to the opening in the rock ahead of us, his wet shirt still dripping in his hand.

"If the soup is gone, I'm throwing them off the Lookout Pier," he says, jerking his chin at Tieg. "He's first."

Dell and Cal erupt in laughter now, earning them both a shove from the boy as he pushes through the fissure.

"Glad you're not swallowed, Jesse!" Zoe calls after him, then begins laughing too. Tieg just rolls his eyes and sighs, too exhausted to care as Veece blows out a breath.

"And you probably can't forget Jesse," he says with a nod at the opening in the wall. "Ty helped him bring you in earlier, and this is Kesh," he adds, gesturing first to another tall, lean boy standing with Myra and Joss, then to the girl with the choppy, dark hair. Kesh nods unceremoniously at us, and Ty raises two fingers to his forehead before taking off the leather pouch slung across his chest, his short brown hair wet and clinging to his forehead.

"It's curfew—come on." Dell looks at his now *very* red stone, then leads us toward the fissure.

This is the corridor we came through—the one where they grabbed us? I think toward Liddick as we walk, and when he doesn't answer right away, I turn to him.

Looks like it, he finally says without turning back, and a cold wave washes over me.

What's wrong? I ask him, then watch him crossing to Dez, a suffocating heaviness in his wake.

Nothing—I'll fix it, he answers, but then Tieg moves to Dez's side, cutting off his trajectory. We fall in behind them, and I feel Liddick's impatience silently explode.

*Hey…*I call to him in my head, and after a second, he finally looks over to me. *Tieg isn't going to give you the chance to fix anything. I can explain to her that you only jumped down the falls after me because we're friends, if it will help?* I offer, but he just chuffs a laugh.

Help who, Rip? You? His words are clipped even in my head and hang in the air as another thrum of adrenaline fires straight through me. All at once I feel seen again, accountable, and this time it makes me angry.

*Liddick, you may be able to read my thoughts, but that does **not** mean you know how I feel,* I answer as my heart starts pounding. He turns to look directly at me over his shoulder, his eyes sparking as he opens his mouth, then bites back whatever he was going to say, forcing the muscles in his jaw to jump as he pushes through the fissure in front of us.

I blow out a breath just as we empty into the same cave where we first met Zoe, Cal, Alec, and Dell. The walls now reflect the deep red glow of the torches instead of the brighter green from earlier, and when we reach the top of the connecting corridor, Center Hall is full of people. Dell and Cal join the tall boy who was intent on soup at the cook pot—*did Zoe call him Jesse?*—where he is fortunately ladling some into a bowl, and I smile at the passing realization that none of us will be tossed off the pier tonight.

Liddick doesn't react to my observation, and I'm not sure if the pressure in my chest now is because of his residual guilt over not explaining his feelings about me to Dez, or really about the moments with him like this when I know he's not entirely wrong—moments when he can see even what I don't want to see. I've made it clear to both of us that we can't be anything more than friends because I can't let myself get caught up...I can't lose sight of consequences the way I do with him, especially not now when there is so much at stake. I look over to him again, but he only scrubs his hands over his face before walking back toward the stone circle where everyone is eating.

"Let's go before Jesse hollows that pot," Kesh says to Arco and Ty, her dark eyes kind, almost maternal, even though she must be about the same age as we are.

"If he hollows it, he'll be the one launched off the Lookout," Ty grins through feigned bravado. "I'll see to that personally," he adds with an escaping laugh as he holds out a hand for Kesh to go up to the cook pot first, and I can't help but smile. He puts off the same kind of warmth as Myra, which is a welcome relief considering the ice wall now between Liddick and me, and I don't even know what to begin to say to Dez.

Kesh smiles, then nods graciously to Ty before they both walk with Zoe toward the others, and Arco's arm tightens around me.

"What's wrong?" he says in a soft, low voice that still startles me. I take a deep breath and look up at him, unsure how to explain.

"Just everything with Dez and Liddick," I finally say, aware of how vague it is, but there's just too much to say and I don't know how to begin. He studies my face for a second before he answers me, and I can tell he's trying to choose his words.

"It was only a matter of time before someone got hurt around him. Maybe he'll be more careful now," he offers, and I feel compelled to remind him that we've been wrong about Liddick—that he was only immersing himself in the virtuo-cines and Skyboard culture to find out more about what happened to his brothers. *How has Arco forgotten this already?* I wonder, feeling an ember of anger start to melt the ice in my stomach. "You know he was just trying to protect everyone," I finally say, trying to keep the note of chastisement out of my voice, but he only sighs.

"He was still reckless with her, and he deserves what he's getting now because of that."

"He just wanted to help her after Pitt..." I trail off, still in disbelief that he's really gone.

"He's been letting her fawn all over him since before anything happened to Pitt. Tieg even caught them making out, remember? He's just careless, Jazz. You can't act that way with someone without it setting up an expectation that you're together," Arco adds, and in the same moment I want to fall through one of the cracks in the walls because if Liddick is guilty of setting up an expectation, then I *most definitely* am, despite trying not to talk about how I feel about Arco until I'm sure myself. *How did this happen*? I smile weakly at him as we walk toward the cook pot where Vita ladles a bowl of soup for him, and I feel distant from everyone as we take a seat on one of the flat stones in the circle.

Crite, you think too much. Liddick says in my head as he finds somewhere to sit. I open my eyes to see him pressing his lips into a thin smile. My own thoughts, everyone else's conversation about the Vishan and about how the Badlanders got down here, all the words running in the background stop as I search myself for a justifying response.

I'd have more figured out if I did, I say, and his mouth pulls to a smile.

Thanks for trying to make him see just now, Liddick adds, glancing at Arco, who is riveted by whatever Veece is saying as everyone finishes their soup. *But everything will always be black and white to him.*

Well, he's not wrong about how Dez feels. Did you forget to tell her things were as casual as you thought?

Rip, how could they be anything else after just a few days? We maybe had five minutes where things got heated, and that's when Spaulding walked up and went atomic. After that, we were escaping an imploding, two-ton Leviathan and burying her brother…no real opportunity for defining the parameters of a relationship in all that, you know? he answers, only half-committing to the sarcasm as he pushes a hand through his light hair, lifting it back to expose the darker roots.

Do you care about her? I ask, and this makes his eyes flash to mine.

Yeah, I mean, as much as can be expected for barely knowing her, he finally answers, then shakes his head and looks away. *Crite, I'm not a sociopath.*

Well, maybe that will just get stronger. Maybe it will be everything you want if you give it a chance? I hear the words in my head, feel them take shape quickly before they lose their nerve, and he just stares at me in that way that's too intense, too focused to outrun.

Is that what you're doing with Hart? *Hoping*? He leans in over his knees and clasps his hands in front of him as his eyes pin me to my seat, and another flare of adrenaline lights in my chest.

This isn't about me, Liddick.

Isn't it? he asks, now with an edge in his voice. *The only difference between you and me is you won't just let your feelings be what they are…you keep trying to make them fit this life plan you're still clinging to, but if you haven't noticed, that blew up the second they slapped these bracelet cuffs on us. We have to make a new way now whether we're ready or not, Rip.* Liddick suddenly darts a glance to Arco, who is sitting next to me, then gets to his feet along with several of the others who then start migrating toward the sleeping areas. *I **do** know how you feel. Does he*?

"Hey," Arco says, nudging me in the ribs, and I look up at him, startled. "Did you hear me?"

"What? No, I mean...sorry. What?" I say, shaking my head to bring myself back into the moment as Liddick disappears behind some of the crowd.

"They're rolling up. Zoe is going to show us where to sleep, and tomorrow they'll take us to the Lookout," he answers, nodding to Zoe, who is waiting for us to follow her. I get to my feet and pull in a deep breath, taking Arco's hand as we walk to the other side of the cook pot where Liddick has disappeared in the mix.

Jax is fast asleep on one of the bedding areas to our left, and Fraya sits next to him on another stack of blankets as she sorts through her pack. To our right, Dell looks like he's trying to facilitate something between Jesse and Tieg, neither of whom look terribly happy to be in the other's presence. I scan for Dez and find her along the wall with Liddick, his brows raised and chin lowered as he holds out his hand to her while he talks. Both her hands suddenly fly up, cutting off whatever he's saying, and I feel the reverberation of it hit him like a crashing wave.

"You'll all be hereabouts," Zoe says, making me flinch as she fans her hands toward the large area in front of us with several neutrally colored blankets stacked up, all of them sitting perpendicularly to the stone wall. None of them are separated by stone dividers like the other areas, and there are no makeshift shelves.

"Thank you," I say, my initial startle subsiding as the sight of the blankets suddenly makes me feel like I haven't slept in a week.

"Not as fancy as some stacks, but we figured your people would want to stay together," she nods, then gestures to the area next to Jax. "Ada's just there in case your walrus needs anything, and I'm right here, plus Veece, Dell, and some other familiars," she adds, motioning to the sections to our right. "Settle where you like, and I'll collect you in the morning for the Lookout. Oh, and Vox wanted me to give you this—said it would help you find your way." She hands me something small wrapped in cloth, then smiles one more time before turning to crawl onto her stack of blankets, her copper hair catching the last of the red light, which is so dark now that it's almost purple.

I let go of Arco's hand to unfold the stiff cloth as I sit on the blankets, which are coarsely woven, but soft, and piled almost a foot off the ground like the rest of the stacks.

"What is it?" Arco asks as he slides his blankets more closely to mine, then sits next to me as I feel a dull buzz starting in the back of my teeth again.

"It's…Vox's *pick knife.*"

CHAPTER 20
Coming Clean

The metal is warm, and the weight of the little knife in the palm of my hand is somehow reassuring...it was the only thing she was allowed to bring from home on her boundary scouting trips, and only because she was supposed to use it to record her path—*to help her find her way*...I think as the last of the light gleams off the thin blade, which is about as long as my little finger, and I resist the urge to touch the sharp point.

"Isn't that what she used to make her map tattoos? Does she expect *you* to do that?" Arco tramples into my observations, and I suddenly want him to go away.

"*Of course* she doesn't!" I snap at him before I even realize it, immediately wrapping the knife and putting it between the folds of blankets. The buzz in my teeth increases just enough that I can feel it surge before it subsides and is gone again, and with it, the reassuring feeling I had.

"Whoa, what—?" he starts to question, but I turn to him and cut him off, outraged that he's doubting me.

"And what if she *did* believe I could make my own map tattoos? Is that really so hard for you to imagine? Who jumped off those falls, Arco? Not you, not Tieg, it was me, and I didn't even hesitate!" My throat constricts on the last words as I lie down and turn away from him.

"*Hey*..." Arco says carefully after a beat and puts his hand on my hip.

"Seriously, could you just not?" I hear the sharp edge in my voice, and then feel his reaction sink into my chest where it starts hollowing everything. He removes his hand, and I hear him lie back on his blankets, then blow out a breath as my heart starts to pound in my ears. I'm compelled to reach for the wrapped pick knife again, to feel that reassurance for just one more second instead of the weight of this whole stupid ocean on top of us. When I curl my fingers around it, the buzzing gets stronger, echoing the pulse in my ears, but after a few minutes, everything calms, and my throat starts to relax enough for me to take a slow, deep breath.

A wave of guilt hits me when the anger recedes, but I don't want to acknowledge it because anger feels better—not right, but better, and right now all I want to do is stop everything from feeling like it's being pulled in different directions. *We're miles underwater, and no one is coming to get us…nothing is how we planned, and we really do have to make our own way, ready or not,* I think to myself.

"You know, I've never wanted anything Wright had," Arco's voice is so quiet I almost don't hear it. "Never envied his girls or his important friends, but when I found out you could hear his thoughts and that he could hear yours—crite, there's so much I don't know how to say," he adds, sighing just before I hear him shifting on his blankets, his voice a little louder now just behind my ear, "It guts me that I'm never going to be able to read your mind like your other Reader Empaths can—like *he* can—but if you can sense anything about me, Jazz, you know I believe you could do anything. Whatever this is really about, just talk to me," he pauses, then takes in a few deep breaths in the dark before the hollow feeling in my chest spreads to my stomach, that gnawing hunger feeling again…his helplessness, and I don't know what to say to fix it until I realize it's really not him who doubts my abilities, *it's me.*

I turn back over my shoulder and feel him right there, strong and solid like a wall holding back the rest of the world, and even though I don't know where I'm going from here, at least I know now where I should begin.

"I'm sorry…" I say quietly, and then feel his hand move tentatively back to my hip. "We just have so far to go, and I don't know where we'll end up. We've always known; we've always been able to see where the roads lead. Now we don't even have roads."

"There are always roads," he whispers, causing a tingle to shoot up my spine and rest at the nape of my neck as I close my eyes, remembering that this is exactly what Vox said back in our dorm. The buzz in my ears turns into a low hum, and in this minute, no matter what Cal thinks, I know she's all right out there when I repeat her words.

"You either find them or make them…"

***

The dull buzzing still in my head wakes me up, and the light is bright even before I open my eyes. It smells like onions cooking along with the dampness of the cave, and I hear voices and stirrings all around me. I blink so my eyes will adjust as I inch out from under Arco's arm, then sit at the edge of my blanket stack and scrub my hands over my face. I comb my fingers through my hair and study the others—the Vishan, the Badlanders, who are all making their way to the Swim and then disappearing down the chute—then scan for everyone in our group. They're all scattered nearby, but still asleep, and the sight of Dez curled against Liddick burns off the rest of my sleepy fog. I take a deep breath and try to cool the jealousy, and when that doesn't work, I force it out. *Good…*I think. *He fixed it. This is how it should be.*

"What is it with him?" Zoe asks in a hushed voice, suddenly looking over my shoulder at Liddick, whose arm is draped over his eyes. She lowers her chin to her chest and looks down at me in utter disbelief when I nearly jump out of my skin, her wide brown eyes afloat in the sea of freckles that spatter her nose and cheeks. "Criminy, Cal's right," she sighs, shifting her leather pouch around to her lower back before pushing up her long, dark sleeves and pulling her fiery hair into a little ponytail. "You'll never make it like this. Come on."

"*What?*" I ask, but she just sucks in a resolute breath and straightens, then grabs my arm and starts walking us toward the Swim.

"First off, that one…" she says quietly, flicking a glance back at Liddick. "How did he know who I was?"

"What?" I ask, still confused. "Where are we going?"

"*You* are going to talk to Cal, but that's second—we're still on first," she whispers without looking at me. "He knew who I was because he went all wondrous at my second name being Frank, and then he just *happened* to figure my mom got pulled through the sand with me? *Pfffft,*" she rolls her eyes. "He knows more than he's offering."

"So just ask him," I say, forgetting to whisper, then look over my shoulder to make sure I haven't woken anyone up. "Why am I talking to Cal?"

"Training for the Rush," she says like it's the most obvious thing in the world. "I've just about got Dell worked into it. Kesh too, and if Kesh and Dell are in, then Alec and Ty are just a matter of asking. As for Jesse, might need to have Ada fashion a pie or—"

"They'll take us to the mountain?"

"Well, no," she says in a normal voice now that we're far enough away from the others. "At least not all of them —that's why you're talking to Cal. The rest can be persuaded to show you how to keep yourself uneaten and all your parts attached while you try. Ready?" she asks with a shrug, but doesn't wait for my answer before stepping over the lip of the Swim opening while still holding onto my arm. The ground falls out from under me, and before I can even process what has just happened, we're at the bottom of the chute.

"*Crite!* A little warning next time?" My words come out strangled as my heart pounds in my ears.

"No fun if you see it coming!" she says as she hops from the edge of the chute, and I crawl after her. Outside, she's waving me past the other Vishan and Badlanders who are gathering along the stream, some of them scooping water from it over their heads and necks while others just stand around and stretch. "Hurry before he's here and gone. It's his day for crops."

She leads me along the stream until we turn the corner and come to a new part of the cavern. The white and yellow glow worms still light the walls, but the ceiling seems to glow with another kind of light. Large sections of green moss also carpet the areas surrounding another pool, which is about twenty feet in any direction, and covered in *steam*.

"Whoa..." I gasp, touching the wall of thick moss next to me, which is cool and soft. When I turn back to ask Zoe about it, I see Dell surfacing in the pool and swimming away from us until he pulls out to his waist at the edge. He lifts his arms to squeeze the water out of his dark hair before letting it fall over his shoulders, the muscles weaving and wrapping into each other before running down the column of his broad back. The random scars there match the ones I remember seeing yesterday on his torso—some of them smooth and shiny, and the one rounded, ragged one that sits to the left of his lower back just like the one over his hipbone. Zoe catches me staring.

"He was in the Rush awhile after another tunnel shark tried to take him back to the mountain. That's what gave him the scar that looks like it's run clean through...must be a year ago now," she says, pulling her hair down from the ponytail she'd just made. "Nanites repair damage inside to out, wise? And a good thing too because his stopped working at the far edge of the boundary. No way he could have made it from there to here with his insides sloshing around, especially not since all the rest of those marks are just from hiking the rainforest system—his repair nanites worked until then," she adds, then walks to the edge of the pool.

Almost in punctuation to her story, Dell palms the ground to hop out of the water, and after my initial shock, I laugh nervously wondering how it's possible that he has *tan lines* when he hasn't seen the sun in a year. He grabs his dark clothes from a nearby rock, then turns toward me after he's squeezed all the water from his hair. Before I see anything that I can't *un-see*, I start walking purposefully to catch up to Zoe at the edge of the water, crossing my arms over my chest and rolling my lips between my teeth until he passes behind us and stops at my side.

"Cal is taking the perimeter today if it's all the same to you," he says to Zoe, and out of the corner of my eye, I can tell he's stepping into his pants just like no one is there. She nods at him, and he brushes my arm, "Then I'll go collect your friends."

"Right, yes…thanks," I squeak in response, still unable to look directly at him. Zoe nods as Dell turns to leave, then picks up where she left off after he's gone.

"So, Cal found him at the crop edge one morning and brought him up to Vita for patching and treatments, and after hearing his story, Cal was set on seeing for himself about the mountain…he was sore about the council sending Vox off without more help, so my advice would be to start with that when he gets here," she says, then drops her bag and *pulls her shirt over her head.* I turn to face the water directly in front of me and clear my throat as Zoe starts laughing.

"I went a whole month clinging to my clothes when I first got here," she chuckles. "My mom and Vita finally had to toss me in the water dressed head to toe because I refused to get natural. After walking around dripping wet clear up until it was time for bed, I just washed up the easy way from then out," she grins, and I'm lost for what to say in response until I see Cal and Jesse approaching out of the corner of my eye. A cold panic hits me as I scramble for her shirt, and I can't get the words out fast enough.

"The boys are coming!" I yell-whisper and shove her shirt at her, surprised when the sleeves rattle like a tin of stones, but she just shrugs and shimmies out of her matching pants that I haven't really noticed until now.

"So," she says, navigating over the rock ledge and stepping into the water. "Parts are parts…mine aren't strange or new."

"*Zoe*—" I start, but swallow it when Jesse walks up next to me.

"Are you all *still* here?" he asks, narrowing his eyes and looking down his long nose at me as he pulls his shirt over his head. It's the same as Zoe's with dark, little scale-like pieces that seem to be sewn together, but I can't get a good look before he drops it to the ground. He turns to the water, and I notice the scratches that ran the length of his side are almost healed, and still partially covered in the same green mud that Ada put on Jax's eyebrow. He catches me looking at them, and I look back at the water just in time to learn that Zoe is a good diver, and that apparently, she has freckles everywhere. *This is not happening.*

"Uh, yep! Still here," I say, frantically scanning the area in every possible direction for somewhere else I can be until Cal walks up and starts untying the drawstring of his pants, at which time I begin a most heartfelt and attentive conversation with the ceiling. "Still trying not to be here, *trust* me…hoping you all might help with that…"

"Getting in? We're going to the crop edge today," Cal asks, and I immediately shake my head.

"Ah, no, I'm… no. You all just carry on," I trip through the words.

"Can't Ghost or Calliope fashion our suits to have a *higic*….a *higee*…what did the other one call it?" Jesse asks.

"Hygienic Climate System," Zoe answers from somewhere in the water. "Fraya said those suits do all but walk around for you," she laughs and splashes me, and I'm surprised that the water is so warm. "Jump in!"

"I am *really* good right here. Hygienic climate whatever and all…" I stutter at the ceiling, which is really quite lovely with the stones shining the way they are, and I make a mental note to ask everyone about it when they aren't all glow-in-the-dark naked right in front of me.

"*Fa na vish,*" Zoe chuckles again, and in the span of five seconds, I'm being dumped head first into the warm, fresh water.

CHAPTER 21
Zephyrs

It's hard to commit to swearing after coughing out the first few words when I feel the warm water soaking into my scalp and running down my face. I clear enough of it to see the skin-blur of Jesse hopping over the rock barrier, and then Cal dunking his blond head.

Jesse laughs at me as he pretends to dust off his hands, and I narrow my eyes at him. Zoe climbs out of the water and slips back into her clothes—her skin tanned with the exception of small, white, circular scars under her arm and down the length of her ribs, her dark freckles, and the long, snake-like scar over her shoulder. But then everything is laser focused once I realize we're all actually back in a pool of water down here.

"What about the worm!?" I cough again, looking around in a panic.

"Worms can't fit through the crevices leading to hot springs. Only water can leak through those little cracks, then it pushes up through there," Zoe answers, gesturing to the pool. "Cal, hurry up if you're running the perimeter, or I'm taking it."

"We get in here once a week…why do you always kill the moment?" he asks, diving under again, and I start making my way toward the edge to climb out.

"Why do you only go once a week?" I ask, then wish I hadn't once I realize I could live my whole life without knowing their bathing habits and be just fine.

"Only need bugs once a week for the crop edge—everyone rotates so it's fair."

"*Bugs*?" I gasp and start looking at my hands and arms as Cal, Jesse, and Zoe laugh.

"You can't even see them without a scope, and they can't hurt you, relax," Zoe finishes chuckling as she buckles her rustling black pants. "They make the crops think that you're native—otherwise the stalks will attack you when you get close enough to pull harvest, which is what we have to go do before we can go to the Lookout. *Cal*!" Zoe straightens and throws a loose stone at him as he floats on his back in the pool. It hits him in the stomach, and the shock makes him jerk his head into the water, then choke. "Tell him I'm taking perimeter when he gets done dying?" she says to Jesse, who is already breathless with laughter. "Come on, Jazz."

My dive suit goes from dripping to damp in the time it takes me to climb out of the pool. I wring out my hair and follow her, looking back over my shoulder to see Cal scrubbing his hands over his face as he coughs.

"Where are we going?"

"Down and down some more, then out," she says as we continue through the corridor. "We have to set the pull tarps for the grain—well, Cal and Jesse have to set the pull tarps. *We* are running the perimeter to make sure nobody gets snatched," she adds, excitement lighting her eyes. "Then we can climb to the Lookout."

I shake my head trying to process. "Did you say so they don't get *snatched*? By what?"

"Zephyrs," she answers as we move downward through a dim, branching part of the corridor where a warm wind suddenly blasts us from even farther down.

"Are those like the tunnel sharks?" I ask, hurrying to keep up with her when she doesn't elaborate.

"No, zephyrs are mostly made of wind, vapors—can't barely see them sometimes before they fly over like they're just passing through, then just suck you right out of your steps. It's harder for them to tell us apart from the ground or the rustle of the stalks if we're wearing these, though," she says, holding up her arm and rotating her wrist so her sleeve makes a *shish-shish* sound. I squint at her.

"You have predatory *food* and *wind* down here?" I ask, stumbling over the dark, uneven stones winding down under our feet until we finally cross onto a stretch of the same green moss that was on the walls by the hot spring pool.

"Everything is predatory down here except us—well, not if you ask the fish in the reservoir, but…" she laughs, then pulls herself through a final opening in the wall, where the wind starts howling. I follow her through to the other side, which opens to a wide expanse of rolling black rock with a field of bright, wispy grain that starts about thirty feet from us and runs even farther back. An enormous white sun burns through the dark sky—can it be a *sky*?—casting yellowish light over everything like an eclipse. The whole area is still and surreal like the calm before a storm until sections of the grain in the distance suddenly toss and whip, and I am stopped where I stand.

"Are those...the *zephyrs*?" I manage to ask before she gets too far ahead of me, then I take a few steps back to the rock wall, which is black and shiny in places just like the ground.

"A few of them. Can't pull anything until they all come, though," she replies, then suddenly looks past me. "There they are."

I turn in the direction she's looking and don't see anything but several tumbling dark clouds, and intermittently between them, small, flickering specks.

"*Stars*?" I say to myself, and Zoe meets my eyes.

"No. It's just more of this," she says, patting a reflective, glass-like section of the black rock we're leaning against.

"That's *a cave wall* out there? That high? But what about these clouds, and that sun?" I ask, incredulous as I look up at the muted glowing disk that pours saturated golden light over everything.

"Not clouds...like I said, those are the rest of the zephyrs, and that's not the sun," she insists. "Dell said they made it at the mountain just like the tunnel sharks— there's a stretch of the same glowing gas over the hot spring. Didn't you see? Anyway, the Council says it's *the source*," she adds, rolling her eyes, "but don't get either Dell or Cal started on that, please and thank you. All I know is it makes the Bale grow." She gestures to the grain in front of us, then picks up several shiny rock chips from the ground and sends them sailing one by one into the stalks.

"The source of what?" I ask, unable to look away from the golden field and the dark, rolling sky that looks like it could be breathing all around it. I try to process how big this cave must be if what I'm really seeing is just more *walls,* but my mind kicks out the concept every time I try to make it stick.

"The source of the original immunity for the first twelve Vishan. Can't see it from this angle, but the homeland mountain is just under that glow. I'll show you when we climb to the Lookout Pier."

"And in between here and there is…"

"The Rush," she says, looking over the grain stalks that stand perfectly still except for pockets of violent whips that swirl them like they're being shaken from below, then stop just as quickly as more of the clouds collect overhead. I cling to the wall behind me.

"Zephyrs are lagging," Zoe adds with a satisfied nod as she steps backward toward the fissure. "Won't stay that way now that they're roused, though." She turns into the fissure, but stops abruptly when Dell and Arco suddenly come through. Tieg, Avis, Joss, and finally, Liddick, Cal, and Jesse appear just after them, and she swallows whatever she was going to shout. "*About time.*"

Everyone from our group stops in their steps just like I did when they look out at the eternity of rolling black and brightly lit grain before us. Cal, Dell, and Jesse walk out a few more feet to stand near Zoe, and then Cal shakes his head at us.

"They're stuck in place just like you two were," he says to Jesse and Zoe. "This never gets old," he chuckles then and backhands Jesse in the chest.

"Where are Myra, Dez, and Ellis?" I ask, looking back through the fissure, sure that Jax must still be resting, and Fraya is probably with him.

"They're talking with Veece and Jove," Dell answers.

"About what?" I ask, but he just shrugs.

"What is all this?" Arco asks, his eyes narrowed, then going wide when he sees the grain whipping around before us.

"How is there…*weather*?" Avis starts walking away from the wall until Jesse stops him with a hand in his chest.

"That weather will pull you straight up and strip you clean, layer by layer till you're gone," he says, stepping slightly to the side so Avis can see the short, explosive bursts of swirling stalks.

"What's doing that?" Joss asks, looking around urgently. "What's running loose out here?"

"It's wind…*predatory* wind," I say, and everyone's eyes snap to mine except Liddick's. He cocks an eyebrow and takes in a breath.

"Zephyrs…they only come around the Bale field because over the years, they've learned that's where they can find us," Dell says.

"Works out fine now that we know how to use them, though—nothing gets the berries off stalks except the zephyrs shaking and pulling. We tried everything from rigging shaker tethers to cutting them free, but even with bugs, the stalks will attack you if they think you're a threat," Zoe nods.

"So, *now* we just set out pull-tarps, run around until *all* the zephyrs gather above and start trying to skin us like rabbits," Jesse explains in an overly upbeat tone, then angles his head at the dark clouds gathering just ten feet or so above the field. "And if we manage to keep our faces on, we zig-zag back and pull in the tarps with the berries that drop." He lets an obnoxious, exaggerated smile interrupt his surly expression for a few seconds, then nods to Cal. "Ready to go?"

Everyone blanches as Zoe holds out her hands.

"It's all regular, don't worry..." she says, shaking her head at Jesse. "See the dark haze forming? That's them collecting. We just take turns distracting them while the others set up."

"Just stay here until we get back—won't take a minute," Cal says to Arco and the others, then nods back at Jesse before they both run toward opposite edges of the grain field.

"You playing fox?" Zoe asks Dell with a wink.

"Unless you're feeling faster today?" He quirks an eyebrow and chuckles as Zoe grabs my wrist.

"What's happening?" I ask, looking back and forth between them.

"Are you split? She's not going out there with you," Arco protests, taking a step forward as he looks over our heads at Cal and Jesse, who are almost to the first row of stalks.

"Stay back—you don't have any bugs!" Zoe raises her voice over the growing wind and throws up a hand.

"*What*?"Arco's face contorts in confusion as Jesse counts to three, and then we start running in opposite directions."*Jazz!*" Arco calls after us.

"It's OK—stay on the wall!" I call back to him, then see Liddick jumping forward with him. *Stay there! Keep everyone there!* I think, but have to turn away before I can see if he's heard me.

Small funnel clouds about the size of a person take shape over the edges of the field where Cal and Jesse have just entered, then dissipate as they drift to the center. Zoe and I stop running once we get to the far corner of the field, and I can't get a deep enough breath.

"The rest are gathering," she exhales, then pulls me down to kneel next to her as she scans over our heads, then gestures to a red rope at our feet. "They're trying to pack hunt Cal and Jesse. Dell is running the front of the field, and I'll run to the far corner and back to draw attention away, then they can set the tarps. They'll yell *pull* when that's done, and you, me, and Dell will grab that red rope handle on our way back, and pull it all the way back with us to the wall, wise? All the way to the wall, and don't look back," she says, her eyes flickering with excitement. "All right, I'll be right back. Get ready!"

My heart pounds, and the low howl the zephyrs start to generate makes it nearly impossible to put words together in response, so I just nod stupidly even though I am absolutely *not* ready to outrun a pack of predatory winds.

Over the whirring, I hear cracks and violent rustling, and it takes everything in me to keep my legs under me. I jerk my gaze to Zoe, who just shakes her head at me and mouths the words *get ready*, but then she takes off running.

Jazz! Are you all right!? I hear Liddick in my mind, and my pulse crashes into my throat, choking off anything I could manage to say even if I could find intelligible words. *They're right next to you — get out of there!*

I can't! Zoe's running; we have to wait for them to set the tarps!

The dark cloud above us spreads until it overlaps the edge of the field, and several funnel clouds begin branching off, three…six…then too many to count, and they all start diving into the rows, shaking the stalks so loudly I can feel the vibration shoot up through the ground straight through to my teeth.

Jazz! They're everywhere! Don't move! Liddick calls again, his voice ragged and stretched. I don't think I've ever heard him so afraid.

"Pull! Pull!" Jesse and Cal call out, and suddenly, Zoe is rushing past me, gripping my arm and shouting.

"Run!"

CHAPTER 22
The Pier

Zoe lets go of my wrist when the outside row of stalks next to us shakes so hard it blurs, and I am sure I have never in my life run this fast. Cal and Jesse run with one of the ropes from the middle of the field as Dell takes another on their far side. At least a dozen tubular, cloth bags follow behind us as the funnel clouds take turns swooping and rattling whole sections of the field at a time.

"Jazz!" I faintly hear Arco calling my name and turn around just in time to see that we're much closer to the dark rock wall than I thought.

"Go inside!" Cal shouts to the rest of our group, and they all head back through the fissure. We follow, then pull the long bags in and drag them over to a section of the cave far to our left that I hadn't noticed on our way out. Jesse lifts a hatch in the ground, then opens the end of his bag of grain into the hole. Each of the others do the same, and then Jesse closes the hatch. Arco's eyes narrow as he shakes his head and holds up his hands.

"What just happened? What are those things, and how is there a *sun*?" he continues, then shoots a glance to Avis, who just shakes his head and blows out a breath.

Dell and Cal both start to answer, but Zoe cuts them off. "Save it all for the Lookout—they'll have a whole bucket of questions up there. Come on."

She walks in Jesse's direction toward the back of the cavern, then slips through another fissure I hadn't noticed in the shadows. Everyone follows her through the winding corridor that slants upward at a steep angle, and by the time we get to the top, my legs are burning. When the ground levels, it opens onto a dark rock ledge that extends out to a point beyond the overhanging ceiling. The walls at each side of us angle into facets like cut crystals, and I can't resist running my hand over one of the smooth, black surfaces. It's cold at first, but then warms after a few seconds, and I hear it start to hum. I jerk my hand away and gasp when it starts vibrating under my finger tips, then jump again when I feel Arco's hand between my shoulder blades.

"Hey…" he says as I jerk around, his hazel eyes scanning my face, then moving past me to the wall. "Are you OK?"

"Yeah, it just felt…electric or something."

"Must be sound waves…" he trails off, pressing his palm against one of the facets. "I don't feel anything."

"Coming?" Zoe calls to us from the ledge beyond the overhang. We walk to the edge, and I immediately feel my equilibrium shift as I look out on the stretches of dark clouds that spread out below us, pieced by dozens of brown and white rock pillars that are spattered in tufts of green. Far in the distance, a single mountain peak also emerges from the cloud cover, and as I move closer to the edge, I see more of the black, glass-like rock giving way to a section of tan directly below us—the Bale field. I crane my neck to the right, but there's just more of the same smooth, black wall wrapping around and bulging until I can't see past it, then look toward the mountain again.

"That's the Rush—the seven biomes—and back there..." Cal says, putting his hands on his hips and staring in front of us. "That mountain is where Vox went," he says quietly like he's still trying to convince himself that it's true. A weight slowly settles in my chest as he looks down at the ground, and I know I have to change his focus.

"Why do the walls back there hum? And why did the vibration heat them?" I ask. Cal looks up at me puzzled, but at least it's a little easier to breathe. *Good, it worked,* I think as Avis raises a feathery eyebrow and crosses back to feel the wall for himself, but then just shakes his head.

"Here? In the obsidian?" Avis asks, his palm pressed to the wall. I nod to him, and he shrugs.

"This used to be magma—you know, lava—could be seismic activity. You said it got warm?"

"Yeah, but how could that have been lava unless we're..." I start, then look at Zoe in disbelief. "Are we inside a *volcano*?"

"Well, technically...no. The volcano is over there," she says, extending her arm out to our left. I look past her, but don't see anything except more of the same dark, shiny surfaces interspersed between rough, porous rock that looks like muddy pumice stone. I follow it upward with my eyes, but I can't see the top.

"You live next to a *volcano*?" Tieg's voice is clipped as he lowers his chin and looks down his long, narrow nose at Zoe, who bristles.

"They're immune to fire, Spaulding. Haven't you been paying attention?" Arco replies. His voice is low and measured, and I can hear his frustration sharpen the edge of each word. I wrap my fingers around his forearm, his muscles pulled taut because of the fist he's making. *Is he still on edge from the zephyrs*? Tieg's eyes shoot to Arco, but I speak up before he can say anything in reply and make everything worse.

"We're not staying here anyway. We need to find Vox and finish what we came to do," I say, then turn to look at Cal. "How do we get there...to the mountain?" I ask, but he just pulls in a long, slow breath.

"You don't understand. Things are different here. I tried to tell her," he answers, furrowing his wide brow, which makes him look years older than he actually is. "It's not just a long walk."

"Then show us. We can't go back to Gaia, Cal," I answer, then nearly choke as Joss speaks up in protest.

"We could go back," he says like the idea has just come to him. "Three months of matriculation means that Gaia would look the other way...chalk it up to us testing our potential or something, right?" he adds, and I can't believe what I'm hearing. This is *Joss* talking now? The same boy who volunteered to help us when he found out that we lost Fraya and Vox?

"You insisted on coming with us. What happened to all that talk about injustice and how we couldn't leave them out there?" I press as Arco's hand moves to my shoulder.

"That was in answer to all of you leaving Fraya and Vox with that cave creature just so you could save yourselves," he answers, his eyes narrowing in the golden light. Arco takes a step toward him, and I just miss grabbing his forearm again.

"You know we didn't have a choice," he says through his teeth.

"You always have a choice. You just chose to be a coward." Joss bites down on the last word. The hard lines of his face deepening as his hands close into fists at his side, and though he's several inches shorter than Arco, he's twice as broad, and seems to know it. They both lunge at each other, but Dell steps in front of Arco just in time while throwing a hand out to stop Joss from advancing from the other direction. He nods to Jesse, who rolls his cat-like eyes and pushes off the wall to move toward Joss.

"You do realize we're on a *pier* up in the *clouds*, wise?" Dell says in a loud voice. "You want to scrap, wait till we have walls again." Dell pushes Arco back toward me, and I thread my arm around his waist to keep him from advancing again. His chest is heaving, and the muscles in his jaw jump under the sharp line of his cheekbone.

"You weren't there—it wasn't so black and white," I say to Joss, but his self-righteous expression doesn't change.

"I wouldn't have left," he answers, his voice leveling as he stares right through Arco. At this, Jesse, who is much leaner but nearly a foot taller than Joss, steps into his line of sight and looks down at him. A heat rises in the center of my chest as Arco tries to restrain himself, but then my stomach also sinks with a suffocating fear...*could Joss be right?*

"Then don't leave now," I say quickly. "We came back for them, and Vox is still out there," I say, and the second

I do, I know it's not me who thinks Joss might be right; it's Arco. I look up and confirm it when I see his expression pressed into a wince as his brows dart in. He *does* feel like it's his fault that Vox is still gone, and I probably didn't help with that by actually *telling* him it was at the time. My chest tightens, but now with my own guilt…he was just trying to protect me, after all.

"Vox made her own choice this time. We can take Fraya back with us," Joss answers, his voice calmer now that Avis has made his way over to his side. Liddick's far away chuckle floats in from somewhere to the side of us all, startling everyone.

"Back to what, exactly?" he asks, pressing his lips together into a thin line and wrinkling his brow at Joss. "You think you can just walk back in there and pretend you don't know that Gaia has been experimenting on people? Or better yet, that they'll even *let you* pretend?" he says with a tired, exasperated laugh.

"What proof do you actually have of that besides the deformed manta ray, which could have just been some random fluke of nature? That, and the voices in your head," Joss fires back as a vein starts to show down the center of his forehead.

"They already tried to kill us, you chutz…were you on that Leviathan or not?" Liddick's voice is cool and steady in response. He folds his fingers around the back of his neck while he shakes his head dismissively, exhaustion on his face like he's been listening to a lecture that has gone on too long. He closes his eyes in a long blink, then opens them slowly as he lets his dark brows drift together, looking at Joss like he's just wasting everyone's time. This is the Liddick I've seen for the past five years—bored, superior, indifferent, and he's so convincing, I almost believe it's really him all over again.

Joss's strong shoulders compress almost immediately, and his eyes scan the ground like they're trying to find what just hit him, his confident presence deflating like a balloon with a slow, undetected leak. Color washes his cheeks and flushes his throat as he shoves a hand through his blond hair, then shakes his head. Tieg starts to laugh, his fingers pinching the bridge of his nose.

"Well, that's just great, then, isn't it," he chuckles. "Nowhere to go but forward, so it's time to rally, right? You have a soapbox speech for that queued up next?"

Liddick tries to give him a tolerant stare, but his eyes narrow, and I feel an ember of anger heat up in my chest again.

"It's what Pitt would have wanted," Dez says, her voice trailing off as she comes through the fissure with Ellis and Myra. They stop in their tracks to stare at the expanse before us. "He would have wanted to see that..." Dez adds absently, and we all turn to face the spread of strange, rolling clouds, rock pillars that interrupt the patches of tan and green, and the dark mountain that sits at the far edge of it all.

CHAPTER 23
The Path

Myra glances over the edge at the cloud blanket, which is torn in places to reveal pockets of green, tan, and black below.

"What's down there?" she finally asks in a small voice, and I narrow my eyes to make out more details.

"Everything," Dell says, gazing out at the mountain in the distance. "And sometimes, nothing."

Arco pulls in a breath, then forces back an impatient sigh as he pulls up our sweep map. The blue 3-D projection hovering at eye level in front of him shows each section of the cave system we are in just like it did when Liddick pulled it up earlier, but now I can also see the adjoining corridors of the volcano next to us, including the wide tunnel down the center of it that runs off the bottom of the map.

"That goes three *more* miles down?" I ask, looking up at everyone. "Are all volcanoes that deep?"

"At least one more is," Cal says with a nod at the mountain in the distance. "They're sisters. She has a drop like that too."

"What's past this grain field?" Arco asks, waving his other hand over the projection. "Are these...*trees*?"

Zoe looks over her shoulder at us and takes a step back from the ledge, then answers when it's apparent that Cal is still transfixed on the mountain.

"It's a rainforest—the first of the seven biomes. We can hear the storms sometimes," she says, nodding to Arco's sweep projection. "All seven biomes are listed on the Origin Wall. It says they're the sources for the climates on the surface…like templates."

Tieg starts laughing, then wraps his hand around the back of his neck and raises his eyebrows. "A *rainforest*, what, five, six miles underwater? Sure," he scowls, pressing his lips into a line and nodding. "Dezzie, do you have something in that medical bag to test for delusion?" he asks, moving to sit next to her underneath the dark overhang, and I notice him gripping the edge so hard his knuckles are turning white. Suddenly my heart begins pounding, and I feel a little lightheaded. *He's overcompensating…he's terrified,* I think, and I suppose I don't blame him.

"I wouldn't have thought a grain field could grow in these conditions either, but there it is," Avis says, standing with his hands on his narrow hips as he looks down on the Bale about a hundred feet below us and shakes his head. "Climate is just a mix of the right gasses and pressures. Add in wind, humidity, temperature, I mean, all the factors are here…somehow," he adds with a shrug.

"There *is* a rainforest," Cal finally addresses Tieg's comment as he turns away from the rock ledge. "We both came through it," he says, nodding to Dell at his side.

"What's after that?" Ellis asks, taking a step toward Arco's projected sweep map and leaning in.

"The Bog," Zoe replies without hesitation. "That leads into the Tanglebush, which turns into the fourth biome. I forget which it is, but we can go back to the wall to see."

"The Sand is next," Dell says without looking away from the mountain. "Then the Freeze, and the Cliffs after that."

I exchange glances with Liddick in the silence that follows, and a knot forms in my stomach. There's something they're not telling us.

"And the last one?" Arco asks after a beat as he closes the sweep map.

"The Woods," Cal finally responds, thumbing the jagged tooth he's wearing around his neck. He looks sideways at Dell before trading glances with Veece and Zoe, then lets the tooth necklace drop to his chest as he hooks his thumbs in his waistband.

"It looks just like the trees and brush on the surface— they surround the mountain—but that biome is shifty… creeps into your head and uses whatever it finds in there against you if you take it as it is," Dell says.

"Nothing is what it seems out there," Cal adds with deadpan calm, then turns back to our group. "That's the first lesson you have to learn."

"The first of more you'll give us?" Liddick asks, raising his chin and kicking his foot up on the wall behind him. Cal gives him a sideways glance, then sighs. Before he can say no, I scramble to ask another question.

"Where is Vox going *exactly*?" I say, remembering the sweep map of the long hollow stretch inside the volcano next to us. "Cal said this mountain and that one were sisters…" I trail off when Dell meets my eyes.

"To the labs at the bottom—that's where they brought me," he says, pushing his shaggy brown hair from his eyes as he leans back against the smooth black wall behind him and crosses his arms over his chest again. Cal rolls his eyes and lets out an exasperated sigh.

"There's *nothing* down there—" he starts, but Dell cuts him off.

"You didn't get all the way down, though, did you? *You* didn't go to the bottom."

"I didn't *have* to," Cal drags his words out like saying them is the most exhausting thing he could possibly do right now. "How many retellings do you need to believe there was nothing but a lake of magma down there? But I hope you're happy because thanks to your story, *that's* where Vox is going!" Cal throws out his hand to the mountain in the distance as he presses his lips into a line that pulls down at the corners, his dimples stretching into vertical lines that emphasize his set jaw.

"*Stop*," I say over them both, then turn to Dell as his face flushes and a wave of violence pushes through my chest. We're never going to find Vox if he doesn't agree to show us, and there's no way he's going to do that if he feels like we believe the Vishan council's story about the labs being a coping device to help him get over being lost in the Rush.

"Can you prove you were really there…that you escaped from those labs?" Liddick asks, evidently on the same wavelength as me…again.

As soon as the words are out, the corners of Dell's thick, dark brows draw together over his hazel eyes. He lowers his chin, and his next words are soft and clear as he pulls his tight worn-white shirt up to his collarbones and angles his body to the side, then meets my eyes as everyone gasps.

"Vox said to show you this," he answers, reluctantly tracing his finger down the long, arcing scar he showed Cal earlier. Up close like this, it looks just like the line I saw on my own ribs in the dream I had that first night in the cave. "It grew shut without their follow-up injections, and I escaped before they could put in the other one," Dell adds, then looks away.

My mouth goes dry, and I try to swallow. I walk toward him, then draw in a breath and move my fingers along the edge of the scar like he did.

"It's...a gill, isn't it?" I ask in the quietest voice I can, and his eyes widen a little as he turns back to me. An echo of the fear I had in my dream attaches like a tether to my sternum, pulling everything down until he blinks again and lowers the hem of his shirt, then looks back out at the mountain.

Cal's sigh deteriorates into a chuckle, which notches a dimple on each side of his mouth. "Plenty out there with teeth and talons enough to have given you that scar," he says, then seems to think better of it. "Look, nobody blames you for not wanting to remember what happened to you in the Rush, but they have to know what's really out there—that there's just another mountain at the end."

I can feel Liddick's eyes on me, and already know what he thinks before he says it.

You have to tell him, I hear in my mind, then turn to him and nod.

"Vox showed me the gills in a dream the first night we surfaced in the air bell. She made me feel the fear of waking up and finding them carved into my sides, and it had to be so that I would know Dell was telling the truth right now," I say, pulling out Vox's pick knife and putting it in Cal's hand. "I didn't understand then but she knew we would need to be convinced, just like she left me her pick knife because she knew we would be just as afraid to go out there…to make a new path."

Dell shifts his stance and faces Cal, hooking his thumbs in the loops of his pants. Cal studies the knife in his hand and traces the vine-like handle carvings with his fingertip.

"Then why wouldn't she just wait for the rest of you before she left?" he asks.

"I don't know. Maybe she wanted to try to forge a path for us. Maybe that's what these messages she's sending me are all about," I answer as everything inside me starts to hum like the slab of glass-rock from earlier, and I know without a doubt that I'm right. Cal closes his eyes and folds his hand carefully around the small knife, then exhales and looks at Dell, who nods.

"If I take you—" Cal starts, but Dell interrupts.

"If *we* take you…"

"If we take you, you have to be treated," Cal adds. "I tried to explain to Vox that those suits won't be enough… not against the elements and organisms in the Rush. Without our DNA fortification, you won't make it through the biomes "

Arco immediately starts shaking his head. "That's not an option," he says, and Tieg gets to his feet.

"We can never go back to the surface if we agree to that!" he adds, but doesn't move away from the wall.

"We can never go back *anyway*. Gaia and the State won't just let us go home—at least not until we have enough evidence against them to take back with us," I say. "But at least if we do get the treatments and continue what we started by following the sweep map, at least we can go forward."

Arco shakes his head adamantly, then pushes his hands through his light brown hair, which catches the yellow light behind him before he looks at the ground.

"Liam is a Biodesigner, he has to be able to undo the DNA bond," Liddick says. "And I *know* he's in that mountain."

"And my dad is an Omnicoder like Jax..." I say. "He will be able to help too. We have to go forward, Arco. We've already come all this way..."

He looks up at me and then closes his eyes in a long blink, then takes in a deep breath before responding.

"And if Cal is right that there's nothing in the mountain, despite this sweep map? If we're stuck down here for the rest of our lives...and that's *if* we can even make our way back through the Rush?"

"Would it be so bad?" Myra asks so quietly I wonder if her question is just a thought in my head. She threads her arm around Joss's, and then speaks again. "We're safe here. It's not what we planned, but at least it's a future. We wouldn't have one for long if we stayed topside—the atmosphere will support four more generations; wasn't that the last report from The Seam?"

"The *Seam*..." Tieg chuffs a laugh. "Those people are paranoid fear mongers—the port-cloud isn't doing anything to the topside environment. It can't trap radiation without absorbing it too, and the State would be reporting integrity issues if that were happening," he says with an arrogant nod on the last word, and I feel an explosion of anger in my chest.

"Yeah, because the State was so up front about *Gaia*, right?" Liddick's eyes flash, then narrow. "I don't remember reading anything about them gene-jacking people in all the promotional material, *do you*?" he asks, but it's clear he's not looking for an answer as he presses his lips into a tight line. Tieg starts to get to his feet with a reply anyway, but Dez grips his forearm and speaks up first.

"I think Myra is right. We don't even have to debate who's telling us the truth or not anymore if we stay here. Securing a future for ourselves, regardless of what we believed that meant, was the whole reason we wanted to get into Gaia in the first place," she says, mainly to Tieg, then nods to Zoe and Cal. "Can't we guarantee we'll have that future by staying here with them...by staying with each other?" she asks, smiling and letting her eyes fall on Liddick. My teeth clench in response until I force myself to look away—until I can stop feeling this ridiculous, unwarranted, *unwanted* jealousy.

"What's wrong?" Arco asks, startling me as he slips his arm over my shoulder. I shake my head too abruptly, then try to swallow the sudden tension that has to be radiating from my chest.

"*Nothing,* because..." I start, but trail off as the concept of actually staying in these tunnels starts to register. The idea is so palpable for a second I can almost touch it, and am amazed that I haven't even considered where we are *now* in my constant focus on where we're going.

Would it be so bad to stay here if Cal is right and there really is nothing in that mountain? It's too late to go back home, and going forward on our same path of relocating to the seafloor after graduating from Gaia was never really an option in the first place. At least not for us.

"Jazz? Nothing is wrong because...*what*?" Arco asks just as I look up and see Liddick studying me, the strange, golden light from the Rush lighting his eyes, and the words are out before I realize it.

"Because at least we would be here together."

CHAPTER 24
The Test

"The Vishan treatment doesn't sound like a long process," Dez says. "We were talking to Jove about it."

"It's similar to how we layered our nanites to third year classification so we could access the Leviathan dock, only the Vishan's way is a bit more...*sophisticated*," Ellis grins, evidently remembering their trial and error bloodletting to keep the nanites viable as they layered them. The image of their indignant faces and their bandaged forearms makes me smile until my chest starts to ache with the memory that Pitt was part of that group too.

"Has *everyone* completely disconnected from reality? Do you understand that you're talking about *staying* down here? Six miles into the earth?" Tieg's surreal blue eyes narrow to slits as he holds out a hand to everyone. "We can go home right now—topside. The Vishan said there are tunnels that lead back to the surface. We can even get help going after Vox and your family...it won't be hard to prove what we're talking about with the sweep map."

"You can't go back," Veece speaks up from just outside the fissure we all came through, and I jump, having forgotten he was still here. "No one from the surface can know that we're in these tunnels...it's too dangerous for our people, not to mention for yours with the tunnel sharks."

Tieg laughs. "You can't *force* us to stay down here."

"We won't have to. We just won't help you make your way back, and without us, it would just be a matter of time before the Sharks found you, or the worm."

Veece doesn't move as he talks. His voice doesn't even register any anger or threat of any kind. He just speaks like he's repeating facts.

"We haven't come this far just to sit here wondering for the rest of our lives if our friends and family are still alive out there somewhere. We have to try," Liddick says but Tieg and Arco both just shake their heads.

"There has to be another way," Arco says, crossing his arms over his chest, and there is a long pause before Avis breaks the silence.

"Why won't our suits be enough in the Rush?" he asks, flipping his blue-edged hair from his eyes. "They regulate for heat and cold fluctuations, right? They have desalinators for water, protein stores for food, oxygen stores, and they negotiate pressure."

"Those suits won't stay in tact across the seven biomes," Cal says. "Didn't you see Dell's scars? It's not a matter of if your suits will be damaged, it's how soon."

"These are made of *carboderm*," Ellis says, turning his long arm out to show Cal his dark, shimmering sleeve. "They build Leviathan hulls out of this material."

"Did you forget what happened to the hull of our Leviathan?" Liddick asks, and Tieg jumps to reply.

"Because it *imploded*? Do we have to worry about *imploding* out there?" he laughs, incredulously raising an eyebrow at Cal, who starts walking casually toward him. Cal slowly lifts the jagged tooth necklace he's wearing over his head and shows it to Tieg, then suddenly slashes Tieg's shoulder with it. It cuts clean through his dive suit *and* his jumpsuit underneath to reveal a thin line of blood pushing through the surface of his skin. He stands in shock for a second until he realizes what has happened, then grabs Cal by his shirt and lifts him in the air like he's going to throw him against the wall.

"Tieg! Stop!" Dez yells, and both Arco and Joss move to pull him off, but they only get a few steps before Cal weaves his arm through Tieg's, then clasps his hands and pushes up on Tieg's elbow from underneath. The momentum knocks Tieg sideways several feet into the stone wall, and when he turns around, his lip is bleeding.

"Whoa…" Avis says, and all our mouths fall open.

"Your suits aren't enough. And neither are your meat paws," Cal adds, looking down at his bleeding palm. He hands me Vox's pick knife and winks. "Suppose I should have put that down first."

I smile at him, a bloom of warmth spreading through me. *He really is going to help us.*

"What is that? A tooth?" Arco asks as Tieg surveys the rip in his suit and the scratch on his shoulder.

"It's from a tunnel shark," Cal answers, putting the necklace back on.

We're not ready to go out there…not even close, I think as Arco speaks up again.

"All right," he sighs, then addresses Veece. "If we get these treatments and we don't find our people, we'll have to come back here, but if we do find them and they can reverse the DNA treatment, we'll take our chances going home."

"Fair enough," Veece answers, and the tension seems to settle until Joss's deep voice crashes through the momentary peace.

"So now we're going to be *fireproof*?" he asks, his voice pitching. "So tell me how this is any different from what you think Gaia is doing to people?" The question sends a rod of ice through my chest as the image of Vox on fire and Fraya crying out flashes in my mind again.

"Maybe it's not, but sometimes you have to fight fire with fire," Liddick says with a wink to me, entirely too proud of his pun as the smirk starts in the corner of his mouth.

Really? I think, and roll my eyes at him.

"This is some kind of joke to you?" Arco asks, stripping Liddick's smile away as fast as it formed.

"I think we all better be able to find the lighter side of this, or we're not going to make it," he answers.

"All right, so we get the DNA treatments in order to find Vox and our families, and one way or another we go on from there. We cross that bridge when we come to it. I don't see another way, do any of you?" I ask the group, and everyone shakes their heads or just looks at the ground as if the answer is there waiting to be found. Arco clenches his teeth, but he can't argue, and finally, his hard expression breaks.

"No," he says. "I don't like it, but no, I don't see another way."

"Then we're agreed on getting the treatments?" I ask everyone again. They all nod, albeit reluctantly, except for Arco and Tieg. "Arco?" I look up, and he sighs in resignation.

"If it's the only way we can go forward," he finally answers.

"Tieg, come with us," Dez says to her brother, the angles of his face made sharper by the rigid set of his mouth. "This is the right thing to do."

Tieg blows out a breath, then pinches the bridge of his long, narrow nose again. "This is split," he whispers a few times before looking back up at us. "Fine," he says, letting his hand fall to his side. "But we test this treatment before everyone gets it. *You* test it." Tieg fires a look at Liddick, and another rod of ice pierces my chest.

"Fine," Liddick answers. "Then let's get it over with." He nods to Veece and marches back through the fissure so adamantly I have to dart out of his way and lean back against the faceted black wall. When I do, I feel the buzzing radiating through my palms again, but when I pull them away this time, the sound doesn't stop. I look at Zoe, starting to feel confused.

"Now? He has to have the treatment right now?" I manage to say, but my voice sounds muffled in my ears under the low droning. *Liddick*! I try to call to him in my thoughts, but I can't focus enough to connect when the only instinct I have right now is to run.

"I don't know," Zoe answers from somewhere far behind me as the golden light of the pier folds into the muted shadows of the corridor leading back down to Center Hall.

***

By the time I get to the bottom of the rise, the buzzing is so loud I have to close my eyes. *No, no...not now, Vox,* I think, pressing the heels of my hands into my eyes to push back the noise, but it only gets stronger. Everything seems to slant sideways, then a sharp pain shoots through my knees just seconds before I feel the warm, hard rock on my cheek. I try to push myself up from the ground, but I see the fire from the center of the room again—the one from the first vision after Liddick and I made our way out of the pool under the falls. It's made up of three colors this time, red, orange, and green, and the glow worms on the walls have been replaced by the green moss from the hot spring room.

Vox, listen to me...send me back. They're going to make Liddick like Arco's sister...like them. They're going to make him fireproof. Vox! I call out, but there's nothing but the fire that starts to grow, spilling over the edges of its container like water overflowing from a tub. The flames widen from the center and I press my back against the wall, skimming the perimeter frantically searching for a way out. The flames lick out at me like they did before, first the green, which narrowly misses my forehead. The orange flame cracks like a whip at my shoulder, but to my surprise, it doesn't hurt. The red flame expands and crashes like a wave over my head; I crouch into a ball and cover my face with my hands, the flickering current of fire pushing in at all the dark corners, roaring in my ears until I shut my eyes as tightly as I can, and then it all stops.

After a second, I open my eyes and see Vox under a canopy of enormous, angular leaves, the largest of which run the length of my arm. They're the same, surreal green as the moss on the hot spring walls, and curl away from her when she kneels over a fallen tree trunk that is half rotted through. She scoops handfuls of brownish-green paste from the center of it, then covers the backs of her hands and the tattooed arrows on her neck. Just before she smears it over her face, I notice the red scrape marring her cheekbone. She looks up at me then and cocks an eyebrow before covering it, too, with the mud.

"It smells like dead fish, but it keeps the mosquitoes away," she says casually, scrubbing her face until it's completely covered in a layer of dark green. She holds perfectly still when she finishes, her round, yellow eyes peering out at me like a tree snake as clicks and rattles, high squeals and hoots come from *everywhere*.

"What is this? Clues? Why do you keep showing me that fire?" I ask, but she just keeps staring at me with that stupid grin and amused glean in her eyes. "Vox! Are you even really here? I have to go back—did you hear me tell you what they're going to do to Liddick?" I sputter out loud, then seize in fear at the guttural, reverberating pulsing sound just behind my head. I duck as it passes over so loudly I feel it vibrating my teeth, my sternum, and every vertebra in my spine. But I don't see anything in the enormous, angular leaves and vines that cover every square inch.

What is that!? I think, terrified to say anything out loud to Vox as her grin deepens, and her eyes narrow just enough to hold in a laugh.

"I just told you. Mosquitoes."

CHAPTER 25
Frequencies

The vision of Vox dissipates before I'm ready, but I can't feel the ground under me even though I'm...*moving*? I force my eyelids open just enough to see a dull, orange light, then blink until I can make out that it's a fire getting closer to me with each jarring movement. Fear seizes my lungs when I realize someone is carrying me—gripping my ribs and my knees so hard it's almost impossible to move, but then I realize it's because it feels like my limbs are filled with sand.

"What the hell happened?" Liddick says, then again inside my head. *Rip, can you hear me*?

I can't put the words together quickly enough to address the urgency in his voice...to find the sounds that make the words, and then arrange them when everything is in slow motion like this. It feels like the ten seconds before completely waking up, the in between place where the body struggles to stay where it is even though the mind says it's time to go.

"I found her lying on the ground, but there was nothing else there, and I couldn't have been more than ten steps behind her." Arco's voice is very close—*he's* very close, and when I try to make myself say *something*, it feels like I've swallowed sand. "Jazz, it's OK...did something hit you?" he asks just as I feel myself lowering until the ground is at my back.

Was it Vox? Did you see something again? Rip, wake up! Liddick nearly yells in my mind, and the shock of it jolts through my chest.

Vox…yes. I think. "Yes," I repeat, out loud this time, coughing, but managing to open my eyes enough to see blurred faces staring down at me.

"Did you see what it was? Hold still because I think whatever it was hit you in the head," Arco says. I fight to tell him that nothing hit me as his warm hand brushes my hair from my face, which is starting to throb under my left eye, but the words just won't come out. "It's OK… don't try to talk," he adds, and frustration pushes against my ribs from the inside.

"Nothing hit her except the ground. She fell when she passed out," Liddick says, and the pressure in my chest subsides a little.

*Yes…she showed me…*I think, but it's all I can manage to pull out of myself.

"You saw that and just *left her* there?" Arco growls.

"Of course not! She got another message from Vox— just give her some space."

"How do you know she got a message?" Arco's voice is barbed again, and I take shallow breaths to speak so I don't cough, but it's too late to stop Liddick from responding.

"Because I just *asked her*, and she just said *yes*," he says, slowly and clearly, and I know he does this so that Arco knows without a doubt that Liddick asked me silently— that he can do something Arco can't, and a weight falls onto my chest…*Arco.* I have to get up before they kill each other, and me in the process.

"Stop," I cough, my throat feeling like it's lined with sandpaper as I try to swallow. The room starts to get sharper, faces come into focus, and the three tone fire I just saw flickers from inside a hollowed out rock in the center of this small cave. The lights dance on the dark walls all around us as Jesse adds silver, shiny rocks to the container, which seem to make the flames spread. "I just couldn't talk yet," I say to Arco as I sit up, each word scraping the inside of my throat. "Vox is in the rainforest. She was digging out mud from a tree trunk," I cough again.

"Vox talked to you? And you *saw* her?" Cal narrows his eyes at me, then looks at Liddick.

"Our telepathy started at Gaia. It's part of the Empath career track—" Liddick starts, but stops abruptly when Cal interrupts.

"She took the NET," he says, locking eyes with Veece.

"Go check," Veece nods to Jesse, who rolls his eyes, then darts back through the fissure in the wall. Veece blows out a breath as Dell starts to laugh.

"This isn't funny," Cal glares at Dell, but this just makes him laugh harder.

"Oh, was it only funny when I told you to bury that thing the second Vox found out about the mountain… what did you say, *she can't even control her fire, how could she control the frequency*?" he adds, and even Zoe starts to smile as Jesse slips back through the fissure.

"Yeah, it's gone," he says as Dell laughs again and raises his arms in triumph.

"We'll see how funny you think it is when I tell Jove you're bringing it back," Veece says through his teeth, then glares at Dell. "I'm going to get a biome map from Kora and somehow convince her that it's for no particular reason," Veece growls at him again, then storms out of the cave. Dell sobers as Cal pulls a hand down his face and lets out a long sigh, then slouches to a sitting position against the far wall and lets his head fall back, the front of his cropped blond hair edging against the rock like a blade.

Control her fire? I think, and Liddick meets my eyes. *Is that why fire keeps appearing in these messages from her*? I ask, but he just shakes his head, as unsure as I am.

"Someone going to enlighten us here?" Tieg asks after a few more seconds of silence.

"Our Neural Enhancement Tuner—the NET...it looks like a tuning fork, and is one of the origin artifacts we use to find anyone who gets too close to the crop boundary," Cal answers, then rolls his eyes. "Not such a problem since most don't venture close, but the Council goes up to the Lookout Pier and strikes the NET once a month as a beacon to remind the ancestors who *went to the stars* that we're all still here," he explains, rolling his eyes and shaking his head.

"And those ancestors are supposed to be one of your grandfathers and one of Cal's grandmothers?" Liddick asks. Cal nods, closing his eyes. "But Veece doesn't even believe any of that story from what you said in the Origin Wall room...why is he so bent about it?"

"Everyone *else* believes. Like I told you before, the truth doesn't matter to them—only tradition matters."

"Maybe Vox didn't take anything...she doesn't need that to talk to me like this—we could do that before we ever got here. Liddick and I can do it too..." I say, hoping this will resolve everything, but Cal just looks up at me and sighs again.

"Have you always been able to see her in your mind when she's talked to you?" Cal asks, opening his eyes and racking his forearms over his knees. I shake my head. "And this time you saw her digging in a fallen tree and spreading green mud on herself?"

"Yes, she said it was for the—"

"Mosquitoes," Cal finishes my sentence with a decisive nod. "She took the NET. That's why you can *see* her and not just hear her—she's still in the rainforest biome," he adds, then lets out an exhausted sigh when we all just look at him blankly.

"That's impossible," Arco says, narrowing his eyes. "How could a tuning fork do that?" he asks, and Cal gets to his feet, closes his eyes in a long blink, then holds up his hands.

"All right, so when sound hits matter, the matter resonates. That movement creates a visual signal..."

"*Yes*," Arco interrupts impatiently, then resets himself. "I know how imaging works, but that's like sonar for 3-D mapping. How could a tuning fork do what this does?" he asks, holding up his forearm Nav unit. "And if it can, if your tuning fork is *actually* strong enough to create a vibration that can paint a whole life-sized scene, why can't the other Vishan see what Vox is sending on its frequency? Why is it just Jazz?"

"I really don't know," Cal answers after a second, then shakes his head and shrugs.

"Wait, the buzzing from before—the sound of Azeris's open channel that Jazz and I can hear...it's because our neural structuring is the same—Jazz and I are both Reader Empaths—that's why we both heard the marlin that night before we left, remember? Liam had configured a channel on the virtuo-cine network like a delivery system to me. Jazz would have seen everything I did if she had gone into them too, I'm sure of it. Maybe this tuning fork creates a similar network for her since Vox is a Reader too," Liddick says, looking around for input.

"Then why can't *you* see what Vox is sending Jazz?" Arco asks, angling his head down at Liddick and narrowing his eyes. "Since you're *the same*."

"Because Ms. Reynolt said we can only talk to each other like this one at a time..." I answer, surprised that it comes to me so quickly. "Liddick could never hear what Vox said telepathically to me, so it makes sense that he wouldn't be able to see it either...I mean, if it's all built on the same connection, right?" I look up at Arco and can see him clench his jaw as he takes in a slow, deep breath.

"It makes sense," Ellis answers, and Arco cuts him a glare.

"So this tuning fork...the *NET*," Avis starts, then nods to Cal, "the NET is basically functioning like a giant antennae for you and Vox—one that lets you see the messages she's sending, not just hear them?" he asks me, then nods repeatedly to himself this time, seeming to have decided on the answer without needing mine.

"You never passed out when Vox talked to you before," Arco says, then turns to Cal. "Why can she receive these messages if only Vishan can use the NET? What's it doing to her?"

"We never showed Vox how to use it. Jazz must be able to receive the messages because of the connection she and Vox already have..." Cal answers, then stands and crosses to me. "Does it hurt when you get these messages?" he asks, suddenly reaching over and pushing up my eyelid with his thumb, then angling my face to look at my cheek. I pull back from him.

"It's just a strong buzzing."

"Buzzing that has gotten stronger since Vox *has apparently* been using that thing to reach out to you," Arco adds, then looks up at Dez, whose long arms are folded over her chest as she suddenly looks up at us when he addresses her. "Can you scan her to see if there's any damage?"

"I tried to scan Jax earlier to measure his concussion progress, but the instruments don't seem to work anymore. We sealed his eyebrow, but since the damage is still there, I don't think our nanites are working either," she says, pushing her straight blonde hair behind her ear, then recrossing her arms.

"So let me get this straight, these suits are the only things keeping us alive right now?" Joss speaks up, flattening his wide palms over his chest panel as I refocus on the conversation.

"Not the only thing entirely," Ellis adds. "From what I read before we left, the baselines they gave us when we first got on the sub to Gaia will continue working so long as they can be charged. So, our internal levels should not be affected as long as we are either near a hub like Gaia or a Leviathan, or as long as we are wearing the suits. The nanites they gave us in the med bay—the repair bots—can't stay online indefinitely without a hub. There are just so many more of them...millions for each of our systems. Our suits just can't keep up with that turnover, so we need to be careful."

"So if this NET *is* causing damage, and her nanites can't fix it? How do we stop the messages?" Arco asks Ellis, then glances at Cal.

"No!" I protest. "Vox is sending us these images for a reason. I think she's trying to leave us a trail to the mountain."

"We'll have to do without the trail, Jazz. You can't keep this up through *seven* biomes, or whatever they have out there," Arco says.

"There is one way," Cal answers, then angles his head at his hand, which sparks with a small red flame.

"All right, enough...I said I would do it. How do we start?" Liddick asks, taking a step toward Cal.

"Only the Council can perform treatments, but we need someone who will come now and be discreet so we can get the NET back before Jove knows it's gone."

"Vita then. I'll get her," Zoe says, and Cal nods to her.

"Hurry."

CHAPTER 26
Bonds

Vita's last name is also Dyer, and I study her face for any resemblance to Vox as she unrolls a cloth with strips of white fabric, a small set of tongs, and several thin pieces of stalk that must have come from the Bale field. She holds out her hand to Cal, who sighs, then pushes up his sleeve as she pulls out one of the stalk pieces. It's pointed on the end, and I feel my breath catch when she sinks the tip of it into the crook of his arm, then pulls a smaller piece of stalk from the inside of it until it's fully extended —*it's like an old style syringe,* I think. When she withdraws it, she nods to Zoe, then to one of the cloth strips, which Zoe wraps around Cal's arm. Vita dribbles the blood from the thin stalk into a small hollow in the rock slab we're sitting on, which doesn't seem terribly sanitary. I start to ask her about it, but she's already in the middle of gesturing to Liddick.

"And now you," she says to him. "The blood needs to be arterial…as close to your heart as possible, where the oxygen is the newest." He blows out a breath and reaches behind his shoulder for the release cord of his dive suit to free his arm.

"No," Cal says quickly. "Vox's nose started bleeding as soon as she tried to take off her suit—took an hour to get it to stop. Your nanites aren't from the land shark. They need your suits to work…it'll have to be your throat."

Liddick swallows again, then takes a seat next to me on the stone slab so Vita can find the artery in his neck. He meets my eyes, and I can feel my heart start to hammer…*it's going to be OK*, I think, reminding us both as I interlace my fingers with his just as Dez crosses to him and puts her hand on his shoulder. She stares down at me with her wintery blue eyes, and I look away, refocusing on Liddick. *Don't be afraid,* I add, gripping his hand, then see the smile tug at the corner of his mouth.

Afraid of the stick she's about to shove into my neck, or of Dez going all pterodactyl on you any minute for holding my hand? he answers, and I can't keep the smile off my face. I take a deep breath at the same time he does as Vita presses her fingers along the side of his neck.

"Be very still," she says, then quickly jabs in another stalk, then draws the plunger up. Dez presses a cloth to Liddick's throat afterward as Vita mixes the blood with Cal's. "Zoe, a stone?" she asks, nodding to the tongs. Zoe reaches for it and scoops out one of the flaming, pebble sized silver rocks that Jesse had added to the three-tone fire, then drops it into the dish, causing the blood to hiss, then ignite.

"*Whoa…*" Joss says, wrapping a wide hand around the back of his neck as Avis and Ellis move closer.

"What's it doing?" Tieg asks, leaning into me as he looks over my shoulder. I give him a sideways glare and take a step forward.

"Binding," Vita answers as the flame dies down, then finally goes out. She pulls the plunger of the makeshift syringe again, and I stiffen as she draws the mixed blood into it.

"Wait, that was just on fire...you're going to inject it into him right now?" I ask, and I can hear my voice pitching as all the muscles in my body tense. Liddick clenches his jaw.

"There will be heat even if it is cool, but it can't be cool for the treatment to work," Vita says without looking at me as she turns again to Liddick. "Lie back."

Liddick's fear crashes into my chest in anticipation, and I grip his hand in an effort to hold off the anxiety suffocating us both. Dez is at Liddick's side, and Arco steps to mine as Vita repositions the point of the stalk syringe over Liddick's throat.

Happy thoughts, I think desperately, remembering what Azeris told me in the Boundaries room to help offset the stress of having to swallow the automators. He smiles at me, but I can feel his nerves fraying.

"This will burn as it makes its way through your body, but later tonight, you'll be like us," Vita says in a quiet voice, then pushes the point in and presses down on the plunger.

My heart pounds so hard that each beat becomes sharp and piercing under my ribs as the dull, aching pulse in my ears starts bludgeoning a path from behind my eyes to the back of my head. The trepidation that lit a million tiny prickles under my skin just seconds ago, or was it hours ago, now sears every surface of my body as Liddick grips my hand. He tries not to scream, but it escapes in pieces through his teeth anyway.

*Happy thoughts...*I think again, clenching my jaw and scrambling for a moment in time that will distract us both. And then it's there, the glowing little fish from the ocean that night he dared me to dive under with him when we were thirteen...the night I got stung by the jellyfish. *Do you remember the fish from that night we sneaked away from the port festival? They were blue and green and white...and no one else ever saw them because we were the only ones brave enough to dive in the dark. We were always the brave ones, Liddick. Can you see them?* I think, desperately trying to pull their colors back into view, to remember the bite of the freezing water on my skin that night, and the way he made me feel—free, invincible...

My teeth are clenched so tightly I don't even realize it until I have to consciously open my mouth to release the tension, and Liddick meets my eyes for just a second.

That was why I started calling you Riptide, he thinks as his eyelids start to fall and his hand relaxes in mine. *I just couldn't...pull away.*

"What's wrong with him?" I ask Vita before my throat pinches completely closed.

"He'll sleep now for several hours, don't worry," she says as she finishes packing up her materials and cleaning the work area. Liddick is asleep as soon as his eyes close all the way, and the raw places inside me start to fade. I take several shallow breaths until I'm sure they're not going to hurt, and then finally, one long, slow, deep one.

"So when he wakes up, he'll be fireproof?" Myra asks the question everyone is thinking judging from the way all eyes move to Vita.

"To all fire except the three together," she answers, angling her head to the center container of tri-colored flames, "but the combination of these three can only mark him; he won't feel any more pain from fire even though he'll have a scar like the other topsiders; his will be somewhere close to his throat…near the injection site," she adds, motioning for us to filter out of the room. "I'll send for you when he wakes up."

"My scar is here," Zoe says, pulling up her sleeve to reveal the arcing, *S* shaped scar on her shoulder, which pulls to a point at the top. Dell does the same as we start to walk, but his is lower on his bicep. When I look at Jesse, he shrugs and starts to pull his shirt over his head, and I hold up a hand to him and laugh.

"No, that's OK!" I say. "I'll use my imagination."

"Promise?" he smirks, then shifts his eyes to Arco and holds up his hands with a chuckle. I look over my shoulder to find Arco's brows drawn together and a scowl pulling at the corner of his mouth, so I push my shoulder into his chest to coax it into a smile.

"So now we just wait? And then if he doesn't implode or something, it's our turn before we all head out into whatever is out there?" Tieg asks, making the air prickle again with tension at the mouth of the fissure.

"No," Cal says. "You'll need to know how to use the gifts after the treatment first."

"Your walrus might need another day before being treated anyway," Dell adds with a nod to me, and a weight drops in my chest remembering Jax's concussion once we're out of the little room.

"I need to go to him," I say, my lungs compressing with a suffocating guilt for not insisting on this sooner.

"Whoa…he's OK, I talked to him before we came to the pier this morning—he's looking a lot better," Arco whispers as he leans over my shoulder.

"I still need to go," I answer, and Arco nods.

"Then if we're not performing any more miracles in the right now, can we *eat* already?" Jesse asks, shifting his weight and putting his hands on his hips as I look back through the fissure at Liddick.

"He'll be down awhile," Zoe says, catching my eye as she winks. "Let's go find your walrus."

***

Dez stays behind with Liddick, and as much as I want to do the same, I don't want to create any more tension between us. It's a short walk back to Center Hall, and the warm smell of bread baking fills the air. My stomach contracts as I remember that I haven't eaten anything except for the five bites of soup I had before I lost it somewhere last night.

"That smells good," I say to Arco as the others walk ahead.

"It's made out of the grain you helped pull in earlier. They were sending people down to get bags of it this morning." He shakes his head and chuckles at the ground, then slips his arm around my waist.

"What's so funny?" I ask.

"I just can't process all this…I mean, there's a whole civilization down here. *Ecosystems.* We must be at least six miles below the surface by now."

"I keep waiting for it to be a dream I'm having. Just weeks ago we were riding a shuttle bus to our interviews, and now we're six miles under water having our DNA grafted with a long lost society's so that we can cross seven different biomes…it's like a virtuo-cine," I add, and we both laugh as we approach the cook pot, which is filled with some kind of porridge, and next to it, a large bowl of biscuits. Jax and Fraya come up behind us with Ada and Ty, all of them with their bright eyes and big smiles generating a wave of happiness that seems to flow over everyone in their path.

"Hi, new sandies!" Ada says, tucking a nearly white curl behind her ear and shouldering Ty playfully in the side when he rolls his eyes at the nickname they have for the Badlanders. He puts his arm around her and kisses the top of her head, then lets her go to take a bowl from the two young Vishan girls passing them out.

"Thanks," he says with another huge smile that makes the two girls blush and giggle.

"Nice to see you vertical again, Ripley," Arco says, clapping a hand on Jax's shoulder. His eyebrow looks completely normal except for three small stitches toward the end, and his eyes are clear again.

"Nice to have the room finally stop spinning. Nanites are a bust this far out, then…" he says with a shrug. "That's inconvenient."

Arco laughs as a smile spreads over Jax's face, and Fraya takes a bowl from the Vishan girls with a nod.

"Thank you for everything you did," I say to her, then to Ada.

"You came for us...we take care of each other," Fraya says with a smile, and I swallow hard to keep my throat from closing up again about this.

"Ada wouldn't know what to do with herself if someone didn't need patching up," Ty says with a sideways grin as he offers a seat to Ada, then sits next to her. I stare at him in awe of how he can be so happy. Wasn't he pulled through the sand by one of those sharks like the others? Taken away from everything he knew, then told he could never go back? But he's there five feet from me beaming, laughing, content with his biscuit and porridge, and as inseparable as they are, I assume Ada must be his girlfriend. *Is that all it takes to be happy here...is that really all anyone needs*?

"How long did it take you to adjust completely to this life?" Arco asks Ty, and I nearly choke on the bite of biscuit in my mouth. *Did I push him to ask that*?

"Me? Whew...let's see..." Ty blows out a breath and interlaces his long fingers over his knees. "I suppose it was hard until I just started thinking about what I still had instead of what I lost, you know? I mean, here I was dragged all this way underground and messed up pretty good along the way. You don't expect to come through something like that, but I did. And it just got easier when I started seeing maybe I even gained some things too," he says, sneaking a look at Ada, whose cheeks are bulging around a giant bite of porridge.

"Wuh?" she tries to say in answer to everyone suddenly looking at her, and we all start laughing. Ty's dark eyes flicker as he leans over and kisses her temple, and it feels like my chest will explode as tears start in my eyes without warning…he really loves her. *All right, what is happening with me all of a sudden? Why is everything so raw?* I blink until I can see clearly again, but can't seem to push aside the feeling of uncertainty, of being lost.

Fraya leans her head on Jax's shoulder as his hand slides over her knee, and I feel the same wave of happiness flooding from them that Ty and Ada generate. He's right…we're alive. We're together, and we even have new friends. I shouldn't feel like part of me is empty, but I do.

"Let's take a walk," Arco whispers into my hair, then gets to his feet and extends his hand to me.

CHAPTER 27
Perspective

Arco takes my hand and leads us back to the rise that goes up to the Lookout Pier, and the empty, lost feeling compresses in my chest. I start to think that it might be coming from Arco, but when I feel it spreading even when he gets several feet ahead, I know that it's me.

"Watch the first few steps…there's loose rock up here," he says as the corridor narrows and the light dims.

"I thought you wanted to go for a walk, not a hike," I say, forcing a chuckle as my legs start to burn with the climb.

"Not much beachfront around here, sorry. The Lookout Pier is the only quiet place I could think of where we wouldn't have to worry about getting dragged off by whatever those tunnel shark things are, or worms, or killer mutant goldfish."

"*Killer mutant goldfish*?" I laugh, this time genuinely.

"I'm sure it's just a matter of time," he says, stepping over the lip of the fissure opening that leads to the Lookout Pier. He turns and offers his hand again to help me through, then leads me to the end of the dark, glassy wall just before the pier starts. The zephyrs have cleared, and the rest of the flat, white cloud shelf has pushed back far enough for us to see what must be at least the first four biomes spreading out beneath the jagged limestone towers.

"Look…that's where the sand starts," I say, pointing to the edge of the last smatterings of green about halfway to the far mountain, then suddenly feel my stomach drop with worry. "Do you think Vox has made it that far yet?" I ask.

"Knowing her, probably," Arco says, almost to himself, then turns to me. "Are you afraid?"

"Of crossing the Rush? Who wouldn't be?"

"Of losing her…" he says quietly, and then in a lower, even quieter voice, "and Liddick."

My heart starts pounding in my chest with the surge of adrenaline that suddenly hits me, and I stare at him, confused.

"What?" I try to laugh again, but it comes out too loud and too fast. He sighs, resigned to say whatever will come next, then leans his shoulder against a smooth slice of the faceted wall and crosses his long arms over his chest.

"I know I can't read your mind like they can, but Jazz, I can tell when something is wrong," he manages, his eyebrows raise just a little, and my defensive gut reaction outruns any concession I could possibly make.

"Well, besides the fact that we're several miles under water, plus inside a *mountain* under the ocean floor? Not to mention these split ecosystems and fireproof people who—"

"You know what I'm talking about," he interrupts with the same patience in his voice, and I immediately feel like I want to disappear. He angles his head at me, his hazel eyes green in this odd, golden light as he unfolds his arms and hooks his thumbs in the dive suit rigging loops at his hips. "I feel like you've just been…drifting," he adds, letting his eyes shift to the ground, and I let out a breath trying to figure out where to begin. We stand in silence like this for a while as a breeze just beyond the pier whistles and hums, and I swear I can smell rain in the air.

"I don't know how to explain it exactly," I force myself to say, and am relieved when the rest of the words eventually find me. "It's like I'm disconnected now. I didn't realize it until Liddick went under and everything got quiet in my head…as stupid as that sounds," I try to laugh, but only manage an awkward smile until the tears start to close my throat and sting my eyes again. I squeeze them shut and shake my head. "Ugh…*this* is what's stupid," I add, swallowing hard and willing this raw feeling to go away.

Arco doesn't answer for a long time, but then he clears his throat.

"You don't see yourself at all, do you?" he asks, still leaning against the smooth, black facet in the wall that shines like it's wet. "That's why you feel cut off without Vox and Liddick now…you told me as much back at Gaia, remember? That maybe you wanted to be like they were?"

"It's not like I need them to tell me who I am, Arco. I know who I am."

"Who? Without them here in your head taking the lead, when it's just your own voice, Jazz. Who are you?" he asks, not in confrontation, but almost in sympathy. The strangled burning in the back of my throat sinks into my chest, burrowing a hole until I'm furious.

"Do you think I need you to feel sorry for me now?" I fire back at him, and his eyes widen before a smile pulls at the corner of his mouth, which only makes me angrier.

"*You* are the last person I could ever pity, Jazwyn Ripley," he laughs. "You *know* that," he adds, then looks straight into my eyes, dousing the outrage in me that was so easy to find…so easy to put in place of thinking for one second that he could be right. *Anger feels better…not right, but better…*I think, then remember that this lost feeling really started after my Gaia interview—when it didn't tell me anything about who I was, what I wanted, or where I fit in the world. *Maybe he's right…maybe I am still looking for me.* "I can tell you who I see, if it helps…" he starts again, and I shake my head, suddenly embarrassed.

"Arco, no, you don't need to—"

"I think my favorite thing is that you'll always be the last one standing," he says, pressing his lips together into a thin line, then his eyes crinkle in the corners with amused confusion as he lets his head rest on the wall behind him. "And I *know* this…I genuinely believe it, so I don't understand why I feel compelled to run interference at every possible turn for you—to protect you from whatever," he adds, shaking his head in astonishment before looking up at me again. "You'll always land on your feet one way or another, just like you always have, Jazz. Can you see that?" he asks with a crooked smile, then just watches me.

Crite, is he actually waiting for me to answer this? I think, as my insides begin to twist.

"I've always been stubborn I guess," I manage, feeling heat run into my cheeks for what must be the third time in the last 24 hours, and I want to change the subject to *anything* other than me.

"Don't minimize it," Arco says almost immediately as he crosses to me. "I've been thinking a lot lately about how sometimes we downplay our strengths to the point that we forget about them. Have you noticed that? I think that's why I choked in my interview...when I let the other guy struggle with the code because I was afraid I would mess it up. But afterward, I knew better...and he died because I didn't step up," he adds after a pause, then grips the back of his neck. "I keep thinking maybe Gaia wasn't really testing us for what we *could* do, you know? I think they were testing us to see what we couldn't," he laughs again, but it doesn't reach his eyes this time. "Guess we fooled them, didn't we?"

I hadn't considered that the interviews might be about seeing which of us would be safe to bring to Gaia... which of us would have the aptitude to do what they wanted us to do without having the nerve to take a big risk, even if we had to. But he's right. Rule followers don't rebel.

"That makes sense," I say quietly. "I never thought about it like that, but most of us had to be pressured into the scenarios in our interviews—that, or when we were pushed to rebel, we didn't fight back until now."

"Exactly. We just have to remember who we are, so whatever you're clinging to in Vox and Liddick...it's already part of you," he says, taking a few steps toward me, then winces as he runs his thumb just under the bruised part of my cheek from when I hit the ground during Vox's last message. "Maybe the pressure we've had to deal with our whole lives with trying to be good enough to get into Gaia has short-circuited our ability to take credit for those traits. I don't know, but Jazz," he continues, combing his fingers through my hair, "you are so much more than what you're letting yourself see. You have to find a way to connect to that."

I stare up at him, the yellow light falling over the sharp angles of his face, softening them in the glow that also bounces off the black, glass-like facets in the walls all around us. The hollow feeling in my chest starts to fill with everything he's just said to me—not just because of how he sees me, but because *I do* recognize Liddick's fearlessness and Vox's stamina in myself, and maybe that means if I believe they'll both be all right, I will be too.

This is the right answer. I know it is, and the certainty is such a relief that I slide my hands over his chest and move as closely to him as I can. He smiles at me as he wraps his arms around my waist, then pulls me into a hug.

He's warm and solid, and I can feel his heart pounding under my hands. I slide them around his neck and press my lips to his, which launches a rush of adrenaline everywhere inside me that scatters in all directions like tiny embers blowing in the wind. He lifts me off my toes and turns so that my back is at the wall, and I sit on one of the flat rock edges. He steps between my knees, his fingers pressing into my hips as he pulls me toward him, then smiles against my mouth before trailing kisses along my jawline and abruptly stopping with a sigh at my collar.

"If it would not *literally* kill us to take these off..." he growls in my ear, sending a jolt of electricity straight through my stomach. I swat his shoulder as a laugh bubbles in my chest.

I lean back and move my hands to his face, suddenly needing to see him. His eyes are warm and soft, and so close that I can see the flecks of gold dancing in the dark, mossy green. I watch my thumb trace over the edge of his high cheekbone, along the rough, dark shadow of his jaw, then over his full, parted lips, which quirk in the corner under my touch. His small smile turns into a wide, brilliant one, and I feel heat pushing through my chest again...the same expanding pressure that Ty radiated with Ada, the same total happiness and gratitude and security no matter what. For a second I wonder again if these are just Arco's feelings I'm picking up, but I can't find the disconnect inside myself anymore like I could when I picked up Ty's. *I really do feel this way,* and not just because I'm afraid or looking for something solid to hold onto...*I'm* what's solid.

"Crite, what's in your head right now" he chuckles, then looks away for a few seconds before meeting my eyes again. "You know you're gambling with your life looking at me like that..." he grins, tugging on my dive suit pull cord as he arches an eyebrow.

"Guess I should have led with being able to take off the dive suits as an argument for getting the Vishan treatments then?" I ask, barely kissing his bottom lip, then pulling away before he can connect.

"There wouldn't have been an argument," he whispers in a rasped voice, then smiles when he presses his hips and chest into mine.

I kiss him again, then laugh, easily now, relaxed and comfortable...happy as I rest my forearms on his shoulders and let my fingers brush through his wavy light brown hair. I find his eyes again.

"Arco, I think I—"

"*There* you are," Jesse's impatient voice crashes into us from the fissure where he stands with a scowl, and the shock makes me feel like I've almost fallen off the pier itself. "Cal said to hunt you up. Your friend is awake."

***

It takes us several minutes to descend the connecting corridor and find our way back to the little cave where Vita and Cal gave Liddick the Vishan DNA treatment. His coloring is darker than it was a few hours ago, like he's been in the sun all day, and the contrast makes his blue eyes almost as bright as Tieg's. Dez smiles sitting next to him on the dark stone slab, his legs hanging over the edge with his black boots planted on the ground, and his hands gripping the smooth rock like he's going to stand and take off running any second.

"Cal said no one has come out of it this fast before," Dez says proudly, but the second I see Liddick, it feels like I've just caught something heavy. *Liddick, crite*...I start to think. *What's wrong?* I feel helpless and awkward standing in the doorway watching him like this, but then he heaves a breath, and the pressure lifts from my chest.

I couldn't get a sense of you, Liddick thinks. *I thought the treatment reversed us—reversed me...*

I try to resist the urge to go to him. Dez wouldn't understand, and while I think Arco might now, I know he wouldn't want to see it. Liddick's chest expands as he takes in a deep breath, and I know he can feel my dilemma as I press my lips into a thin smile.

"Welcome back," I say as casually as possible. He clears his throat and nods, and just like that we are back within our lines again.

"So when do I get to start lighting campfires?" he asks. Everyone laughs at this, even Arco, and Vita moves to Liddick's side to angle his jaw upward.

"This will scar, but it won't cause you pain," she says, tracing a red line that looks like the letter *S* stretched at the top to a point.

"It's like a little fire," Myra says just as Vita smiles at Liddick.

"This is the mark of the Vishan. Now, you are one of us."

CHAPTER 28
One of Us

"What does being one of you mean, exactly?" Liddick asks, looking down at his palms. "This itches a little."

"If you focus on the itch...focus on making it worse, it will—" Dell starts, but Liddick immediately jumps off the stone slab when a flame bursts from the palm of his hand like a small explosion, and then is gone. "It will *light*," Dell finishes with a laugh. Ellis and Avis move quickly to Liddick as Dez examines his hand.

"Are you burned?" she asks.

"No...it just surprised me," he says, then swallows. "My hands tingle like they're asleep," he adds, blowing out a breath, then notices the back of his hands. "When did I get a sunburn?"

"That will darken after some time. It seems to be a side effect of the DNA bonding," Vita answers. "Leave your suit on for the next 24 hours, and then you can be sure you are climatized."

"Pressure proof," Avis adds helpfully, and Liddick gives him a tolerant grin.

"Thanks," he says, nodding with a thin smile as he closes his eyes in a long blink.

"You'll be able to pick up the NET's signals now...the bond expands our neural channel," Zoe adds.

"What if we have more paths than one? Are they all enhanced?" Liddick asks, suddenly rigid. "Or at least are they all preserved?"

"That's right, you have a *splice*," Tieg laughs. "I forgot about your port-*carnage* death wish. Did your cannibal install that?"

"That *cannibal* is the only one watching our backs right now, so if you ever want to get out of here, I would stow it," Liddick says, then raises an eyebrow at Tieg. "If I recall, you didn't make a great first impression," he adds, tapping his teeth with his index finger the way Liddick's Badlander friend, Azeris, did when Tieg insulted him back in the Boundaries room back at Gaia.

"So he's watching us right now?" Dez asks timidly.

"No, it's not like that. He adjusted my port-carnate splice so it could also serve as a direct link between us. He was going to align our coordinates with Liam's and Jazz's dad's and send us map updates, but so far all I've gotten is visual of his digital signature—the wavy letter *A* repeated on the walls from before—and some hellacious buzzing in my ears from the channel feedback."

"Wait—didn't you see those letters in the walls too?" Arco asks me, and I nod.

"I didn't at first, but I could after I concentrated, why?" I answer. Arco turns back to Liddick.

"You said she could see everything Liam sent out—the marlin, and if she'd gone into the virtuo-cines, all those messages you'd received in there too—because you're *the same*, and he'd hacked into your neural channel through the virtuo-cine network, right?" Arco asks, narrowing his eyes at Liddick, who takes a stiff breath and angles his head in a warning back at Arco. "But you just said that's not how Azeris is sending you signals, so how could Jazz see those letters in the wall without a port-carnate channel splice too?"

I feel heat rush into my face at Arco's implication and turn to face him.

"I was the one who insisted that port-carnate was too dangerous," I say, feeling the pulse in my throat pounding all the way through to my teeth. How could he think I would be all right with physically teleporting, and especially after it nearly killed Liddick? "You actually think I'd somehow secretly get a *splice*?"

"I never said I thought you'd do it," Arco answers, his brows pushing together and his eyes softening for just a second before he shoots a glare at Liddick. "But he would. That's why Azeris pulled her in that automator launch with you. It wasn't to help stabilize you because her neural structure was the same as yours, it was to copy your splice onto her neural channel. She's rigged for port-carnate now too, isn't she?"

Arco's chest heaves with his quickening breath, and I feel his anger boiling up like acid behind my ribs, leaking behind my collarbones and climbing up the back of my skull. At the same time I feel like I'm falling, unsure of what actually just happened. I bring my hands to my head and look at Liddick with the question I can't seem to verbalize because I'm terrified that once I do, it will be a real possibility that's loose in the world.

Liddick? I think…

"*Isn't she!*?" Arco yells through his teeth, the violence in his voice and the pointed steps he takes toward Liddick jostling my attention back to him. Dez jumps in front of

Liddick and holds out her hands to Arco, who stops abruptly.

"Spaulding..." Arco shouts, but Tieg is already only a step from ushering Dez from his path. Arco takes several more steps toward Liddick after she's clear, but the delay has given Dell and Jax enough time to scramble to Arco and seize his arms.

Everyone else turns to me—Zoe, Avis, Ellis, Vita, Joss, and Myra... even Dez and Tieg—and I feel everything flying into me all at once: fear, anger, pity, jealousy, but it takes a minute for my own feelings to work their way up from under the pouring deluge of everyone else's. Liddick meets my eyes, his, laced with apology, and I can only shake my head.

*I'm sorry...*he thinks. *It was just the only way to make sure I could get you out if things didn't work.*

"If what didn't work?" I say out loud, feeling ice crawl up my spine. His eyes widen a little, and he angles his head.

The channel...all of it. We had to get out of there, Rip...you heard Liam, you saw the experiments they were doing on Lyden and Arwyn. Will you just talk to me? he thinks again.

"You mean like you talked to me about copying over your *port-carnate splice* while letting me think I was *helping* you?" I say out loud again. "Is that why you grabbed my hand and wouldn't let go, so the circuit would go through me too? Is that why we were supposed to think of *happy thoughts*, Liddick? Were we supposed to get on the same frequency or something? Just get out of my head, all right?"

"Rip, it was the only way to make sure you'd be safe—you wouldn't have taken the risk because—" he says out loud now, but I don't want to hear it.

"It was *mine* to take or leave, not yours," I say, letting the ice racing through my veins freeze each word.

"The splice is just insurance...it can't hurt you," Liddick says out loud again, looking at me now like there is no one else in the room—the same sincere blue eyes, the same full lips held just on the edge of smiling like when we sat on the dune the night before we left for Gaia, and he told me about getting messages from his brother Liam. The angle of his jaw shifts when he clenches his teeth after I don't respond, and I hear him again in my head. *Do you really think I could ever do anything that would hurt you?*

"I didn't until now. Get *out* of my head," I say aloud, and watch the tremor of it move over his face. His brows contract as he presses his lips into a hard line, then swallows before walking out of the small cave. Dez tries to follow him, but Tieg intercepts her.

"Let him go," he says as Ellis nods in agreement, evidently heading after Liddick himself.

"Arrogant *ass!*" Arco hisses, then pushes his hands through his hair and turns into the wall.

"Guess training starts now," Dell says to Zoe through a long exhale just before turning to follow Ellis.

Arco resets, then walks back to everyone with his hands on his hips and his eyes on the ground. He looks up at me and sighs. "It's going to be all right. The splice can be taken out...we'll just need to get back to some kind of data hub like in the Boundaries room," he says, reaching for my hand.

"He said it can't hurt her, though?" Joss speaks up. "Is it really so bad to have an extra channel?"

"That's not the point," Jax says, biting off the words. "What did he think he was going to do? Port-carnate them both out of Gaia?"

"Calm down," Fraya says at his side. "She's all right."

"And he wouldn't have done it if he thought she would be in danger," Myra adds. "He must have known she would be OK."

"Well, it's not *OK*, Myra. You can't just make decisions about other people's lives like that," Arco says, bringing a hand to his temple in frustration.

"Why not? If it's the difference between them living and dying?" Cal asks abruptly, then folds his arms over his chest.

"*What*?" Arco squints at him, a few words forming on his lips before he shakes his head and starts over. "That's the same kind of thinking that created this situation in the first place! What gives you the right, any of them in that mountain, or back at Gaia, or anywhere the right to alter people? What's *wrong* with you?"

"Your one-track world where everything stayed in the lines is gone, sandy. Down here, we don't always have the luxury of being idealistic. You either learn to bend, or you're going to break in the Rush," Cal says as he pushes past Arco and stops at the cave opening, then turns back to us. "Liddick's cells will be turned over in a few weeks, but you'll be able to see the full effects of the treatment by tomorrow. We'll treat the rest of you tonight so that you're all ready to leave at the same time," he adds, then nods to Jesse. "Help me find Veece."

Jesse rolls his eyes and pushes himself off the wall, then follows Cal through the opening. Vita smiles at me as she puts the rest of her materials into the cloth and holds them to her chest.

"Don't be angry with him for too long. Crimes are not reflected in the outcome, but in the intent. His intent was to protect you," she smiles softly. Arco huffs, but she just lowers her blue eyes in a small nod before following Cal and Jesse.

Everyone's eyes are on me again, except for Dez's. She looks off to the side, and the only thing I can feel from her is an ache in the back of my skull that spills into my jaw, then down my neck. It pinches everything like it's trying to shrink the muscles in my shoulders, pulling them tight to the point that it feels like they will snap. I squeeze my eyes closed and turn away from her, then scrub my hands over my face to dislodge her confusion, her anxiety. I want to explain to her that I didn't know, that it wasn't my fault he chose me, but I get the sense she already knows this, and that's part of what makes this so hard for her—I didn't even want him to.

When I open my eyes, Tieg is talking firmly with her and Jax is making his way toward me with Fraya. He pulls me toward him like I've had a bad day, then palms the back of my head with his huge hand.

"He shouldn't have done it, but he was right that it can't hurt you, especially since you're not actually going to try to upload your consciousness and send every atom of your body into the port-cloud, right?" Jax laughs, trying to find the bright side of things like he always does. A spark flickers in my chest for just a second at the idea that *I actually could* upload myself into the port-cloud now, then rematerialize somewhere else. The thought is quickly snuffed out by the flash of Liddick's bloodshot eyes after returning from his port-carnate trip with the automators that helped us map our way out of Gaia. Not to mention the deluge of public service announcements warning about misaligned body parts and scrambled insides. I must grimace at this because Arco grips my hand and Fraya brushes my shoulder.

"A splice is just like our regular neural channel for the Network…virtuo-cines, school feeds, weather, and with the new nanite constructions from Gaia, port-calls. It's just an extra path, Jazz. You're upgraded!" she giggles, which is infectious, and I feel my own smile starting.

"And since you can tap into his Badlander friend's feed now, we don't have to rely entirely on Liddick for path updates once we get out in the Rush," Jax says, elbowing Arco just as a low hum starts in the base of my skull, then vibrates my teeth.

After a second, I start to see fiery green flashes materialize into thick, dark brows. They push together over a set of round, brown eyes—older, scrutinizing eyes that suddenly widen from behind a large, strong hand with veins that run between the battered knuckles. It falls away from the man's face to reveal dark stubble flecked with gray. The man starts to speak, but then the image breaks apart and is gone. I blink a few times and shake my head, still trying to understand what I just saw…

"*Azeris*?"

CHAPTER 29
Fireproof

Jax and Arco look at me expectantly, and I realize I've just said Azeris's name out loud.

"I saw him…just now. It was like he was looking into a screen or something, and I think he saw me too," I say, every word helping to convince me it actually happened.

"You saw what?" Tieg asks from across the room, which cues everyone else's attention.

"Azeris. It was just for a second. He was going to say something, and then the image just fell apart. I need to find Liddick," I say, moving toward the door. Arco holds out an arm, blocking my path, and I turn to him impatiently.

"Jazz, did you forget about the port-carnate splice he put in your head without you knowing? About how Azeris probably helped him with that?"

"I didn't say I forgave him, but I have to find out if he got the rest of whatever that message was supposed to be. Wasn't this treatment supposed to enhance our neural channel, or…*channels*," I add tentatively. "Maybe I only got part of what he saw because I haven't had it yet."

"Jazz…"

"Arco, come with me or stay here, but I need to go," I insist, then turn to Zoe. "Did Dell say something about training?"

"I'll show you," Zoe answers, suddenly seeming anxious as she blows a strand of copper flyaway hair that has escaped her little ponytail, then rubs her freckled nose with the back of her hand. "We'll pass the entry to Center Hall on the way to the training circle if anyone wants to leave off there instead," she adds over her shoulder to Arco, then hooks her arm in mine, guiding me through the fissure and into the corridor.

We walk for several minutes before I recognize the opening to the small cave that leads up into Center Hall, but no one opts to go through. The torchlit corridor slopes downward, past the opening to the Swim, past the Origin Wall room and the Pinch where those stupid, gooey blue bats live, and past the hot spring room with the strange, mossy walls. Then I recognize the dark gray, porous rock showing in places and the smooth, glassy black rock from this morning when we went to the grain field.

"Are we going back out there? To the Bale stalks?" I ask Zoe, and she shakes her head.

"No. Under it."

***

We pass through a large cave with more torchlit walls, but these look too straight to be naturally occurring in the rock face. When I look more closely, I can see grooves and scuffs cut near the corners. Ada, Ty, and the young Badlander boy with the little, blue bat from earlier are feeding Bale berries into a flat, stone grinder on the other side of them. It looks like two old clock gears, but neither of them are moving. Calliope, the Badlander girl who fixed Dell's tooth when we first arrived, looks like she's trying to repair it as the same two Vishan girls who giggled when they gave Ty his soup pick some of the green berries out, then throw them in a separate bowl at the end of the little processing area.

"And who is on Bale rotation today that you don't know…you meet Ty's little brother, Ghost, yet?" Zoe asks, and the sandy-haired boy who is about thirteen looks up from adjusting a stone plate and nods. "He's handy at fixing things like Calliope—*things,* not so much people. Don't think you've met Kora and Myka…" Zoe gestures to the two Vishan girls with long, straight blonde hair who are spreading more Bale berries on the stone countertop slab in front of them.

"No, but the tall one helped Jax through the doorway after his concussion, and the little one was trying to calm down Cal when we first came through Center Hall, right?" I ask quietly.

"Right. Myka is the tall one, and the bug with dimples is Kora, Cal's sister. She talks him down from his episodes a lot—just about the only one who can," Zoe says, raising her eyebrows and shaking her head. "I'm surprised Myka doesn't have a critter running loose after her…likely hard to keep it out of the Bale, though. You get bit or clawed down here, Myka is the one to see about it. And well, Ada too," she adds with a shrug.

Myka, the tall, thin, blonde girl with the wide brown eyes smiles at us, then whispers something to Kora, who pokes Calliope in the back. Calliope looks up from the flat stone she's trying to balance on some kind of spool and scowls, then talks around the three pins sticking out of her mouth.

"*What*? It ain't like this is particular and requiring my complete concentration or anything, wise? I said tell me about him later if you can stand it," she fires, and Myka clears her throat and angles her head at us.

"Happen to see Dell come through here with two of their lot in between all your concentrating?" Zoe asks, darting a glance at me, then gesturing to Arco and the others who walk up behind us. Kora and Myka see Dez and Tieg and start whispering again as Calliope gets to her feet and takes the pins from her mouth.

"They went with Kesh over to The Circle—and, *hello*," she says, fitting the pins into place around the stone disk, then tucking a wild, dark curl behind her ear and winking at Arco. I raise an eyebrow at her, but she doesn't look at me.

"Hi," Arco says, trying to swallow a chuckle when I glance up at him. Calliope smiles, and I clear my throat. She waves absently like she's telling me to wait a second as she looks him up and down, then nods to me with approval before turning her attention back to Zoe. I roll my eyes.

"Anyway, do me a solid if you're going back there and tell Kesh to hurry up, wise? Grinder is fixed now, and I'm not trying to finish her rotation," Calliope nods decisively before returning to her work, then looks back at us quickly, her wide, green eyes lighting with a smirk at Zoe. "And besides, I need to check Dell's mouth again," she adds with another wink.

"I'll lay it out to her," Zoe smiles, widening her eyes at me with a laugh once we're out of earshot, then move through another fissure. "In case you felt your skin creeping, you're the first from Skyboard down here," she says over her shoulder to Dez and Tieg. "So it was just your eyes and other particulars that set Kora and Myka whispering—they didn't mean anything by it," she adds.

"Veece said he was going to get a biome map from one of them, right?" I ask, and Zoe nods.

"They catalog everything, gather the vein rock for the green flames, keep records of the artifacts, and maintain the Origin Wall," she adds.

"Vein rock?" Avis calls from somewhere behind us, but it's too narrow now for me to see him behind the others. "Can I see some of it?"

"Sure, it's all about in the training circle walls. Just don't carry any off because this is the only place to find it. Can't make the treatments or Gathering fires without it."

We emerge from the corridor on the heels of Zoe's last word. Green torches line the length of another small corridor, but this one not as narrow. The white, jagged ceiling is lined in green torches that seem to be pulled upward like there is a vent opening somewhere we can't see. The walls are also jagged and white, but with striations of silver running the length of them. Avis moves quickly over to a wall and picks up one of the silver pieces of rock from the ground.

"Is this the vein rock?" he asks. "It's just boron," he says. "Your secret fire dust is boron?"

"We call it vein rock," Zoe says, holding out the inside of her forearm against the white wall, where the dark gray lines of boron deposit do look like veins in an arm. Avis nods and shrugs.

"Well, it's boron," he whispers to Jax and Arco as we follow her through another opening, this one unfolding to a large, round cave with the same green torches running the perimeter of the ceiling, the flames being pulled upward again to some unseen vent. Kesh stands with her hands on her hips as Dell and Ellis kneel in front of Liddick. For some reason, he has dropped to one knee and is leaning over it to support his forehead with his hand.

"What happened!?" I shout, running into the training circle to kneel next to Liddick. Kesh looks down at me and pushes a hand through her short, erratic black hair.

"I was going to show him how to control his flames, but then he said he heard a buzz and glassed over—just dropped right there," she answers.

"He said Azeris's name a minute ago," Ellis adds. I nod to him.

"I think I saw the beginning of a message before it cut out. He must still be in it."

"Can he hear us?" Avis asks, taking a step forward as the rest of our group files in behind me.

"I don't think so. We tried talking to him, but he's—" Dell starts just as Liddick takes a deep breath and rubs his eyes, then sits down and racks his forearms over his knees.

"Liddick?" I say, trying to align my eyes with his, which are still glassy. "Did you see Azeris?"

He blinks several times, then swallows hard and nods.

"It was like he was right in front of me," he swallows again and shakes his head.

"What did he say? I saw him for a second just now too, but the connection cut out right before he was going to talk."

Liddick scrubs his hands over his face, then gets to his feet.

"He said he'd been working on tracing Liam's message ever since he got back from helping us in the Boundaries room, but he could never get the link to stay connected," Liddick meets my eyes for a second, then scans the ground before moving his hands to his hips and looking out at everyone again. "But he just locked onto Liam and your dad, Rip. They're alive, and they're in the bottom of that volcano on the other side of the Rush. Dell is right. *There are* labs down there."

Everything is silent for a second except for the subtle whipping of torch flames all around us and the sound of air pushing through small spaces.

"He talked to them?" I ask quietly, afraid that I will shatter the possibility if I'm too loud. Liddick nods, fixing his eyes on mine for a long time before I hear him in my head.

Your dad has been there all this time, Rip—there was no hydrogen plant explosion...he really is alive.

I feel my throat constricting with the threat of tears, so I bite the inside of my lip to push them back, then look up at Jax, whose jaw is locked as Fraya interlaces her arm with his and Arco's breathing quickens at my back.

"Arwyn and Lyden...are they...?" I ask, but can't bring myself to finish the sentence, and I grip Arco's hand.

"They're alive too, but they're moving them into something called Phase Three. Your dad told Azeris it's a facility like the one they're in now, but it's somewhere in this classified layer of atmosphere..." he trails off, then takes a deep breath. "The only way in is port-carnate transfer. That's why the tech exists at all. Somehow it leaked underground, I don't know, but this is *the State,* not just Gaia...this is..." he says through clenched teeth as he presses the heels of his hands into his eyes and then lets a scream of frustration rip from his throat. He turns his back on us just before crossing the arena to lean against the wall. Tieg laughs and shakes his head.

"Isn't that convenient?" he chuckles. "Port-carnage tech is the only way to get there just after you were outed for splicing Jazz...you must be the luckiest man alive, Wright."

Liddick's eyes blaze when he looks up at Tieg from the wall, the sharp cut of his jaw and cheekbones shadowed in the downcast green light from the torches above us.

"You think I'm spinning this to clear myself?" Liddick asks through his teeth, his voice even and low.

"Of course not..." Tieg laughs again, taking several purposeful steps toward Liddick. Jax follows him and puts a hand on his shoulder to bring him back, but he just keeps pressing forward. "I *know* you're spinning."

Before the words have time to fall through the air, Liddick springs off the wall and rushes Tieg. His shoulders light in peals of fire that engulf his neck, face, and his hair, but he's not burning. Jax jumps out of the way, crawling and kicking backward as Liddick shoves Tieg so hard he hits the wall several feet behind him, then lies gasping for breath and coughing before rolling to his hands and knees. Liddick stands in the center of the training circle, then turns toward Jax, who is still struggling to get to his feet.

"He's got potential!" Kesh says, clapping her hands as Liddick reenters the little arena. Dell throws an arm around him, and his flames slowly disperse. His breath is ragged when he shrugs off Dell's arm and marches toward me, then takes my hand and flattens it over his chest

*Read me. I'm not spinning this...*he thinks, but before I can say anything, Arco shoves him back, breaking our contact.

"Back up!" he yells, then takes a step toward Liddick.

"Stop!" I say, trying to get between them. "He just wanted me to read that he wasn't lying. He's not, Arco. He's not spinning any of this."

Fraya is at Jax's side when he gets to his feet as Tieg finally straightens, but continues to cough.

"I don't think anything is broken," Dez says to him. "Just breathe slowly."

"It came on like that for Vox, too," Fraya says to everyone. "It was like she didn't even see me when she was trying to get to Kesh. Provocation made her so strong. Liddick, you have to relax before the fire starts again."

Liddick's chest heaves, and he shakes his head, seeming disoriented as he looks around at everyone's horrified expressions.

"I'm sorry..." he says with more confusion than regret.

"Well, if you can already knock down the cloudy, you're pressure stable," Dell says, pulling his shirt over his head, the silver and white scars scattered over his torso catching the light from all the torches. "Take off that dive suit before you burn it off, and let's see about firing you up again."

CHAPTER 30
The Itch

"Vox was here in this training circle with Kesh, not Fraya? She was on fire?" I ask Zoe as Dell kicks off his boots. She nods, but doesn't look away from Dell and Liddick in the little arena.

"Once they figured she was Vishan, they tried sparking her in Center Hall, but it didn't work until they brought her down here with all the vein rock," she explains, and I meet Liddick's eyes as Dell fights with his other boot. "Kesh did about what Dell's doing now, poked at her until she lit. Fraya tried to stop it all, but just wound up on her backside," Zoe laughs.

It's true…Vox was standing right there on fire, Liddick, just like in her message from the corridor. She's trying to show us where she's been, I think, but Liddick doesn't have time to respond before Dell calls to him.

"I'm sure I have *yet* to hear the end of Cal's complaining that Vox didn't have enough training before she left, and I'm not trying to have you on my conscience too. Let's get on with it already," Dell says, tossing his shirt to the outside of the training circle.

The long scar running vertically down the side of his chest is silver in the torchlight, and I can't help but wonder what could have made it. The light isn't bright, but there's enough of it to see that the smaller scars over his sternum are actually parallel, like they could have been made by a claw. I swallow my gasp and look quickly over at Liddick as he takes off his boots and socks. He straightens, then reaches behind his shoulder to pull his dive suit cord, which makes the back panel fall away. He pulls his arms from the sleeves and steps out of the legs, then kicks his dive suit up to his hands and folds it in half before setting it on the stone ground several feet away.

"So we just need to learn how to control this fire, and then we can start out for the mountain?" Liddick asks, crossing back to the center of the little arena.

"At the rate you're getting all your burnables off, that's looking like a far off someday. On my life, princess, you are *shy*," Dell says, shaking his head and bringing a finger to his lips, which makes the faded brown *S*-shaped treatment scar on his bicep jump. Liddick jerks down the invisible zipper of his blue jumpsuit top and yanks his arms free, then steps out of it, too, and tosses it in a wad over by his dive suit.

He stands in the training circle in his dark base layer shorts and tank top, the latter clinging to the swells and ridges of muscle I didn't know he had as he takes in a deep breath. After a second, he peels the base layer top over his head and throws it onto the pile of his other clothes, and my heart starts to pound in my ears. Unlike Arco, I *haven't* seen Liddick with his shirt off while playing gravity ball with Jax, so heat flushes my cheeks when I catch myself staring at the sections of his stomach and the indentations over his hips. I clear my throat and refocus my attention to his *S*-shaped treatment scar, which is red and about three inches tall, starting just above his collarbone and winding over the...rise of his chest—*crite, stop*! I tell myself, then clear my throat again and find Arco, who is talking with Jax against the far wall.

"Leaving your britches on, Dell? *That's* hardly fair," Zoe says in a thick voice as she drapes her arm around me. I look back at Dell, and he winks at us.

"Just so it's crystal, I'll oblige on account of you just don't deny a woman who's requesting you out of your britches..." Dell nods to Liddick with some kind of man club camaraderie, then turns his grin back on us. "And *not* because I'm worried I'll burn through." His smirk widens to a toothy grin as Zoe laughs and fans herself with her hand. Fraya chuckles at her, then quickly covers her mouth when Dell unties his makeshift cord belt, and my eyes flash to Zoe.

"Go on, then!" Her laugh is infectious as she throws her other arm around Myra and shoots me a grin. Dell kicks his pants upward and catches them, and I notice his base layer bottoms are dark and cut just like Liddick's.

"Standard issue State skivvies," Avis says. "Well, there...I'm convinced he's officially from secret volcano Gaia."

Jax and Arco laugh, but Liddick either doesn't notice, or doesn't care.

"Just stay in control your breath," Kesh coaches him from outside of the training circle, but he doesn't seem to hear her either.

"So we're supposed to fight or what?" he asks Dell, taking clockwise, measured steps as he shakes out his arms.

Dell is bigger than Liddick—thicker in the chest and torso like Jax and Joss—but so is Tieg, and Liddick knocked him to the ground just a few minutes ago.

"I suppose that's one way to do it," Dell says with a shrug to Kesh, then quickly closes the distance between him and Liddick in a few steps with a hard punch to his stomach. Liddick drops to a knee and coughs, clearly not ready, but when he looks up again, his eyes light on Dell the same way they did on Tieg. Tufts of red flames rip from his shoulders before immediately dissipating as he gets to his feet. Dell takes another swing at Liddick, but he ducks, then elbows Dell in the back of the ribs as he passes him. Dell loses his footing for a second, but then regains it as he rubs his kidney and tries to laugh.

"He does have potential!" Zoe shouts, then whistles through her teeth at Liddick, whose shoulders glow with low level red flames from one end to the other.

"Keep control of your *breath*," Kesh calls again, more adamantly this time.

"Well, now, that didn't take long. Hate to break it to you, ladies..." Dell chides, then rounds on Liddick and punches him in the side, taking advantage of his guard being up by his face. "He's a fast burn..."

Liddick recovers more quickly from this punch, and his arms streak with more red flames when he turns back to Dell. In seconds, he's engulfed again, and Kesh shakes her head, then puts her face in her hands, resigned.

Liddick, he's just trying to get in your head—think of it like the bugs in the termite code from the Leviathan. It's not real... don't listen to him! I think, and see the words reach Liddick when he meets my eyes. He takes a deep breath, then another, and walks clockwise again as his flames start to dissipate.

"There you go," Dell says, clapping a few times. "That's how you control the itch. Now let's see if you can maintain it," he adds, walking quickly and directly at Liddick. The flames flicker at his shoulders for just a second before they recede, but flicker again when Dell pulls back for another punch. Liddick sidesteps, then lands a punch of his own at Dell's midsection, but even then, the flames don't rage like they had initially. Liddick draws in a deep breath through his nose, his eyes narrowed, and slowly, the remainder of the small, red flames slip away until they're completely gone. Dell coughs, then nods until he can get his breath back.

"Good," he says around another cough. "Next time we work on channeling it," he adds, straightening up, then turning out his hands in front of him. They light with red flames that stretch until they meet in an arc above his head, then ignite something in the ceiling, which makes a little yellow-green explosion like the color of the torches along the perimeter.

"The orange flame alongside the red and green can mark you, so you have to know how to pull the red back, especially in the Rush—vein rock is everywhere, and the lightning will start an orange fire if it strikes…you can't lose control," Kesh says as Liddick takes a step back.

Dell closes his hands into fists, and the red flames disappear with a whip of air that snaps after they're gone. The green flames dance on the ceiling for a second more until they, too, flicker out. He crosses back to his clothes and steps into his pants, angling his head for Liddick to do the same.

"That's it? That's the training?" Liddick asks, and both Kesh and Dell laugh.

"Going to be hard enough for you to stretch out comfortable tonight. You'll feel it proper when the fight wears off, but that pain will stop too when you're done cooking tomorrow," Kesh says, throwing Liddick his clothes.

"When he's done *cooking*?" I ask Zoe, apparently too loudly because Kesh answers before Zoe has the chance.

"Meaning when all the effects of the DNA bond come about…the treatment doesn't repair injuries, just makes them harder to come by—thickens the skin so to speak, and that ain't painless," she says, putting her leather pouch back over her shoulder and adjusting the strap across her chest. Dell sits to pull on his boots as Myra's hands fly to her mouth. He chuckles.

"Doesn't really thicken the skin, sunshine," he says with a wink to her as Joss pulls her close. "Just makes us a little harder to kill."

Liddick gingerly pulls his base layer shirt over his head just after I see a few red marks already starting on his side. My chest tightens, and I have to fight the urge to make sure he's all right as he steps into his blue jumpsuit.

"Did you burn through, pyro?" Ellis asks, inspecting Liddick's shoulders, which look a little darker than the rest of the jumpsuit. "Looks like the material absorbed most of the heat," he says, then crosses to pick up the crumpled dive suit just outside the training circle. "This too, so I guess you're accident-proof for at least a few minutes, but it wouldn't hurt to learn some yoga, eh?"

This finally puts a smile back on Liddick's face as he puts his dive suit back on, his coloring already darkening to a golden tan from the reddish cast he had just hours ago.

"You're going to want to eat anything you see as soon as the nausea passes," Dell says, "so we should get some food squared away so you can have it later."

"I'm not nauseous," Liddick answers as he pulls the dive suit cord up, then lets it retract.

"Heh, you will be. Lots to look forward to tonight!" Dell laughs, then claps Liddick on the back before leading the way out of the training circle cave. *Are you OK?* I think, but I can't focus long enough to connect to Liddick with the barrage of words Calliope fires at Kesh after we make our way back through the corridor.

***

When we reach Center Hall again, Vita and Liv are passing out bowls of tuna and greens, which everyone except Liddick devours almost immediately.

"How long did you say it will take for his cells to turn over completely?" Dez asks Cal, who takes a seat on one of the flat stones near the cook pot.

"The nausea will pass by tomorrow, but the turnover won't be complete for two weeks," Cal says, eyeing Liddick.

"Which means the DNA bond won't be permanent for a few weeks either, right?" Ellis asks. "And don't we want to be able to reverse it once we get to Liam and Ripley's dad?"

"You won't be stable, and the Rush is hard enough without worrying about your inner bits making peace with the changes. They're not just physical..." Cal warns, nodding to Dell. "Tell them."

Dell tips the last of his bowl upward, and I see the long scar stretch across his forehead as his brown, feathered hair falls back from his face. He sets the stone bowl down next to him and pulls in a breath.

"The first week after the treatment is harder than the second. Can't say I would have kept my wits if I'd been in the Rush then," Dell answers.

"What happens during the first week?" Arco asks the question we're all thinking, and Dell looks up.

"Bursting into flames when someone shoots sparks at you for starters," he grins, then angles his head at Liddick, who rolls his eyes. "Sometimes it's hard to breathe or to regulate temperature, but your suits will likely deal with that. The paranoia, though..." he says, shaking his head. "The treatment enhances your neural channels, so you'll see and hear a mess of things like the messages from the NET and stray feeds—images with no story to them. Might not happen for everyone, but can't say it's a risk I'd want to take in the biomes. Bad enough some things there shouldn't be real, but are," Dell continues.

His words pass over all of us like a cold wind, and no one says anything until Cal nods, then gets to his feet when he sees Veece entering through the fissure.

"We'll treat the rest of you before curfew so you can sleep most of the suffering off, and tomorrow we'll train. In the meantime, figure out how to bury your axes before you leave. There are enough surprises in the Rush without backdoor conflicts *and* your imaginings in the mix, and the two of us can't lead with all that distraction." Cal nods to Dell again, then turns to intercept Veece.

"The three of us," Zoe announces as she watches him walk away, and we all look up at her, surprised. She turns back to us, then meets my eyes. "The Badlander you saw in your vision earlier was called *Azeris*. That's my father's name."

CHAPTER 31
Treatments

"You knew who I was when I told you that my second name was Frank," Zoe says, fixing her wide brown eyes on Liddick. "Why didn't you tell me my father was helping you?"

Liddick rubs his eyes with his thumb and forefinger, then scans the dark stone ground, which reflects the dancing torchlight that is slipping into a deeper orange. "I wasn't even sure Azeris *was* your father, and it's not like that's a topic you can un-broach," he answers, sounding exhausted when he finally looks up. Arco chuffs a laugh, and Liddick's eyes dart to him. "You have something to say, Hart?"

"Plenty, but how about I just limit it to what else are you keeping from everyone?" Arco asks. My stomach lurches in response, and I'm not sure if this is Liddick's initial reaction or mine, or maybe it's both.

"I was waiting to say anything until I was *sure*," Liddick says directly to me, and I meet his eyes. "I'm *not* hiding anything."

"Just like you weren't hiding the port-carnate splice you and Azeris put in Jazz's head," Tieg adds, tossing the last of his bread into his mouth. Liddick bristles, but I've suddenly had enough of all their testosterone.

"All right, were you not here five minutes ago when Cal said to bury the axes? Can we just do that before they wind up getting us all killed out there? We can't afford to doubt each other," I say to Arco and Tieg, then glance at Liddick. "It's reasonable he wanted to be sure before he said anything about Azeris, and by the way, *I'm* the only one who has a right to be upset about the splice," I add. To my surprise, I have to suppress a smirk when Arco, Tieg, and Liddick actually stay quiet.

"And now that you're sure and all, how do you contact him?" Zoe blows a loose strand of her red hair from her eyes as she angles her head at Liddick, and I lower my eyelids at her for interrupting my moment of being impressed with myself.

"No," he answers, shaking his head. "Liam and Jazz's dad were able to talk to him from the mountain, but so far, I think the channel is only set up for me to receive the messages Azeris sends," he answers, and Zoe shrugs.

"Then I'm going with you to find Liam and Jazz's dad," she confirms.

"Zoe," Arco says in a quiet voice. "You know the only way we're coming back here is if we *don't* find our people…remember?"

"Could be you don't get to leave at all," Dell says, gesturing to Veece, who is marshaling Cal and Jesse back through the fissure. "If you're all still interested in getting treated tonight, we should go cool that down," he adds, then sets his bowl next to the cook pot on his way toward the fissure.

***

We move through the opening in the wall a few at a time so we don't draw attention to ourselves, and finally catch up to Veece in the little cave where Vita bonded Liddick's DNA with Cal's. Vita and Jesse are trying to explain something to Veece when we walk in, but Cal interrupts them.

"Jove would have treated them anyway! Do you want the NET back or not?" Cal holds out a hand.

"That's not the *point*," Veece says through his teeth, biting down on the last consonant. "How many times have you told them only tradition matters, *vig-rhovo*? Tradition! Now I have to explain the missing NET *and* the unsanctioned treatment," he adds, then looks up at us all. "It is just one, right? Or have you already treated them all?"

"Just him, and we don't have time for this," Cal says. "You can stand here boiling about traditions, or you can finish their treatments so we can find the NET."

"It's not just about the NET…aren't you listening? We have a *way*," Veece says, trying to compose himself now that we've all funneled into the small space, but Cal just starts selecting silver rocks and setting them next to the little fire like Jesse did during Liddick's treatment.

"*Vahg om*, when we catch up to Vox, I'll send a message that I took the NET so I could lead the new sandies to the mountain, all right? I'll say I treated them too, which is what I'm firing up to do now," Cal says without looking up at Veece, but then abruptly stops adding rocks to the flames and meets Veece's eyes. "Or maybe *you* fancy going out into the Rush while I stay here and tell Jove what I think about our ways?"

"Hate to harsh your debate, but standing around trading swipes ain't about to resolve anything," Dell says after clearing his throat. "I venture Jove will forgive the unauthorized treatments if you just swing it like you were taking initiative to get the NET back, seeing as how you're the son of the Council leader and all," he adds, looking at Veece. "Could be an opportunity to show you've got the chops to run it yourself someday, wise? And the Council already gave the nod for helping Vox's people when they turned up, so lay it all out like you were just following through." Dell leans against the wall and slips his hands into his pockets, then cocks his head to the side.

Veece exhales and moves his hands to his hips, then cuts a glare at Cal.

"Can't exactly pull back halfway through the jump now…and I suppose they used *your* blood on him?" he asks Cal, who nods. "Then if we're doing this now, the rest of the treatments will have to use mine," he adds, rolling up his sleeve and gesturing to Vita, who pulls another reed syringe and other equipment from her bag. I turn to Zoe and grip her arm.

"What's happening?" I whisper, afraid that I already know the answer.

"The treatment makes us harder to hurt and all, but it takes longer to replace blood that's lost. Since they tapped Cal earlier, he shouldn't give any more for a few days," Zoe explains, but I shake my head.

"No, I mean is he saying we're being treated *now*? All of us?"

"Looks that way," she says. "Got your wish, little sister," she adds with a wink.

"Who's first?" Cal asks our group as he finishes stoking the multicolored fire, and Vita collects the first small syringe of Veece's blood and puts it over the tiny rocks.

My heart jumps into my throat and pounds in my ears as my eyes dart to everyone else's, then settle on Jax's. His brows are knit together, and I feel the beginning of a weight pressing in on my chest...his will for me to stay still, to stay quiet because he is about to volunteer, but I tear my eyes away from his and step out from Arco's hand, which has just moved to my shoulder.

"I'll do it," I say, my voice sounding clear despite the muffled pulse in my ears, and when I try to push up my sleeve and can't, I remember where the syringe will need to go. Ice water fills my veins at the realization as Vita pushes back the hair from my shoulder and looks into my eyes. Hers are wide and clear blue like the slivers of sky we used to see closest to the horizon sometimes, and though everything about her is small and delicate, I feel an overwhelming safety with her, a strength that makes me feel like she will personally make sure I'll be OK.

"After it's done, we will need to move you all quickly to your blanket stacks so you can sleep," she says in a soft, warm voice. "I'm adding a sedative so you will not wake up while everyone else is asleep after curfew. It will be disorienting when you awaken, so we will make sure someone is there to help you in the morning," she adds, then looks around at the rest of our group and nods before meeting my eyes again. "It is all right to be afraid," Vita smiles, and the small lines around her eyes make me think of my mother. "But know that the pain you will feel is growth, and all growth, no matter how painful, is good. Are you ready?" she asks, and I take a deep breath, then nod.

I'm here, Rip. You don't have to do this alone, Liddick says in my mind, but I can't take my eyes from Vita's.

"Guess I'll think twice about scaring you from behind now that you'll be able to shoot a fireball at me," Jax says, then grips my shoulder as Arco moves to my other side and takes my hand. I smile, and Vita slips her fingers inside my collar to pull it back as I feel the sharp tip of the syringe on the side of my throat.

"This will be the withdrawal of your blood. The next time will be the treatment," Vita says as she extracts the syringe, which doesn't hurt as much as I thought it would. Jax holds a cloth to my neck as Vita ejects the syringe and mixes my blood with Veece's, and a small pop of fire jumps from the bowl when she adds one of the silver rocks Cal had arranged. "All right, please be very still," she says, then prepares the syringe again with the blood mixture. She angles my jaw away from her, then slips her fingers back inside my collar, and I realize I'm clenching my jaw. I try to make myself relax, but the pounding in my ears is like a drum beat that keeps getting louder. Arco moves closer to my ear, then leans his head against mine and squeezes my hand.

"I love you, Jazz. It's all right...you're all right," he says, and a rush of adrenaline pushes through my chest.

We're going to make it, Riptide...we're going to find your dad, Liddick thinks, causing another surge of adrenaline to hit me at the idea of seeing my father after thinking I never would again. I swallow hard and close my eyes when I feel the sharp point of the syringe press into my throat again, then grip Arco's hand. Ribbons of searing heat run down my neck and shoulders, then multiply and spread until my whole body feels like it's on fire.

I lock my teeth together to keep the screams from coming out, but then it feels like I can't get them out in the heaviness all around me…like I'm swimming through something thick and dark. It pushes against my eyelids and nose, and when I open my mouth to gasp, my chest won't expand. I try to struggle until I feel arms wrapping around me, which somehow makes the heat and pressure dissipate a little, then a little more until it's cold like wind on my skin just after coming out of the water. It gets colder when it seeps inside my muscles, into my bones, unless…I'm just going numb? Pins and needles push into me from every direction as a soft buzzing begins in the back of my mind.

Go to sleep, I hear. *You can do this.*

CHAPTER 32
What I Feel

I hear sounds of sleeping all around me, and my mouth is so dry I almost can't swallow. My muscles burn as I try to take a sip from my desalinator tube, but there is no more water.

After a few seconds, my vision starts to adjust, and I see the dim, red light through the fissure that leads to the small cave Zoe and her crew hauled us into when we came out of the falls. I remember that the freshwater stream isn't too far from there, then try to sit up. When I do, every muscle in my body protests, even if I just turn my head.

Crite, did I fall off a cliff in my sleep or something? I think, noticing that it actually hurts to blink.

I felt like I woke up inside out for a while after my treatment too, I hear Liddick in my mind. *Though, Vita said you'd all be knocked out for that part after she gave you the root powder. Guess you didn't get a big enough dose.*

How long have you been awake? I ask, trying again to sit up, but I can't move without feeling like my insides are igniting.

How do you know you're not just dreaming about me? Liddick thinks, and I can hear the grin in his voice.

Because I don't ever dream about my veins being filled with acid, I reply with a silent laugh, which I instantly regret when pain stabs through my torso. *Crite, how long does this last?*

The more you move around, the easier it gets. Hang on, I'll help you take a walk.

I clench my fists and try to swing my legs down from my blanket stack without waking up Arco, whose bedding is still pulled close to mine.

I'm OK, I reply, finally managing to brace against my knees and push myself up, but I lose my balance until an arm slips around my hips and steadies me. I stop the startled breath in my throat from turning into a shriek, and the muscles in my stomach rip with searing pain all over again.

It's me, relax, Liddick thinks, chuckling for a second, then suddenly wincing next to my ear. *Crite, sorry. I didn't mean to scare you,* he adds. *Didn't you get a drink from your tube?*

What?

*You're still thirsty…*he thinks.

My suit is empty—how did you know I was thirsty? I ask, squinting to see the dark, uneven path to the fissure opening in the far stone wall.

I felt it…that's what woke me up, he answers, then pulls up a small red flame in the center of his palm as we walk, which lights our path a little better.

*What do you mean you **felt** it?* I look up and find him smiling as the dim red light flickers in his eyes. He clears his throat.

I'll explain once we get through the corridor. My suit is empty too—we can refill them by the stream…come on, he thinks, tightening his arm around my waist to help me walk. This close, he smells like fire smoke and leather, the latter of which I don't understand until I feel the wide strap across his back.

Are you wearing a Badlander bag? I think, desperately trying to find footing that doesn't feel like I've stepped into a hornets' nest.

It's Zoe's, he answers with a quiet laugh. *Azeris made it for her. She gave it to me to wear tonight in case I get another message—she wants him to see that we found her. I told her I didn't even think he saw me during the last message, but I guess she put the bag on me when I was sleeping anyway.* I smile, forgetting about the pain shooting through me like fireworks for a second as I imagine Zoe tiptoeing through the darkness just to drop off her bag, then tiptoeing back to her bed all satisfied with herself and full of hope. The thought falls apart, though, when Liddick lets out a low whistle at the descending path on the other side of the fissure. "That's going to hurt," he says out loud, then moves in front of me. "Your legs won't handle this decline yet—just lean on me."

He walks down sideways with one arm posting against the smooth stone wall at his side. I brace against his shoulder as I find the wall with my other hand too, but after a few steps, the pain of descending the short, narrow corridor is almost unbearable…like it's somehow echoing in my muscles.

My heart is racing by the time we step into the opening of the little cave where we first saw Zoe and the others, and I can hear the stream rushing past just outside of it. I stumble in my excitement, and pain paralyzes every nerve in my legs and stomach when Liddick catches my arms. A prickling itch starts immediately in the center of my palms, and I'm terrified that fire will light in my hands.

"Rip, focus on your heartbeat," he says out loud again as he squares himself in front of me. "You have to slow it down…are you OK?" he adds, gripping my hands in his and holding them just under my chin.

"How did you…?" I start to ask, but then see red flames slipping between our fingers.

Just breathe when I do, and don't look at the fire, Liddick thinks, tightening his fingers with mine so our palms seal in the flames. *You just have to get ahead of it,* he thinks again as he lowers his chin to meet my eyes, and another flame snaps from our hands.

"It's not working!" I say out loud, then try to move toward the water so I can douse the fire, but Liddick shakes his head.

"That won't work either," he says, then closes the remaining space between us by pressing both my hands flat against his chest, which finally smothers most of the flames. He wraps his arms around me to stop the rest, and in the same second, the pain in my muscles starts to give way to a warm feeling that compounds the longer we stay still. "Can you feel this…what I feel?" Liddick whispers next to my ear as his arms tighten around me. "Can you physically feel it?"

I can't find my voice to answer him when I realize that his heart is beating in rhythm with mine, slowing it down, and everything else falls away—all the pain, even being thirsty. *How are you doing that?* I think, but I don't know if I care about the answer.

I don't know, he thinks as he moves back to meet my eyes. *When Vita injected you, I just felt the treatment all over again. I felt when you were thirsty a little while ago, your fear about lighting up just now...I even felt the itch starting in your palms right here in mine*, he adds, covering my hands at his chest again with his. The heartbeat in my ears starts pounding harder and faster, and right now, I don't know where I end and where he begins. "You're just...what I feel," he whispers, and we are so intertwined that I don't realize he's leaning in until his lips brush mine.

I jump back from him when flames shoot out from under my hands, not even sure what has happened until I stumble into the hard rock wall.

"Sorry!" I startle, then try to smother the fire until everything seizes with the pain pouring back into my muscles like scalding water from a tap.

"Hey, *hey*, it's all right..." Liddick says over the sound of the rushing stream. "It's all right, just breathe, remember?"

I squeeze my eyes closed and force myself to take a deep breath, then let it out as slowly as I can. The itch in my palms eventually subsides, and when I open my eyes again, the only red fire is from the torches that line the stone ceiling.

"Liddick, *what* is happening?" I say with the last of the breath I'd just taken, then see that my hands are shaking as he helps me off the wall and through the opening on the other side of the cave that leads to the water.

"It must be the treatment...I didn't understand either when I first felt it—when I first felt *you*...like this," he answers in a low voice, closer to my ear now as we walk.

*Can he hear and feel **everyone** like this now*? I think, blindsided by my own words and their accompanying panic. I don't mean for him to hear them…for him to feel that in me, and my stomach crashes in embarrassment the instant I realize he has. We slow down when my whole body floods with adrenaline, but then he leans his head against mine.

"No. It's just you, Riptide…" he whispers. "There's only you."

We kneel carefully next to the rock ledge of the stream as my heart pushes into my throat, making it even harder to swallow the handfuls of water that I wind up splashing over my face. I start to feel dizzy with all the thoughts and feelings now swirling everywhere inside me, so I rest my forehead on the wet rock, letting my arm collapse over the short barrier wall. I feel Liddick flip the intake valve of my desalinator tube, then submerge my hand in the cold water, which helps clear my head a little.

"Did you push those feelings for me? The pain? And… the rest?" I finally say, keeping my head down and my eyes closed to stop the room from spinning.

"I don't know," Liddick answers. "I just wanted to help you focus, but then there was…*more*," he adds from somewhere in front of me, and my head spins again in reaction to the sudden swell in my chest.

Is this you now…is this what you feel? I think, lifting my freezing hand from the stream and bringing it to my cheek to help my mind stop swimming. I lift my head off my forearms so the cool mist can spray my face and neck, but it doesn't help the heaviness from building in the back of my skull. *Liddick, where are you…* I think, reaching out to reestablish which way is up and which is down. He quickly lays his hand over my shoulder and then I hear his quiet, gentle voice.

"That nausea will be a lot worse soon—don't drink any more," he says, then secures my desalinator tube and guides my arm over his shoulder. "Maybe you can sleep through the rest of this…come on. I'll help you get back."

A million hot needles push up through my legs with each step I take, especially when we get to the short rise that connects the first small cave with Center Hall, and wave after wave of dizziness echoes through me. I have to stop for a second and swallow hard when we come through at the top, positive that I am going to pass out until Liddick pulls me closer to him.

We're so close now…count your steps, he thinks, but all I can think about is how he managed to stay vertical when he went through this after his treatment.

How could you have felt like this when we were eating earlier? I think, closing my eyes as we start walking again.

It wasn't this bad, he answers. *Take shallow breaths, Rip… we're almost there,* he adds, pulling me in even closer as I hear him take in a few short breaths of his own.

Crite, you can feel this, can't you? What I feel now? I think with a pang of regret that he's suffering again.

Small price to pay, he thinks after a long pause, and I feel the warm rush from earlier rising in my chest. I want to reply, to ask him what he means, but the room starts spinning again as the haze thickens in my mind, and I can't find the words. *Here, hold on to me,* he thinks again just before I feel something soft under my head, and then everything finally stops moving.

Thank you...for helping me, I say in my mind, feeling like my whole body is filling with sand and sinking into the ground.

Just repaying the favor, he thinks, but his voice is getting quieter. *Do you think a dose of my nanites would help you reset like yours did for me?* he adds after a second. I feel his hand brush my cheek, and another rush of that warm current runs through me with the memory of him kissing me after his port-carnate accident back at Gaia. I could feel him, all of him—his clarity and determination, his clever mind and passion, but I can't let myself fall into that again because now everything is different, and I know I might not be able to find my way out this time.

*Liddick, we...*I start to think, then feel his lips on my forehead, light and soft just before I hear his voice echo in my mind.

Goodnight, Riptide.

CHAPTER 33
Waking Up

I open my eyes and nearly bite my tongue when I see Zoe sitting cross-legged next to me with her chin propped on her fists. She raises her rusty eyebrows, and a smirk tacks the corner of her mouth.

"Don't hurt yourself," she laughs, then gets to her feet. For a few seconds I am too afraid to find out how painful it will be to move, so I just stare at the toe scuffs on her black boots and the frayed ends of the laces. "Need a hand up?" she adds, then extends her arm down to me.

I start to turn my head, expecting it to feel like someone is trying to saw it off, but to my surprise, my neck is only a little stiff. I hold my breath and try to sit up, bracing for the hundreds of imminent stabs to my torso, but the pain is actually dull in comparison to last night when Liddick had me walk to the stream. I reach up and grip Zoe's forearm, then smile when I realize I might just be over this part of the treatment.

"Thanks," I say to her, then turn around when I hear Arco stirring. He shifts to his side and stops in place as his thick eyebrows crash together in a wince.

"*Crite...*" he groans without opening his eyes, then takes in a shallow breath. Zoe giggles, and I laugh a little too.

"Sore?" I say, kneeling down next to him, surprised again that it's so much easier to move.

"Up and about," Zoe says, kicking the bottom of his sock feet with her boot. "Pain should only last a few minutes. Vita gave you all flint root before we stacked you out for the night."

"Ow," he groans again, and now I can't help but laugh. Arco tries to sit up, but just manages to exhale a quick breath as he freezes again. Zoe rolls her eyes.

"Boys are always wailers," she sighs. "You feel all right enough to tend to him?" she asks, tilting her head at Arco, who has finally managed to open his eyes a little. I smile and nod at her. "Then I'll go see about rousing the walrus and Fraya. I'll come back to take you all to the training circle, wise?"

"Thanks," I say, and Arco lifts up to his elbows as she walks away shaking her head. He starts to smirk, but then suddenly abandons it.

"Hurts even to smile, doesn't it?" I laugh, then nod at him. He looks up at me, surprised.

"You're not sore?" he answers as he sits the rest of the way up.

"Not really anymore..." I say. "I woke up last night dying of thirst, but my suit was empty. I had to go to the stream, and then it was really bad."

"What did you do? I didn't hear you get up."

"Liddick helped me," I say hesitantly, then scan quickly until I find him grinning over Ellis, who's pressing the heels of his palms into his eyes. Arco doesn't say anything after this, but I can feel my chest tighten with anxiety. "He was already up. My hands lit up too just like his did right after his treatment..." I add, and his eyes flash back to mine, waiting for the rest. "I mean, it was scary, but he told me how to get it under control. I still don't think I can completely do it, though," I try to smile casually, but thinking about this pulls me back into last night, into the way I felt with Liddick, which I can't seem to sort out. Arco must sense this because he moves himself to the edge of his blanket stacks, then pushes up to his feet all at once, swearing under his breath at the aftershock he must feel as his muscles protest.

"Sorry," he says once he's completely upright.

"I've heard worse," I smile, but Arco doesn't react. I sigh, then rub my hands over my face trying to decide if I should just tell him about Liddick—about us physically feeling what the other one feels now—but if I do that, it's just going to give Arco one more thing to worry about. *Maybe it's only temporary anyway,* I think, and if it's not, I'll just have to figure out how to compartmentalize it. Liddick seems to be able to censor what he thinks from me when he wants, right? There must be a dial for this new development too…there has to be.

Zoe finds her way back to us with Joss and Myra in tow, and I see that Dell and Cal have rallied Tieg and the others, and are heading toward the Swim opening on the other side of Center Hall. Jesse meets Liddick, Ellis, and Avis at the lip, and just as soon as I make them all out, they disappear down the chute.

"Ready to see what you can do?" Zoe asks with a dangerous look in her eye, and I'm not really sure if I am ready. "You got all your aches and gripes out of the way?" she asks, looking up at Arco over my shoulder. He stretches his neck to the side, then the other and nods.

"I'll do," he answers. "Lead on."

I slip my hand into his, and try to find something to say to help ease the tension that's starting to build all around me as we approach the opening to the Swim.

"Seems like you're not going to have to deal with the nausea, and maybe not the itchy hands and random fire snaps...do you feel queazy at all?" I ask, looking up at Arco. He meets my eyes and shrugs.

"Not really. I mean, eating is about the last thing I want to do right now, but I don't feel sick. Did you get sick last night?" he asks, and I immediately regret bringing this up.

I nod, then Arco nods, and the tension dials up another notch between us. "Liddick helped you through that too?" he asks after a few more steps, and I sigh, feeling the struggle flare up in him again between his understanding of the way Liddick is connected to me in a way that he can't be, and his insecurity about it. He lets go of my hand to scratch the back of his head, but he doesn't take it again afterward.

"Arco," I start, then slow down to create a little more distance between us and Zoe, who is already several feet ahead of us. "You know I don't want to be with him like that. Like *this*...with you," I say, reaching for his hand again to reassure him, then feel pressure in my chest like I'm impatiently waiting to say my peace in an argument, but I force it out.

"I know you don't want him, Jazz," he finally says. "That's the hard part," he adds with a small smile at the ground that is already wilting when he glances up at me again, squeezing my hand once before he lets it go again as we walk on.

I understand what he means more than I can even begin to explain to him since my feelings about Liddick are just as unresolvable lately—I can't control feeling drawn to him just like Arco can't control feeling jealous or fearful that I am, even though we both know I *don't* want to be with Liddick. Last night was just...more getting caught up in the storm of him. It had to be because I know *perfectly well* that my draw to him is because he's a reminder that I'm not the only one who feels the way I do when I want to run, or when I want to rally and fight, or when I just want to stop the world for five seconds so I can make sense of it, and it's this *reassurance* that makes me feel less fractured and scattered and searching when I'm with him. This *has* to be right...

I mean, until recently, I've needed to hold onto that security, but I can't believe that's love. It's camaraderie... it's friendship, and maybe those are forms of love, but it's not the same thing that draws me to Arco. I don't have to cling to him to feel like I'm secure because I already am secure with him. So, if love means being able to bring *myself* to a relationship like I'm starting to believe it is, I need to be self-sustaining like that, right? Otherwise, what am I really able to bring?

My head starts pounding, which makes me realize I've been clenching my teeth. I relax my jaw and take a deep breath, and to my surprise, I actually feel a little better. Did I really just figure this out? It seems like it was too easy. It *can't* be that simple, but the certainty that falls over me makes me stand up straighter, breathe easier, and I can't help but feel like no matter what happens next, I'll be able to handle it because with Arco, I finally feel like I have…*me.* That's the missing piece in all of this with Arco and Liddick. *That's* the difference.

I take another deep breath and watch Zoe sit on the edge of the Swim, then slow down until I'm almost stopped in place. Arco turns to me, and I study his face, which looks darker now, the yellow-green light casting shadows under his high cheekbones. I reach up and run my fingers over the rough stubble starting along his jaw, then trace the strangely curved *S* scar that looks like a three-inch fire just over his collarbone. We've come so far, and we have so far yet to go, but I can't imagine being here without him. I know it's impossible to plan everything ahead of time after all that has happened since we took the submarine to Gaia. Maybe we never see what's coming, but I know I can handle whatever that might be now, and so I'm not afraid of it anymore.

"What is it?" Arco shakes his head a little and tries to find the answer in my eyes as I feel a smile pull at the corner of my mouth. "What's in your head all of a sudden?" he asks.

"I…love you," I say, then watch his eyes widen for a fraction of a second before he swallows, then takes a deep breath as a smile spreads over his face and his chest rises and falls.

I let my hand slide down from his treatment scar and feel his heart is pounding hard and fast beneath it when he wraps his arm around my waist, then pulls me into him. His other hand moves through my hair as he lifts me to my toes, squeezing me so tightly that I can't suppress the bubbling giddiness that is pushing up in my chest like a geyser. I laugh as he kisses me, then forget for a second where we are.

"Say it again," he finally whispers against my lips, making our teeth click together since we're now both grinning like idiots.

"I love you, Arco" I say, and then laugh out loud when he wraps both of his arms around me and lifts me off the ground in a bearhug.

He looks up at me as I brace my forearms on his shoulders and meet his eyes, which are bright green in the yellowish torchlight and crinkling in the corners. I lean down and kiss him again, then hear Alec's voice just a few feet away.

"Or *don't* turn into a human bonfire in the middle of everyone maybe?" he says, clapping Arco on the back as he passes, but I don't understand what he's talking about until Arco puts me down and I see red flames out of the corner of my eye.

"Whoa!" Arco says, jumping back from me and closing his hands into fists, which only makes the flames snap out from the sides. He tries to put his hands under his arms to smother the fire, but this only gives him flaming red wings. His throat and cheeks blotch with color, and I can't stop myself from giggling.

"OK, just take a deep breath and concentrate on blowing it out. Just focus on your breaths and your heartbeat… " I say, trying to remember what I did, what I thought as Liddick coached me through the same thing.

Arco nods and closes his eyes, then takes several deep breaths. Slowly, the flames shooting from his hands start to dissipate, and he opens his eyes again.

"I don't know why that suddenly...I mean...I didn't even know that I..." Arco stumbles through an attempted explanation, and I just shake my head and laugh again as I try to get enough breath to remind him that the same thing happened to me. "Oh, that's funny, huh? I'm funny?" he nods quickly. A wide smile spreads over his face before he puts his arm around my waist and pokes my ribs until I squirm the rest of the way to the Swim. We stop then, look down over the edge, and get ready to jump.

CHAPTER 34
Do What You Can

When Arco and I walk into the training circle cave, Veece and Cal are already talking with Kesh and about five or six other Badlanders, including a big one I haven't seen before. He stands with his back to us at first, but turns when he hears us come in. He's missing his right hand from the wrist down, and I freeze in my steps as he looks directly at me with large, yellow-gold eyes that are set like a panther's against his dark skin. For a split second, I think he's Mr. Tark, our Endurance and Survival instructor from Gaia Sur, which sends a wave of prickly heat down my spine until I see that he's much too young to be Tark, though, no less intimidating.

"Who is *that*?" I whisper to Arco. "I thought he was Mr. Tark just now."

"I thought the same thing when I first saw him the other day. Jesse called him 'General,'" he says, quirking an eyebrow.

"*General*? Like, the old military rank?"

Arco shrugs again, "I mean, look at him...he's at parade rest or something," he says through a small laugh as General stands with his feet shoulder width apart while listening to Kesh, his chest pushed out and his one hand gripping the wrist of his other arm behind his back.

The green torches glow all around the perimeter of the ceiling, highlighting the stripes in the walls that everyone calls *vein rock.* Kesh nods, then walks with the other

Badlanders to the far edge of the training circle, and after a few more minutes of everyone talking, Veece turns to the rest of us.

"Vox left before we could prepare her for the Rush. I take responsibility for that," he says, cutting a glance at Cal, who pulls a stray thread from the hem of his loose, thermal style shirt, then raises steely blue eyes at Veece. "But the *rest* of you will learn to control the fire before you cross the barrier," he adds, holding out his palm. After a few seconds, a small, bright red flame flickers, then grows until it surrounds his whole hand.

"Why is it red?" Tieg asks, standing with his arms folded under his broad chest as he tilts his head to the side and narrows his eyes, which seem to glow an even more surreal blue in this light.

"It takes on the color of our blood," Veece says, concentrating on the flame to make it grow and shrink, then spill to the floor and encircle him before he somehow pulls it back into his hand. He takes a small, white cloth from his pocket and holds it just above the snapping flames. It starts to blacken and curl, then vanishes in a whoosh of fire, leaving only flecks of char floating in the air like some kind of disappeared phantom. "It burns...it just can't burn us," Veece adds. "You shape it by picturing it moving to where you intend —any shape, and direction, but its size will depend on your control. If you're careless, the smoke of whatever you set on fire can still kill you, so be careful...aggression is the fastest ignition, so we will start there," Veece says, then turns to Cal, who starts walking toward us. "Pair them up."

"Pick up where you left off with Dell," Cal says to Liddick as he passes him, then waves him on with a nod over his shoulder. Dell grins and cracks his neck.

"It's our second date, Princess," he smirks, and I try to stifle a laugh when Liddick rolls his eyes.

"You're with Kesh," Cal says, surprising me at my shoulder. I look around, but don't see her until she startles me from behind, moving like a shadow just beyond my peripheral vision. My heart starts to pound in my ears.

"Ready or not," she says as she passes in front of me, making a clicking sound with her mouth like I'm her pet and she's calling me to her. A wave of anger pushes up from my chest and makes my face hot. I glance at Arco, who raises his eyebrows, then nods at me while forcing back the smile that he must know will make me kill him if he actually let's himself laugh.

"Whoa…it'll be OK," he whispers through a chuckle, then clears his throat, clearly knowing how close to the end of his life he is when I angle my head at him. "She knows what she's doing—we wouldn't have made it out of the falls without her," he adds, and this relieves some of the outrage percolating just under the skin of my palms. He blows out a breath, and I nod back at him before following Kesh. When I look back over my shoulder, I hear Cal telling Arco to wait for him in the middle of the training circle, then watch him point Jax toward General.

General…I say his name again in my head. *Does he really go by that*? My thoughts stop when Zoe's voice cuts a path in the air as she crosses to Dez.

"So, if you don't have any individual teeth in there, what happens when I hit you…the whole soap dish falls out?" she asks, then laughs in satisfaction as little snaps of fire immediately whip into and out of existence from Dez's arms and shoulders. "There! Now we can work," Zoe nods, still grinning when I catch her eyes. She winks, then angles her head to something behind me. I turn around right into a blur of white and a whoosh of air, which makes me instinctively jump back, then fall hard on the stone ground.

"What the—" I start, but Kesh is already walking toward me, spinning and tossing a small knife just like Zoe did after she and her crew hauled Liddick and me into the little cave by the falls. I scramble to my feet.

"Hey! Whoa! I thought we were *fire* training!" I stammer. Kesh stops in her tracks and raises her eyebrows at me.

"We are," she says, pretending to straighten her short frenzy of black hair as she dips her chin at my shoulder. I follow her eyes and discover several licks of flame shooting up through my dive suit, which I quickly try to take off before it burns through. I pull the cord that releases the back panel, then shimmy out of the sleeves and fumble for the invisible zipper of my jumpsuit. I find it just in time to unzip it and pull my arms out, but between last night's pyrotechnics and now this, a small singe line mars the left shoulder of my jumpsuit, which is still smoking.

"Great…" I say, dropping the sleeve at my side, then roll my eyes. Kesh snickers, and I glare up at her. "What's so funny?"

"You look like a squid," she says, angling her head at the double set of sleeves hanging around my waist. I roll my eyes and step out of both suit layers, then feel the damp air on my skin. It sends a line of chills down my spine, which somehow, are warm. "They give you all the *same* skivvies?" Kesh asks, incredulous. I look down at my base layer shorts and tank top style shirt, which fits more like a bathing suit than an actual shirt.

"Apparently," I say, feeling the tingle in my palms spread over my arms and shoulders more strongly now. I jerk my eyes away from her and inspect my forearms, which prickle. Flecks of red sparks seem to strike, but then immediately disappear, and for a few seconds it looks like my arms are covered in glitter the way they catch the light. Out of the corner of my eye, I see Kesh advancing toward me again.

"Tunnel sharks, zephyrs, worms…none of them tend to wait for you to finish admiring yourself before they grab you," she says, excitement flashing in her brown eyes when she sees the sparks of red fire at my shoulders, which crackle and pop near my ear. "Think of the prickling like water running down your arms and into your hands. Then throw it at me," Kesh adds, darting toward me and slashing her knife again, this time nearly cutting my base layer shirt. "The mosquitoes out there have talons," she winks, and my heart jumps into my throat. I swallow hard so I can breathe again, and try to focus enough to envision the little pin pricks all over my arms turning into water. I almost have it, but then see General rush Jax, driving his shoulder into Jax's stomach and knocking them both to the ground as another large

Badlander boy with short blond hair moves in. Flames immediately engulf Jax as General rolls off him, but he doesn't have time to regroup before the other boy takes a swing at him. Jax ducks, but when he stands up again, his base layer shirt burns through at the shoulder and falls across his chest.

"Better put it out, boss. I give you one more flame out like that before you light your wick," General says in a low, casual voice that hovers just on the edge of a laugh. Jax takes an angled step and rips the rest of his base layer shirt away, then quickly tries patting the red flames that are traveling down the groove of muscle in the center of his chest to his stomach. He pulls in a deep breath when the patting doesn't work, and finally the flames stop their southern trajectory. The cords in his neck stand out as the muscles in his chest start to twitch with his effort to control his breathing, and I'm sure the only other time I've seen him this angry is when he confronted Arco about leaving Fraya and Vox behind in the cave during our explorative run in the Stingray ships.

In another blur and flash of white, I feel a sudden burn on my upper arm. I look up to see Kesh dancing back from me, then wiping her knife on her pants. At the site of the burn a long, thin cut is starting to well up with blood, so I close my hand over it.

"What is *wrong* with you!?" I hiss at her, but she just shakes her head at me like I'm the most pathetic person she's ever met and starts coming toward me again. I feel the prickle in my arms doubling, quadrupling, and spreading to my legs until I'm sure I will blow up like a volcano. *Water…think of the water*, I remind myself, and take several steps back from Kesh while holding my upper arm. To my surprise, a wave of pins and needles rushes downward until I can feel it pushing against the ends of my fingertips, and when I let go of my arm, a few small, explosive bursts turn into two large streams of red fire pouring from my hands. They travel about five feet before they hit the ground and form a red, flickering pool at Kesh's feet, then dissipate.

"Well, see there? Some people have to bleed before they know what they're made of," she says, then puts her knife back in her boot. I take a deep breath and swallow the acid in the back of my throat, then hear Cal from somewhere behind me.

"That's what you do when you can see something coming—but what about when you don't?" he says. I jerk my head in the direction of his voice only to find Dell sparring with Liddick and General trying to show Jax some kind of twisting throw movement with the other tall Badlander boy. The second I register that I don't see Cal anywhere, my air is cut off as an arm closes like a vice grip over my chest, pinning my elbows to my sides while fingers close over my throat and jaw. "This is how the tunnel sharks will carry you—what can you move? What's free?" he asks close to my ear as I struggle uselessly to breathe. "Don't think about your air. The tunnel sharks want you to think about that—about what you *can't* do instead of what you can. Everything in the Rush wants you to *react* instead of act," Cal adds, and I feel the pins and needles stirring under my skin again. I kick backward and connect with nothing, then try to stomp on what I hope will be his foot, but again, find nothing. A scream starts to strangle in my throat as my fingers curl into fists, but I can't lift them high enough to visualize any fire moving to them. I feel heat prickling my shoulders and arms, then see flames catch and fly like they did last night—uncontrolled and everywhere.

"The sharks are immune to the fire like we are—that won't do any good," Kesh coaches from somewhere I can't see as Cal's grip around my ribs and jaw tightens. I struggle against him, but I don't gain any leverage. "What *can* you move?" he presses. "What is *free*?" I scream in frustration and see a curtain of fire drape in front of me. "What is *free*? Focus!"

My legs....my legs are free, I think to myself, but only accomplish more panic and frustration when I kick, but again, don't connect with anything.

"Swing your legs!" Kesh yells, and tiny flecks of light dance in the flames before me as my struggling somehow only increases Cal's hold on me.

"I can't...breathe..." I gasp.

"What *can* you move!?" Cal yells near my ear.

"Swing!" Kesh calls again. With the corners of my vision starting to darken, I kick out instead of back, pretending I'm in a swing at the playground. It doesn't feel like I've accomplished anything at first, but when I swing my legs back, I feel Cal's grip loosen enough for me to slide my arms out from under his. I plant my feet on the ground and stand up, then pull downward on his wrist, which is near my throat. To my surprise, he flips over my shoulder and rolls to a stop in front of me before springing up, a wide grin spreading across his face.

"*That's* what you do when you don't see it coming."

CHAPTER 35
Boundary Lines

The Lookout Pier is surreal after curfew—after the orange light of the torches fades to red, then to purple, which only provides enough illumination for me to find the edges of the walls and the very next foothold in the corridor that opens over the Rush. I take off my dive suit so I don't accidentally burn it one too many times when I start practicing with my fire again, then walk as far as I dare over the smooth, black pier so I can look out at the distant volcano where my father, Liddick's brothers, and Arco's sister are being held in the labs somewhere at the bottom. The white, limestone towers pierce the cloud blanket and glint in the light that has changed from a sun-like ball to strips of parallel, iridescent bands in the sky…which I suppose isn't really a sky, but the vast ceiling of the cavern Zoe explained we're actually in. The saturated gold light seems to pour from the glowing gas strips and plunge into the dark pockets of clouds that aren't really clouds either, but dormant zephyr winds just waiting for someone to walk through the Bale field so they can suck them into their hidden miniature tornado mouths, skin first, then one layer of their body at a time until the unlucky person is just…gone.

How can we possibly survive out there, I think, then dig my fingernails into my palm, which has started to itch. A small red flame breaks through my fingers and flickers until it whiffs out of existence just as fast as it appeared.

Just like we'll disappear when those things catch us crossing the boundary line, I think again, then shake my head and try to concentrate on bringing the flame back so I can practice directing it in spite of the dark, ghostly zephyrs in the distance putting me on edge. *I can't freeze out there when I'm afraid. I can't panic,* I tell myself, then squeeze my eyes shut against the low howl that trails off into a chittering sound coming from what must be somewhere in the Rainforest biome, the first biome just beyond the Bale field boundary line. *If I can't control what's out there, at least I can control myself,* I think.

Since we started training several days ago, I've been coming up to the Lookout Pier on my own after everyone else goes to sleep. I can't seem to sleep anymore, not really. Not like before the Vishan's DNA treatment when my thoughts, Liddick's comments, or the buzzing from Vox's occasional messages were the only other sounds in my head. Even they weren't constant like these echoes of strange whale songs, or whispers of conversations that I'm not *sure* I hear because they just seem to float in the background of everything else. Dell said we would start picking up more random signals because the treatments would enhance our neural channels, but he also said we might become paranoid, so don't know what is actually happening or how much I should be worried about it. All this is supposed to last two weeks while we finish *cooking,* as Cal put it...two more weeks of this until our DNA finishes bonding with the Vishan's. Whatever is happening, I'm starting to fear heading into the Rush in the morning with these distractions in my head, but there's no other choice if we want to get to our families before our treatments become permanent…before Lyden and Arwyn are sent to wherever the Phase Three location is for the sick mutation experiments Liam said Gaia has planned for them next.

You're up late. I jump when I hear Liddick in my mind, then turn around abruptly to find him leaning on the black wall at the threshold of the corridor that leads down to Center Hall. "Sorry, I was trying *not* to scare you," he adds out loud as he takes off his dive suit to reveal his blue jumpsuit underneath, then folds it next to my dive suit against the side wall. "I can help you practice if you want," he adds as I pull up another pathetic little flame in my hand so I can try to extend it in an arc over my head like Dell and Veece did in the training circle, but it dissipates before it gets past my shoulder.

I let my hand drop to my side, frustrated as Liddick crosses to sit on the smooth ledge that juts out of the otherwise jagged wall next to me. The muted, glowing light hits the angular lines of his face and filters through his blond hair, making the dark roots disappear against the backdrop of the poured black wall behind him. He looks like an apparition again just like he did against the dark sky that night on the dune…the night before we left for Gaia when he told me about the messages from Liam. Thinking of this reminds me all over again of the years everyone misjudged him for being shallow, vain, and obsessed with Skyboard North virtuo-cine culture when all he was really trying to do was find his brothers without endangering anyone else. That seems like a lifetime ago, but I still regret not seeing it...not helping somehow.

"How did you know I was up here?" I ask, trying to bring up another flame when I feel the dull itch returning at the base of my fingers.

"I had a *feeling* you were practicing," he says, gesturing to the palm of his hand and winking at me.

"Of course you did," I reply, trying to sound casual, but I can't keep the anxiety out of my voice. I'm still not completely sure what to do about us now being able to physically feel what the other is feeling. I was *just* starting to keep clear lines between us with the telepathy we already have. With this new layer of connection, I can't risk losing sight of where he ends and I begin again. I feel a dull pain in the base of my chest after realizing this, and have to look away from Liddick.

"Is being able to physically feel things like this now with each other why you've been avoiding me?" he asks.

"It's just...this is too much, Liddick," I sigh, closing my eyes and shaking my head, suddenly exhausted. "This is all just too much." I try to relax my hands when prickling heat starts to race down my arms, then take another deep breath and push back the doubt I feel about being able to handle whatever is waiting for us in the Rush, especially if I can't even keep myself together around Liddick.

"If it helps, Vita said we won't be able to feel each other's physical reactions after the DNA bonding period. I guess everything just goes a little outer ring before it's permanent for some people," he adds, and I can feel the dull ache in my chest spreading like something cold has spilled inside me: disappointment...his disappointment, which is quickly blotted up by my own anger.

"You *told* her we could feel each other's physical reactions?" I ask, the ache sharpening to a stabbing panic at the idea that Arco will find out and think it's just one more thing Liddick and I have, but he and I don't.

Liddick straightens, his brows darting together as he angles his head at me. "Crite," he says through a wince as he presses a hand to his chest. "She's basically the Vishan doctor, Rip. I had to find out what was happening with us, didn't I?" he adds, trying to smile through the shock in his eyes, which then narrow in disbelief. "If you're *this* worried about Hart knowing..." he starts to say, gesturing to the hand at his chest, but then abandons the thought and shakes his head.

"What? Finish what you were going to say," I press. He takes a deep breath, then lets it out all at once.

"If you're worried this much about Hart knowing that you and I have another level of connection, then maybe what you think you have with him isn't what you want after all," he says evenly, like he's been working on the theory for a while. Suddenly, all my accumulated frustration hits me like a crashing wave—the last several training sessions that end with me losing control, and the follow-up nights of failed practices here on The Lookout Pier where I still can't shut out enough of the world to focus.

"How would you react, Liddick? What if Arco could feel what I felt, hear what I thought, and you couldn't? Can you imagine that for a minute? What if I were with *you*, and I couldn't pull away from *him*?" The words are out before I consider their implications, caught up in the whirlwind of building pressure and fear and confusion as I dig my fingernails into my palms to keep the itch at bay. He meets my eyes as the striations of muscle in his jaw release, and now he has confirmation of his suspicions about me being as drawn to him as he is to me. The piercing anger in my chest softens and warms, then swells against my ribs as I take a deep breath and wait for him to flesh out the *rest* of his reaction—to say it again...to tell me we fit and *that's* why it's so hard for me to pull away from him. I can feel it just below the surface like I'm about to say it myself, but it's not what he says when he responds.

"You're hearing the sounds now too, aren't you? The whales and whispers?" he asks, pushing my hair behind my ear after a few seconds. I stare up at him.

"It's not the paranoia..." I say too quickly, both a little relieved and a little disconcerted because if Liddick can hear them too, if it's not just the paranoia Dell was talking about, that means the whispers are real. "Can everyone else hear them? I didn't want to ask because..."

"Because you didn't want anyone to think the paranoia hit you...that's why I didn't say anything either," he nods in understanding, then lets his eyes drift to the ground as he smiles, but that falls away after another second as he tenses again. "I felt you pushing away, Rip—pushing me away, but I thought you just needed time, I don't know. The physical feelings...this new connection. I know it was...*it is* a lot," he adds, starting and stopping until he abandons that path and returns to a safer one. "Anyway, the others hear some of it—Dez hears the whales, but I think you and I are the only ones who hear the rest."

"Why do you think it's just us?" I ask. He meets my eyes again and takes my hand.

"Because we're the only ones who can't sleep any more."

He doesn't look away when he lets out the long, slow exhale that tells me he's been with me the last several nights lying awake on his blanket stacks just thirty feet below while I've been up here watching this new, impossible world spread out before me, trying to train myself not to be afraid. I cross my arms and turn back to look out over the Rush because I feel myself getting pulled into him again…into the comfort of not being the only one who sees what I see and feels what I feel.

"So you made up with Dez," I say, clearing my throat and changing the subject so I can redraw the ever fading lines that separate Liddick from me.

"I suppose she doesn't want to kill me anymore," he says with a quiet laugh in his voice.

"She's good for you if you'll just give it a chance," I answer, feeling my heart start to pound in my chest as I hear him walking toward me.

"Why do you keep playing this game with yourself, Rip?" he says quietly over my shoulder, giving into the need to say it again once and for all. "You think if you just ignore how you feel, you'll stop feeling it or something, but it doesn't work like that," he says in the same quiet voice against the distant sound of muffled whale songs and whispers.

"Liddick, it's *more* than that—" I start to say, feeling his hands rest on my shoulders as carefully as they did when he checked my back for the gills I dreamed I had that first night after we escaped from Gaia. This time, his hands slip into my hair when I turn to face him, his clear blue eyes reflecting the golden light of the Rush behind me as his thumb traces the line of my jaw, and the way he looks into me makes me forget to breathe.

"You're right. It is more," he whispers, leaning in, and turning away from him is like trying to resist gravity. I can't move except to ball my hands into fists to prevent the fire from escaping again as I fight to take a slow, deep breath, to disappear in him and forget about everything else, at least for a little while.

"Liddick…" I finally manage just before his lips touch mine. "This pull I have to you…isn't what you think," I say, lightheaded as my heart pounds in my ears. He pulls back slowly and scans my eyes, then furrows his brow in confusion when I don't say anything else. After another few seconds, realization spreads over his face, and my throat constricts with all the words I haven't said, but don't have to now.

"You *love* him…don't you?"

CHAPTER 36
Into the Storm

Liddick takes a step back from me, nodding to the air over his shoulder, and I feel like someone has punched me in the stomach. I didn't even completely realize that I *do* love Arco until recently, but it still feels like someone is squeezing my lungs because Liddick had to find out from reading me rather than me telling him myself.

"I didn't even know that's how I felt until before we all went to the circle arena for training that first night...you were right about me needing some time to think I guess," I say, hoping to take the edge off of the news for him, but he bristles instead.

"So you were planning to tell me this when... somewhere in the third biome when we're outrunning tunnel sharks or giant taloned mosquitoes or something?" he asks, narrowing his eyes again and pressing his lips into a thin line as his teeth lock together, making his jaw contract.

A gust of anger hits me, which I know is his, and I know he's angry because he's hurt...but the heat rising in answer is mine, and it's because I'm so done with him not accepting what I've been telling him from the beginning.

"Liddick, I told you within five minutes of you kissing me after your port-carnate debacle that we couldn't be together, remember? And when you told me I was what you were coming for—when you told *Arco* as much with me standing right there—I told you again that you and I couldn't be together like that," I say, then take a deep breath so I can control my tone. His narrowed eyes widen, and I can see the red outlines near the edges. He hasn't been sleeping much either.

"And the times since then—these past weeks…all the times I felt you needing *me*, Rip, not Hart," he says, pointing toward the dark fissure opening, which is awash with glinting specks of reflected light from the Rush. "When you were the most afraid, you looked for *me*—when we first surfaced and everyone was wrecked over Pitt dying…and when you were coming through the squeeze with your nanites failing? When you had to take a breath or you were going to—" he stops abruptly and closes his eyes, then swallows hard and pushes a hand through his hair, gripping it in a clenching fist as he turns away from me and moves to lean back on the black, glassy ledge that is so shiny in places it looks wet. I watch him for a few minutes with all those scenes racing through my mind before I manage to pull together a response.

"You're right…" I say, then take a deep breath, which I hold a second before letting it out as if it will buy me some time to find the words that will pull him back from this harsh, lost place that's twisting in my own stomach now too. "I was…I *am* pulled to you, Liddick. We can *literally* hear each other's thoughts, feel each other's feelings," I add, but he still doesn't look up at me. "Knowing I'm not the only one who feels the concentration of everyone's emotions all the time on top of my own is probably the reason I've made it this far without losing my mind down here," I say, taking a step toward him. "But I disappear in you, Liddick. I just melt down and reform into this soldered rebellion with you against the rest of the world. We turn into this strength for each other when things spin out, but at the core of that, I don't see myself anymore. I just see you, or us. I can't even tell the difference. Don't you think that's... *terrifying*?"

"No," Liddick answers casually and immediately as he straightens, gripping the black rock ledge at either side of him and shaking his head adamantly as he drives his bottom lip against his teeth. "No, Rip, I don't. I think that's what people go their whole lives trying to find— someone who gets it. Someone who can just look at you, and you *know* you're everything to them because you're *that* intertwined. There is no *you* or *me* when it's right like that...there's *us. That's* love, Riptide. Going all in and not looking back. Tell me you really can't feel it—a level of connection that no one else could ever have with you? Tell me we don't have that," he says, reining in his voice and angling his head. His brows pull together as he tries to soften the rigid set of his mouth.

I take a deep breath and feel tears burning the back of my throat, then welling in my eyes as everything inside me feels like it's being ripped out. I shake my head, feeling my heart breaking...his heart. *Ours*? I can barely find my voice to reply.

"But how do you know you're everything to someone when you disappear?" I manage, and his eyes narrow like he's trying to wall off my words. "*Of course* we have that connection, but it's *because* we're so intertwined that this isn't good," I say, hearing my voice failing under the weight of the words. "You've felt me need you, felt that I've wanted to be with you, and you were right, but don't you see how you've run those feelings through your own filters? We have different definitions of love, Liddick. I don't *want* to disappear. I don't want to have to wonder if all the things that I think make me who I am are just reflections of you, or *us*, or whatever. Can't you see that? Can't you feel *that* in me?" I ask, watching his bloodshot, blue eyes ignite as they glass, and his dark brows crash down in an effort to stop them. He swallows hard again and locks his jaw, forcing the muscles to jump and outline the sharp angles of his face as the cords begin to show in his throat. I watch his pulse jump under the small *S* scar of his treatment injection just above his collarbone until his chin lowers to his chest. He grips his elbows like a cold wind has just blown over us, and the chill runs through me like a blade. I just want him to talk, to say something. *Liddick?* I think. Several more seconds pass before he sighs, but he still doesn't look up at me.

All right, he finally answers in my mind, then nods to the ground a few times before turning back toward the shadowy fissure, which flickers as he passes in front of the reflecting light from the Rush behind us. He stops abruptly with his back to me, then stands still for a second before turning around and pulling something from his pocket. He walks a few steps back to me and reaches for my wrist, his hands warm as he folds my fingers over the smooth, cool stone he puts in my palm. It's bright red with spots of gold marking one end—a Cycle stone like Zoe and Dell had earlier to tell the time.

"We leave in the morning—when this turns green in about five hours," Liddick says out loud, then silently to me as he closes his fingers over mine, his eyes bright blue with fatigue and narrowed like he's fighting against too harsh a light. *At least that's one thing we can see coming down here,* he thinks, then forces a smile, but doesn't meet my eyes again before he grabs his dive suit and disappears into the fissure. I sit down and stare at the rock, running my thumb over the smooth, flat surface, then stare out over the Rush. The white, limestone pillars stab upward through the bellies of the seven biomes that unfold for miles into the distance under the floating zephyr nests and striated, muted gold light of the gas clouds above.

***

It feels like I've barely closed my eyes when the sensation of drops hitting my face forces them open, and I startle at the crack of thunder that follows about three seconds later.

"Good way to get yourself sparked, sleeping up here all exposed like that," Zoe says from behind me as I scramble to my feet and move back to the overhang of the Lookout Pier with her. "I was just about to start throwing pebbles to rouse you," she adds, then lets the handful of dark stones in her hand spill to the ground. "Come on—they're dishing breakfast, and Jove wants to talk to everyone before we push into the Rush. We need to light out while it's storming…harder for the zephyrs to make us out during storms," she says, jerking her freckled chin at the weather beyond the edge of the pier, which I haven't really looked at until now.

"*What is that*!?" I gasp at the huge, cylindrical tubes of dark clouds that cover the entire sky, bunching in places like thick, rolled blankets against what looks like a bright, intermittent light on the other side.

"Storm clouds," Zoe shrugs.

"*Those* aren't storm clouds. They're…layered!"

"You heard the crack, right? And you see those flickers up inside them?" she asks, cocking an eyebrow at the sky. She nods at the same time I do and shrugs again. "Storm clouds. Come on."

I can't tear myself away from the tubular bands that seem like they will drop down from the sky like an unfurling curtain at any second, and Zoe suddenly jerks my elbow. I turn abruptly and follow her down the rise to Center Hall to find everyone standing around the cook pot—everyone, that is, except Arco and Dell, who are talking off to the side. I scan the room for Liddick but don't find him near his blanket stacks, or anywhere else nearby the others.

"Where's Liddick?" I ask Zoe as we make our way to the food.

"Last I saw he was sliding down the Swim. Haven't seen him since," she answers.

I try to focus my thoughts enough to call to him, but once we pass through the opening to the large room, there's too much noise and commotion to hold him in my mind for more than a second or two without actually having him in sight.

"Maybe he went to practice in the circle arena," I say, but Zoe doesn't seem to hear me as she reaches for the bowl that Myka, the tall Vishan animal expert with giant brown eyes, is passing her. Myka glances at me, then does a double take before looking over her shoulder.

"Have you talked to Liddick?" she whispers as she leans toward me and pushes her straight, blonde hair away from her face.

"No, why?" I ask, surprised, and now suddenly feel like something bad has happened, or is about to. "What is it?" I press when she just looks at me blankly and straightens.

"Bale muffins today," she says abruptly in her regular voice, then narrows her round doe eyes at me before she lets them dart to Vita, who is putting little muffins into stone bowls. I shake my head just a little…confused, until I realize she's trying to avoid us being overheard. When she's sure Vita isn't listening, she leans in again and offers me a bowl. "He was already in the Origin Wall room when curfew lifted this morning…only Council members, Kora, or I can go in there so early, but when I tried to tell him that, it's like he couldn't hear me…he was talking to someone who wasn't there about *you*."

"About *me*?" I ask. "What did he say?" I add, a little too loudly, apparently, as Arco walks up behind me and puts his arm around my shoulder. He kisses my cheek as he steals one of the little muffins from the bowl I'm holding, then looks around for one of his own.

"What did who say?" he asks, popping the muffin into his mouth, and Myka stiffens. Arco raises a heavy eyebrow at her as he chews, then looks at me and raises the other.

"It's OK if he knows," I say quietly with a nod to Myka, then watch her delicate shoulders relax as she exhales.

"He was…angry," she adds under her breath, and I feel the wave of her fear push over me like a sheet of ice.

"*Who* was angry?" Arco asks just after he swallows, concern spreading over his face and forcing a crease between his eyes. Myka looks at me apologetically as Vita gives her a steely sideways look and clears her throat.

"Sorry, I have to go," she says, then takes a few bowls from the ground and helps Vita fill them with muffins. I blow out a breath, torn between excitement that Liddick must have been talking to Azeris somehow, and guilt because I know he was angry because of me.

"Jazz?" Arco says, startling me out of my thoughts, then shakes his head impatiently when I don't answer right away. "What is she talking about? Did something happen this morning? You were gone when I woke up."

"I fell asleep up on the Lookout Pier last night," I say, spotting Jove talking with Cal and Veece at the opening of the Swim. Arco starts choking on his muffin as I set my bowl down and get ready to head toward them. He clears his throat to stop himself from coughing, then catches my elbow.

"Wait…" he coughs once more, then clears his throat again. "The Lookout Pier is open to *the Rush*, Jazz…to those zephyr things," he says, his brows darting in on the last words.

"I didn't plan to fall asleep up there…"

"How did that even happen when you'd already fallen asleep next to me?" he asks. I sigh as I turn back toward the Swim, knowing I'll just have to tell him about practicing…and about Liddick.

"I've been getting up the last few nights to train with my fire after curfew," I say, turning back to him and stopping. His eyebrows jump as he opens his mouth to reply, but I hold up a hand to stop him. "*I know*, I know it's open to the elements and whatever else is airborne in the Rush. I tried to go to the circle arena first, but General was posted out there with Jesse. They wouldn't let me pass," I explain, but Arco's expression doesn't change.

"Well, no—not with that worm threat and the tunnel sharks. Why would you risk that?" he asks, shaking his head in bewilderment.

"Because I have to be able to control myself," I say, turning from him to head toward the opening to the Swim again. "I can't go out there without knowing I can do that, Arco."

"Jazz, will you *wait*?" he calls to me as I pass Jove, Cal, and Veece.

"I can't get swept up and lose sight of everything," I add, then step over the threshold to the Swim chute.

CHAPTER 37
Threshold

General and Jesse are still on watch when Arco and I climb out from the bottom of the dark chute. Jesse glares at us, making me stop in my steps until I realize he's actually looking at the two boys, one tall, blond Badlander and one shorter Vishan, who come out after we do.

"Finally! You're late," he growls, looking down the narrow bridge of his nose at them.

"Sorry, sorry," the tall blond one laughs, "but Wade was just—"

"Why do you think I care?" Jesse says, pushing his hands over his face and into his short, brown hair before he fixes his dark eyes on mine, then gestures over his shoulder to the stone path that leads to the circle arena. "Jove said to wait in there until he comes to send you off. Should be any minute. Is there any food left up there?" he asks, but doesn't wait for me to answer before he turns to go, slapping General on the shoulder.

"Right behind you," General says in a low voice that reverberates all around him. His golden eyes flash, and again, I'm reminded of Mr. Tark. "Good luck out there," he adds with a smile to us that stands out against his dark skin.

He adjusts the wide leather strap across his broad chest, the V-neck opening of his dingy, white knit pullover stretched beyond buttoning, and a long, wooden club shifts behind his back. *He's even bigger up close,* I think as he nods to us, then follows Jesse through the fissure at our side.

"Thanks," Arco says, returning his nod, then looks back at me. "What's going on with you? What was all that up there about not losing sight of everything?" he asks, the greenish torchlight casting shadows over the sharp angles of his face as we head down the stone path to the circle arena.

"Nothing," I say, already having forgotten our conversation as the reality of finally leaving for the Rush hits me even harder now that I can hear the winds crashing against the other side of the dark rock face all around us. "Do you hear that? The opening to the Bale field is just up there," I add, looking behind us at the rise that climbs up and out into the grain stalks.

"Should be interesting heading out," he answers, darting a glance over his shoulder at the source of the sound. "But Dell said the zephyrs would be less likely to see us in the storm," he adds pushing an overgrown lock of sandy, wavy hair out of his eyes. "*Anyway,* what's wrong?" he presses, and I blow out a breath.

"I told Liddick. I told him that I love you," I say abruptly, then feel a tingle run down my spine and through my fingertips as I say the words again. "He read it in me, actually, and he didn't take it well...I still feel like someone shoveled a scoop out of my chest," I add, bringing a hand to the base of my sternum as I take in another breath. Arco nods slowly and tries to hold back the smile that threatens to break free at the corner of his mouth, but he can't keep it from touching his eyes, which flicker with the green-gold light of the torches all around us when he presses his lips together.

"I imagine. That would wreck me to hear if things were reversed," he says after a pause, his voice low and soft. "What are you worried about losing sight of, though?" he asks again, then pushes hair from my shoulder and lets his fingers brush my cheek. I bring my hand to his and interlace our fingers, then try to gather the nerve to tell him what I should have told him several days ago as we walk toward the training circle.

"Arco…it's harder to separate from Liddick now," I finally say, then clear my throat and take another breath as my stomach and chest suddenly tighten, and I know this is in response to how he's now feeling.

"What does that mean?" he asks without looking over at me.

"Ever since the treatments we've been able to, um…to feel how the other one is feeling. Physically, I mean. He felt my treatment like his was happening all over again," I say, but now Arco stays quiet, keeping his eyes forward as we walk between the long stone countertops of the Bale processing room, the walls showing dark, broken lines of the vein rock that run the length of the walls in the arena and the small corridor that precedes it.

"So, you're even *more* connected to him now?" Arco finally says, his jaw muscles jumping as he presses his teeth together when I look up at him. I feel him fight to keep the accusation out of his voice as he lowers his chin, then turns to face me. His heavy brows pull in, and the dancing flecks of gold in his eyes that were just there have faded into the muted backdrop of dark green. "And it's been like this since your treatment?" he asks, which only increases the tightening in my chest.

"I'm sorry I didn't tell you," I say. "I knew I could figure out how to untangle from him—but *I* had to figure it out. I had to do it without being distracted by you worrying in the background because I didn't want that to be a crutch. Does that make sense? I didn't want feeling guilty about how you might react to be a reason I pulled away from him," I say, looking up at him and tightening my hold on his hand. He swallows and nods again after several more steps.

"No, I get it," Arco says after a second more, but the heavy feeling in my chest all of a sudden tells me that he really doesn't get it.

"Arco…it's not like that. How you feel matters to me, but I had to be sure there was nothing that I was burying," I add, and he pauses for a long time before responding.

"Sorry…I shouldn't be so close to this edge—so afraid you'll decide it's just easier with him or something," he forces a chuckle and lowers his chin again.

"I don't think easier is the word I'd use to describe any of this with Liddick," I say through a laugh that outruns my discretion. Arco's smiles broadly, then slows our pace and studies the ground for another second before finally looking up.

"I guess part of me still doesn't believe you chose me," he nearly whispers, muffling another small laugh as we walk.

"I didn't," I answer after another beat, then immediately feel a wall of ice push through my chest as his eyes dart to mine and his expression falls. I smile up at him. "I chose *me.*"

His lips quirk, and after a second more, the freeze in my chest melts away. He stops walking and brings his hand to my face, then pushes it through my hair as he brings his mouth to mine, his full lips warm and soft. His other arm moves around my waist and pulls me closer to him as everything inside me feels like it has been cut loose from the tethers that held it all in place. The sensation of it floating away makes it seem like I'm falling, but his arms are strong as I move my hands over the hard curves of his shoulders and let my fingers run through the curls at the nape of his neck. I feel him growl from somewhere in his chest as he pulls me even more tightly against him, which sends a jolt through me like it does every time he makes that sound.

His hands move to my hips, his grip tightening as he pulls me closer, deeper into the kiss, but then he stops himself and holds me back a little, resting his forehead against mine as we both catch our breath. The muscles in his chest twitch under my hands, and when I let them slip to his torso, his stomach is also tensed and quivering.

All at once, I want to see him, to feel his skin under my fingertips and hear his breath catch like it did when I was examining his ribs for injury when we first surfaced in the air bell cave a few weeks ago. The memory of his eyes following my every move sends a wave of heat through me, and the second I feel it, he takes a deep breath and tightens his hold on my hips again.

He exhales slowly, controlled, and takes in another deep breath. I feel him wrestling with his restraint and watch his chest expand as another explosion of heat radiates through me, and in nearly the same moment he brings his mouth to mine again. I slip my fingers into the dive suit rigging loops around his hips and pull him toward me. His fingers wrap around my waist and push up to my ribs as he presses me against the wall and kisses me again, harder this time, until I feel him consciously slow down and relax his grip. He draws in a quick breath and brings his hands gently back to my face as his tongue coaxes mine...*crite, he's a good kisser*, I think absently as my stomach leaps and dives. In the next second, from nowhere, it feels like everything that had been floating away inside me crashes fast and hard into the stone ground, then shatters into a million pieces that tumble end over end, scattering into all the dark corners of the rock corridor. I break the kiss abruptly and stare up at him. His eyes are wide, reflecting my own confusion as well as his.

"What happened? What's wrong?" Arco says, worry spreading over his face as his thumb strokes my cheek, searching for some external cause of my sudden shift. "Crite, Jazz, what is it?" he says more intently, raising his eyebrows in helplessness, and I remember his Empath Receiver latency...how he can pick up on strong feelings like this, though he can't tell the cause. "Are you...*hurt*?" he asks.

Yeah, Liddick says in my mind, and it's so soft I question if it really is one of my own thoughts. I turn then and see him in the short corridor just before the circle arena several feet in front of us. He meets my eyes, his, a stormy sea gray in this light as they seem to be fighting collapse under the weight of his brows. He presses his lips together into a hard line and clenches his jaw. "Sorry..." he adds aloud, but under his breath, then clears his throat.

"Liddick—" I start to say, but he just closes his eyes in a long blink and shakes his head a few times to stop me from saying anything else as he holds up a hand, which is electric with crackling static flashes of red flame that die as soon as they appear. He clenches both hands into fists as soon as he notices it, then drops them to his side as his knuckles turn white.

"We're leaving as soon as Cal and Jove get here. We can't miss the storm," Liddick says when he opens his eyes again, then makes his way past us without looking at me. The empty feeling in my chest spreads and sharpens the closer he gets, then dissipates as he moves farther and farther away. Arco lets out a deep breath once he's sure Liddick is out of sight.

"That came out of nowhere...that shift...the second he appeared," he says, looking down the corridor after Liddick. "I don't like him being able to transmit feelings like that to you...even I felt it that time. Are you OK?"

"I'm fine," I nod, taking a deep breath as the suffocating pain in my chest starts to subside. "Except... Arco...*we're* the ones who made *him* feel like that. What you felt...what I felt was the backlash of him seeing us. It was because of me," I say as my throat starts to close. I'm confused all over again when my eyes start to burn and blur with the threat of tears, which rise up in response to the shock of the last three minutes and also to the aftermath of the pain I know Liddick is still feeling. "I don't want to hurt anyone," I say, hearing my voice crack.

Arco's arms wrap around me as he sighs.

"It's not your fault. Liddick needs a hard line," he says into my hair as another gust of wind howls and throttles the rock face that separates us from the storm. "Better he sees it now than out there, too. Come on…"

Arco pulls me in as we walk through the small, dark corridor and into the circle arena where Dell and Zoe are strapping on packs with everyone else from our group. Zoe angles her head at two more packs on the dark ground at her side, then meets my eyes and whispers.

"Ready to go?"

CHAPTER 38
The Rush

Jove, Veece, and Cal enter the circle arena a few minutes after Arco and I put on our canvas packs, which are full of small pouches that I didn't investigate, and a corked glass jar of foaming white water from the hot spring—this must be for us to what, pour over ourselves? To put on the *bugs* from the spring that Zoe said will help us get past the Bale field stalks? I scan for Liddick, but don't see him anywhere.

We're all wearing our black dive suits, but Cal, Dell, and Zoe have long-sleeved brown leather shirts over the worn thermal ones they normally wear, as well as two straps around their legs, which hold a knife and a small leather pouch. Jove wears the same light colored tunic he wore the night of the Gathering for the younger Vishan when Liddick and I first arrived. His piercing blue eyes are narrowed, and my stomach clenches as he scans us all. I watch him cross to the center of the arena as a loud crash from beyond the walls makes everyone jump...*the storm is getting worse.*

"At the behest of Cal and Dell, the Council began assembling your packs as soon as the storm started this morning," Jove starts, letting his eyes narrow just a little more as he darts a glance at Cal. "Inside them, you will find Avo paste for wounds, food, spring water to assist in passing the Bale stalks, and a Cycle stone to help you keep track of the days and nights, which are not reliable in the Rush," he adds, then lets his eyes fall to the ground as Tieg huffs a laugh and wrinkles his wide forehead.

"*Days and nights* aren't reliable?" he asks, and Cal quickly looks up at him.

"No," he says in a firm, even voice, locking eyes with Tieg. Jove takes a breath and raises his hands to stop any further exchange between them.

"Understand, the biomes of the Rush are the templates for the surface world. They are concentrated and ungoverned…the original essence of everything you know, and everything you do not know yet," he says, folding his hands at his waist as he raises his chin to Tieg, then scans the rest of us again. I find Jax, who is already looking at me, his brown eyes focused and intense as he mouths the word *breathe* to me just like he did when we stood across from each other the morning of our interviews, lined up with our teachers on opposite sides of our school hallway. I nod back to him and take a deep breath. "We are not a confrontational people, so we will not stop you from going, as we did not stop Vox, but you must be aware that you are not simply entering a place of varying climates. The Rush is a living thing. It is the divine garden of the Motherland, the raw materials of the world above." Jove takes a step toward the rest of us like a lecturing teacher, and Myra feverishly begins twisting the tips of her long, reddish-blonde hair around her fingers. "Enter it peacefully, or it will purify you," he nods once more to Tieg, and I feel the reverberation of the warning ripple over us as he turns the floor over to Veece. He's wearing the same lightly colored woven thermal as the rest of the younger people here wear—no leather shirt. He does not have a pack, and now I remember that he is not coming with us.

"What is that supposed to mean?" Tieg speaks up again, this time with an irritated edge in his voice rather than mockery. "Purify us how?"

"The Council does not think you will come back," Veece says, squaring his shoulders and lifting to his full height, which puts him at eye level with Tieg. "And while what my father just explained about the Rush is true, we have two reasons to believe you will make it," he adds, gesturing to Cal and then to Dell.

"That's great, but what does *purify us* mean?" Tieg insists, his voice lower and more menacing now. Veece smiles without feeling, apparently trying to maintain the balance in the room.

"It means there are things out there that feed off of trouble," Cal says, crossing to Veece's side. "The Mountain protects itself from sabotage by not allowing destructive energies near it," he explains, looking out onto the rest of us. "The Rush sees those energies in you somehow, pulls them out of you and drops them in your path so you have to destroy them yourself before it will let you pass. The more consumed you are by anger, jealousy, revenge...the harder your road will be," he adds, then looks over to Dell, whose eyes fall to the ground.

"Coming from or going to that mountain doesn't matter either—it'll find you either way," Dell adds, almost as an afterthought. "Suggest you all get right with your sentiments, or else hide them real good."

"Where's Liddick?" I whisper to Zoe, who is a few feet away. She shrugs as she tightens the lacing around her wrist.

"He knows when we're lighting out," she whispers.

"All right, just wait…" Arco's voice is suddenly loud and startling next to me. "You're saying this land between here and that other volcano is going to be able to read our *motivations* or something? But we have people in there. *Of course* we're not coming in peace."

"The fact I'm having the chance to tell you at all is more than Vox had, so all I can say is try not to fixate on what you think happened or is happening to them. This is going to be a one hour at a time kind of trek. Wondering about anything past that just makes the road longer and harder," Cal answers, grinding his teeth together on the last word, which makes his jaw and temple jump in unison.

"So it's rigged to sense an attack? *The mountain* is rigged against an ambush? That's what you're *just now* saying?" Tieg asks through an incredulous laugh as Dez grips his arm and whispers something to him, apparently in an effort to dial him down.

"Listen, cloudy," Dell says in an amused voice as he takes a step toward Tieg, whose guffaws disintegrate as he raises his eyebrows and squares his stance like he's preparing for a fight. "You go right on thinking what a gut-roll everything is out there, and we'll see how funny it is when the trees don't like the smug look on your face and start conspiring to remove it—your face, wise? The look comes with it."

Tieg blinks his narrow, unnaturally blue eyes and swallows, quickly returning his expression to neutral.

"We did not anticipate that you would be leaving right now," Jove adds. "But…it has come to my attention that you have all been treated, and that you believe someone in the Motherland can reverse it. Our own ancestors also pursued this path, and we will not stand in your way," he says, but is interrupted by another crack of what sounds like thunder before he starts again. "The storm will give you shelter from the zephyrs who plague the Bale field boundary, but you must go now. Your treatments will be permanent in eight days—if you reach the Motherland after that, do not attempt to surface. You will not survive. Return here, and we will make a place for you." Another crash of thunder interrupts Jove and rumbles out after a long roll. "Go now. You are in good hands," he says, extending his hand toward the fissure. When I look toward it, I'm startled to see that the other Council members have joined us, along with Kora, Myka, Ada, and all the Badlanders who have helped us. General nods at me, his golden eyes reminding me again of Mr. Tark's smile of approval after the beach attack virtuo-cine.

"This way," Dell says, moving back through the fissure. Everyone touches his shoulders as he passes, and Calliope gives him a hug. Veece and Cal exchange glances, and Cal nods to him.

"I'll bring back the NET," he says quietly, then crosses to Jove, who grips his shoulder in response with a nod. Cal turns to follow Dell through the tunnel of people that is slowly forming, and Veece brings his hands to Zoe's face when she crosses to him. He touches his forehead to hers as he says something in his Vishan language, and after a second, she wraps her arms around his neck and kisses him, which seems to startle him. Jove closes his eyes in a long blink and lets out an exasperated sigh, and I can't help smiling when she makes her way to me with both of them in her wake.

"What? Think you're the only ones with amenities?" she whispers, winking at me and raising a copper eyebrow to Arco as she passes us. "Better close that before something flies in," she adds over her shoulder, clicking her teeth and darting a glance at my mouth, which has apparently fallen open. Arco coughs a laugh and shakes his head, and I feel heat flooding my face when I see Fraya and Myra grinning stupidly at me.

"Thank you for everything," Dez says to Jove and Veece as they move through the fissure together with Tieg, Joss, and then Myra, who echo the sentiment. Jax is the last to shake Jove's hand before he crosses back to Arco, slapping a broad hand on his back.

"Well, let's go get our people," Jax says with a nod, and then meets my eyes. "Let's go get Dad, Jazz."

I nod, and follow him, Fraya, and Arco to the fissure, hugging Kesh and Vita as I pass, but I can't help turning back around to take one more look at the silent arena. *Where are you?* I think, but Liddick doesn't answer me.

***

The tubular clouds I saw this morning aren't gray anymore with intermittent light behind them. They're the color of soot now, and the flickering light is so constant that it's almost not a flicker at all. I can see the zephyrs darting in and out of the Bale stalks, but only here and there. The rest of them start to dive, but then stop when the lightning flashes or the thunder cracks, which is almost every few minutes. The overly saturated gold of the stalks stands out even more against the dark gray backdrop, which reflects off the inky black, volcanic rock under our feet.

Cal, Del, and Zoe pour their spring water over their heads and instruct us to do the same before leading Joss, Myra, and most of the rest of our group start to follow them, but Arco, Jax, and Fraya must still be coming up through the corridor. I look around frantically for Liddick and finally find him leaning against the outside of the rock face watching the zephyrs high up in the storm just a few hundred feet away.

There you are! I think, relieved, but he doesn't turn away from the sky as another crack of thunder sends the zephyrs scattering from the Bale stalks. *What are you doing up here?* I ask him in my head.

Making my peace, he thinks on the tail of the rumbling, and I don't know how to respond. *Myka said you were looking for me earlier...*I add, grasping for something to offset this stiffness between us now that he knows how I feel about Arco once and for all. Liddick nods absently without looking at me.

"I talked to Azeris last night...after I left the Lookout Pier," he says out loud, pushing a smile to the side of his mouth and shaking his head with a huffed laugh. "Almost fell down that stupid rise when the message hit," he says, then pushes off the wall and takes a step toward the others as he looks over at me. "The biodesigners are moving Lyden and Arwyn to Phase Three in two days, not two weeks," he adds abruptly, hooking his thumbs in the side rigging loops of his dive suit and looking toward Cal, who seems to be giving instructions to the others.

Arco, Jax, and Fraya appear from the fissure just behind me before I have a chance to respond to Liddick, and by the time I turn back around to find Dell making his way over to us, Liddick has joined Cal's group.

"Come on! We're going to cut along the perimeter—stay out of the field!" Dell shouts to us over the roar of the wind as he waves us to join Cal and the others. Heavy, warm drops the size of marbles start to fall, and I'm immediately startled by how hard they hit—like someone has flicked my shoulder, my cheek, the top of my head with their thumb and finger.

"We need to get out of this!" Tieg shouts as we close the gap between groups, but Dell quickly cuts him off.

"Stay close together—no holes in the line!" he calls from the rear of our group as we start to approach the outer row of Bale that seems to meet up with the trees in the distance. "We'll be clear of the zephyr pack once we cross the line!"

Zoe falls back and closes the hole just behind me, jogging a few steps as her voice strains over the howling wind. "Liddick is with Cal—in the front, you saw?" she asks, and I look back over my shoulder to see him just in front of Joss and Myra. I nod to Zoe.

"Thanks," I say, trying to be loud enough for her to hear me, but quiet enough so the zephyrs don't. I fail on the latter as the group of Bale stalks right next to me immediately bend into my path and begin shaking so hard they blur like they did when Zoe and I came out here harvesting. I startle so badly that I stumble and fall on my knees trying to jump out of the way, then look up right into the eye of a little gray, wispy tornado, which is as big as I am.

Rows and rows of fine, pointy teeth swirl in opposite directions like hundreds of tiny wheel cogs, and I don't even have to make myself stifle the scream I feel pushing up from my chest because the instant terror that accompanies it forces my throat closed. *I can't move...I can't move...*is all I can think, until several pairs of arms jerk me to my feet and pull me forward as we all break into a run toward the tree line, holes appearing in our line as more little funnel clouds materialize overhead. Their low, reverberating buzz finds its way into my teeth and behind my eyes where it vibrates my skull and muffles Dell's desperate calls for us all to stay together, but it's too late. Joss is near the front of our group, and is suddenly jerked into the air by one of the rotating dark clouds, which instantly begins passing over him end to end so quickly I can't even see it anymore. His skin gives way to red as two other zephyr clouds begin racing over him too, peeling the layers of his skin and muscle away so fast now that I don't even have time to blink before his muffled screams stop, and he's just completely...*gone.*

"Stay together! Close the gaps!" Dell shouts as Cal waves Myra toward the trees, and the deafening hum in my ears fades in the presence of her shrill, anguished sobs as we cross the boundary line into the Rush.

CHAPTER 39
The Rainforest

The heavy, marble sized raindrops pelt us from the sky when we finally get past the Bale stalks and the packs of zephyrs darting after us. Here in the rainforest, all I see are vines and walls of green.

"Up here! Move!" Cal calls back to us, then points to a huge tree with visible roots that look like pythons twisting and gripping the ground, until they disappear well beyond the tree and into a carpet of enormous leaves. "Get inside!"

Get inside? I think, puzzled, until I get closer and see that the front of the tree is nothing in comparison to the width…it must be twelve feet deep and just as wide. The inside of it is dark and smells like musty earth as another flash of lightning forces my eyes closed, followed by the giant crack of thunder that I feel vibrate through my bones. I bring my hands to my ears too late, and only manage to muffle the ringing left by the thunder clap.

"Everyone OK?" Dell asks, filing into the tree with Liddick, who looks like he's going to kill someone. Water streams down the angles of his face as he shoves both his hands through his long, wet hair, the rain coloring it as dark as the tree behind him. His hands crackle with light that he quickly snuffs out by making fists and taking a deep breath. His eyes are wild, and I feel my heart start to pound in answer to the pace of his.

*Liddick…Liddick, listen to me…*I start to think, but it's so hard to shut out the feeling—*his* feeling—of thousands of tiny irons being shoved into my veins. I panic for a second when I remember that the Vishan treatment has made it so we can physically feel what the other feels…I don't know if I can do this all the way through the Rush. *What if one of us is hurt, or…killed?* I wonder, but the thought washes away in the flood of wanting to hit something…to hit *someone* until I can force whatever this is out of me, and it feels like any second that's exactly what I'll do. *Liddick! Look at me!* I shout to him in my head as I move to him. I grip his biceps and meet his eyes, which are still wild and murderous. "Look at me!" I say out loud over the barrage of rain pounding the ground outside and beating the outer bark of the tree. His eyes focus and lose their violence when he finally registers what I'm saying, and his dark brows snap inward as he wipes more streaks of rain from his face and pushes them through his hair again. He locks his hands behind his head and walks past me to sit against the tree wall where Dez moves quickly to his side. He grips the back of his neck with both hands and props his elbows against his knees as his head falls forward, and an ache starts in my chest.

Arco moves to my side and pulls me against him. I turn into his chest and close my eyes, but then open them immediately when I see the image of Joss being yanked into the air and then the obscene, white bulge of his eyes against the red, wrapping muscles of his face—

I choke on the gasp I suck in and cough, then feel my heart pounding again in my ears.

"It's OK…we're OK," Arco says into my hair, and I let go of him to find Myra. She's shaking, curled into Fraya with Jax at their side. Our eyes connect, and his chest heaves as he shakes his head in shock and disbelief.

Tieg wipes the water from his squared face and covers his mouth as he brings a hand to his hip. He takes a deep breath, then shakes his head just like Jax. Ellis wraps his long arms around himself and clenches his jaw over and over again, making the muscle in his cheek pulse as Avis sits against the wall and hugs his knees, then rocks back on his heels over and over again. Zoe pushes her rain-soaked red hair off her forehead and crouches next to Myra, then starts pushing Myra's wet hair from her face.

"It was quick, wise? It was quick…" she says softly and repeatedly, but Myra doesn't say a word, or even blink.

"We need a fire," Dell says, blowing out a breath and searching the ground, then moves to the side of the tree and pulls the knife from his leg sheath. "Could you dig a hole?" he asks over his shoulder and tosses a piece of thick bark to Cal, who nods and moves a few feet from the tree opening to start gouging at in the ground.

Zoe pushes the last of Myra's hair from her face, but keeps repeating the motion anyway as she sings a quiet song to her. A steady stream of tears drip from Fraya's cheeks as she watches them, and Jax puts his arm around her. Zoe nods to him, taking Myra into her arms as she continues her song. Fraya buries her face in Jax's chest, and he rests his chin on the top of her head, kissing it as his brows crash together. He looks over at me and I nod to him quickly to let him know that I understand and that he doesn't have to hold back anything just because he's my big brother by one minute and 18 seconds. I nod again to him, and then again until he finally lets the tears come. He closes his eyes and leans into Fraya's wet hair, and I keep nodding even though he can't see me anymore. I just keep nodding.

"Hey...*hey...*" Arco whispers from somewhere far away, so I'm surprised when I feel his arms wrap around my shoulders from behind and his warm breath on my neck as he talks. "Come here," he says, loosening his arms enough for me to turn into him if I want to, but I can't lay my cheek against his chest and feel warm and safe enough to close my eyes only to see Joss again, suspended ten feet over my head, being stripped and peeled. I shake my head to clear the thought, which keeps finding me every time I manage to escape it. I pull my hair through my hands and wring out the water, then lean back against Arco, his arms crossing over my shoulders as I watch Cal finish digging the hole, then teepee the pieces of wood Dell has been cutting from the inside of the tree.

"The fire will keep animals out—we'll be safe in here until the storm passes," Cal says, just before looking up at Avis, who is still rocking back on his heels against the tree wall. "Avis...*Avis—*" he says, but it's not until the second time his name is called that Avis stops rocking and turns to him. "We need a core and some rings..." he says, nodding to the beginnings of the fire pit. Avis blinks several times as he comes back into himself, then wipes the water from the broad planes of his face. He shuffles over to Cal, who nods again and passes him the collected wood, then gets out his knife to help Dell sheer more from the tree.

Liddick has lifted his head, but has buried his face behind his interlaced hands as he sits with his knees still pulled up, and for a second it looks like he's asleep. He must feel me watching him because he opens his eyes and stares into mine. Dez has entwined her arms around his and is resting her head on his shoulder, her eyes closed and her face still wet either with tears or the torrential downpour or both.

*Don't do that again, Liddick...*I think. *Don't close off. No matter how bad it gets out here. I almost couldn't find you.* The ghost of a smile touches the corner of Liddick's mouth, but then disappears.

I almost couldn't find me either. He was right next to me, Rip...right there next to me and then... he trails off, then closes his eyes again and leans his head back against the tree. Avis pulls a small red flame from his palm and lights the wood scraps, the glow illuminating the wide smile that spreads over his face, liberating his troubled, deep-set eyes.

"I did it," Avis says to himself, then looks up at Ellis and nods. "I did it," he repeats. Ellis smiles, exhausted, and Avis returns his attention to the fire, adding more of the wood shavings, and then larger pieces all around it. After several minutes, the flames stretch the circumference of the pit, and Dell stacks the rest of the wood against the inner wall at his feet. I look over to Myra again, whose eyes are still wide and staring as she sits cradled in Zoe's arms.

This is a vacuum…a swirl of twisting pain that is somehow forced into the center of a void I can't reach. It's everything and nothing at the same time—a silence that is much too loud to bear. I feel it most when I exhale, but I know there's more breath inside that *will not* release. I take another half-breath, and then another, knowing I must lose a second of each of them through some kind of one-way membrane inside me, and no matter how hard I try to push them out before they accumulate and suffocate me, the closest I can get to them is trying to draw out a yawn that never comes.

Cal puts the last of his wood next to Dell's and both of them sit with their legs outstretched near the fire. Cal grips Avis's shoulder and nods to the flames, which makes Avis beam with pride.

"We have to let the fire thaw us out before anything can really soak in from back there, wise? We just have to let the fire work," Dell says as the flames grow and the wood in the little fire pit begins to pop and smoke, the latter quickly wafting toward the opening in the tree and twirling into a little cyclone on its way out.

I feel Myra before I hear her…the scream out of the void pushing up through my chest, but dismantling itself before it reaches my lips—Myra's lips, which open and close like a fish out of water as her boots scuff at the ground.

"Myra…*Myra*," I say, leaning forward into Arco's forearms until he releases me. I drop to my knees and try to block her view of the smoke, but it's like she can see through me. I hold her shoulders in place and try again. "Myra, it's just the smoke. The fire smoke, OK? Myra, stop looking at it. *Myra...*" I say, grabbing at whatever words I can find just so I can keep putting one in front of the other for her like a wall between what she's seeing and what she's imagining. Her fear hits my chest in several dragging points...a claw stabbing through and ripping upward. I wince against it and wonder for a second if I can feel Myra's physical feelings too, or if her fear is just this bad. "Myra, listen. It's smoke. *It's just smoke*," I repeat, trying to push calm and focus into her.

Finally, her scream gives way, fractured and grasping until she finds her breath and with it, her voice.

"It's coming back! It's coming back!" she squeals, the pitch of it so piercing I feel compelled to cover my ears, but I can't risk letting go of her arms.

"No, nothing is coming. It's from the fire," I repeat, trying to keep my voice level, but it doesn't help. In the next second Liddick is moving behind me into the twirling smoke. I turn in time to see it hit his stomach and bellow out, and Myra stops screaming.

"See? Just smoke," he says, then kneels and wraps his arms around her when her face crumples again. His brows crash together as her breath catches after a second. She rests her cheek on his shoulder, and her tears finally fall, heavy and hard like the raindrops that ride the thunder down from the sky.

CHAPTER 40
After the Rain

"We should get moving," Dell says after several hours of weather. "There's a break in the rain, and we need to try to make it to the edge of this biome before nightfall. Should be several hours off yet, but we'll have to watch the source."

"The source of what?" Ellis asks.

"The source of the light—the gas accumulations overhead. If those start to scatter, it'll get dark quick," Cal answers.

"So night could be hours off, or it could be any minute? And we're just supposed to start hiking knowing that?" Tieg asks, indignant again.

"That's why we brought the Cycle stones—they'll help generate light. We don't want red flames here in the open with the vein rock everywhere and threat of lightning, remember?" Cal explains, then sighs when Tieg's expression doesn't change. "Bringing the green flame from the vein rock and the orange from the lightning together with our red flames will mark us—remember Liv's and Rav's Gathering…when they received their Vishan scars?" Tieg shakes his head and looks down his nose at Cal.

"No, because I was pulling one of your minions off the top of the waterfall about then." Cal narrows his eyes at Tieg, then closes them in a long, tolerant blink after Tieg pushes past him toward the opening of the tree. "What's that buzzing?" Tieg asks.

"Just be ready to fish out your stone if those flickers start going out," Dell snaps. "They fade altogether, and we'll just have about five minutes before we can't see a foot in front of our faces, wise?" he adds, then turns to the rest of us. "Should be some fallen trees somewhere. We'll need some of that mud to repel the skeets. Keep an eye out."

"*Skeets*?" Fraya asks, and Dell takes a patient breath.

"Mosquitoes," Zoe answers, pulling still wet strands of her copper hair out from the inside of her collar. Fraya smiles, looking relieved until Zoe leans in closer and whispers to her. "No, see, they're about as big as a little brother. Best you should know," she adds with a quick wink, then crosses to help Myra up. Arco and Avis bury the embers of the fire in the middle of the tree hollow, and we all start toward the opening. Just as we're all almost out, Myra jerks her arm from Zoe and shakes her head.

"We're just going to leave? That's it? That zephyr thing just *killed* Joss!" Her words hang in the air over everyone like a net we can't escape, and I scramble for something to say to calm her down.

"It did," Dell answers almost immediately in a quiet, even voice. "And something else will come along *for us* if we don't hitch up right now."

Myra's face blanches at his abruptness, and her lower lips starts quivering uncontrollably. Her eyes well up with tears again, and Liddick glares at Dell before moving to Myra's side. He puts his arm around her, but the red flames that suddenly leap from her shoulders startle him back.

"Myra…we're not going to forget him," Liddick says, and I can feel the same fear in her that he must be trying to address. She looks up at him and pushes her sunny hair from her eyes, then repeats the motion as several long strands stubbornly stick to her cheeks.

"Like we didn't forget about Pitt? He should be here with us too right now, but what's the last thing anyone has said about him? He and Joss should *both* be here right now," she says through choking sobs. "But we just move on, right? We just have to keep going! How is that *fair*!?" she shouts, and I begin to hear the low, menacing buzz that Tieg must have been referencing a few minutes ago.

"Myra, listen," I say, the words falling into place one after the other before I know what I'll say next, before I realize I'm crossing to her and holding onto her shoulders. "Just listen to that sound…can you hear it? The humming?" I ask.

Her eyes widen as the flames at her shoulders dip, then leap like a gust of wind has just blown over them.

"What is that?" she asks in a rattled voice.

"You knew Joss better than any of us. Ask him what that sound is…what he wants you to do about it. Close your eyes and ask him, Myra, OK? Ask him right now."

"We don't have time for—" Dell starts with a sigh, and I shoot him a cutting look. He rolls his eyes and holds up a hand dismissively, then turns his back to us and scans upward beyond the threshold of the tree opening.

"What does he say, Myra?" I ask, gripping her shoulders more tightly as my heart feels like it will crash through my ribs a little more with each hammering beat.

"That the buzzing is the mosquitoes…like the ones you saw in your vision with Vox," she almost whispers, then erratically giggles through the tears streaming down her face as she continues. "He'd say that Dell should shut his vent…" she smiles, wiping these new tears from her face as she keeps her eyes closed, then sobers. "But that we have to listen to him…that we have to…" she says, her bottom lip quivering again as more tears spill from her eyes. "And that we have to go on."

My eyes blur with my own tears as she finally looks at me in understanding, the shock slowly fading from the wide, innocent blue of her eyes, which are red-ringed and puffy. Her normally even skin is blotched and smeared with dirt as she tilts her head to the side, nodding in answer to the question I haven't asked…yes, she's ready to go now.

"OK. And you can ask him what he thinks next time you're afraid, all right? Whenever you need his help… just think about what he would tell you," I say, squeezing her shoulders.

Myra nods quickly, tears running down her face in rivulets now, and I know her grief has only just begun.

"I will," she says between sobs, then throws her arms around me, her heartbeat crashing against my chest, or maybe it's both of ours crashing against each other's as her flames dissipate. The bared skin of her shoulder brushes my chin, her jumpsuit and dive suit having burned through, and the low, reverberating hum of the mosquitoes sounds like it could be getting farther away. She meets my eyes one more time with a small smile, then wipes her face again and takes a deep breath. She walks to Fraya, who pulls her in close as they make their way out of the tree and into the green with the others.

Liddick lingers a second more, pressing his lips together and lowering his eyes in a subtle nod to me.

*That was brass, Riptide...*he thinks, then tucks the beginnings of a smile away before it can surface. *You've always been brass...*he adds after he turns to follow the others out of the tree, and it feels like he takes the ground I'm standing on with him.

"That was pretty incredible," Arco says at my back. I turn to face him, feeling like everything in me has been emptied out as I swallow hard and pull in the deepest breath I can.

"She can't figure out how to let go...maybe we can never let go of the people we lose, Arco," I say, hearing my voice break on his name. He pulls me into a hug, and I fight to keep my composure.

"Maybe we don't have to...not if we can take them with us like you just taught Myra."

I nod against his shoulder and push the hair out of my face, then swallow hard again just before we follow the others out of the tree.

***

Nearly a quarter of my Cycle stone has turned from a vivid yellow-green to orange, so I know we've been hiking through this forest for at least a few hours when we *finally* come upon a fallen tree like the one Vox found in my last message from her. Dell leads us to the edge of the caved-in trunk, which stretches about eight feet out from us and three feet across.

"Won't need much of the mud, just enough for a coating over any exposed skin," Dell says, which is the first thing anyone has said since we started walking. He pushes back his dark hair, then pulls the top of it into a ponytail with a scrap of elastic he's torn from the cuff of his sleeve. I had forgotten about the long scar over his forehead, which is usually covered by a wing of feathered brown layers that are falling into his eyes. I remind myself not to stare.

"Ugh, this smells like rotten fish," Avis announces as he spreads a glob of the green mud over his cheeks and neck.

"Skeets won't stick you if they think you're rotten fish," Dell answers, slathering a layer of the mud over his neck like he's putting on cologne. Jax smears a finger scoop of mud over Myra's nose, which, after a startled second, finally prompts a small smile from her. It's not much, but the fleeting break in her sadness sends a ripple of warmth over me. After another long pause, she flicks some of the mud back at Jax, who feigns outrage, his normally narrow brown eyes widening as his dark brows shoot up. He wipes the spatter from his face and gives her a devilish look as he scoops an enormous handful of mud from the rotted tree trunk and bounces his eyebrows at her. She swallows a little squeal and tries scrambling to her feet, but only slips and falls forward. She catches herself with her hands, which puts her just inches from Jax and his giant mud pie. His mouth shifts into a silent *oh* as his brows shoot up again, and he wobbles the mud in his hand in mock threat just under her chin. Without missing a beat, Myra pushes Jax's hand toward him, covering his face and neck.

Arco laughs out loud, and soon, so does everyone else. Jax wipes the mud from his eyes, then spits to his side.

"Crite, it tastes like rotten fish too!" he complains, then shakes furiously like a dog, splattering mud flecks on Myra and Fraya, who groan in unison.

For just an instant, we all come up from under the weight of the shock and loss of the morning, and I'm so distracted by the temporary levity that I don't notice the dull buzz in my ears at first. All sense of relief disappears when the happy scene before me starts to burn away. The buzz in my ears increases, and so does the rate of the decomposition of my surroundings...the green giving way to endless drifts of tan...of sand, and then...of Vox standing on the edge of a deep, sweeping sand funnel, which must be twenty feet wide at the rim.

I start running toward her, my feet sinking into the sand under my feet as I remind myself that she can't really be here, that I can't really be here because I'm still sitting on the log while we're all putting on mud, aren't I? It doesn't matter because either way, it doesn't stop me from calling out to her.

"Vox! You made it to the Sand biome! That's what this is, right?" I shout. She turns to me abruptly, her yellow-green eyes blazing with anger as she holds up a bare arm, her dark map-work of tattoos interrupted by streaks of deep, red scratches.

"It ate my suit!" she yells to me as indignant as I've ever seen her. I'm stunned into stopping as I replay her sentence in my head, trying to understand what she's talking about.

"*What*?" I ask, shaking my head.

"It *ate* my suit, sand dollar," she overly enunciates, then rifles through her leather pouch and pitches a rock to the bottom of the sand funnel where enormous black pincers lie perfectly still. *They must be nearly five feet long!* I think, sucking in a gasp, and with it, a mouthful of dust when I notice that there is also a cluster of round, gelatinous sacks, a few of which have burst around a long wooden spike that sticks up from the hairy black...*crite...it's a head*!

"What is that!? Where's the rest of it!?" I yell out to her, then bring my hands to my mouth.

"It's *dead*! That's what it is!" she snarls, then curses and pitches another rock, this one ricocheting off one of the pincers and rolling to an abrupt stop in the sand. She sits down hard, well away from the edge and digs in her pouch again, this time pulling out a small jar of green paste like the kind the Vishan packed into Jax's eyebrow when he split it open. She starts spreading it over her scratches, and I call to her.

"Vox?" I say, folding my hands into a megaphone, but she just flips her burgundy hair out of her eyes and continues muttering more curses to herself. "Vox! Did you take the Vishan's tuner—their NET—to talk to me... to show me what's in the Rush?" I call out again.

Vox stops her slathering and swearing and lowers her chin for what seems like the specific purpose of staring up at me like I'm an idiot.

"Yeah, I took it," she says, then spits into the giant funnel of sand just beyond her feet. The glob arcs high in the air, then falls almost straight down as she juts her bottom lip out and nods, clearly impressed with herself. "But I don't know how to make it work," she adds, returning her attention to her arm. When she's finished, she packs the little jar back into her bag and gets to her feet, dusting off her legs as she looks at the sky. "I took it that first night with the Vishan because I knew they'd have to send Cal after it. Then you jellies would at least stand a chance of getting past the zephyrs. Have you *seen* those things?" she asks, suddenly animated as she turns her gaze from the sky back to me, her eyes widening as her forehead wrinkles. I nod slowly, then chew at my bottom lip trying to figure out how to tell her just how well we know about the zephyrs.

"Vox…" I start, then start over again, still not quite sure how to explain that we've lost two of our friends, let alone that one of them was Joss…the one chink in her armor—the one person she wouldn't admit she felt something for when we were still at Gaia. "Vox, we lost Pitt. He got infected by the spores, and then—"

"I know," she says abruptly. "I found him after what he did to that manta ray," she adds, then curses again.

"It wasn't his fault. He couldn't have known it was only trying to reattach his fingers," I say on Pitt's behalf, but she just looks out over the endless sand. I take a deep breath. "And the zephyrs…they took Joss when we were heading for the boundary line," I finally manage, and am surprised when her expression hardens even more.

"Cal didn't...?" she starts to ask something in a distant voice until her already pale face blanches in understanding. The dark diamond tattoo warps between her eyes as her eyebrows dart in for just a few seconds, and once she realizes this, she tries to force a neutral expression.

"Cal was with us, and Dell and Zoe. One of the zephyrs just dove close to us, and everyone panicked. We got too spread out..." I explain. Vox sets her jaw and looks back up at the sky.

"So how are you locking onto me like this?" she asks me, completely pushing aside everything about Joss as she presses a palm to her ear, then sticks her finger in it, and I know she's changing the subject in an effort to lift the heaviness that's starting to suffocate us both. She shakes her head as she studies the clouds overhead. "Look, can you manage to contact me next time without this head ringing?" she asks with a clip in her voice.

"I'm not doing it at all," I answer after I swallow the lump in my throat, which just moves like a rock into my chest. "I thought it was you. It has to be you since you have the Vishan's NET." I add, watching her bring her hands to her hips.

"I don't know. Seems like whenever I see something to warn you about, you just show up," she says, then shrugs. "I thought one of your boyfriends hacked a channel for you or something." She still doesn't look at me, but squints at the clouds and raises a hand to shield her eyes.

"Yeah, funny…it's just Arco, by the way. What are you looking at?"

She raises an eyebrow, then angles her head at the strangely lit, stacking clouds above.

"I have to go," she says. "When they band up like that, it's going to rain. A lot. Then those giant antlion things in the funnels wake up." Vox spits again, gesturing to the dead insect, whose head and pincers are as big as she is. She kicks a wave of sand down over it, then takes a deep breath. "He's really gone?" she asks, looking up at me now for just a second, the diamond between her eyes warping again, but this time, she lets it. I nod slowly a few times, and after a beat, she nods back, pulling in another breath and letting it out like a curtain coming down, the official end to the grief she'll allow herself. She rights her face just before she turns away, and I blink hard against the dust that rises up in the sudden gust of wind. It blows the endless sand over my image of Vox, then from the vines and leaves and trees that appear first in strips, then patches, until they are all I see again.

CHAPTER 41
Skeets

Jax's face is the first I make out, though I have to blink several times before I'm able to recreate the context of why he's covered in dark greenish-brown mud. He meets my eyes and lowers his chin at me as his brow wrinkles.

"Nice nap? Hurry up with the mud so we can—?" he starts, but interrupts himself after a second more of studying my face. "What's wrong?" he asks, getting to his feet as Liddick sits down hard next to me on the part of the fallen tree that hasn't collapsed.

"You saw Vox again, didn't you? Just now?" he asks, his hand gripping my knee to get my attention. He's the only other one not covered in mud when I look at him and nod, then notice Arco, Dell, Cal, and the others starting to move toward us.

"She's in the Sand biome," I say, but my voice sounds far away. "She killed a huge bug at the bottom of a sand funnel," I ramble, then feel Liddick gripping my knee harder.

"Did she tell you she was hearing buzzing—like the kind we've been hearing?" he asks, but his urgency is confusing. "*Rip!* Could she hear it?"

"Hey, you can back up," Jax says, taking several steps toward Liddick, who just fixes his wild blue eyes on mine and reaches out to square my shoulders with his.

"Rip, did she hear it *or not*?" he presses like we're the only two there, and somehow running out of time.

"Really." Jax takes another step toward Liddick, but Arco jumps in front of him before I can say anything.

"What is your *problem*?"Arco shouts, hauling Liddick up by his arm, but Liddick jerks away as soon as he plants his feet on the ground, then pushes Arco so hard in the chest that he stumbles backward into Jax.

"Get off me, chutz!" Liddick shouts, suddenly as if he's another person. His chest heaves, and for a second I think he will go after Arco, who regains his composure just long enough to lose it again.

"*Oh*, I've been waiting for this," he says in a low voice as he takes a few steps toward Liddick, but he barely finishes the last word before Liddick lunges at him. His shoulder drives into Arco's stomach, the momentum bringing them both to the ground before Jax pulls Liddick back, then shoves him toward Dell and Ellis, who both take an arm.

"Zone!" Jax yells as Liddick struggles out of their grip.

"I'm fine!" he says, then walks a few steps away from them, balling his hands into fists to smother the flames whipping out. He turns to me, his eyes still blazing. "So did Vox hear the buzzing or not?" he growls, and I pause in answering as I notice Jax pulling Arco to his feet, then putting a forearm against his chest to keep him from advancing.

"Yes," I say, confused until I feel the desperate ache he's projecting push into my chest, but that's all I can process before a deep, droning hum fills the air. I look around for the source, but only see trees and vines all around us.

"Skeets!" Dell shouts, pulling out a long machete from a sheath on his back. "Come on!"

"But the mud!?" Myra calls as we all scramble to follow Dell.

"It's too late for it to work—they already found us!" Cal shouts over everyone. "Go! Go!" he adds, waving us on as he brings up the rear.

We only get about ten feet before one of the mosquitoes breaks through the leaf canopy and dives at us, its long, spindly legs dangling like several loose, fraying ropes. I almost can't keep my eyes open long enough to make out the rest of it with the reverberations of its wings beating sheets of air against my eyes. But I do see two hooked talons at the ends of its forearms, its translucent, bulbous body with spider webbed veins running to its pointy stinger-like tip, and the silver needle beak that must be three feet long.

I stumble backward over a downed tree, landing hard on the backs of my hands. Jax helps me to my feet, and I see our reflection in the mosquito's black, empty eyes. Each ones spans the entire side of its head, which juts out of its hairy, humped shoulders. It seems to see us too as the dangling ape-arms spread wide and its thick, spiny back legs drag along the ground just before its talons swipe at us. I look around for something to use as a weapon, but only find more vines.

"Jazz!" I hear Arco yell, then see Dell with his machete out of the corner of my eye, but it's too late. I feel the itch in my palms and the prickle in the hollow of my jaw. *Fire! I have fire!* I remember, then immediately see a curtain of it unfold in front of me, catching the hairs on the mosquito's legs, which blacken and curl as the fire peels back toward me along the ground and disappears into the soles of my boots. The mosquito slashes its talons in every direction as a high-pitched squeal pierces my eardrums. It thrashes as it burns, slamming into nearby trees, then ricocheting off the ground and into more trees before the smoldering body falls in a bouncing crash at my feet, then rolls so fast I don't have time to move out of the way before my legs are pinned underneath it.

"Get it off!" I scream, trying to pull myself free as its antennae dart back and forth and its talons twitch, either in death spasms or in one last frantic attempt to find me. "Get it off!" I grip the vines closest to me as Jax scrambles to his feet, then starts pulling me from under the charred body of the mosquito.

We're running within the next three steps. Tree limbs sting my face as they whip past while more bone-rattling humming pours down over us from somewhere above.

"There are more of them!" Tieg's voice bellows from behind me.

"Keep moving!" Cal yells from somewhere near Tieg as another crack of thunder explodes all around us, and marble sized raindrops start to fall again. Dell curses, then stops abruptly.

"Wait! Bring those leaves!" he shouts, pointing at a collection of small trees just to our left. "Help me bend the saplings!" he calls to Tieg and Jax, who move quickly to him as he lowers himself down a small ravine just ahead. "Bend them down to me!" Dell shouts, reaching upward as Tieg and Jax arc the trunks of several small trees. Dell takes one of the nearby vines and ties the grouping in place, the beginnings of a bowed shelter taking shape over him. "More! Get the rest!" he calls up as Cal starts hacking giant leaves from nearby plants.

"Zoe! Bring your blade!" Cal yells, and Zoe moves to help him cut.

"Come on! Help run the leaves!" Arco shouts to everyone else, and we all make our way to deliver the giant leaves Cal has cut so far.

"Weave them up and under the sapling trunks!" Dell instructs as the rain starts to fall more quickly, making it feel like someone is hitting my back and shoulders with tiny hammers.

"This won't hold up out here!" Tieg yells down to Dell, whom I can't see anymore through the leaves we're placing.

"Just keep layering!"

After several more minutes, Cal rushes up behind us and motions everyone into the small shelter, which butts up against a grassy ravine that is veined in a gnarled root system. Everyone is dripping, the green mud on their hands and faces nearly gone as the rain pounds on the makeshift roof of leaves over our heads, which leaks water in several small streams.

"This won't hold for long, but it will give us a few minutes out of sight from the skeets. They probably just started burrowing to get out of the weather…we'll need to run again in a minute, wise?" Dell asks, taking an overdue breath as he wipes the mud dripping into his eyes with the back of his wrist. Most of us nod, but absently, still in disbelief of what just happened. Jax turns to me.

"Are you all right? Your legs?" he asks, surveying the damage caused by the burning mosquito body. Nothing hurts, but as I follow his eyes, I see singe marks burned all the way through to my blue jumpsuit just over my knee, and just under it, another patch is burned all the way through to my skin.

"I'm fine, it doesn't hurt," I answer, suddenly cold as the rain sinks in. Arco maneuvers next to me, then pulls me into a hug.

"Are you OK? Did it cut you?" he says, out of breath, and I shake my head as Liddick stands against the twisting tree roots with his arms crossed over his chest, trying to ward off the cold that I know he feels sinking in too…the same cold that forces my teeth into chattering spasms when I meet his eyes.

*I'm sorry…*he thinks after a second, but trails off as water drips from his long, rain soaked hair and falls over his lips. He wipes them with the back of his hand, then pushes through his hair as the same heaviness I felt before with him settles in my chest again. He rests his forehead against one of the tree roots, then closes his eyes, and no matter how much I focus on trying to connect to him, he won't let me in.

Another crack of thunder booms overhead, and we all startle.

"Can't risk this lightning…we'll have to wait this out in here!" Dell says over the ringing in my ears, then shakes his head at Cal. "If one of them sparks out there again…"

Cal nods reluctantly, then turns to face the rest of us.

"Downpours don't last long—just stay calm! The Bog isn't far off!" he says over the storm.

My teeth chatter more violently after a minute, and I wrap my arms around myself trying to decide if I should risk closing my eyes and seeing that mosquito all over again. Arco holds me against him, but I can't seem to let myself relax.

"What was that out there?" Jax shouts over the hammering rain, and my eyes jerk back to his. He's shaking his head at Liddick, who just narrows his eyes without answering. "Why did you tweak about Vox?" Jax reiterates, but Liddick still ignores him.

"It was Azeris…" I answer too abruptly, suddenly putting the pieces together as I look over at Liddick. "From this morning, wasn't it? When Myka saw you in the Origin Wall room. What did he tell you?" I ask, stepping out of Arco's arms and trying to make myself heard over the rolling thunder. Liddick looks up at me and takes a breath.

"He said he was going to look for Vox…if she's hearing buzzing, it's him. He found her."

"He told you that? He said he found her?" Tieg yells from the far side of the enclosure, only half his face still covered in the brownish-green mud. It makes him look like an exotic wild animal huddled in the shadows with his unnatural, electric blue eyes.

"No. He said he was going to try, but if she's hearing buzzing, then he found her," Liddick answers, clearly out of patience. He turns to me again, and I know there's more he's not saying.

Another crack of thunder explodes all around us as Liddick turns to Zoe, whose question hangs in the air without her even asking it. Liddick thumbs the leather strap of Zoe's satchel, which he still wears across his chest. Her smile starts slowly, then breaks free and lights her whole face.

"He saw it? He knows?" she asks, and Liddick nods to her.

"He knows we found you," he explains, and another chill runs down my spine.

"Can he get into the mountain? Does he know how to find us?" Zoe asks, barely able to stay ahead of the words.

"He's working on it," Liddick answers, but I can still feel him holding more back.

What did you start to say about Phase Three...? I think, bringing up the story that he started to tell me before we set out past the Bale field. He turns to me again, but his expression instantly hardens, and I feel him *trying* to push me out of his head. Arco must misunderstand the wall that goes up because a wave of heat pushes at my back as he suddenly starts shouting.

"I'm done with this!" he says, then maneuvers from behind me and advances until he's just inches from Liddick. "What are you telling her now? What do you know?" he presses, and before I can blink, Liddick pushes Arco back in my direction.

"You want to know, Hart? Lyden and Arwyn have two days before they're sent to Phase Three. *Two days*, not two weeks before they're launched into the atmosphere, *all right*? And we can't get there in two days! That's the message I got from Azeris in the Origin Wall room this morning!"

Arco straightens, and I grip his arms to keep him from retaliating as small flames shoot from his shoulders and

from Liddick's palms. The combination of their anger feels like something is trying to claw its way out of my chest as a flash of lightning temporarily blinds us, and the almost immediate explosion of thunder leaves another ringing in my ears.

"Put it out! Put out your fire!" Cal shouts over the rumbling, but his voice sounds distant and hollow in the wake of the thunderclap. Ellis crosses to talk to Liddick while Jax moves in front of Arco, and I can't hear what either are saying over the rain. After a few minutes of listening to Ellis, Liddick is the first to get his fire under control, but he's had a lot more practice than Arco. It takes another few minutes for the periodic flames to stop snapping from Arco's shoulders, but they finally subside as the thunder starts to disintegrate into a slow, distant roll.

"If you're trying to melt your faces off, by all means keep flaming up like that out here with lightning and vein rock everywhere!" Dell scolds as he rounds on us inside the small shelter. "Lightning will spark an orange fire if it strikes, and if you spark red anywhere near the vein rock, the green will ignite—all three colors together will mark us, wise?" he says, pulling up his pant leg to reveal a swirling burn pattern on his leg, which looks like an old pinwheel branded into his skin. "Bury your axes!" he shouts one more time, then closes his eyes in a long blink and pushes his hand over his face in exasperation.

Arco sighs as Liddick stands with his hands on his hips, shifting his weight from one foot to the other like a big, caged cat. Arco clears his throat.

"All right, I'm sorry," he finally says to Liddick, the rain still pelting the leaves overhead. "I overreacted," Arco adds. Liddick stops shifting, but his eyes are still narrowed when he acknowledges Arco with a begrudging nod. Arco offers his hand, and the hot feeling in my chest turns into a bubbling tickle as Liddick's eyes widen just a little. The corners of his mouth twitch like he is trying not to laugh, and I glare at him.

We can't keep going with you both at each other like this. Do you want to get to the mountain or not? I think, focusing as hard as I can to penetrate the wall Liddick has up. His eyes dart to mine before he can catch himself, and I watch the muscles in his jaw flex as all traces of amusement fade from his expression. He grips Arco's hand after another second and meets his eyes, each of them refusing to look away first.

CHAPTER 42
The Edge

The rain slows, and I'm paranoid that every click, chirp, croak, and rustle is something that will try to kill us. I notice that the tubular clouds have spread out again in the muted sky—or, actually, they've spread out against the walls of this enormous *cave*, as Zoe keeps reminding me. I wonder if there are other impossible creatures living in plain sight like the zephyrs…creatures that I can't even imagine, let alone see coming.

We've been walking for what has to be an hour now, and while our dive suits and boots managed to keep us mostly dry, my hair is saturated with rain and sticking to my face. I look over my shoulder and see Liddick walking with Dez, Ellis, Myra, and Tieg, but he might as well be walking alone for all the interacting he's doing. He meets my eyes, and for a second, his are not hard or narrowed like they have been all day. He hasn't spoken since his episode with Arco back in the shelter we made against the rain, and I hope he can feel how much I wish he would stop shutting me out.

"The canopy is thinning," Cal says as we walk through the dense foliage covering the ground, which is so thick it comes halfway up my shins with each step.

"What does it mean if the canopy is thinning?" Ellis asks from behind Arco and me.

"It means we're crossing into the Bog biome," Cal answers.

"Is that why it's about a hundred degrees hotter now?" Zoe asks, then starts to take off her leather over-shirt. "Can you imagine being out here without our treatments? Topside folks would fry up like fish in oil. Can we stop a second?" she adds, holding her pack with one hand and shaking her other arm free of the sleeve. Dell and the others start to slow down, and I lean against a nearby tree to take a swig of water from my desalinator tube as Liddick and the others catch up to the rest of us. Cal smothers a laugh at Zoe's remark and hesitantly removes his own leather over-shirt.

"We'll have to put these back on when the green gets thick again. Too many things crawling in these trees," he says, and immediately, I start to move away from the one I'm leaning against. After just a few steps, Dell holds up a hand to stop me in my tracks.

"Jazz, don't move," he says evenly. Fraya's hands fly to her mouth, and my heart starts hammering in my chest. I move my eyes wildly from Fraya to Dell, then to Ellis, whose mouth has fallen open.

"Why not? Why shouldn't I move?" My voice sounds like it's coming from somewhere outside of me, but Arco holds up his hands like he's about to say something.

"Jazz, it's OK, just hold still." He takes a step toward me, but Dell shifts his hand to stop him. Arco's face blanches, and his lips press into a stiff line.

"Everyone just be still," Dell's voice is low and steady.

"Then get it off her!" Jax commands.

"Get *what* off me!?" I ask, trying to keep my voice level, but I hear it shaking anyway as Myra folds her hands over her mouth and Tieg's face contorts in a grimace. *"Get what off!?"* I say with the last of my voice.

"Just relax and don't talk. Breathe and pull your flames back," Dell adds, and I feel my throat start to close with fear. *My flames?* I think, then notice the itch in my palms and the whipping sound behind my head. "Pull them back now, Jazz. Right now," Dell says again, his voice pulling tightly around the words as his forehead wrinkles. His wide eyes fix hard on mine. I swallow and try to take a deep breath. "Good, Jazz..." Dell coaches, nodding as he takes a slow, careful step toward me, but the terror behind his eyes makes me lose my focus, and I hear the whipping just beyond my ears again. I clench my teeth together and try to keep my chest from heaving, but my breath is getting harder and harder to control.

*Rip, listen...*Liddick thinks. *Close your eyes. Don't look at anyone. Their reactions are making you tweak...it's just a stupid bug on your arm. We'll get it. Just don't move, and don't look at anyone, OK?* I hear everything ten times more loudly when I close my eyes. Something is scurrying several feet above my head, something else is pecking a steady rhythm to my left, and I can even hear the shallow hum of wind through the leaves. The whipping behind my ears starts to fade, and then it's gone...replaced by cracking twigs and the sound of sucking mud...footsteps.

Is that Dell? What's happening? Is he coming? I think in a rush, and it feels like I'm running in the dark. *Liddick!*

I'm right here. It's OK. Dell is walking toward you. I told you we're going to get it. It's just a stupid ant, Rip, he thinks, but something in his tone is forced. The levity, the casual, dismissive humor surrounding his measured words.

Why was everyone tweaking if it's just an ant? *How could they even see an ant, Liddick*? I think, starting to feel dizzy because I'm too afraid to take more than shallow breaths.

"Jazz, you have to put your fire out. Count your breaths…you have to relax," Dell says, which sends a crashing wave of anxiety through my stomach.

They were tweaking because they're jellies. You're going to feel like such a mollusk for worrying when you see this thing. Just hold still. Liddick answers, but he's nervous under it all, and I know he's holding something back. Myra starts to whimper, then tries immediately to stifle it.

Tell me the truth, Lid—! I shout in my mind as I fight the urge to open my eyes, but stop when I feel a heaviness on the side of my head, then a faint tickle just under my cheekbone. Everything in my body freezes solid: the breath in my lungs, the blood in my veins.

"Just like that…good," Dell sighs like he's finally let out a breath he's been holding in. "Keep still just like that and breathe so your fire stays out," he says, sounding a little closer now. The tickle on my face turns into small prickles as the heaviness shifts in my hair until I feel something clinging to my cheek. Tears constrict my throat and rush into my eyes, which I don't dare open.

"Dell!" Arco says, his voice sounding forced through his teeth, and my chest instantly tightens so much that even my smallest breaths are sharp inside my ribs.

The multiple, small prickles start moving over my lips, and I fight to keep my mouth closed against the pulling sensation. I hear a strangled scream in my throat and swallow as slowly as I can to keep it from coming out. Tears fall from the outside corners of my eyes and burn the sides of my face, and when I hear a hissing, high-pitched chirping, I start to see stars in the blackness behind my closed eyes.

*Rip...breathe. Crite...all right, Dell is almost there. Just breathe. You can't pass out, OK? You have to be still. Don't move...ten more seconds...count them. Count, Rip. One... two...*Liddick says, and his voice warbles in my head like he's talking under water. It feels like everything around me is starting to spin when I hear him again, louder this time. *Three! Four!* But on four, something cold and sharp touches my cheekbone.

"Don't move, Jazz. Don't even breathe for a few seconds, wise? Just a few seconds..." Dell's voice is low and calm, and as if by some magic command, his words stop the breath in my chest again. I feel nauseous just before I hear a *whoosh*, then feel burning on my cheek. Before I can open my eyes or even breathe, someone... Arco, wraps his arms around me. I fall into him.

"It's gone...it's gone..." he repeats, stroking my hair. As soon as I can feel my feet under me again, I open my eyes and move back just enough to look around.

"Where is it?" I scan the ground frantically, then cross to Liddick. "Where is it?" I ask, grabbing the black dive suit fabric over his chest, which gathers and bunches between my fingers. "Liddick, where—"

"Dell killed it. It's gone, Rip," he says in a quiet voice as he meets my eyes and covers my hand with one of his. He brushes my face with the other, and I notice a sting just over my cheekbone. His eyes are so clear and so blue under his thick, dark brows and lashes, the blond ends of his hair dripping either water or sweat or both over his temples as he studies me. Standing this close to him—feeling this close to him again—fills the hollow that terror just carved out of me, but I can't tell if this is his relief or mine because we're both occupying the same space inside each other again.

Thank you…for talking me through, I think. He swallows hard and nods, then brushes the wet hair from my face as the start of a smile pulls at the corner of his mouth.

Just one little scratch…right here, he thinks, running the edge of his thumb just under the stinging part of my cheekbone. His hand is warm…everything about him is warm. *That's all, Riptide. You just have one little scratch.*

I lose control of my breath all over again when I realize I'm being folded into the gravitational pull of him, but then Dell's voice breaks my focus.

"Bullet ant…" he says with an exhale. I turn abruptly from Liddick to see the black, hairy corpse impaled on the tip of the machete Dell holds out.

"That was on my *face*!?" I shout because it's as big as my hand, and when the long, spindly legs twitch, the ground feels like it gives way under my feet. My knees buckle, but I catch myself before I fall, and Liddick supports my elbow until I stand up straight again.

"Are you OK?" he whispers. I nod, still unable to take my eyes from the ant.

"These ants sting," Dell says, then lifts the point of the machete straight up so the ant's body arcs toward the ground. "It's named after old bullet guns, so if it would have been singed at all by your fire, or if you would have twitched even a little, the sting would have felt like you were shot…and that would have been the *least* painful part of it," Dell adds, pointing to the ant's sharp, curved stinger. Everything inside me gets cold again, my skin feels clammy, and my mouth goes dry.

"And that was on *my face*?" I ask again, trying to keep the darkness pushing at the corners of my vision at bay.

"They climb to the tops of the trees to eat the fruit… probably another half-mile to the Bog, and we'd have been clear of them," Cal says, scrubbing his hands over his face and then shoving them through his short, white-blond hair. "We need to get there and make camp before it gets dark, which will be anytime now," he adds, looking at the sky again, and I remember that once the clouds spread out, night can come out of nowhere. I take a few absent steps from Liddick, and Jax moves to my side, wrapping his huge arm around me.

"Come on," he says in a low, steady voice close to my ear, and I feel sick as the aftershock hits me and the adrenaline floods my veins now that I'm safe…now that I have the luxury of falling apart. My hands start to shake uncontrollably, and I feel tears burning my face again, but it doesn't feel like I'm crying. They just fall like they're part of some completely separate biological operation that I don't control.

*It's just shock, Rip…*Liddick thinks from behind me, and I remember he must still be feeling the physical lash of my feelings. *It'll pass. I promise, it'll pass,* he adds. I try to turn to acknowledge him, but my motor functions abandon me when Dell flings the dead ant into the brush, and I actually hear it land in a thud. Everything sounds muffled after that. Jax and I walk side by side, the solid mass of him like a building or a mountain, like nothing could knock him down or force him back. In this moment the wave of homesickness that passes over me is so debilitating, I almost have to stop walking.

*I want to go home...*I think, but I don't consciously form the words; they just come. They just rise up in me like flood water and crest until I'm submerged in them, and I don't care at all if I go under as my lungs start to burn.

It's all right, Riptide. We'll be all right no matter how bad it gets out here, remember? As long as we're together, Liddick thinks, his desperate, exasperated words floating to me like a buoy on the water of my disembodied thoughts. I'm sure they'll drown me until I see Arco's lost, grateful, conflicted face, and I'm startled into breathing again.

CHAPTER 43
The Bog

The trees have completely thinned out, and ahead of us, they seem to give way to a grass field clearing. Jax and I walk along in silence with everyone, and even though the air is stickier and somehow heavier in the span of what can't be more than half-a-mile of walking, he doesn't take his arm from around my shoulder, and I don't want him to. For just a few more minutes I need to be able to close my eyes and shut this place out...the impossible reality of stupidly sized bugs, of Joss being gone now just like Pitt. He was here when we woke up this morning, and in the span of less than a minute the zephyrs just took him. It could be any of us tomorrow, couldn't it? Or right now? One minute from now, another one of us could be gone forever. What if it's Jax? What if it's Arco...or Liddick? *What if it's me?*

Another wave of nausea crashes over me at the thought of losing anyone else. How can we *not* come apart out here knowing that everything we've ever been taught hasn't prepared us for any of this? I can't schedule my way through it. I can't juggle responsibilities to free up time or force myself to study for good marks. Those actions all depend on constant variables...on outcomes that I can't predict out here.

"Stay out of the clearing, it's mainly water. Welcome to the Bog biome," Dell says, breaking the silence. "Those gas clouds aren't coming back together, so we need to start making camp by the trees," he adds as we follow him and Cal to the tree line where everyone starts gathering fallen wood.

"Lay the wood down in a rectangle as a barrier—things…crawl out here. Clear a spot, then put leaves down so you don't have to lie directly on the ground," Cal says to everyone, then turns to Arco. "We need to dig a trench for the fire…about twenty feet in diameter. Try to keep as many trees out of the circumference as possible so we don't have to deal with what might be in the branches."

Arco nods, then looks at me quickly like he's waiting for me to answer a question. Cal slaps him on the shoulder, then hands him the long, thick stick he has just sharpened with his machete before scanning the ground for another one to sharpen. Arco takes it, then starts digging.

"Do you think anything we've learned our whole lives is of any use now?" I ask Jax, interrupting whatever he's about to say when he turns to me. "All we've ever done is fight to stay in the top ten so we could have a chance to get into Gaia. It all seems so worthless now," I add. His lips quirk in a small smile, and he studies the side of my face where the scratch must be.

"I think fighting to stay on top has taught us how to survive, you know? We've learned that we don't give up," he says, then meets my eyes again. His are a deep, warm brown and kind, just like I remember our father's. The smile spreads across his face, and he nods reassuringly as he grips my shoulder. "We're going to find dad, Jazz. That's our one thing, just like the top ten got us through all those years of competing. Just imagine seeing him again…we're going to make it. We're going to see him again, OK?" he adds, somehow knowing what I've been feeling like he always does, somehow seeing my loss of focus. His eyes light with hope and purpose, his thick, heavy brows moving upward as if to get out of the way of his determined vision, which I feel starting to catch inside myself now too. He nods one more time in question, and I nod back in answer. "OK," he says, then hugs me, and for a few more seconds, I believe nothing can hurt me out here, or anywhere.

Dell, Tieg, Arco, and Jax finish digging the circle trench while the rest of us gather wood and leaves. Cal fashioned some kind of a rake to sweep the area inside the circle to make sure we don't inadvertently build bedding over any nests or burrows, and the idea of actually having to worry about things like that makes me shudder. We can't take anything for granted.

"Probably just short of an hour before the light goes, but storms don't rise up in this biome, so we can light an open red fire," Dell says, driving his pointed stick-shovel into the ground next to him as he nods to Avis. "Want to do the honors again?" he asks, gesturing to the perimeter trench. Avis smiles, then returns the nod before depositing scraps of wood in the trench for the fire. Arco drives his stick into the ground and looks at his hands.

"I made a place for you," I say, walking toward him. "Crite…Arco," I add, noticing the torn skin on his palms.

"I'm fine," he says, letting his hands drop to his sides as he looks anywhere but at me.

"Here," I say, reaching for his wrists. "Keep them up." I hold my hand under his and pour some water from the desalinator tube in my other sleeve over the cuts. He winces, but quickly closes it off with a sharp intake of breath. "Sorry," I say, looking up at him for a second, but he doesn't meet my eyes. "Why were you digging so hard?" I ask, but the heavy feeling pushing into my chest from him answers before he has the chance.

"Because I could, I guess," he says as I stop the water and pull my pack around to dig out a bandage wrap and the jar of Avo paste the Vishan packed for us. "I don't need that," he adds, shaking his head and recoiling when I open the little jar.

"If you want those cuts to heal before tomorrow you do. We have a long way to go, and you'll need your hands," I say. He sighs impatiently, but doesn't say anything else as I apply the mud. "I think this is the same thing we were putting on to keep the mosquitoes off," I say, then look up at him again, but he just keeps watching his hands.

"I don't know how to do this, Jazz," he says abruptly. "I thought I did, but I don't."

"We just have to keep going. We just have to focus on getting our people back, and that will get us through this place," I say, relating Jax's advice, which has been helping me.

"I don't mean this place," Arco says with a quiet edge in his voice. "I mean you and Liddick."

I finish dabbing the Avo paste over his cuts, then wrap a thin bandage over them and squeeze it in place over the backs of his hands.

"You're the one I want to be with, Arco," I say, and he finally looks at me. His hazel eyes are tired, red around the edges, and strained under the weight of his furrowed brow.

"You went to him because he talked you through dealing with the bullet ant, didn't he?"

I swallow, trying to find a way to answer that will lessen the impact, but I can't find the words. I nod. Arco nods in answer, then looks off into the trees.

"It doesn't mean I want him instead of you," I finally manage. "It doesn't mean that I don't love you."

The anchor in my chest seems to pull down harder at this, which starts an ache that wraps around my ribs and squeezes.

"But I couldn't help you. All I could do was watch, horrified when that thing started crawling on your pack and then—" he stops abruptly, then clears his throat. "I told you when those Badlanders came out of nowhere and held that stick to your throat back on the virtuo-cine beach in Tark's class…I told you I couldn't watch you like that again and not be able to do anything. So if he can get to you…if he can help you when I can't, then maybe you should be with him instead of me."

The ache in my chest intensifies, squeezing more tightly until I can't take a full breath.

"You don't get to make that choice, Arco. You don't get to decide who I'm with because that's up to me, and I choose you, do you understand?" I say, trying to control my voice. Arco closes his eyes in a long blink, then sighs.

"I don't know how to be with you when I have to accept that when you need someone most, he's the one in your head. He's the one who's right there. I'll never be able to do what he can do for you, Jazz, don't you see that?" he asks, now struggling to control his voice too.

"You're blowing this up into more than it is. I can't get tangled up with him because I lose sight of myself if I do, and I don't want that. I've told him that."

"But how can you *not* be tangled up with someone who always knows everything you think?" Arco asks without hesitation, then waits a few seconds as I search for an answer that never comes. "Thanks for fixing my hands," he says after a deep breath, then nods once before walking to one of the last two bedding stacks. I follow him to the other as the light fades, and Avis kneels near the circle and lights a fire that encircles us all.

***

Arco is turned away from me when I wake up, and the last of the red fire glows in the circle all around us. We didn't talk anymore before we fell asleep, though as I run through the possibilities of what more I could have said, I can't think of anything that would be new information. Maybe he's right…is it easier this way? I never expected him to save me from anything, and I'm not going to be able to convince him that it's not somehow his responsibility. We all need to help each other however we can out here, and he'll have to find a way to accept that. He turns to me as if he's heard me say this, and I smile at him. He smiles back, but then his expression withers to something unreadable as he sits up and turns away from me again. I catch Liddick's eyes from across the circle as he lies on his side with Dez curled in front of him, and just like last night, neither of us seems to know what to say.

"We need to get moving," Cal announces over everyone, and I startle. "The gas clouds are packed together again, so we should have plenty of light," he adds as people start getting to their feet. Cal kicks dirt over the fire embers, then hammers a hole in one of the trees. A steady trickle of water spills from it, and he refills his bottle. "Top off if you need to," he says.

Ellis and Avis walk toward the clearing with Tieg and Myra, and I have an unsettling feeling that makes me want to call them back, but I don't have a good reason why. Didn't Dell say it was mainly water over there? And we're refilling our stores, aren't we? I shake the thought loose and get to my feet.

"How are your hands?" I say, looking down at Arco, who lifts the bandages I put over his cuts last night. He chuffs a surprised laugh.

"You were right about the green paste," he says. "Almost healed up," he adds, then looks at me for a long time as if he's going to say more, but Jax interrupts as he gets to his feet across from us and brushes off the legs of his dive suit.

"When they put that stuff on my eyebrow, Ada said it only took a day for it to heal a Vishan's cuts, but for me it would take a week or so. Looks like those treatments are coming in handy," he says, bouncing his eyebrows at Arco. "Get it...*handy*?" he says, then nods ridiculously. Arco laughs, more at Jax than at his stupid joke, and a ripple of levity falls over us. Jax grips Arco's forearm and pulls himself to his feet, then starts a conversation that I can't hear, so I pull the desalinator tube from my sleeve and head toward the tree. I press the button at the cuff of my sleeve so it vacuums the water that's pouring in a steady stream now, and when the little light on my cuff turns green several minutes later, I press the button again and turn around, almost directly into Liddick.

"Oh! Sorry," I say, muffling a surprised laugh, then look toward the clearing after Ellis and the others as the unsettling feeling I had surfaces again.

"You'd think we couldn't sneak up on each other by now," Liddick smiles as he steps up and positions his tube under the water, but then my heart starts pounding and a prickling cold runs down the back of my neck.

"Something's wrong out there," I say, mostly to myself.

"Where are they going?" Liddick asks with a new tension in his voice, then seems to feel the same unease that I do. "No…Raj! Stay out of there!" he calls after Ellis, then sets out running. Dell and Cal pull up the sharpened sticks they stuck into the ground last night, and I take off running after Liddick. "Raj! Stop! Stay away from the clearing!" he yells again, and Ellis turns around abruptly to face us just as the most enormous alligator I've ever seen charges behind him. Tieg, Myra, and Avis stop in their tracks. "Look out!" Liddick screams as the alligator's jaws open, completely back-shadowing Ellis, then snap down just short of Ellis's legs. He jumps out of the way and falls, then tries to scramble to his feet as the alligator charges him again.

"Where did that come from!?" Ellis shouts as it snaps at him again, and from this angle, I can see that it must be at least twenty feet long. Flames shoot along Ellis's arms, but they don't seem to make a difference to the alligator.

"Hey! Over here!" Liddick screams to get the animal's attention. "Everyone run behind it and come back this way!" Liddick picks up a rock and throws it, hitting the alligator in the head as he starts yelling again. "Right here! Over here!"

"Liddick!" I shout when I see the jaws opening again as it turns to face us.

"*Why* did you follow me!? Go back!" Liddick yells over his shoulder at me as Ellis and the others manage to get behind the alligator, then run past it back toward our camp.

"Don't run! Don't run!" Cal yells from near Tieg and the others as Dell circles around to Liddick and tries to aim his sharpened stick at the alligator.

Liddick's arms move out to his sides, his hands spread wide...*look bigger, and you'll feel bigger*...I remember from Ms. Wren's communications class, and know that's what he must be remembering too. He brings red flames to the palms of his hands, then aims them at the open jaws, but the alligator only jolts back for a second. It doesn't advance any more, but doesn't retreat back to the water even when Liddick starts running toward in a wide arc that leads away from me.

"Stop going toward it! Everyone is safe, come on!" I shout as the gap between us widens.

"Rip, *go back*!" Liddick yells without turning around.

"Come with me!" I call to him again, but he's apparently trying to use his fire to force the alligator back into the water, but it just turns away from him and starts advancing in my direction instead.

"Hey! Here!" Liddick yells, then pulls back his flames and picks up another rock from the ground. He hits the tail, which only makes the alligator run toward me more quickly. Dell runs in my direction as Liddick starts yelling again, and I start to see my own fire out of the corner of my eye. As I try to remember how to aim it, Arco flies past me gripping the long stick he used to dig the trench. Flames shoot up his arms as he slows, holding the sharp end out to the alligator and jabbing the air with it as he shouts, trying to drive it back into the water.

"Go on! Go!"

It opens its jaws even wider, then charges him. Dell throws his stick, but it just bounces off the alligator's lower jaw.

"Arco!" I scream, and in the second the alligator turns toward me, Arco drives his stick into the roof of its open mouth, letting go just in time to avoid the jaws snapping down on his arms. The stick shatters as Dell's fire explodes in front of us, and the sight of it helps mine light in my hands. Just as I raise them, the alligator retreats, finally, backing away with its jaws still open until it disappears into the invisible, grass covered water.

CHAPTER 44
Burning Down

I run to Arco, whose bandages have completely torn loose from his palms and whip in the breeze. Cal stands with Ellis, Myra, and Tieg on the far side of the clearing, and Dell stands between Liddick and me. I see the last snap of the fire in Dell's hands, and before I know it, I'm running directly at him and screaming.

"Why didn't you tell us there were giant alligators out here!? You said it was mostly water in the clearing! Mostly water! Not tree-length *alligators*!" I yell, shoving him as hard as I can once I reach him. He stumbles backward, and I shove him again. He falls this time, and I lunge at him.

"Rip!" Liddick shouts, then holds up his hands as he runs toward me. "Calm down! He didn't—Rip, stop!" he says, but I push past him and shove Dell off balance just as he gets to his feet. He falls again, and as I try to jump at him, an arm reaches around my waist and pulls me off my feet. I try to pry it loose, then just start kicking.

"Put...me down! They could have been eaten by...that thing! Put me down!" I yell.

"Rip, stop! *Stop*! We need to get away from the water! Do you want another one to come! Stop!" Liddick shouts.

"Let me...*go*!" I say, blind with violence to everything except hitting Dell as hard as I can. Dell gets to his feet again, his eyes wide in amazement as he pushes his hair out of his face. I see a flash of his long scar, and for some reason, it just makes me angrier. I kick harder and elbow Liddick's shoulders and arms behind me, then his jaw, but he won't stop dragging me away from Dell.

"Damnit, Rip!" he shouts, and I hear a long, guttural scream fill the air, then vaguely realize that it's mine.

"Jazz...*Jazz!*" I hear Arco's voice as I swing both of my legs back, then kick them out at the same time like I did when Cal was training me in the circle arena. The momentum breaks Liddick's hold around my waist, and I start to run at Dell again, but this time Arco intercepts me, gripping my arms and lowering his eyes to mine.

"Get out of my way!" I scream at him, crashing my shoulders into his chest in an effort to move past him, but he just pulls me into him, his arms locking behind my back as I struggle against him, hitting his chest with the sides of my fists as fire starts to blaze all around us.

"Get out of here!" Arco calls to Dell over his shoulder. "Take them all back to camp!" He looks at Liddick next, then nods adamantly. "Just go, I'll handle it!"

I watch Dell moving out from behind Arco through the curtain of flames and try to lunge at him again, but I can't break Arco's hold.

"*Let me go!*" I scream again so loudly this time that I feel something pull in my throat.

"Come here...come here...listen to me..." Arco says, burying his face in my hair. "We're going to be standing here naked in a second if you don't breathe, OK? Breathe or this fire..." he laughs, "...this fire is going to burn everything up," he says laughing again, and the sudden absurdity of it all makes me stop struggling. "OK...there. Take a breath," he coaches, then meets my eyes and nods.

One of his hands moves to my face as the side of his thumb brushes my cheekbone, and I watch the remnants of bandage evaporate in the flame that catches at the end of it. *His hands...*I take a deep breath, then another until the fire all around us starts to dissipate, and then is completely gone. I reach up and move his wrist outward so I can see his palm, which is better, but still not completely healed, and there are now a few fresh cuts, no doubt from the stick he'd just shoved into the alligator's jaw.

"Your hands..." I say, my words cracking and broken from screaming. He smiles and shakes his head, then thinks better of it.

"You can fix them up again," he says with a small nod. I laugh, then feel the sob rising up in my throat and the tears burning my eyes. His brows push together, and I wrap my arms around his neck, the convulsive sobs catching in my throat and choking me, but I don't care. His arms tightens around my waist, and I try to take a breath.

"I thought...first Pitt and then Joss...it almost happened. It almost happened, again, Arco," I stutter through the sentence, squeezing my eyes shut when all the words won't come out. The floodgate breaks with this final frustration, and I cry so hard I can't get ahead of it. The silent convulsions come in one continuous wave that just keeps crashing as his arms pull me tightly against his chest.

"It's OK, I know. I thought the same thing. It's OK, we're OK," he says, resting his cheek over my head as he talks into my hair. "Can you walk? We need to get away from this water. Can you walk with me?" he asks, but I can't get enough of a breath to answer him, so I nod. "All right…all right," he says, and I don't fight him or feel embarrassed or stupid because there's no room inside me right now for any of that. Not with the sudden deluge of everything else spinning out again. I've spent my whole life preparing to get into Gaia only to learn the whole thing was part of a conspiracy to experiment on people, which I still don't fully understand, then we lost Pitt and almost Arco, all this with being torn about Liddick—of needing him, but knowing he's not what I need, and then Joss…*crite, Joss*…the insect attacks, new worlds that shouldn't even exist…

"What's wrong? What's wrong with her?" I hear Jax's voice, and it pulls me out of the tossing sea inside myself.

"She's OK," Arco says as Jax moves in front of me and meets my eyes, pushing my hair from my face.

"Are you hurt?" he asks, but doesn't wait for my answer. His eyes soften, and his lips press together as he takes a long breath and lets it out slowly, then folds me into a huge hug. He kisses the top of my head, then whispers down to me. "One thing. Just remember our one thing, OK?" he adds, and I nod against his chest as more tears come, but these are not as violent, and suddenly, I'm so impossibly exhausted.

"Dell didn't know about the alligators out there," Liddick says from somewhere, and I imagine he must be talking to everyone. "I asked him why they didn't tell us what was in the water when he came out there, but they just didn't know."

"Neither of us ever saw them when we came through the Rush before," Cal says. "We're just going to have to operate on the knowledge that if something could be somewhere out here, it probably is. At least we're almost halfway to the mountain. The Bog isn't a big biome, so we'll be through it soon. We'll all needs spears, and we'll stick to higher ground."

"And no more small groups," Dell adds. "Everyone stays together…that was too close."

I open my eyes and turn from Jax, then wipe my face and see Ellis, Myra, Avis, and Tieg, who look pale and rattled. I clear my throat, which sends a wave of pain through my ribs.

"We're going to be all right. We're going to make it to the mountain…all of us together," I nod, trying to convince myself as much as I am them, and with each word, I believe it a little more. "We just need to focus on getting there. On getting home."

"Let's walk soft and carry some big sticks, then," Zoe says with a decisive head bob. "Well, come on, I'm not fetching the mess of them," she adds, winking at me and waving me to her. I step out of Jax's arms and look back over my shoulder at him. He nods and smiles, claps his hands once, then rubs them together.

"OK, then," he says, holding out an arm to Fraya, who moves to his side. Liddick is standing right next to him, and sends me a stiff-lipped smile, then touches his ribs.

*Sorry if that's because of me…*he thinks, and I realize the pain in my own again, as well as a throbbing in the far corner of my jaw.

Sorry for elbowing you, I think, bringing my hand to my cheek. He smiles to the opposite side of where I hit him.

Remind me never to clip you off, he answers. I laugh, knowing there is more that is unsaid between us, but I don't know how to start that conversation, and neither does he. I turn back around to find long sticks with Zoe, then see Arco standing just a few steps from me. I stop, then motion for Zoe to go on without me.

"I'll catch up; I just have to do something first," I say to her, then get the Avo paste and another bandage out of my pack. Zoe nods and crosses to walk with Avis, Dez, Tieg, and Myra, and I hold out my hand for Arco's wrists, then pour water over his new cuts. This time, he doesn't wince. "Sorry," I say anyway because I know it hurts. I dab the Avo paste into his cuts, then wrap the bandage over them just before I look up to find him watching me. He doesn't say anything for a long time, and it almost makes me self-conscious. "Why are you looking at me like that?" I ask, looking away, but then meeting his eyes again.

"Because I think I believe it," he answers, and I raise my eyebrows at him in confusion, "Maybe there is something I can give you that he can't..." he raises his freshly bandaged hands to my face, then leans in to kiss me softly before resting his forehead against mine.

"Does this mean you do know how to be with me now…knowing what he can do?" I ask.

"No," Arco says, which empties the breath in my lungs. "But I'll figure it out because I don't want to know how to be without you," he answers, then kisses me again for a long time before abruptly stopping to announce random thoughts that seem to have just come to him. "And did I mention there are things I can do that he can't?" he asks, quirking an eyebrow. "I'm taller than he is, which helps with leverage for starters, and I'm funnier too, both of which are damn convenient when my girlfriend is so clipped off she's burning down the world because a giant alligator tried to eat me. Who knew those were the winning skills?" he says, nearly straight faced until I start laughing. "You'd have been elbowing Liddick in the face totally naked," he says, then kisses me again, talking against my lips every few minutes. "And then you'd have to wear...a leaf bikini...which, down here...would probably come to life...and try to eat you..."

I start laughing so hard as he growls and pretends to take a bite out of my neck that I can't even keep my eyes open. He starts laughing too, then pulls me into a hug, and I wish everything could stay like this. *Remember our one thing*, I think, hearing Jax's words, which help me find my way again as my laughter subsides and I hear Zoe calling to us.

"I love you," I say against Arco's chest, which expands as he takes in a deep breath and pulls me in more tightly, then whispers into my hair.

"I love you back, Jazwyn Ripley."

CHAPTER 45
Tanglebush

Dell walks near the front of our group, but not as part of it, and every time I look in his direction it feels like I'm stepping into a damp basement, the air heavy and cold. I need to apologize to him. It wasn't his fault about the alligator, and I know the pressure of being responsible for everyone has to be weighing on him even more now.

"I'll be right back," I say to Arco, who picks up the long tree limb he's using as a walking stick with each step, then puts it down again. I catch up to Dell, and as soon as I get close to him, my stomach twists and my chest tightens. If I had any doubt that he's beating himself up over what almost happened with the alligator, this feeling chased it away for good.

An old, white handkerchief tied over his head keeps his hair out of his eyes, and I try not to look at the long scar over his eyebrow. He looks older somehow with his shaggy, straight brown hair pulled back like this. Maybe it just makes his dark eyebrows more prominent, or the set of his full mouth, always seeming like he's either about to say something or trying to keep himself from doing it. He grips the two leather straps across his broad chest, one holding his pack in place, and the other holding his machete. Veins run up his forearms, weaving through the muscles and random scars, and I remember that he came through all seven biomes *by himself.*

"Look, I just want to—" he starts after several tense minutes walking side by side, but I interrupt him.

"Dell, I'm really sorry for attacking you," I say, and he looks over at me, surprised. "It wasn't your fault about the alligator. Everything else just caved in on me then," I explain. He presses his lips into a line that almost turns into a smile, then nods at the path ahead of us.

"Losing people is a lot to handle, then this place. It has a way of finding you," he says. *What could he have gone through to arrive at a philosophy like that?*

"Zoe said you've been with the Vishan for a year, but you made your way through six-and-a-half biomes before that. I can't imagine being on my own out here..." I say, letting the sentence trail off as the full weight of the accomplishment settles over me, and I shake my head.

"Sounds more impressive than it is," he answers like he's giving me the solution to a simple math problem— basic, obvious. "I wasn't going back into those labs, and the only other option was waiting for something to end me out here. Didn't make much sense to go through all the trouble of getting free just to give up on the other side," he says, then angles his spear a few feet in front of me. "Watch yourself," he adds, pointing to a big puddle in my path, which I jump over.

"Thanks," I say, noticing the fine white scars over his battered knuckles as he grips the spear. "But for all you knew, it wouldn't end. You didn't know about the Vishan, did you? How long did it take to find them?"

"I just saw another mountain in the distance. Figured I could make my way topside, but found out otherwise once I got in there with them," he says, and now a grin does pull at the corner of his mouth. "Can't really say how long the coming through took—I didn't have a Cycle stone, so the days and nights were random. Long enough that I looked born wild by the end of it, or so they told me." He aims his gaze at the ground as his eyebrows push together just long enough for me to notice, then he resets his expression. "That was a long time ago, though."

"Zoe said it was a year ago. You're brave," I say, struck with admiration for him and everything he must have gone through, first in being pulled down into the labs by the tunnel shark in the first place, then enduring the experiments…the gill they put into his side, which is healed over now, then navigating the Rush on his own.

"You just get through. The other options weren't too appealing," he says with a chuckle.

"I mean, you came back out here for us. You must have demons around every corner, but you came back out here to take us into those same labs you risked your life to escape. That's brave. I don't know if I could do it."

He turns his round, hazel eyes on me, then narrows them like he's trying to read something far away. He shakes his head and looks forward again, planting his wooden spear as a walking stick and picking it back up.

"I gather if you thought you could stop some wrongs that would otherwise go on, you'd go too," he says decisively, then looks at me from the corner of his eye like he's trying to see if I'm paying attention. "And it wasn't being brave that made me come back out here. It was seeing you were fighting for a purpose in all that swinging you were doing." I must look confused when he turns back to me because he chuckles again, wiping the sweat from his top lip on his shoulder. "Some people just thrash around because they're cage-rattled, wise? Swiping at everything that walks by. Other people pound the lock," he says, then finds my eyes and nods at me like this is a secret between us. "Those are the ones who get out."

As we've been talking, the terrain under our feet has turned from soft and muddy to dry and firm, scattered with angry bushes, sharply spiked with thorns and briars that stick to the laces of my boots.

"It's different here…the ground is dry," I say, the thought falling out in words without any conscious effort on my part.

"We're in the Tanglebush now—the desert, close to the Sands. This is the halfway point to the mountain," Dell says, then scans the horizon.

"What are you looking for?" I ask as a chill runs down my back.

"Tunnel sharks."

***

We stop to eat under one of the last trees before the landscape stretches out into an expanse of red dirt, which is littered with rounded green shrubs.

"What else did Azeris say when he messaged you by the Origin Wall? You said there were only two days left for my sister and your brother?" Arco asks Liddick as he takes a seat on a rock next to me. Liddick pops the last bite of his bread into his mouth and leans over, bracing his forearms on his knees before interlacing his fingers, and I realize this is the first time since we left the Vishan tunnels that we've all been able to stop and breathe.

"He said it's called Phase Three," Liddick answers, swallowing the mouthful of bread, then pulling a draw of water from his desalinator tube. "I don't know what that means other than Phase Two is where they made Liam and the Ripley's dad assist in making Arwyn fireproof, and Lyden..." he stops, searching for the words. "When they put the gills in Lyden. Azeris was working on configuring a channel to Vox since she was so much closer to the labs than we were. If she could get in there and sabotage something, cause some trouble, it could buy us enough time to get there before the Phase Three transfer to somewhere in the atmosphere."

"You keep saying that—what atmosphere? Like a space station?" Dez asks Liddick. I notice the edge in her voice, and that she's not sitting near him.

"I don't know," he answers. "All Azeris said is that Liam told him there was another facility where they were testing the next level of experiments. They wanted to send Arwyn and Lyden because they were still strong. Apparently, most of the subjects don't last the duration of Phase Two," he adds, and I feel my chest constricting as his must be. He takes another pull from his desalinator tube, then clears his throat.

"So Azeris was the source of the buzzing Vox was hearing when I saw her in the message she sent me... when she was in the Sand biome? That was Azeris getting through?" I ask.

"It had to be. The timing was right. Why else would she be hearing buzzing—we're a long way from the neural interface Gaia was using to send us announcements," Liddick answers.

"And her channel is probably amplified since she has the NET. Every time she made contact with Jazz, it was like sending up a flare," Cal adds, squinting against the bright light from the gas clouds before stepping under the tree and sitting in the shade with us.

"Can't you just call to Vox? Initiate a message?" Tieg asks me, and I notice how hard his face has become, his narrow, almost glowing blue eyes piercing everything he sees. Red dirt smudges the sharp angles of his face, and I wonder if he's been burned or hit.

"I don't know how to call her. She didn't know how she was calling me either, but she said whenever she ran across something she wanted to warn me about, I appeared," I answer, then nearly jump out of my skin when Tieg suddenly leaps to his feet and starts tearing at his dive suit.

"What's wrong? Tieg, what's wrong!?" Dez shouts, frantically looking him over as he tries to find his dive suit pull cord.

"There's something…on me!" he yells through his teeth as the back panel of his dive suit finally falls away.

"Crite—there!" Avis says, pointing to his shoulder where the end of a wide black bug about the width of my palm crawls toward his blue jumpsuit collar. I choke on the involuntary gasp that forces itself into my throat when I see hundreds of its yellow legs moving at different times.

Tieg reaches behind his neck and grabs the enormous, foot-long centipede just as it starts to make its way down his shirt. Myra screams as he throws it to the ground, then pulls back and yells in pain.

"Back up!" Dell shouts, pinning the shiny, black insect with the blunt end of his spear, the barbed, orange tail of it curling as all the bright yellow legs writhe in different directions.

"It bit you?" Cal asks Tieg, who is holding his hand while a single stream of blood drips between his knuckles.

"You could say that!" Tieg answers, and Dell flips his stick to the sharp end, then spears the centipede. Bright yellow ooze spills from the puncture, and the tail end flails and thrashes until it slows to sporadic twitches.

"Burn it, or a hundred more will find him—it has your DNA. They hunt to stay hydrated," Cal says, gesturing for Avis to bring up a flame to ignite the bug.

"And do it quick—they're all connected. These aren't like topside centipedes. Down here, they live in nests, and they'll track you. Show me the bite," Dell says to Tieg. He opens his hand, and Dell pours water from his bottle to wash away the blood, then looks at Dez. "Get the Avo paste from his pack," he nods. She complies, then puts it on Tieg's bite, wrapping it with the same kind of thin bandage I used on Arco's hands earlier.

"We should move," Cal says, pulling his leather pack over his shoulder and grabbing his long wooden spear.

Liddick and I look up at each other at the same time, with the same thought. *Telepathic bugs?* we both think, too horrified to find any humor in it.

No, they can't be. That's why he said to burn it. The others will trace the DNA if they find the body, I think.

Then why is Cal in such a hell-bent hurry to get out of here? Liddick replies, and cold shoots down my neck.

"Stay close. I've seen tunnel sharks in this biome," Dell says, then turns to Cal. "You?" he asks.

"In here, in the Sands, and in the Woodlands," Cal nods.

"These are what pulled you and Zoe through the topside sand?" Ellis asks.

"The things that are *mostly* people?" Fraya says, twisting her long auburn hair around her finger like she always does when she's nervous. Jax puts his arm around her and pulls her into him. He nods at me, pressing his lips together as if to tell me it will all be OK too.

"Won't be any mistaking them," Zoe says, her voice unusually heavy. "They have shark heads—beady black eyes and no necks. Their teeth run in all directions like zippers connecting little mouths all the way down their body, so no matter where you try to hit them, they just bite off whatever you put out there...a knife, your fist," she says, and I remember the hand that General, the huge Badlander from the Vishan camp, was missing.

"If they catch you, gouge their eyes before they can fold you into their fins. You won't be able to move if the spikes on the inside stick you in place," Dell explains, and the blood drains from Dez's face.

"*Spikes*?" Dez asks, her voice pitching.

"They stick you first thing and inject the nanites if they drag you from the surface, and you knock out for a few hours until it's too late for you to find your way back even if you could get free," Zoe adds, lifting her shirt to show the several white, circular scars under her arm.

"If you struggle anyway, they'll spear you somewhere that will keep you still with a horn that comes out of their shoulder, so just sit out the ride." Dell adds. "If they don't kill you right there, they'll take you to the labs, and we'll come for you."

Myra nearly starts to hyperventilate, and Tieg tries to put his arm around her shoulder, but she shakes him off.

"Hell of a gamble, no?" Arco asks. "Not fighting back because you're hoping they won't kill you?"

"Everything is a gamble," Dell says. "They're not bright…they're just programmed predators. If you're not dead in the first thirty seconds, they don't aim to kill you, but they'll keep you quiet," he says, pulling up his shirt to reveal the fist-sized scar that sits over the notch of muscle in his hip, then turns to reveal its match on his lower back.

"Crite…" Avis says, pushing his blue bangs off his forehead.

"Just keep your eyes open and stay close," Cal says. "Especially when we get to the Sands."

"Because *you're* going to protect us from something like that?" Tieg asks, looking down over Cal, who is probably a foot shorter than Tieg and much leaner. "Why don't you let me carry that machete," Tieg adds, apparently having forgotten how Cal threw him back on the Lookout Pier.

Cal flicks a small, black scorpion out of his path with the end of his wooden spear, and my stomach drops as it sails through the air, then lands several feet to our left. Myra's hand moves to her mouth and her eyes widen as it skitters away.

"The bigger they are, the less of a threat they are," Cal says, smirking up at Tieg. "It's the small ones that will kill you."

CHAPTER 46
Tunnel Shark

The shrubs that seemed to be everywhere just a few minutes ago are suddenly sparse, replaced by thorny, winding brambles and dark, twisting branches that look like some kind of landscape circulatory system over the red ground, which is also starting to fade to a desert sand color.

"It looks like this whole place got burned down," Avis says, squinting as he looks out at our surroundings.

"It's not as hot either," Dez adds. "Did we cross out of the Tanglebush?"

"Almost," Dell answers. "Just over that hill. This is the last of anything we'll see in the way of plants for a while. The Sand biome, and the Freeze, which comes after that, are the shortest in the Rush, but they're extremes. They'll knock you about, wise?"

"What do you mean?" Ellis asks, looking down his long, thin nose at Dell, but there is worry lacing his voice.

"I mean they're the hardest to take—always good to have your wits on call so you can catch things before they jump out, but out there…it's quiet until it's not, and then it's too late."

"What do you mean it's too late? Why do you always talk like that?" Ellis asks, shaking his head in exasperation.

"I mean you don't see anything coming. It's just there on top of you," Dell says like it's the most obvious answer in the world.

"*What* is there on top of you?" Ellis presses, his voice constricting, and I glance at Liddick.

He's starting to fray, I think. *Ever since the alligator.* Liddick nods.

I know. I've got him, he replies.

"Funnels for starters," Dell answers. "They just look like pits in the sand, but giant antlions live at the bottom of them."

"That's what I saw when Vox messaged me," I say. "She had to kill one with a long stick because the rain woke it up."

"Rain? Does it look like it ever rains out here, Jazz?" Ellis snaps. "Everything is in a state of rigor mortis!"

"It's not normal rain," Cal says with an extra calmness in his voice as he darts a look at Dell. "It's mineral rain. Not strong enough to burn anything, but enough to poison whatever would grow. Don't let any of it get into your eyes or mouths if we get caught in a downpour."

"Or what? Let me guess? It will eat our faces off?" Ellis says, his voice crackling into a neurotic laugh on the last words. Cal narrows his eyes at him, and Liddick moves to his side. He grips Ellis's shoulder, then talks to him in a quiet voice.

"Raj, you're coming loose, man. Take a deep breath, OK? We're going to make it. If it rains out here, just deploy your helmet like in *Xenotrope 6*—remember how we saved the planet in that virtuo-cine?" Ellis nods quickly as a grin starts in the corner of his mouth, but can't quite take hold. His lips twitch, and he blinks repeatedly. "So take a breath. Take a few. It's just a cine, OK?" Liddick adds with a few pats to Ellis's back.

Ellis swallows, then takes a few deep breaths and nods again, normally this time.

I look up at what should be the sky, and notice the clouds are starting to band into those bruised, cylindrical twists like they did when we first left the Vishan tunnels. It is going to rain. *A lot,* as Vox said.

"We have to hurry—look at the sky," I say. "The rain is coming."

"If you slide…even if you start to slide into a funnel, dig your sticks into the ground in front of you to stop yourself. Get a good grip, wise?" Dell says to us all in warning, but underneath, it sounds like a plea.

He feels like we're on his watch, Liddick thinks, picking up the same feeling I am.

He told me he came with us because he knew we would fight to get to the mountain. I think he's getting nervous that not all of us will.

He might be right, Liddick answers, and I look up at him as he grips Ellis's shoulder in reassurance again.

***

The threat of the mineral rain increases as the clouds above thicken and swell, twisting into arcing columns that squeeze out the light from the gas pockets above them, but fortunately, there is no lightning behind them this time. It seems like dusk back home with the last of the light shining just brightly enough to see what is nearby, but not enough to prevent the shadows in the distance from becoming whatever they want to be.

"How dark is it going to get? What if we can't see where we're going and we slide into one of those funnels?" Dez asks too quickly.

"The Cycle stones," Arco says at my side. "They're like little flashlights, remember? If it gets any darker, we can use those."

Cal nods, and Dell confirms with a nod of his own.

"We have a little while before any of that, but have them ready all the same," Cal says.

Jax and Fraya move to walk with Arco and me as Liddick keeps Ellis close, enlisting Avis to walk on his other side so he's not exposed to the open *rigor mortis* bush plateau.

"People are starting to tweak," Jax says to Arco. "That's dangerous."

"I know. We just need to keep them talking—pull them in...but Spaulding won't fall in with me. Have Fraya reach out to Dez, and he'll follow. He trusts you. Get Zoe to bring Myra in with you too. Wright looks like he's got Raj, and Ling has his back."

Jax nods. "And you?"

"We're good," Arco says, then looks down at me. "We're good, right?"

I nod, "I fixed things with Dell," I say, and Jax smiles.

"I knew you would," he says. "All right. I'll get it going. Looks like things are about to get uncomfortable," he adds, taking another look at the sky.

Arco presses his lips into a line and nods again, but then his resigned expression shifts to surprise as the ground starts to rumble under our feet.

"What's that!?" Myra yells.

"Listen, stay tight. I mean it, stay tight. No space between us, understand?" Dell says, a different edge to his voice...cold and menacing.

"What's happening? Why did the ground shake like that?" Dez demands as Tieg changes positions with her, bringing her to the inside of the group. Zoe does the same with Myra and slides her machete under her arm, then grips the handle as the ground rumbles again.

"*What the hell* is that?" Tieg echoes.

"Maybe a tunnel shark," Cal says, his voice low and cool like Dell's. "But I've never seen them come through the ground until we get to the looser sand."

Myra starts to cry, sending a biting fear over me, which I can feel seeping into everyone else too. Liddick meets my eyes.

We have to push them before they tear everyone apart, he thinks, jerking his head at Ellis, then angling it to Myra. *Myra's been tweaking, now Raj, and Dez just started. It's going to spread.*

How do we push them all at the same time? I ask.

Project, just like you did in Tark's virtuo-cine with the Badlander cannibals. Do you remember how you did it?

I didn't do anything except try to convince myself, not anyone else. I just kept thinking about what you told me...how the rocks were cold in the sun, so it couldn't have been real. But this is real, Liddick.

Not anymore. Not for everyone, he answers after darting another glance at Myra.

The ground rumbles again, and my heart starts to pound in my chest. Flames light Myra's shoulders, and Dell swears.

"Myra, pull that in! Right now—focus!" he says. "Bring her to the middle!"

Zoe guides Myra until she's in the center of everyone, then talks adamantly into her ear until her flames dissipate, but Zoe's expression blanches a second later when Myra actually starts *giggling.* I feel the ricocheting hysteria weighing down the back of my head, making me dizzy, and in this moment, I know that she has just completely detached from reality. The ground shakes more violently, and longer this time.

"Weeeeee!" Myra shouts at the top of her lungs, and a chill runs down my spine when I see that her eyes are so wild it looks like they might pop out of her head, and her mouth is open to the point that it looks like she's going bite something. Zoe suddenly looks lost, then lets go of Myra and meets my eyes. I shake my head at her.

"Don't let her go!" I yell. "Hang on to her! She thinks she's on a ride!" Myra's arms fly into the air as she starts to sway, first to the left, then to the right, which edges Dez and Zoe out a few steps. "Keep her close!" I shout again to Zoe. "Myra, you have to lock in, OK? Lock in or you'll fall out!"

Myra's mouth shifts from the wide, psychotic position it's been in to the word *oh,* then she nods at me like I've reminded her of something very important. She brings her fists to her chest like she's holding onto the pull bars of a solarcoaster, and to my relief, she stops swaying. I almost lose my footing when the ground moves this time, and Dez suddenly screams hysterically at Myra's side as a sheet of red flames engulfs them both.

"Let go! Let me go!" Dez yells at the ground.

"It's the shark! I see it!" Fraya shouts, jabbing the sharp end of her stick at the long, dark gray fin, which stretches through the ground to the length of a human arm, then wraps around Dez's calf up to her knee. Dez screams in pain as Tieg fires his stick at the ground where the fin emerges, stabbing a hole through it, but it doesn't let go. He stabs through it again as another fin shoots up and grabs Fraya's stick, flinging it several yards away, then whips back in one fluid motion and wraps itself around her thigh. She screams, and Jax drives his spear into the narrow part of the fin just above the ground where it isn't attached to Fraya. Dez passes out just as Tieg manages to stab enough perforations in the fin to sever it. He drops his stick and picks up Dez, jostling her shoulders and shouting her name.

"Dezzie! Can you hear me!? *Dezzie!*"

"She's just knocked out from the nanites! She'll wake up! Stay in the middle with her!" Cal shouts, his machete in his hands. "Jax, back up!"

"It's got her!"

"I know! Back up so I can cut the fin loose!" Cal shouts again, but Fraya's screams are the only thing Jax can hear as he keeps rifling the point of his stick at the fin and flames shoot everywhere.

"Ripley!" Arco yells. "Ripley, back up!"

The ground sounds like thunder as the huge, gray nose breaks through the packed earth, reddish, then black dirt crumbles and rolls down its face as the jagged teeth zipper down what should be a throat, then open into hundreds of differently sized pocket mouths, which open and close sporadically, some slowly, some so quickly that they blur just like the Bale stalks when the zephyrs were hunting us.

Jax stabs his spear into the center of the tunnel shark's throat, but one of the mouths just bites the stick in half.

"Its eye! Aim for the eye!" Arco shouts.

"Back up! Damnit, get clear!" Dell shouts to Jax, but he won't be moved. Fraya screams again as the other fin, which is severed in a ragged line at the tip from Tieg's stick, wraps around Fraya's hips, pinning one of her arms. She screams again, the kind of blood curdling scream I know I'm going to hear for years to come. Jax stabs at the tunnel shark again, and two horns like elephant tusks shoot out from its shoulders, which now break free from the ground.

"Back the hell up if you want her to live!" Dell shouts as he, Zoe, and Cal try to take aim at the eyes, but the tunnel shark is moving so erratically, they can't get a fix with my brother in the way.

"Jax!" I scream. "Jax, back up!"

"No!" he yells in reply, stabbing again at the shark only to lose more of his stick to its snapping mouths.

Arco wraps his arm around Jax's neck to drag him backward, but Jax elbows him in the face, knocking Arco to the ground. He scrambles to his feet, blood spilling from his nose as Liddick has no choice but to hit the back of Jax's legs with the side of his spear, knocking him to his knees. Arco jumps on top of Jax then and holds him to the ground.

"Now! *Now!*" Arco yells to Dell, who swears when he realizes that he's too far away to take out the shark's eye. He swings his machete clean through the base of the fin wrapped around Fraya's thigh instead. The other fin is still wrapped around her hips, and I grip my stick now that there is room to take aim at the eye. Once I'm about three steps closer, Fraya's head falls forward just like Dez's, and Jax lets out an anguished scream that freezes me to the bone. I raise my stick, then pull it back just before accidentally running it into Cal's arm as he punctures one of the tunnel shark's eyes before I can. The shark's body jerks violently toward him, whipping Fraya into me and knocking me to the ground.

My lungs stop working so quickly that I am terrified they've somehow been ripped out of my chest. No matter how hard I try to breathe, I can't make any air enter. *How am I drowning?* I hear myself wondering. *There's no water…how am I drowning?*

"Rip!" Liddick shouts, but I can still only see hundreds of little round, white lights.

"*No!*" Arco yells, and I try to grab onto something solid, but my fingers only dig into the crumbling ground.

Someone lifts my head and shoulders, then moves me to my side.

"Little breath! Take a little—*oh no…*" Liddick says.

"Stay there and hold him! Arco, hold him! It's not dead yet!" Dell yells in the distance as Zoe shouts over everyone, and Myra giggles hysterically.

"I have a clear line! Run interference!"

My lungs feel like they're on fire, and a thousand little stabs run up my chest. *But how...how am I drowning?* I think.

You're not drowning, Rip! Listen, you're fine...you're fine. You just hit the ground full tilt. It just knocked the wind out of you, OK? OK...? Myra! Liddick shouts, but he sounds so far away.

But there's...no water...in the desert, I think as the white lights get brighter, spreading out until they touch each other, and the searing pain in my chest starts to subside.

Rip! Crite, please...damnit...Rip, I love you—I know you can hear me. I love you...fight! You have to fight!

"Watch the spikes in her thigh—unwrap it slow!" Cal shouts along with all the other noises in the background of Liddick's fading screams.

CHAPTER 47
The Channel

"It's you, by the way. You're the one calling me," Vox says. "At least this time."

I blink until the blinding white light clears, then notice the floor I'm lying on is metal and freezing cold. When she comes into focus, she's leaning against the wall with her knees up and her boots turned in, one bare, map-tattooed forearm hanging over her leg as a few ragged scraps of dive suit sleeve dangle from her shoulder. She props her other hand on the ground and leans into it, then turns her head absurdly on edge to meet my eyes.

"Vox?" I ask, surprised to hear my own voice sound so muffled, like I'm talking under water.

"Well, yeah. You linked into anyone else's head? Oh, you remember Azeris?"

"What?" I say, pushing myself up on my elbow, relieved when my voice starts to sound normal again.

"Hello, Jazz," Azeris says, bringing two fingers to his forehead in a salute as he stands, leaning against the wall. He's wearing dark pants, which are tucked into his boots just like they were the first time I met him in the Boundaries room at Gaia. This time, though, his shirt is faded tan with a thermal weave like the young Vishan and tunnel Badlanders wore. He smiles, and his white teeth stand out against his dark stubble and tanned skin.

"Your lung is punctured by the way. I hope that chutz stops jostling you back and forth with all that *I love you* rag," Vox says, then sticks out her tongue like she's gagging. Azeris shoots her a look, which makes her hold up her hands in faux surrender just before she turns to me and rolls her yellow-green eyes. "OK, well you need those nannies from the tunnel shark, or you're going to die, so tell Liddick, yeah?" she adds with a thin-lipped smile, and I start to feel nauseous.

"*What*?" I manage to ask, and once I do, the other questions spill out in a deluge. "Where are we? Why is it so cold? How did I—"

"Look, can you just not die first? Because that would kind of end our conversation here. Go ahead and think really hard, sand dollar. *Nnnnnannies*!" Vox interrupts, holding out her hands like she's just finished a performance and is waiting for applause.

"Nanites," Azeris corrects, then locks his hands behind his neck and takes a deep breath.

"Oh, yeah sorry…*nnnnnanites*! Think it, Jazz."

"Vox, I—"

"*Think it,* or **you. are. going.** *to die*," she enunciates. "And I did not come all this way through giant bugs and talking ravines just for you to die at the front door of everything, so can you stow it and think *nanites, please*?"

I try to concentrate on the word, but nothing happens. "It's not working!" I say, shaking my head against the clatter of voices pushing into the corners of my focus.

"No," she says, closing her eyes and shaking her head. "Picture Liddick. He was wrecked, remember? He's still wrecked…I can hear him wrecking *all over* the place, and the only way I can hear him now is if you can hear him, so *listen* and connect."

"Close your eyes, Jazz," Azeris says, pushing a weathered hand through his dark, curly hair.

I close my eyes, trying to listen for Liddick's voice, but everything is just as jumbled as it was, especially with the overlay of buzzing and the distracting, sharp pain in my chest again.

"It hurts," I say, trying not to take a deep breath.

"Good, that means you're closer…you're connecting back to your consciousness there—to what's happening around you right now in the Sand biome," Azeris says.

She needs the tube! Cut it! A voice shouts, but it's too far away and warbled for me to identify.

Is Dez awake yet? I can't do it!

"Myra… that's Myra!" I say.

No, so you have to do it! The first voice says, closer now.

"Jax?" I ask, trying as hard as I can to hear him.

"Jax can't hear inside your head! Call to *Liddick*!" Vox sounds like she's right next to my ear, which is so loud and so abrupt that I'm shouting his name in my head before I even realize it.

Liddick!!

"Tell him to get the nanites!" Vox yells again, but her voice is farther away now. "Hurry, Jazz!"

Nanites! Tunnel shark nanites! I think as loudly as I can, picturing Liddick's face, replaying his voice, strained and desperate. *He said…he loves me?*

Rip!? Crite…yes! Hang on! I hear you! Hang on! Liddick says, but his voice sounds like it's coming through a wall, and I start to feel heavy and tired as all the other sounds sink under me.

*You **heard** her? What did she say!?*

Hart, move!

We need the fin!

I know, Ripley! Cut it! Hurry up!

No! It has to be attached! Drag it here before that thing dies! The last few voices muffle again in the wake of the growing buzz, and something cool starts hitting my face.

"He heard me..." I say, bringing my fingers to my cheek before I open my eyes. "What's this?"

Vox exhales. "It's rain," she says just as I blink, then see that she's touching her face too.

"You can feel what I feel back there?" I ask, placing my palm on the ground to push myself up a little more, but I don't feel the same cold that I feel with the other palm. "Wha—?" I start to say, looking at Vox for an answer. She moves her other hand to the ground, and then I feel the cold.

"You can only feel what you feel there, and what I feel here. Trippy, yeah? This chokes by the way..." she says, lifting one of her hands to the side of her chest and wincing in pain as she raises a dark red eyebrow at me. "No pun intended."

"If I can only feel what you feel, then how can I see you if you can't see yourself?" I ask, confused.

"This, I guess?" she says, pulling the Vishan's NET artifact from inside the collar of her dive suit and holding the flat, metal Y-shaped bars out at an angle, making my view of her ripple. "Whoa, yeah, it's this," she laughs. "Sand dollar, you're bendy!" she almost sings as she turns the bars from one side to the other, which stretches her head and shoulders to the ceiling, then her torso and legs until they're just inches from my fingers.

"Stop!" I say, pushing the heels of my hands into my eyes to stop the nauseating distortions, then hear her laugh echoing like it's in a canyon as I wince from another sharp pain.

"He did it," Azeris says, tapping something onto a small blue screen that hovers over the palm of his hand. "Your lines are regulating," he adds with a quick glance at me. I try to get to my feet, but the stabbing feeling in my chest puts an immediate stop to that. I bring my hand to the source of the pain, but there's nothing there. Vox chuckles.

"You're not really here—you won't be able to see the damage because you haven't actually seen the damage yet. Only your brain is in my channel, sand dollar," she winks. "Though, maybe I have to stop calling you that because trying to cyclops a tunnel shark was pretty brass," she adds with a nod as she cocks her eyebrow.

"You were there? You were with me?"

"*No*, I saw it because it was the last thing *you* saw before you hit the dirt. Are you listening to me or what? We can feel what we would normally feel, and what the other one feels. You're still in the Sand biome with everyone else just like I'm here in what is apparently the freezer room of this stupid mountain Gaia," Vox explains, and after a second Azeris clears his throat. "What? She *is* still there because I couldn't make her all bendy if she were really *here*," Vox says, rotating the flat, metal Y-bars of the NET artifact in her hand again, and immediately, both she and Azeris twist and pull in opposite directions around the room.

"*All right*," Azeris says through his teeth, then closes his eyes and pinches the bridge of his nose as I nearly roarf. The sensation is pushed back only by the overwhelming need to laugh as I wonder if I would be throwing up in Vox's head.

"So are you going to get your doodle plate out or what?" she asks Azeris, rolling her bright green eyes as she returns the NET artifact to the inside of her dive suit. She squints suddenly to study the scratches on the underside of her arm just as my own arm starts to itch in the same place.

Azeris sighs, then pulls up the glowing panel in the palm of his hand again, which projects about a foot into the air this time. He draws two big circles inside the blue projection with his index finger, then connects them with parallel lines before looking up at me.

"Jazz, this is your channel—your consciousness," he says, pointing to the first circle, then to the other. "And this one is Vox's. This pathway between them, that's your channel bridge," he explains, pointing to the two parallel lines connecting the circles. "You can see and hear her consciousness, and she can see and hear yours. Normally, you'd just meet in the middle of the channel bridge and see each of your environments behind you, but the NET must be overriding that and pulling you all the way into Vox's environment somehow—into her channel," he says, then draws another circle with two more parallel lines that intersect the others. "When I uplink to your channel, but you don't uplink to mine, I can see what you see in just that time and place too. I can see into your channel," Azeris adds.

"So the buzzing we've been hearing...that's just you connecting so you could keep track of us?" I ask. He nods and starts to elaborate, but Vox cuts him off.

"Or, it's me trying to get this thing to stop vibrating the teeth out of my head," she says, pausing her arm inspection long enough to reach for the collar of her dive suit again.

"No! It's the NET, I get it!" I say, throwing out a hand to her, which sends a wave of nausea over me again. She grins, then goes back to scratching between the healing marks on her arm as Azeris scowls at his palm display.

"Those nanites are lagging..." he says to himself, then looks up at me. "Jazz, even though you're linked into Vox's channel, part of your mind is still in the Sand biome. That's the part reporting the pain in your chest... when you move, or when you get close to waking up there, you can feel it more. Think of it like your consciousness is water being poured back and forth into glasses on a scale. The more water you have in one glass, the more information you process from that environment —it tips the scale of your awareness, wise?" Azeris asks, and I'd almost forgotten that he was a Badlander. His thick, dark brows raise in question, and several lines crease his forehead as he waits for my answer.

"I think I understand," I say. "But *you're* here? Really here with Vox in the mountain?" I ask, and he nods.

"I used port-carnate tech as soon as she made it here. When I was able to lock onto her channel before that, it was easy enough to find yours at the end of the bridge between you," he says, gesturing to the hovering blue grid over his palm again.

"That's what Liddick was trying to tell us," I say, remembering how adamant he was that Azeris had found us.

"You're going to knock out any minute from the dose of tunnel shark nanites, but when you wake up, tell Liddick this," he adds, then draws three triangles with three corresponding symbols: a wave on the first, the point of an open arrow on the second, and three undulating lines on the third. "Phase One," he says, pointing to the wave. "Phase Two, Phase Three," he adds, pointing to the arrow, then, to the three wavy lines. "Tell him that Liam and I are almost finished with the Phase Three bridge—I don't know when I'll be able to connect to him now that we're here in the labs," he adds, and I try to nod.

"A *channel connection* to Phase Three?" I ask, shaking my head in an effort to keep everything straight.

"Yes…this one is an encrypted path that will connect the labs here to the counterpart site just outside the port-cloud. Do you remember launching the automators into the system back at Gaia?" Azeris asks.

"When you put the *port-carnate splice* in my head—yeah, I remember that," I say, narrowing my eyes. Azeris's mouth quirks.

"Just doing my job," he answers, "and I aim to finish it. The bridge will connect the hub here to the Phase Three hub inside Admin City. There's a—"

"Inside *what*?" I ask, looking from Azeris to Vox, who shrugs.

"Giant floating candy bar," she says, nodding like this will explain everything.

"*What*?" I squint at her as Azeris sighs.

"Ask Liddick about Admin City. There's not enough time to explain it right now. Just tell him about the symbols and their corresponding phases, and that we're almost done with the bridge. He'll tell you the rest, wise?" Azeris asks, then flips his hand, which brightens the blue, hovering screen that had almost faded out. "You have about two minutes before those nanites make it to your brain and put you down for a few hours, so try—"

"My dad…is he OK?" I interrupt, feeling my stomach drop in panic that I will run out of time before I find out everything I need to know from Azeris.

"He's fine, for now. He's in a holding tank because he sabotaged the last Phase Two test for Lyden and Arwyn. The biodesigners have to wait another 48 hours now before they see the results of the test they had to redo. Your father bought us another few days," Azeris says with a small, proud smile.

"What are they going to do to him in that tank?" I press, feeling my heart starting to pound hard against my ribs, which makes my side ache again. Azeris's screen beeps, and he jerks his eyes from me.

"Look, you're going to bleed out if you don't relax… the nanites they gave you are already weakened because that tunnel shark was on its last fin."

"Then tell me!" I demand. He takes a deep breath as the door panel behind him slides open and a tall, lean man with messy blond hair and wide blue eyes appears.

"Are you ready?" he says to Azeris and Vox, and when I focus on his face, I see the thin, white scar running through his left eyebrow…just like Liddick's.

"*Liam!*" I shout. Azeris's eyes flash back to mine as he shakes his head.

"He's not connected to this channel—he can't see or hear you."

"Who is it?" Liam asks, looking around the room. "Liddick?"

"No, it's his girl, but he's close," Azeris answers just as everything starts to fade and muffle.

"Wait! What are they going to do to my dad!?" I yell, panicking with the spreading blur.

"They're not going to do anything because we're going to get him out," Azeris calls back, his voice getting quieter as all the details of the room bleed together. "It's the tunnel shark nanites…you're knocking out, Jazz. Don't forget the message for Liddick, wise? The symbols, and the Phase Three bridge!" he adds.

"Wait! Make it slow down!"

"Come back to life, sand dollar! And go through the glacier in the Freeze biome—the crystals are wild!" Vox's last words echo until the light gets so bright I can't make out where she is anymore, and in a blink, everything is dark again.

CHAPTER 48
The Freeze

My lips taste metallic and cold, but it's warm on the right side of my face. Everything feels warm on my right side, and I turn my head toward the heat. The bright glow is immediate, making me squint before I even open my eyes, and though my chest still hurts, at least I can breathe now.

"Jazz...don't move, OK? There's a tube in your side," Arco says in a low, quiet voice as I feel a hand brush my cheek.

"Why?" I try to say, but it comes out as a creaky whisper.

"Because you landed on a tanglebush—under your right arm... a branch punctured your lung," he answers.

"The nanites?" my voice creaks again.

"Yes...you have them. We all have them now. Everything is going to be OK, just stay still," he says as I open my eyes.

"Arco..."

"I'm here..." he smiles.

"Tell Myra thank you...for the tube. It was...scary for her," I whisper, then try to swallow as Arco's brows draw in.

"How did—?" he starts, but Myra interrupts him and kneels next to me.

"You're welcome," she says, her eyes clear and blue instead of wild and bulging, then she grips my hand and smiles as the fire blazing behind Arco comes into focus. I smile back at Myra and feel a hand brush through my hair from the left, then turn to see Jax's dark eyes wrinkling in the corners as he smiles down at me.

"You heard me, didn't you?" I whisper to him, and his brows flinch.

"Heard you?" he asks, angling his head.

"The nanites…" I whisper again, his eyes widening and reflecting the dancing fire. He presses his lips into a thin line, then pulls in a deep breath and nods.

"I guess so," he says trying to control his voice as he strokes his fingertip over the bridge of my nose, right between my eyes like he did when we were little. "I guess I did."

"I'll get you some water," Myra says, then stands. Liddick is sitting behind her with his elbows on his knees and his fingers interlaced in front of his mouth like an adamant preacher. When he sees me, he lowers his hands and raises his chin like he's about to ask a question, but then doesn't. His chest expands in a slow, deep breath, which he lets out just as slowly.

Hey… he finally thinks.

Hey… I reply, and he smiles so widely that he's surprised by it. He smothers it with his hand, then shakes his head.

I thought—crite, Rip…I thought you… he trails off, and my throat constricts, making it harder to breathe again. *When I couldn't hear you anymore…*he restarts, closing his eyes as he takes in another deep breath.

I'm really sorry, I think, unsure if the stabbing sensation in my chest is from the tube or from him. It fades a little when Liddick laughs abruptly, then looks over at me with a wide, incredulous smile just before he gets to his feet. He hooks his thumbs in the rigging loops of his dive suit and meets my eyes again like he's trying to see straight into me, and in that second, I remember that he can.

Arco turns to face him, breaking his line of sight. Liddick moves to the other side of the fire and kneels next to it as I squeeze Arco's hand and smile at him, his hazel eyes dark when he turns back to me, but in the shadow from the fire, I can see a half-healed cut about an inch long over his cheekbone.

"You're hurt?" I ask, reaching to touch his face. He wraps his hand around mine and brings it to his lips, then shakes his head, and my throat tightens.

"Not anymore," he whispers. Brushing his thumb just under my bottom lip for a few seconds before leaning down and kissing me.

Myra returns with a tube sticking out of a cylinder of water. I must make a strange face because she giggles.

"The straw is the first part of your desalinator tube—the rest is in your side. Ellis can put some of it back in your suit when you're better, but we'll need to find a way to roll up your sleeves so you can get a drink until then," she smiles. I take a long pull from the tube, not realizing how thirsty I am, then notice the strange red hue of everything around us.

"Where are we?" I say, my voice feeling a little stronger.

"At the edge of the Sand biome, almost to the glacier," Dell answers from several feet away. "We weren't far off when the tunnel shark attacked," he adds, and suddenly, I remember everything: the shark, the fins, all its mouths, and…Liddick.

A current runs through me, pushing away all the violence with the memory of him calling to me, of him shouting that he loved me. The force of it spreads in my chest, igniting everything until I make myself shake it loose. We have different definitions of love, and *I know* that. *He* knows that. I push these thoughts aside as soon as I'm aware of them too because the last thing I want is for him to eavesdrop on my thoughts and hear me rationalizing this all over again.

"Are Dez and Fraya OK? Where are they?" I ask abruptly, then try to sit up.

"*Whoa*…stay still. They're fine," Arco says as Ellis moves in behind him.

"They woke up from the initial nanite infusion, but are asleep again now—they got a big dose, especially Fraya, so it will take a little longer for their bodies to regulate," Ellis says with a small nod. "Welcome back."

"Ellis…you're OK?" I ask, and he nods again as his lips quirk into a smile.

"*Xenotrope 6*," he says, angling his head at Liddick. "I was brass in that cine," he adds, and I laugh, but it hurts.

"And the others?" I ask, looking around for them. Ellis moves out of the way, and I see Zoe, Tieg, and Cal sitting on rocks about five feet from the blazing red fire, which Avis is stoking with what looks like the remnants of one of the long spears we made in the Bog biome. I squint, trying to make out what the massive charred thing in the middle of the fire is.

"Is that—?"

"The tunnel shark's head," Liddick answers before I can even finish the question. He doesn't look up from watching it burn, and I feel a ball of ice form in my stomach after a second, which tells me that it was him, in the end, who killed it.

***

I don't remember falling asleep, but when I wake up again, we're not in the same place. Long, light blue crystals shoot out in every direction from the milky walls, as well as from the ceiling that is somehow moving. My head bounces off an uneven surface, and when I try to sit up to see what it is, the ground underneath me creaks.

"She's awake," Fraya says. "Jax, stop..."

The ground shifts under me, and then I realize it's not the ground at all when I grip the sides for balance. I look down and see gnarled, gray branches weaving in and out of each other.

"What is...?" I start, but trail off when Arco and Jax appear, then Myra.

"It's a sled. We made it from the tanglebushes at the edge of the Sand biome to get you, Fraya, and Dez out of there after the..." Myra says, pausing and glancing over her shoulder at Liddick. "After the tunnel shark," she says under her breath, then gestures to me. "I took out your tube—sorry about the hole in your suit," she says, rolling her lips between her teeth. I feel under my right arm and find that the hole in the fabric is a few inches in diameter, but the exposed skin there is raw and pink, and the ache feels like it goes straight into my spine. It's better than the searing pain from before, though, and I take a hesitant breath, expecting the stabbing sensation to return, but it doesn't.

"You fixed it," I say, smiling up at her as Arco kneels at my side.

"Does it still hurt?" he asks, moving his hand over my leg. I shake my head.

"Not like before. It's just an ache now, but at least I can breathe," I say, and the tightness in his jaw releases. I swing my legs out of the sled, and he slides his arm around my waist to help me up. Jax sets down the sled and moves to my other side.

"Are you sure you can walk?" he asks, and aside from my legs being a little stiff, I feel surprisingly strong.

"I'm good. Where are we?" I ask, looking down the long, blue crystal corridor that stretches out in front of us.

"Ice caves," Zoe says, then whistles through her teeth to call everyone at the front of the group to us. "Welcome back," she says with a wide smile that puts little apples in her freckled cheeks. Fraya walks around the sled and hugs me, then hooks her arm in mine as the others gather around, and I start to feel a little awkward with everyone just looking at me and smiling.

"Thank you…for helping me," I say, nodding to the group and wishing someone would talk. Liddick steps out from behind Ellis and finds my eyes.

"Nothing you wouldn't have done," he says, the blue light hitting the side of his face and making the scar through his eyebrow stand out—the one he got from falling down the dune as a kid. *Liam*...I think, suddenly remembering the message I'm supposed to deliver.

"Azeris said that he and Liam were almost finished with the bridge to Phase Three," I blurt, making everyone's eyes widen. "He told me to remember the symbols, and I just saw your scar, and *I saw Liam*! Azeris and Vox made it to the mountain. I mean, Azeris got there through port-carnate, but Vox made it, and Liam is helping them. And my dad...*Jax*...dad..." I say, whirling around to find my brother, but then the room starts to spin.

"Hey..." Jax says, catching my arms. "Sit back down." He tries to help me into the sled, but I don't want to go back to sleep.

"No, I'm fine," I say, biting the inside of my cheek to help me focus as Myra takes my pulse, and after a minute, the room goes back to normal speed.

"We had to guess at the nanite dosage..." she says. "So you're probably still regulating like Dez and Fraya had to, but it's taking longer because you had such a bad injury too. You just have to take it easy for a little while more," Myra adds as Fraya nods at her with a big smile, and I feel the underlying confidence she must be feeling as her eyes sparkle in the blue cave light.

"OK, I'll try," I say, and the proud smile finally breaks free over her face as Jax's hand moves to my shoulder.

"And dad?" he asks.

"They put him in a holding tank..." I answer, trying to pick up where I think I left off. Jax's expression shifts from worried to proud as I explain what Azeris said about our father ruining the last experiment needed to send Lyden and Arwyn to Phase Three…that he bought us a few more days.

"What happens in Phase Three?" Dez asks Jax instead of me, as if *he* knows somehow. Aren't I right here *explaining* everything to him? A small ember sparks in my chest at the idea that she is probably just refusing to talk to me out of her own jealousy over Liddick, and all at once I'm exasperated. *Crite,* we're in the middle of an ice crystal cave under the seafloor fighting giant mutant-people sharks, and she's worried about me *stealing her boyfriend*?

Rip, that's not it…read why she's—Liddick starts thinking, but I don't want to hear it.

"Azeris drew three wavy lines for Phase Three," I say out loud over his thoughts as I try to push my frustration aside. "Phase One was a wave, Phase Two was a little open arrow or mountain, and Phase Three was three wavy lines…*air.* The atmosphere!" I say, the overdue epiphany rising in me like a geyser as I jerk my attention to Liddick, but then wobble when the room takes another spin.

"Slow! *Slow…*" Arco says, putting his arm around my waist again until Liddick crosses to me.

"Before we left the Vishan tunnels, you said Azeris told you Phase Three was a facility in the atmosphere somewhere. What's the rest? He told me that he and Liam were almost done building a bridge to Phase Three, and that you knew the rest. Liddick, what is Admin City?" I say, gripping his arms.

"He told you about *Admin City*?" Liddick's dark eyebrows shoot up in surprise as he takes a step back from me to lean against one of the facets of blue ice crystal jutting from the wall.

"No, there wasn't enough time before the nanites put me to sleep. He said *you* would tell me," I say. Liddick sighs.

"Don't get so worked up..." Tieg answers. "Admin City is just what the Seam and the rest of the conspiracy theorists call some *covert* interior level of the Grid where all the subliminal programmers code our next thought for us," he adds, rolling his eyes. "It's supposedly this giant floating rectangle that magically sits right on top of the port-cloud servers and virtuo-cine studio platforms in the atmosphere. But of course, it's invisible," Tieg adds, his biodesigned blue eyes widening as he nods slowly for effect, then squints like he's just witnessed the stupidest thing he's ever seen.

"A giant floating candy bar..." I say to myself, remembering Vox's description.

"Uh...sure? You should probably sit back down, Jazz," Tieg chuckles and shakes his head, and I narrow my eyes at him before turning back to Liddick.

"Azeris said Phase Three was in Admin City. Why did he want me to tell you about the symbols, and that he and Liam were almost done building the *bridge*? What does that mean?" I ask, holding Liddick's eyes with mine so he can't deflect or reroute again. He takes in a breath, and after a second, finally just resolves to say it.

"He wanted you to tell me about the symbols as a confirmation code so I would know that no one else hacked into your channel...it was so I would believe what you said about the bridge," Liddick answers, and I raise an eyebrow at him. "The symbols were the first real breakthrough Azeris and I found when we went back through the virtuo-cine code that Liam used to warn me about Gaia. Lyden had actually written it to keep *Liam* from going to Gaia before me, but neither one of us figured it out in time. No one else knows that, so..." Liddick explains, crossing his arms over his chest. I swallow hard, trying to keep my focus.

"So Lyden wrote those symbols into the code when he was still working in the Grid?" I ask.

"Your brother worked in *the Grid*? He's a Quantum Programmer?" Tieg asks, and Liddick gives him an exhausted look.

"Yeah, before they put *gills* in him," he flares. I grip his shoulders to get him to focus again.

"All right, what was the code supposed to tell you—that the symbols were all Gaia tags? A wave for Gaia Sur, the arrow thing for where we're going now, and wavy lines of air for *another* Gaia in the atmosphere? No wonder you didn't figure it out in time," I say, and Liddick shrugs.

"Only part of the code ever got through the mainframe firewall anyway...that's the same reason we only heard part of your dad's message with the marlin," Liddick answers.

"Wait a minute..." Arco says, holding out a hand. "The wave symbol, that's a State geographical key. It doesn't mean water though, it means coastal land, like home... like Seaboard and Skyboard. The arrow tip with an open bottom means hilly terrain over sand, like the Badlands, and three wavy lines means..." he adds, his cheeks and nose red in the cold until he blanches with realization. "Three wavy lines means water. Those symbols are...*pull sites*," he says as Avis covers his mouth.

"Right," Liddick says, pressing his lips into a thin line. Tieg closes his eyes, then drops his chin to his chest and blows out a breath.

"What does that mean?" Myra asks, shaking her head.

"Phase One subjects are pulled from Seaboard and Skyboard communities like ours, and then are sent to Gaia Sur. Subjects for Phase Two come from—" Arco starts, but Dell interrupts.

"The sharks pull them through the sands in places like the Badlands..." he says, darting a glance at Zoe. Cal sighs, then studies the ground.

"And Phase Three subjects come from under water— from the homesteads and from Gaia Sur," Liddick finishes. "That's why your dad and Liam were trying to keep us from going there at all."

"So the State *knows* about this?" I ask, incredulous as Jax chuffs a laugh.

"That would explain why Mr. Paxton was sweating like he was standing in a cook pan at the port-festival. Remember?"

"Who's Paxton?" Zoe raises an eyebrow.

"He's our head councilman...like Jove," I say, recalling how nervous Paxton was when he announced us at the port-festival.

"So he *knew* he was sending us somewhere they might experiment on us?" Fraya asks.

"Our council leader was rattled too," Dez speaks up. "She's usually so polished, but she always loses her footing during the Skyboard North port-festivals. It's kind of a joke back home..." she adds, trailing off as she and Tieg exchange glances.

Avis pushes a hand through his blue-tipped black hair until it's pulled completely off his wide forehead. "They just sold us out," he says, then startles with a new question. "Did our *teachers* know too?"

"No, there's no way Ms. Wren knew. She was too cautious about giving me hints to help me pass the interview. She was excited for me," I answer without hesitation.

"And what about this *bridge*?" Arco asks, pinning Liddick to the wall with a level stare. "Why was Jazz supposed to tell you the bridge to Phase Three was almost finished?"

Liddick darts an apologetic glance at me, and my stomach falls.

"Because we're going to Phase Three..." he finally says, and the blood seems to drain from my body through some opened valve in the soles of my feet.

"We're *what*?" I ask, locking my eyes with Liddick's.

"We have to force the Gaia mainframe to cannibalize itself, or they'll never stop, Rip. They'll just keep taking people from the pull sites like they've been doing for the past eighty years. They'll keep using Gaia Sur as a funnel for getting rid of people who get in their way, and for recruiting others who can be manipulated into helping them. Everyone else is just a pawn in the game—don't you see it?" Liddick explains, his brows drawing together in preparation for what he must know is coming.

"We planned on going into that mountain to get our family out, Liddick. No one said anything about going into *space*!" I say, biting off the ends of the last few words. Arco laughs out loud from behind me, then turns to Dell.

"And I suppose you knew about this? That's what caused your sudden change of heart about helping us?" he asks. Cal and Zoe exchange confused glances, but Dell clenches his jaw and squares his stance. "You *did* know," Arco hisses, narrowing his eyes.

"They have to be stopped," Dell finally answers like it's the most obvious thing in the world.

"So you agreeing to help us because you saw I was fighting for something more than just being *cage-rattled*? All that about wanting to help me *pound the lock* on the cage instead...?" I trail off, trying to decide if I was manipulated or not.

"That was the truth," Dell nods immediately. "But I never said I thought you were the only one pounding. If the State keeps snatching people from *all those* places, and somebody is aiming to stop them, I mean...ain't that just the biggest lock of all?"

CHAPTER 49
The Cliffs

I push my hands over my face trying to make everything slow down. If the State is actually behind what Gaia is doing to people, how can we possibly stop them? *It's too big...*I think just as Liddick meets my eyes.

There are others who know, Rip. They've known for a long time. We're not alone in this.

"So what exactly are we walking into here?" Avis asks in a thin voice, and I can feel the cold pressing down on us while trying to process Liddick's ridiculous suggestion that we are now somehow going *into space.*

"We're not going home after we get to the mountain..." Myra says like saying it out loud will help her accept it. In the same breath, I feel a ripple of anger shoot out from everyone, which I feel hit Liddick too.

"We can't go home," he says defensively, exhausted by the concept. "Don't you think that's the first place they'll look for us? Right now, Gaia can't tip their hand. They can't let anyone topside know that we're gone, so our families are safe, at least for now. But if we try to go back...you saw how they made the Ripley's dad disappear," Liddick explains, and Arco shakes his head and narrows his eyes.

A dull ache starts at the bottom of my chest and quickly turns to a sharp, unrelenting stab. When I look up, low level flames are running across Arco's shoulders and down his arms, and the cords in his neck pulse with his heartbeat.

"*Arco...*" I say quietly, but then Liddick turns to face him and makes everything worse.

"And if *Nann* were next?" he asks. "What if they took Jazz's little sister next, Hart, and you had a chance to stop them, but chose to quit while you were ahead?" he pushes, which only makes Arco's fire flash. Jax takes a step forward and grips his shoulders, but not before sending a level glare at Liddick.

"Take a breath, man. You can't light up in here—look around," Jax says in a low voice just before a few drops from the melting ice ceiling fall onto Arco's cheek. He blinks, then squeezes his eyes shut and takes in a long breath. His hands close into fists, and slowly, his flames recede.

"Why didn't you just tell us?" Zoe asks Dell the question everyone must be thinking.

*Why didn't you tell **me**?* I think toward Liddick. He turns back to me slowly, then sighs and angles his head in apology.

Rip...I had to be sure, he answers just as Dell speaks up.

"Because everyone believed me about the labs in the mountain, right? Anyway, didn't see the point in getting everyone all worked up with questions until we got all the details worked out," Dell says casually.

"What *details*?" Cal shakes his head, pinching the arrow-scarred bridge of his nose. My chest compresses when I look at him, desperate for more information that will somehow offset his feeling of...*betrayal*?

"Well, for starters, we didn't know the bridge would be fit for traffic until about ten minutes ago. Seems a little unnecessary to get all your skivvies in a bunch over zipping to space if it turns out we don't even have a ride, wise?" Dell explains like this is the most obvious answer in the world, and I see how he and Liddick are more alike than I ever realized. "I mean, don't that make sense?" he asks after a few seconds.

"But it's not the *point*," Arco growls.

"We need to know everything. Right now," Jax says, staring right through Liddick as I brace against the wash of mixed emotions…anger, by far what everyone is feeling most, including me, but also excitement, hope, fear, panic…*admiration*? If I'm honest, I think the latter might be mine.

"That's everything," Liddick starts. "We were going to tell you when we had confirmation that the bridge could work—it's not like it's easy to hack into a channel for Admin City—but as deep as this goes, heading there was inevitable the second we decided we were getting out of Gaia," he adds, scanning everyone's faces for understanding, which he doesn't find. He resets, exasperated. "Look, I don't know what fantasy land you're living in if you really think they are just going to let us walk out of that mountain with our people and go back to the surface…" Liddick stiffens, then nods at Arco. "That's what you think, Hart? We're just going to climb home through some tunnels?"

"There are protocols…agencies in place that—" Arco begins, but Liddick's guffaw interrupts him.

"Agencies!? You must be kidding...wake up, man—did you really think for five seconds the State was innocent? See, your problem is that you don't know anything about the world beyond the Seaboard beach. They've been lying to us our *entire* lives, don't you get that yet? Do any of you get it?" Liddick throws out his hands to the group just as Arco's flames snap from his shoulders again. He advances, and I hold out my arm.

"Arco, *stop!*" I say, then see the surprise register on his face. "Just hear him out," I add, which doesn't walk him back, but it makes him take a minute. He heaves a breath, and Jax brings him in with a few words close to his ear that I can't make out.

"What they're doing is wrong," Liddick starts again. "None of you are stupid, and after *everything* we've found out so far, the only reason you're not half-split with outrage just like I am is because you're still holding out for that Gaia career and lifestyle fantasy. It's an easy lie to believe, but it's still a lie. The sooner we start accepting that, the faster we'll be able to do something real about it," he adds just as another dull ache starts behind my eyes and in my teeth. My heart pounds in my ears, and in that minute, I know he really believes every word of what he's just said. And also, that he's right. I have to speak up.

"After my interview didn't tell me anything about what I was supposed to be, I didn't know how to let go either," I say, turning to Arco, then to everyone. "But we really can't go home. We can't go on with our Gaia paths either, and we knew that the minute we escaped...we just weren't ready to believe it. At least I wasn't, and I haven't known what's going to happen next since then. It's terrifying, but what makes me feel better is that we're together. Pretty soon, we'll get to that mountain, and we'll have more help. The only way out of this is through, I think. All the way through."

No one says anything in reply at first, but the desperate feeling in my chest gives way as Avis and Ellis start nodding, and then Arco takes a deep breath.

"I don't like you, Wright," he says to Liddick, who bristles and narrows his eyes. "I've never liked you, and I probably never will because how you operate is mind bending."

"Arco..." I start, but he just keeps going.

"Maybe I just don't *understand* your justifications for what you do, but you know what, I really don't care. I don't *want* to understand...and that's how I know it's personal," he adds, confusing me with his sudden change of course. "I'm good with that, honestly," he shrugs, then glances at me. "But a leader has to be objective," Arco says, taking another breath, and I smile at him. "So, I can't set the tone on this—if everyone accepts this new trajectory, I guess we're going to space..." he pushes out a breath, closing his eyes and shaking his head before meeting Liddick's eyes again. "But you better be up front with developments from now on," he continues, narrowing his eyes. "It's not just you in this boat anymore." It's so quiet when Arco finishes talking that I can hear everyone's breaths in addition to seeing them in the cold air, and all eyes fall on Liddick.

"Fair enough," he answers after a few more seconds, and for the first time, I believe they might actually be on the same page about something. "So what's your verdict?" Liddick asks, looking out at our group.

No one says anything at first. I look at Jax, and we nod to each other at almost exactly the same time. Fraya nods too, and I raise my eyebrows hopefully to Tieg. He sighs, pressing his lips into a line, but then also nods.

"All right...then we're doing this," I say after registering everyone's assent, and the air seems electric until Zoe starts hopping up and down at the front of the group next to Dell.

"So, not to harsh everybody's soliloquies and all, but some of us aren't wearing your smart suits with the climate controls. Can we giddy-up here now?" she asks. Her teeth start to chatter erratically until she locks her jaw in a panic, and I'm not sure if the rush of bright pink in her cheeks is from the cold, or from the embarrassment I feel immediately spilling out of her. Dell belly laughs and throws an arm around her, rubbing her arm quickly until she elbows him in the side as we start walking again.

"You aiming to friction fire this whole igloo or something?" she laughs until her teeth chatter again, and she slaps her hand over her mouth.

"So we're about to go fight for the *planet* is basically what you're telling us?" Ellis asks from the other side of Liddick. He raises a thin, dark eyebrow at him that then gives way to a smirk.

"Good thing it's not our first scrap," Liddick answers.

"Dibs on naming the virtuo-cine they make about us. *Cloud Rider* has a nice ring to it, no?" Ellis adds, and there are only a few groans among the chuckles that pop up from around the group as the tension officially recedes.

Thank you, Liddick thinks from just ahead of me. *You didn't have to take up for me back there.*

You were right. It just took me a while to let go…it's a hard thing, I answer, watching Dez weave through the group to walk next to Liddick.

I fought it for a long time before I read the writing on the wall…before I stopped clinging to the way I thought things were supposed to be and just started letting them be what they were.

Dez weaves her arm around his, and I roll my eyes at the ridiculous parallel he's trying to set up.

I know what you're doing, I think. *This isn't the same thing as you and me. Liddick.*

I didn't say it was…but it's interesting you saw enough similarity to argue about it, he says, and I don't have an answer for that. We walk on for several more minutes before Arco finds his way to me after talking with Jax, and I smile up at him when he takes my hand. *By the way,* Liddick starts again. *Dez thinks she had some kind of fever dream after the tunnel shark. She said she called you every name out there because I was shouting that I loved you for the whole world to hear. Now she's too embarrassed to face you, even though she didn't really do anything. Isn't that funny?* he asks. Heat pushes over my throat and into my cheeks, pulling me to him all over again as I remember him calling out. At the same time, I feel completely stupid for thinking Dez had some kind of agenda and shake my head, trying to clear the whole thing before I lose sight of everything.

Liddick…it just won't—

"How far are we?" he calls up to Cal and Dell, stopping my thought before I can finish it.

"We just need to cross the Cliffs into the Woods, then come out the other side at the foot of the mountain," Dell answers, then jerks his chin forward to the sparkling blue, shadowy corridor that extends in front of us. "The chasm is right at the end of this."

***

I walk the rest of the way with Arco's arm around my waist. I'm not dizzy anymore, but it seems to temper the air around him. I rest my head on the side of his chest and can't stop feeling like there's something unsettled, something unanswered in him…an uneasiness that being close to him helps to offset. Just as there's finally an opportunity to ask him about it, the crystals in the cave start to shift from blue to white as the light from the gas clouds returns, and I have to raise my hand to shield my eyes until they can adjust to the brightness. After a minute, green grass peeks out through the packed ice and dark rock just beyond the edge of the crystal cave, and evergreen trees spring up in all directions. In the distance, more mountain peaks shoot up from bases I can't see, and the air is biting and cold.

"These are the Cliffs," Cal says. "The Woods are across that," he adds, lifting his chin to the ravine that looks like the edge of the world in the distance.

"How are we supposed to get over there?" Tieg asks, looking first to the left, then to the right.

"See the ridge?" Cal answers, pointing toward what looks like the empty center of the ravine until I see the edge of a jutting, narrow rock ledge bridging the two sides of the cliffs. "It's the only way," Cal says. "I tried to find *any* other way..." he adds, rubbing his mouth with the back of his hand after he takes a drink from his container. Dell nods just before he looks at the ground, and their combined sense of foreboding thickens the air all around us.

"What's the problem?" Liddick asks, obviously feeling the heaviness too as he lifts a hand to the ridge. "We can't just walk across?" he adds. Dell and Cal exchange glances.

"It's only about a foot wide in places, maybe less," Cal answers.

"And there's a wind. It tries—" Dell stops himself, then seems to decide something. "It tries to make you do things. That's the only way to say it."

"*The wind*? Because it's not enough it can just blow you right off the ridge, right? It has to jack with you first?" Tieg nods, then throws his hands in the air before pushing them through his short sandy hair. He turns his back to us and then startles everyone when he screams at the tops of his lungs. The sound echoes just as loudly before *the echo* repeats itself in the canyon too, making the hair on the back of my neck stand on end and my skin prickle all the way down my spine.

"It comes from the Woods—the whispering is in the trees there too," Cal adds.

"This is *stupid*! How are we supposed to fight that?" Tieg shouts back to us. "You got any ninja moves or machetes for whispers? Of course not," he adds, then clasps his hands behind his neck and walks a few more steps away from everyone.

"What if we cover our ears? Like Odysseus said to do for the Sirens, wise?" Zoe suggests, her red eyebrows shooting up in optimism.

"Doesn't work," Dell says. "The wind will just go through your nose or your eyes to get into your head. The only way around is through."

"So how do we do that?" Avis asks.

"Find your reason. The one reason you've come this far—the one reason you have to get to the other side no matter what," Dell answers, then cuts a glance at me. "It's the only way to get out of here."

Jax grips my shoulder, and I take a deep breath as Dell and Cal gesture for us to follow them toward the edge of the cliff where the ridge starts.

My heart hammers in my chest with each step we take. It feels like I've forgotten something important that I'm going to need….a desperate kind of fear that makes me scramble inside myself for an alternative. Arco grips my hand and looks down at me.

"Hey, are you OK?" he asks, "Can you breathe?"

I nod, but my heart feels like it's pushing against my ribs with every beat.

"The hole is all healed," I say, bringing a hand to my side. "I just can't get my feet under me," I add, and my throat starts to close.

"Listen," he says, studying my face as he brushes my cheek. "It will be all right. It has to be because we've come too far. I have to believe—" he starts, then swallows and regroups. "It just can't all be for nothing now. We're going to cross. We're going to get into that mountain, and we're going to find our way home…eventually," he nods, then brings his other hand to my face. "Don't accept anything else," he adds, nodding once more before he kisses me, softly at first, but then like it will be the last time. I hold onto his wrists as he rests his forehead against mine. "I love you so much," he whispers, then pulls me into him, wrapping his arms around me and sending tiny prickles down the back of my neck. He blows out a quick, hard breath like there's a candle just past my ear a few seconds later, and I realize why when he chuckles. "Get that out of your system now…no lighting up on the ridge, OK?" he laughs, then sobers and meets my eyes. "Only one outcome…" he whispers, and I nod just before he grips my hand again as we approach the cliff edge.

Dell kneels at the edge and puts his hands on the rock under his feet, then lowers his head and closes his eyes. He picks up a rock in each hand as he rises, then turns to face everyone.

"Just walk your line. There's nothing else—no monsters except the ones you bring with you, so leave them here," he says, then takes a deep breath. "Don't look down, and don't look back, no matter what happens, no matter what you hear. Nothing is real until you're on the other side, wise?"

My heart thrashes against my ribs like they're iron bars, beating against them so loudly I almost can't hear anything else. Dell looks at me one last time and nods just once before he turns around and starts to walk across the ridge, which is about three feet wide and covered in veins of limestone that spill into the chasm below. *Other people pound the lock*…I hear echoing in my head, a stray, secret weapon thought stored away for just this moment, and it is exactly what I need. I lock eyes with Jax, and he mouths the word *breathe* to me. I take a deep breath, and raise my index finger to him. *Our one thing*, I think, and I know he understands.

Cal and Zoe start walking next, and Arco crosses his arms over my shoulders, pressing his chest to my back as we watch them. He leans down and whispers in my ear.

"I'm right behind you," he says, then kisses my temple. I look back at him and nod, then see Liddick standing just off his shoulder.

Just one more cliff edge, Riptide, he thinks. *Nothing to fear, not even in falling…remember?* He flattens his hand over his heart, and I feel the beat of it competing for space in my chest, pushing everything else out of the way…all the nerves, all the fear, and then I feel it beat against the palm of my hand at my side.

We start walking to the cliff edge, and I look over my shoulder again at Jax, Arco, and Liddick, then take two short breaths and one more, then none at all as I look out over the long, narrow path before my first steps over the chasm.

CHAPTER 50
The Wind and the Chasm

The wind comes up within the first ten feet of crossing the chasm, and although it's cold, my steps feel sure because the ridge is at least three feet wide. I keep my eyes fixed on Dell, whose fists at his sides hold the rocks he took from the solid ground we just left. I know they're a reminder of his one reason—his concrete, solid reason for needing to get to the other side, but I don't know what that reason is other than maybe he believes that demons can't find any footing this high up, on this difficult a path, and with nowhere to hide. Maybe he needs to be free once and for all of his experiences in this place…to put an end to what Gaia is doing before anyone else has to go through it.

Other people pound the lock…those are the ones who get out…

The wind starts reverberating, and for a second I wonder if the hum in my ears is the precursor to another message from Vox, but her voice never comes…just the low humming of impossibly sized insect wings beating at the back of my teeth.

It's not real…the mosquito is gone. I killed it. I watched it burn. I will cross—I will cross because we have come too far. I will. I will…

Flames break through Zoe's shirt sleeves in front of me and I feel my breath hitch in my chest. She's losing her focus, and she's not even halfway across the chasm.

*Breathe…breathe…*I think, trying to push her…trying to send the message somehow on the very wind that's whipping her fire into a tangle over her head.

Her right sleeve falls away in a ball of red flames, and I have to force my eyes from following its trajectory into the chasm. Ash swirls upward from it, twisting into a little cyclone, and I see Joss's face in the sky—his neck and arms, his skin peeling away, his muscles fraying, disintegrating. I hear him screaming, and then see my own red fire in the corner of my eye.

Breathe…I'm right behind you…I'm right behind you…

I make my hands into fists and push down the tears that are burning the back of my throat.

I will cross…I have come too far, and I will cross!

But the tears come anyway. They burn my face until the wind hits them, and then they cool to a tickle that I don't dare move to rub out. The howling wind compresses until the low moan of it sounds like a pinched off scream, then a squeal that breaks into squeaks, then chirps and clicks, and every tickle on my cheeks becomes the dragging of legs, of stingers just waiting for an excuse, waiting for the slightest provocation like Dez and her ice lately, her cold shoulder because she thinks I want Liddick.

Some people are cage-rattled…

First Pitt…not him too…she can't lose him too…

Other people pound the lock…

My breath hitches again and I feel my heartbeat getting louder.

Pound the lock…

Breathe…

I'm hearing it. I'm hearing the wind just like Dell said we would…but he's wrong. It doesn't try to convince us of anything…it's just amplifying what we already know, at least deep down. *Liddick is another anchor for Dez…I think. She can be the bridge again. She can keep the peace between Liddick and Tieg just like she did for Pitt and Tieg. He puts her world back together.* The thoughts fly loose in my mind, and I almost feel dizzy, like my chest is cracking open and spilling everything inside into the chasm beneath me where I'm sure it will just keep falling forever. *No wonder…crite, Dez, no wonder you're so afraid…*I think, trying to keep my throat from closing up again.

Breathe…breathe…

But then she screams from somewhere behind me, and I'm instantly afraid that she fell.

No, Dez! Please, no!

I can't lose them, I can't lose them…

Dez, hang on! Liddick, tell her to hang on!

Just one more cliff edge…we'll do it together.

No! Liddick! Wait!

I don't know how to be with you when I have to accept that when you need someone most, he's the one in your head. He's the one who's right there.

Arco!

In the next breath, I see Nann, my little sister, pulling at my sleeve.

Jazz, will you port-call me?

My mother is waving to me as our shuttle pulls away, but then it sinks into the ocean, and she just keeps waving. She just keeps waving with Nann as we sink…as the water covers the little port window.

Welcome to Gaia, Jazwyn Ripley...

Ms. Rheen's red hair turns into fire, and her red dragon-lady nails scrape my arm when she clamps on my Gaia bracelet cuff.

Get out of my head...Get out of my head! I think, trying to push the wind out, but the flames from Ms. Rheen's hair turn into a *curtain* of fire. Inside it, I see the zippered mouths of the tunnel shark as Dez starts screaming all over again. *Get out of my head!* I think, then realize that the fire I see is real. It's my fire all around me! *No...no... breathe...I can't tweak out here. Not up here...breathe...*

Pound the lock! Pound the lock!

I will...I will!

I take a deep breath and blow it out, then another, and another, timing them with each of my steps. In....out...

I'm right behind you...

Count, Rip...just ten more seconds...one...

I told you I couldn't watch you like that again and not be able to do anything. So if he can get to you...if he can help you when I can't, then maybe you should be with him instead of me.

Arco! Wait!

Little breaths, Rip...two...

How can you not be tangled up with someone who always knows everything you feel and think?

Arco!

Three...four...I've got your back.

I'll never be able to do what he can do for you, Jazz, don't you see that?

The clouds thicken all around me, and I can't see Dell or Zoe anymore up ahead. I can't see anything anymore.

"Arco!!" I hear myself yell out loud.

I know it hurts, but just take little breaths…it doesn't make it wrong just because it scares you…

Liddick is next to me on the dune, the dark roots of his hair disappearing against the backdrop of night, which makes him look like a beach apparition. Then his lips are hard on mine in his room after his port-carnate disaster. *South American villages…*I hear him saying, then hear myself laughing from far away.

I love you—I know you can hear me. I love you…
The words echo all through the canyon, and then so does Arco's scream.

***

Something pulls me forward, and I land hard on the rock. I look at my stinging hands and see blood—real blood, my blood. But when I look around, I'm alone. I struggle to my feet only to fall again in the first step, hitting my knee on another rock in exactly the place where the material there is burned clean through. I watch the blood pool on my skin, hypnotizing me for a second until the wind howling in my ear pulls me out of it.

"Hello!" I shout, but I still don't see anyone. Dell, Cal, and Zoe were ahead of me. If I've finished crossing, they have to be here. "Dell!"

No one answers. I turn around to see who is coming after me down the ridge, but there's only rolling fog covering the chasm…*where's the ridge…they won't be able to see the ridge in that…I think. What if they're all gone? What if they all fell?*

*Our one thing…*I remember Jax's words. *Remember our one thing…*

But I don't want to remember. I want my brother, I want my friends…

"Sand dollar, run!"

I hear her. I actually hear her voice.

"Vox…*Vox!*" I yell her name out loud, but she doesn't answer me, and all I hear now is the steady buzz in my ears of where her voice used to be. *Vox!* I think.

Run, it's coming!

What's coming!?

The wind! Run! she answers in my mind this time, and I look around like it must be everywhere—anywhere, then I see the fog rising from the chasm out of the corner of my eye. It twists into the tubular dark rain clouds that look like the buckling blankets from over the Bale field, and then again from over the Sand biome, but then the clouds stack on top of each other three at a time in the same symbol that Azeris wrote on the Phase Three triangle he drew. I look back at the chasm now that the fog has lifted, but the ridge is gone.

"Jax!" I yell into it, taking a few running steps toward the cliff edge until the three wavy clouds start to swim toward me like synchronized snakes, slowly at first as I skid to a stop, then more quickly as I take steps backward. I turn to run again, and within a few strides the low howling fills my head.

"Jazz!" I hear Arco's voice coming from somewhere in the distance, and I run toward it, but then hear Liddick's voice coming from the place I just left as the fog swirls all around me.

"Rip! Riptide!"

I skid to a stop again, then slide on the slippery grass under my feet. I try to stop myself with my hands, but just manage to grind dirt into the scrapes on my palms. I dig my boot heels into the ground and stop sliding, then hear Tieg screaming.

"It's your fault! He's dead because of you!" he yells, but I don't see him anywhere.

"Dez! Tieg! Where are you!?"

"You already know I couldn't want anything more than that with her, Rip. I told you what I was coming for."

"Liddick!" I yell, but then hear the too fast, too high squealing of the marlin from our port-festival the night before we left for Gaia.

"I never saw it coming—I never saw it coming—"

"Stop! *Stop*!" I scream, then crawl under a big evergreen tree and push my fists against my ears, pressing my nose and mouth against my knees, then I squeeze my eyes shut so I can disappear inside myself.

And then I do, or it feels like I do. The wind stops howling, and the only thing I hear is the rustling and crunching of dried leaves until I see a long-eared brown rabbit, though I'm sure I haven't opened my eyes...*have I?* I'm afraid to move to find out. Its nose twitches, and then it looks right into my eyes.

"Our one thing," it says, then twitches its whiskers again, and now I'm sure I open my eyes as I push back from the rabbit, but it's not there anymore. The howling returns, and it feels like there's a boulder on my chest as I try to catch my breath.

*OK...OK...stop tweaking...*I think. *Why am I out here... why do I keep going? Dad...my dad. Even if everything else is gone, especially if everything—if everyone else is gone. But they can't be. They can't be gone because we've come too far.*

I get to my feet, and the wind picks up as if it's watching me—as if that's its countermove. It's biting cold, scraping my face again like the tree branches from when we ran through the Rainforest biome. The twisting clouds are gone, and the sky now is the same dark gray with surreal yellow light as it was back at the Bale field. As I remember this, the wind starts to feel like hands pushing me back—gripping and pulling me all the way back to the beginning of the Rush, or at least trying to, which only confirms that I have to go in this direction.

I have to go just like I had to stand up to Mr. Tark when he tried to intimidate me after the virtuo-cine beach attack by the Badlander cannibals. He wanted me to see that I could stand my ground. That's why he was proud of me so suddenly—why he gave up the act. That was the real test. This is the right direction—the mountain has to be on the other side of this wind because it wouldn't be pushing against me so hard unless it was trying to keep me away...stuck in these woods with the whispers and voices of all my fears and shortcomings, but I will cross out of here.

"I will cross out of here..." I yell. "I will. *I will!*"

"I'm right behind you..." I hear, but I'm afraid to turn around and discover he's just another trick of the wind. I don't move when I feel his hands on my shoulders, then his arms wrapping around me and pulling me back against his chest, and it's so much like him that for just one second, I don't care if it's real or not. But the second passes, and I know if I don't pull away right now, I may never see my dad, or anyone again. I try to push out of the hold, then hear my own sobs crashing in front of me.

"Just let me go...you're not him. I'm going to get my dad...I'm going..."

"And I said I'm right behind you," Arco says, still holding me against his chest. He *really* says it. I feel his warm breath on my neck and his fingers pressing into my shoulders like he's afraid I'm going to fall through the ground. "I'm right behind you..." his voice breaks, and he buries his face in my hair.

"Arco...?" I say his name, but my voice is so hammered flat by the pounding in my ears I'm not sure I do.

"The fog came. You screamed for me, and then you were...gone. *Crite*, you were gone..." he says, his voice collapsing on the last words.

I turn into him and throw my arms around his neck, clinging, gripping the fabric of his tattered, burned, torn dive suit until I feel his skin under my fingertips. He's holding me so tightly I can't breathe, but I don't care. I don't need to breathe because he's here. He's really here. We drop to our knees, and for a second I'm terrified all over again, pushing back from him so I can see him, but I can't see anything because of the tears burning my eyes, so I wipe them away with the back of my hand. I bring my fingers to the sides of his face, which are scraped and dirty except for the clean lines of new tear tracks.

"You're *here*…? You're here?" I say with the quietest voice I can so I don't alert anything that could be watching and waiting to take him away.

He nods, then swallows hard and kisses me like he's not sure I'm real either, like I'm made of glass…or air.

"Jazz!" Jax shouts, and by the time I look up he's already picking me up in a bear hug that crushes my ribs. I try to yell his name but I can't get enough of a breath, and I start coughing. "Sorry! Sorry…" he says, his heavy, dark brows knit together as he puts me down and starts pushing the hair out of my face. "You're OK? You're all right?" he asks, completely out of breath. I nod frantically because my voice is still choked off, then I see Ellis, Dell, Cal, and Zoe approaching. Tieg and Dez, Myra, Fraya, and Avis follow…but not Liddick.

"We thought you fell…crite, Jazz, we all thought you fell when we heard you scream for Arco," Fraya says, throwing her arms around me.

"No…no," I say, choking back tears. "Everyone disappeared in the fog, but that's when I crossed, I think. I landed on the rock at the edge of the Woods—these are the Woods, right? We're in the Woods biome?" I scan everyone's faces until I find Dell's.

"We're here. We made it," he says with a nod, then pushes his hand through his feathered brown hair, which clings to his temples with sweat.

"Liddick? Where is he? Where's Liddick?" I ask, and Dell's expression tenses as he shakes his head, pressing his lips into a line.

"He didn't come off the ridge behind me," he answers after a long minute.

"How do you know that? I came off the ridge behind you and you didn't see me. Liddick!" I shout, but don't even hear an echo.

"Jazz..." Dez says in a broken voice, then shakes her head as tears stream down her face.

"No! He's here somewhere. I would know if he were gone. Vox!" I scream into the trees. "Tell Azeris! Tell Azeris to find him!"

"Jazz! Stop...please stop..." Dez crumples into Tieg's chest, and Myra aggressively wipes the tears falling down her own face as she convulses in an effort to swallow her sobs, but I look away, refusing to acknowledge their fears.

"He'll head for the mountain," I say in an even, cool tone. "That's what I was doing. He'd know that...we need to keep going. We'll find him. I'll find him."

CHAPTER 51
Out of the Woods

The fog settles around our feet, but not so thickly that we can't see the grass, which gives way to black sand, and finally, the same volcanic glass and porous rock that was back at the Lookout Pier.

"This is it," Dell says. "We're out of the Woods."

"So, now we climb up there?" Arco asks, still gripping my hand as he cranes his neck to see the top of the volcano in front of us.

"No climbing," Dell answers while looking over his shoulder at the trees behind us, and I start to hear a low buzzing in my ears again as the light shifts and pulses on the ground several yards to our left.

"We *don't* climb up there?" Cal confirms under raised eyebrows, which wrinkle the diamond and arrow scars on his forehead. He shakes his head in disbelief as Dell aligns himself with a tall poplar tree that is situated between two evergreens, then walks back to the base of the volcano and runs his hands along the wall.

"Here," Dell says after several minutes, then pushes something that opens a panel in the ground exactly where the light was just shifting. "Let's go," he adds before disappearing through the opening, and I can feel a cold twist of anxiety in his wake.

Cal is speechless, his mouth hanging open until Zoe reaches over and taps the bottom of his chin, what's left of her leather sleeve burned to a gnarled edge at her shoulder.

"Can't wait to hear how you spin this for Veece," she says, then clicks her tongue against her teeth before slipping through the hole in the ground after Dell.

Inside, a narrow, white corridor wraps down a flight of stairs just beyond the hatch we've just come through. The passage reminds me of the relay sub that took us to Gaia Sur, and for a second, my stomach swims at the memory of the matter board and Vox creating a parson fish that almost got our entire cadet class disintegrated.

"Where do we go now?" Myra asks.

"We need to find Azeris and Vox," I say. "They were in a coolant room when I saw them in the vision."

"That's for the computer servers…this way," Dell says, taking us down the next set of stairs that eventually disappears straight into a white wall.

"Excellent—now what?" Tieg says, gripping the railing and looking over the edge, which leads to nothing but a white floor several flights down.

"Like I said, this way," Dell repeats as he puts his arms through the wall in front of him, then disappears into it. We all exchange incredulous glances, then push through after Dell and find him waiting on the other side.

"It's a *hologram*…" Myra says, and Dell knifes a finger over his lips. Once we're all through, he leads us around a corner toward a door with an unlit control panel, but I see another door with a panel of scrolling letter *As*— they're moving just like the ones Liddick and I saw in the Vishan caves when we first surfaced in the Stingrays. The panel is about ten feet ahead on the other side of the corridor, and the low buzz still in my ears gets stronger as I walk toward it. This must be where we need to go.

"Jazz!" Dell hisses at me, waving me back to everyone, but I shake my head and point to the door next to me.

"Azeris marked this one. See the letter *As*?" I answer, forgetting that only Liddick and I can see them until Dell just squints at me.

"The coolant room is this way!" he hisses again.

"Nobody is in there," I whisper back, then look at the holographic keypad. *How do I open you...*I think, and like they were magic words, letter *As* appear in succession over certain numbers...*1...1...1...3.* The pattern runs twice before I catch on, then push them in the order they flash. The panel slides open, and I look back at everyone just as surprised as they seem to be. "Come on," I say, walking through the doorway into a small room with nothing in it except a series of built-in metal console stations that stop abruptly against the metal back wall.

"There's no one in here," Dell says.

"They have to be in here...they coded the door," I say, confused until I see the back wall glint, then shifts into an *A* when I look directly at it. *Liddick?* I think, but don't hear anything in response. I walk toward the wall and lay my palms flat against it as I hold my breath and close my eyes, trying to push everything out of my head except for him. *You have to be here. You would know to meet up here just like I knew. We've come too far, Liddick...*I think as my throat closes, but I swallow and shake my head against the growing buzz that tries to drown out the words in my mind.

Jazz? I hear just as the wall in front of me dematerializes, and I see her sleeve shredded to the skin all the way up to her shoulder, her winding map tattoos marred with red scratches just like in my vision. Her burgundy hair is braided back from her face in several rows, and her light green eyes widen.

"Vox," I breathe her name, then watch the recognition spread over her face.

"I *knew* you'd make it..." she says, smiling until her expression falls as she scans our group. She looks back at me, and I can feel her pity starting to surface.

"Where's Azeris? Is he looking for Liddick?" I ask so abruptly that she flinches.

"After he programmed the false wall behind you, he went to jailbreak your dad. They locked him down when they found out he sabotaged the last test on Lyden and Arwyn—see?" she says, motioning to a series of embedded panel screens along the wall behind her. The one on the left shows footage of Azeris at a control panel in front of a large, clear box enclosure...*my father's.*

"Jax!" I call, motioning him over as the door to the enclosure suddenly opens. My father rushes out of it, and he and Azeris run through the lab doorway that closes immediately behind them. They slip around the corner just as a man in a long white jacket stops to key something into the door panel of the room they've just left.

That brief second of seeing our dad there makes the time between my heartbeats stop. For that frozen moment I can't move because I almost don't believe he was really there. I look back at Jax and nod, too shocked to cry, to talk, to do anything but look up at him and know that we've come all this way for a reason, and we're not going to stop until we're free. *All* of us.

"It's him…that was really him in there right now," Jax says at my side.

"That's what I just said," Vox adds, making her way past us toward the door. "Come on, we have to go."

"Wait!" I almost yell. "Liddick is still out there…we have to do something. How did you find me when I was in the Woods?" I ask, but she just shakes her head.

"I didn't…those clouds over the Woods weren't there when I came through. I didn't know what was happening when *you* transmitted to *me*…but when you did, I felt it coming for you," she says, her eyes widening again like she is afraid to blink because in the very second she does, something will jump out at her. "I just kept trying to talk to you telepathically. I was just as surprised as you when it worked."

"I didn't transmit *anything*," I answer. "I don't know how to do that. It had to be the NET," I add, but she just shakes her head and turns her eyes on Cal.

"How does it work?" she asks, but she's met with a level blue glare.

"It's different for each person," he finally starts to answer. "It's like a homing device—reads your frequency and projects it to others on similar frequencies," he adds, keeping her pinned in place with his eyes. "Want to tell me why you took it?" he follows, sharpening the last few words. Vox takes in a breath, then sighs as she tilts her head like she's trying to hear something far away. "*Well?* Of all the things, why take that?" Cal presses, pulling his bottom lip between his teeth as he raises his eyebrows at her. She looks back at him slowly with the beginnings of a smile.

"Because I knew they would send you to come after it," she answers, and we both feel the wave of nervous adrenaline that suddenly radiates from him. After several seconds, Cal fights back the smile by pressing his lips into a hard line, but his dimples betray him, and so do his eyes. He forces his eyebrows together and nods at the ground, and a grin spreads over Vox's face.

"All right, then give me the NET," I demand, turning back to Vox with my hand out. She looks at Cal, but I intercept his protest. "We have to try," I say. "Please..." After a second more, he nods to Vox, and she reaches into her collar to pull it from the chest panel of her dive suit. I wrap my fingers as tightly as I can around the metal Y-shaped bars, which are warm and heavy in my palm. *I know you didn't fall. I know you wouldn't leave me out here. I know you're coming to the mountain...*I think, trying to hold him in my mind as the NET suddenly vibrates the bones in my hand and wrist, the current of it running all the way up into my skull before it subsides. There is no vision of Liddick like I had of Vox when she had the NET, so I put it inside the chest panel of my dive suit in the same place she kept it. It hums again, but I still don't see anything. "OK, let's go," I say, clearing my throat and resolving not to spend one more second afraid.

***

We move through the long corridor, and for a second it feels like we're back in the passageways of Gaia Sur—the same lightly colored, rounded corners where the walls meet the ceiling and floor, the same seamless, opaque doors, and any doubt I may have still had about Gaia's... no, *the State's* agenda evaporates. It's really true. Our whole lives have just been a game to them. I feel my heartbeat jump when I realize this is almost exactly what Liddick said too. *I know you're coming. Just get to the mountain...*I think, hoping he can hear me even if he can't reply.

"Wait, this way!" Dell stops our group and looks at the walls, then nods to himself. He starts counting something in the flooring as he takes backward steps, then drops to his knees and drives the tip of his machete between the squares of two tiles. The illumination of one tile flickers, then goes out when Dell lifts one of the corners with the leverage from his blade. "We need to get to the labs first," he says.

"We don't have time for that!" Vox protests.

"I'm not leaving people behind again! The guards here are droid clones. If you can make it through the Rush, you can handle a few of them without me if you have to —I'll catch up," he says, slipping through the opening as Cal moves to follow him.

"I have to help him—after everything I doubted..." he trails off, looking at Zoe. "Can you take point?" he asks. Zoe nods after a second, and I see the smile start in the corner of her mouth as she raises an eyebrow at him.

"You mean I get to scrap without you two frogs underfoot for once?" she asks. Cal grins at her. "Well...

then *get!*" she adds, jerking her chin at the displaced flooring and throwing out an arm like she's trying to shoo him off. He nods to her with a wide smile that tacks dimples on each side of his mouth, then disappears after Dell. Her shoulders rise as she takes a slow, deep breath before she turns around to face us. "All right, then," Zoe says, rubbing her freckled nose with the back of her hand just before unsheathing her machete. "Let's go start a fight."

CHAPTER 52
The Bridge

Vox leads the way down several flights of stairs to rooms that look exactly like the ones I saw in the message my father and Liam sent during my advising session with Ms. Plume...the message showing the water filling in Lyden's enclosure, his gills appearing, and Arwyn lighting on fire, but not burning.

We pass lab after lab, some with the same transparent cube enclosures, standing pillar consoles, and seated console stations like the ones in the Boundaries room back at Gaia Sur. We walk a few more lengths of the corridor before Vox stops at a door panel, and a green holographic keypad appears. She punches in a code, which makes the readout scramble until the door slides open.

The room is white-walled, and looks like a mini amphitheater with two giant metal cubes where a stage would be. Three curved rows of seated panel stations that remind me of the ones on the Leviathan's navigation deck rise to the back wall on either side of the stairs, and a series of waist-high white pillars stand in an arc along the upper level back wall.

"Where is everyone? Lyden and Arwyn are supposed to be in here," Arco says, crossing behind one of the white pillars on the upper level next to the door. He taps the air above it until a green holographic screen appears like a little table, then chuffs a laugh. "These are programmed like the stations in the Boundaries room back at Gaia Sur," he says, then eyes the huge metal cubes at the front of the room and continues tapping the screen. I jump when the door behind us suddenly slides open again.

"Whoa, stop," Liam says, charging into the room wearing a silver, shimmering jumpsuit like our blue ones from Gaia Sur. "What did you press? Never mind—look out," he adds, catching his breath as he takes over the console where Arco is standing.

"*Liam*?" Arco asks, then shakes his head.

"The one and only—well, not technically, but I can't fix that yet. Are you spliced? Crite, I got here just in time…" Liam says, typing something onto the screen. "You almost lowered those walls…how did you even—? Never mind. Are you *spliced*?" he exhales, then looks up at us with the same intense blue gaze as Liddick. My heart drops into my stomach when I see the matching white scar running through his left eyebrow, but after a second, my eyes are pulled to a ring of light that appears on the floor between the two metal cubes. Liam nods to us. "So? Port-Carnate splice? Do you have one yet?" he asks Arco again, who shakes his head absently while looking at the cubes.

"What? No? Why can't the walls—" he starts, but Liam cuts him off.

"Then get in the coding field down there. Hurry up, we don't have a lot of time," he says impatiently.

Arco looks at me and raises his eyebrows, then starts for the circle, but I grab his sleeve.

"Wait! What about the nanites?" I ask, remembering how they almost killed Liddick when he tried to port-carnate transfer before we left Gaia, and my chest tightens at the thought of him again. Liam blows out a breath as he continues typing.

"Your repair-class nanites from Gaia Sur are dormant because you're out of range, and the stabilizer-class nanites are standard…neither of them will interfere with a transfer. The tunnel shark nanites Azeris said you had should be dormant by now, but if they show up in the scan, I'll purge them," Liam answers. "Let's go—get in the coding field!"

"Hang on!" I say, gripping Arco's arm again as he tries to walk toward the glowing circle. "Liam, listen, we have Vishan treatments now too…our DNA has been adjusted so we could come through the Rush," I add all in the same breath.

"*I know*, Vox already told us—that strand came from here, so it's in the database already. I'll strip it in the transfer before you get to Admin City…trust me, I've done my homework. Now, *please* get into the field!" Liam says through his teeth to Arco, who nods at me.

"It's all right. I'll be all right," he says, gripping my hand before he makes his way down the stairs to the circle, which glows brighter and starts to hum when he crosses into it. Liam pushes another button combination on the holographic screen, and Arco immediately doubles over gripping his knees.

"Whoa…" Jax says at my shoulder as everyone else exchanges worried glances.

"Hang on!" I try to shout above the low hum that sounds like it's coming from the inside of my head, then remember the feeling of my stomach being pulled away from the rest of my body when I was being rigged for port-carnate…when I thought I was just helping Liddick launch the piggy-back code before we left Gaia. The NET starts to vibrate over the ache in my chest at the memory, and I hold my breath as it passes.

"All right! You're good—next!" Liam says as the circle light dims and Arco stumbles out of it. I rush under his arm to help him stand.

"Are you OK?" I ask, but he's already nodding.

"Just dizzy," he exhales, wrapping his arm around my shoulder as he straightens and presses his thumb and forefinger against his eyes.

"Here, sit down," I say, leading him to a seated console panels like the ones in the Leviathan. Jax moves into the circle next, then Fraya, then I stop noticing—I stop breathing when I see Azeris come through the doorway with my father.

He's older than I remember, and of course he would be. It's been five years, but he looks like he's aged twenty. His dark, curly hair is streaked with gray, and his narrowed brown eyes that are just like Jax's are edged in lines. His heavy brows dart together when he sees me, and it feels like my chest is going to explode.

"Jazwyn…" he says, but my name sounds like it's made of air. He meets me at the bottom of the steps, then moves his hands over my face.

"Dad!" Jax calls as he makes his way to us, stumbling out of the circle after his splicing.

"Jaxon!" our dad shouts, gripping the back of Jax's neck and pulling him into a hug with us, and for this one second everything else is quiet. I make it quiet. I force out the scramble of everyone's emotions swirling around me, especially the doubt that keeps trying to pull me into it like a black hole. I force out Liam's hurried, shouted commands, and I grip the white fabric of my father's jumpsuit, which is thick and smooth under my fingertips. I grip his arms to make sure he won't disappear, and he doesn't.

"They told us you died at the hydrogen plant in an explosion," Jax says into our father's shoulder, and he pulls us in even more.

"I'm sorry. I couldn't stop them until now," he says. "I promise I'll tell you everything, but right now Arwyn and Lyden—" he starts, but is cut off by Zoe rushing past us on the stairs to jump into Azeris's arms.

He presses his cheek into her shoulder, lifting her off her feet and holding her there in total stillness for what seems like several minutes before he puts her down and brings both hands to her dirt-smeared, freckled face, then pushes the hair out of her eyes.

"You look just like your mother…" he says in a rough voice. Zoe curls her fingers around his wrists, and his eyes catch her gold adjoining *As* bracelet. He swallows hard as his jaw tightens, "Crite, just like her." Azeris looks up hopefully. "Is she…?" he starts to ask, but abandons the question when Zoe shakes her head after a second more. He nods quickly and presses his lips into a hard line as Liam clears his throat.

"Everyone is spliced. We don't have a lot of time since they expedited the Phase Three transfer—did you jam the doors?" Liam asks my father from the pillar console.

"I could only program a seize code in the time we had, we might be cutting it close," he answers, and Liam blows out a relieved breath. "Did you launch the reroute coordinates?" my father asks, and Liam nods.

"I did it as soon as I heard about the expedited transport—should be at least five percent encoded by now," he answers, then turns to Azeris. "How close is Liddick now?" he asks.

The temperature in the room falls when Azeris just takes a deep breath, but I shake my head, refusing to let in any doubt.

"His channel frequency is offline, but that could be interference from the environment," Azeris answers after a long pause. "He knows where to go...I coded the path from the edge of the Woods all the way to this room, and he knows the bridge plan," he adds.

"What exactly is the bridge plan again?" Tieg asks, crossing to one of the seated consoles to put his arm around Dez, whose tears have started all over again. My father sighs as he turns to face the rest of our group, all of us now mixed throughout the rows.

"The quick version is that we couldn't get through the firewall to cancel Lyden's and Arwyn's port-carnate transfer to Phase Three, but we found a way to reroute it to different coordinates in Admin City," he starts to answer, then nods to the metal cubes behind us. "Liam and Azeris built a data bridge that connects those hubs with Phase Three. I encrypted it so no one can use it to follow us," he says. "Rheen and Styx won't know where we land once we transfer."

"What's their reroute status?" Azeris asks, looking over at Liam.

"Twelve percent—almost there," he answers, glancing at his screen. Azeris nods.

"Wait, so they're in here?" Arco raises his eyebrows at the metal cubes and straightens in his seat.

"Yes, but we can't lower those walls until the new coordinates are at least 15 percent encoded, or the magnetic field down here could alter them," my father answers. "It won't be long now. As soon as Lyden and Arwyn transfer, we'll follow, and our contacts from Admin City will help us enter the virtuo-cine network. We'll destroy the Gaia mainframes from the inside... including the one for this facility."

Ellis suddenly shakes his head and holds out a hand like he's trying to stop someone from advancing.

"Are you saying that we're going to port-carnate our *own* atoms into the virtuo-cine network? Not our hologram with the port-cloud atom overlays?" he asks, narrowing his eyes as he leans back against the side wall with Avis, who clasps his hands behind his neck.

"These won't be your typical virtuo-cines," Azeris grins. "15 percent!" he says, then types onto his screen, and the tall, metal walls of the cubes at the front of the room slide into the floor.

CHAPTER 53
Transcending

The metal walls of the cubes in the front of the room disappear into the floor to reveal two clear enclosures that are the same size as the original cubes. Arwyn is standing in one of them with her hands pressed to the wall that faces us, her long, light brown hair falling half-braided over her shoulder. Her silver jumpsuit is like Liam's, but hers is singed at the cuffs. Arco's breath catches, and he pushes to his feet.

"*Arco...*" she says, but I can barely hear her muffled voice.

"Open the door!" he shouts, knocking over the chair of the seated console station. It clatters to the floor as he crosses to his sister and presses his palms to hers through the wall.

"Can't. The transfer already started," Azeris says from behind one of the pillar consoles along the back wall of the room's upper level. "She'll die if you open it now," he adds, which makes the blood run out of Arco's face.

"You got so tall..." Arwyn says as tears stream over her high, delicate cheekbones—her wide, hazel eyes just like Arco's closing tightly and opening again as she blinks back tears. Arco clears his throat, and it feels like my chest is being compressed on all sides.

Can you hear me? A voice says from all around me, and then I realize it's in my head. I instinctively turn to Lyden in the other cube enclosure. His eyes are clear and blue like his younger brothers', but his hair isn't blond with dark roots like Liam's and Liddick's. It's brown and shaggy like Dell's, and the veins in his forearms stand out as he clenches his hands into fists and holds them against the wall that separates him from the rest of us. *Jazwyn, listen,* he thinks again, and I nod, stunned that he can talk to me telepathically.

You're a Hybrid too? A Reader and a Coder? I ask.

Yes, listen to me. I lost Liddick. I was leading him here through the Woods, talking to him like this, but then I lost the connection. It could have been because they started the port-carnate transfer, but it could be that—

I know what Lyden wants to say, but I won't hear it. I won't even let him think it.

*You said you lost the connection in the Woods? Then he made it over the Chasm. I knew he didn't fall...*I swallow hard, then try to concentrate on Liddick again. The NET resonates against my chest, but I still can't see or hear him. *Why doesn't this stupid thing work*!? I shout in my head, then turn around to find Vox, who is already on her way to me. I reach into my dive suit and pull out the NET, then extend it to her.

"I can't—" she says out loud, shaking her head as her burgundy eyebrows dart upward.

"You made me see you, and you could see me out there," I interrupt. "Make him see you. Find him. You're Vishan, it must only work for you," I say too loudly, but she just shakes her head again.

"I don't know how it worked—I told you," she says, shoving the NET back at me. I try to protest, but she doesn't give me a chance. "Look, *you* showed up in my neural channel when you were in trouble. *You* found *me.* We've been over this," she insists.

"So why can't I find *him*?" I ask, then hear Azeris from the back of the room.

"Closing in on twenty percent DNA transfer!" he calls, reading the floating screen in front of him.

"Bridge integrity?" my father asks, climbing the stairs to Liam and looking down at his screen.

"It's good. They're on course," Liam answers.

Jazwyn, Lyden thinks again, and I turn back around. *I don't have a lot of time. Listen, I don't believe Liddick is gone. Maybe we lost the connection because he's blocked—because he saw something out there, heard something in the Woods. The wind can get inside your head...I know because I coded it to do exactly that. If he's lost, you have to show him where to go.*

"We're at thirty percent!" Azeris calls out as Liam types as fast as he can.

"Still on course—the bridge is holding!" Liam says, then shifts his attention to Lyden. "Hang on! You're almost there. Is Liddick past the Chasm? Why isn't he here yet?" he asks. Lyden tries to answer loudly enough to be heard through the enclosure wall, but I can feel that he's not strong enough now. He meets my eyes, and I know I'll have to explain what he said about Liddick. "It's OK, just be still...too much of your base has transferred. We'll meet you on the other side of the bridge, all right? Calyx will be there when you arrive. Hang on!" Liam says as Lyden slides to his knees, then leans against the side of the wall.

"Arco, you have to back up…your sister is all right, but she has to stay perfectly still," my father says, and Arco reluctantly backs away from Arwyn's cube.

"Where's Liddick?" Liam asks, crossing to Azeris as my father takes over his console.

"I don't know. I can't get into his neural channel," Azeris says. "It's still offline."

"How can it still be offline? Lyden tracked him crossing the Chas—" Liam stops abruptly, and the hollow in my chest opens again at his dawning fear.

"No! He's coming!" I yell, feeling the crushing doubt all around me pressing into my lungs again. "Lyden just said he lost the connection in the *Woods*. He didn't fall into the Chasm, Liam. He's just…lost."

"Then I'm going to find him," Liam says, taking a step toward the door panel that leads out of the room.

"Stop and think!" my father calls to him without looking up from his hovering screen. "You won't make it to the drop floor entrance before they find you, let alone into the Woods. Guards will be flooding the passages as soon as they crack the seize code I put on the doors, which won't be long now," he adds.

"Fifty percent!" Azeris shouts. "Get everyone into position!"

"They're disappearing!" Arco lunges toward Arwyn's cube, but Jax catches him.

"They're transferring—it's normal. Both of you get back before that current surges!" Azeris calls.

"I can't just leave him out there!" Liam shouts to my father, and in this minute he both looks and sounds exactly like Liddick.

"He's come this far, and he beat the Chasm. He's navigated enough virtuo-cines *and* their alpha channels to know how to handle any of the anomalies out there. He'll make it, son," my father says, lowering his voice and raising his eyes to meet Liam's.

"We're at seventy percent!" Azeris says as my dad punches something else into his console. He grips the sides of it when Liam starts to protest again.

"Listen to me, I just preloaded our hop, but it's still going to take about thirty minutes to initiate," he says, then gestures to the cube enclosures at the front of the room. "When they complete their transfer, I need everyone locked inside those hubs right away so no one can stop us. Get everyone in position, all right? We will find Liddick, I promise," he says.

Liam nods after a second as the muscles in his jaw jump and twitch. He takes a deep breath and pushes his hands through his hair just like Liddick does when he's frustrated, pulling the blond back from his forehead to reveal the same dark roots.

He blows out a breath and makes his way to the lower level with the rest of us, but as he does, the buzzing in my ears starts again. At the same time, the metal bars of the NET in my hand start to resonate, then pull at my fingers like they're somehow magnetized. My heart starts to pound as I scan for Vox to see what this means, but then I freeze in my skin when the door to the room slides open.

***

"Jack Ripley! I've always said you were more trouble than you were worth," Styx says, stroking his pointed black beard just like he did in my Gaia interview. He glides halfway down the wide steps of the room's entryway, the edges of his lab coat flying away from his white military uniform. Two of the six guards in black with him drag my father away from the pillar console along the back wall while two other guards in white remain at his sides. He waves a hand casually at Azeris before taking a seat on one of the long, flat stations that arcs into the wall on the far side of the steps. Azeris quickly types something onto the hovering screen of his console, then blows out a breath just before two of the guards in black grab him too.

"They transferred into the hub across the hall and broke the seize code. I just locked everything down again —the codes on the rest of the doors are still in tact!" Azeris calls to my father as I shove the NET back into my dive suit, then feel Liam grip my upper arm. He pulls me under the console where I'm standing, and I see Vox already crouched in front of us near the aisle.

"It has to end, Eros," my father says as the guards in black drag him down a few of the stairs to Mr. Styx. Jax starts to advance from behind a seated station across from us, but Arco holds him back.

"Oh, but it's just begun!" Styx says, extending both hands out to Arwyn and Lyden, who are slumped motionless against the walls of their cube enclosures at the front of the room. "After all, these two are perfect thanks to you. The first candidates no longer to be limited by water, by pressure, or by heat. The cold and the atmosphere of Phase Three are all that stand in the way of us being able to transcend our environment...and *oh look,* they're on their way there now! I hope you understand why we didn't ask for your consult with the expedited transport. You have a history of...complicating things," Styx adds.

"Transcending the elements is *not* worth this price! There are other options! How much blood is on your hands already? Yours and Rheen's?"

"You give us too much credit, Jack. This is bigger than transcending the elements. This is bigger than all of us. It's the future, and unfortunately, you are the past," Styx adds with a shrug, then looks over his shoulder directly at Jax. "So good to see you again, Mr. Ripley," he says, still smiling at Jax as he angles his head to the remaining guards in black. "Take him."

CHAPTER 54
The Connection

I start to shout as the guards in black uniforms advance on Jax, but Vox covers my mouth, and Liam catches my arm before I can get all the way to my feet.

"Listen, *listen!*" Liam says. "Light will flood those cube hubs any minute. When it does, we have about ten seconds before Lyden and Arwyn finish transferring. When the light stops, the queue will start. You need to get inside then, understand?" he says, looking first to Vox, then to me. "*Don't* close the doors until everyone is in—your dad wrote chaser code that will lock them once they're shut, then camouflage the bridge coordinates so no one can follow us to Calyx, our contact in Admin City, all right?" he adds before nodding at us. "Get ready to shield your eyes. I'll start funneling the others to you when the light goes out." He nods once more, then crawls to the outside aisle and up to the back wall where guards are holding Azeris.

You can take your hand off my mouth now, I think, pushing Vox's arm away when I realize she's still holding onto me.

Then stop trying to use it to get yourself killed, she answers, but I can't say anything else before a tidal wave of light starts at the back of the room and rolls forward.

"Sir, there seems to be a problem with the trajectory!" the guard at one of the pillar consoles says. A second later, the cubes next to us fade into the blinding light.

We start to head for the cube doors when we can see again, but Jax and Arco put their hands in the air as a guard behind each of them holds a white baton to their backs, just waiting for them to move. I stop, then see Liam typing something onto the hovering screen of a pillar console along the back wall. Almost immediately, all the guards except the ones in white uniforms standing with Mr. Styx collapse into motionless heaps.

"DNA clone strand B-17, goodnight!" Liam says with a satisfied laugh, then waves us into the cube enclosures. "Go! Get in!"

"Jazz, hurry!" Arco shouts as Vox grabs my shoulder.

"Time to go," she says, but I pull out of her grip when one of the guards in white shocks my father with a baton, making him drop to his knees. I race up the stairs to him.

"Jazwyn, no!" Liam yells, but I'm already too close.

"Bring her to the labs!" Styx shouts to the white-uniformed guards, and my father coughs violently when the one who shocked him grabs my hair and holds the baton to my throat.

"My pleasure," the other guard in white says as she pushes back her beret, then sneers as only one other person I know can.

"*Sarin?*" I say, barely recognizing our classmate from Seaboard North, ranked number seven out of our top ten. She looks down her long, broomstick nose at me with eyes that are now a strange shade of lavender instead of brown like before, and her normally olive skin seems lighter too. When she smiles, even her teeth have been changed to look just like Dez's and Tieg's solid, bioengineered white bar, but there's no mistaking the shiny black hair tied back so tightly I'm not sure how she can blink.

"Don't struggle, Jazwyn, and you won't get hurt," the guard behind me says. I turn my head just enough to see pieces of choppy blonde hair and a cold, unnaturally blue gaze under the beret of Quinn Stallwart, who was ranked fifth in our class from Seaboard North.

"*Quinn*? But...why?" I whisper.

"What did you think would happen when the long-term clones you made of yourselves back at Gaia expired after a few days, Jazwyn? You were all so *careless*. It was illogical to side with you when Ms. Rheen approached us," she says with almost no facial expression at all, and I'm stunned at how robotic she sounds, even for her.

"Let her go!" Arco shouts, already halfway to me with Jax, but Quinn tightens her hold on my hair and wedges the baton under my jaw.

"Stay back!" she yells, stopping them on the stairs.

*What can I move...what can I move...*I think, remembering Cal's training lesson in the circle arena at the same time I feel a prickle running down my arms and into my hands...*think of it like water*, I remember Kesh saying. Before it's too late, I raise my hands high enough so the fire shoots over my shoulders. Quinn must be immune to it like the other guards, but it distracts her long enough for me to grab her wrist as I twist into her, making the baton slip over my shoulder and into hers.

The last thing I see before the current runs through her and into me is Arco and Jax running up the rest of the stairs, but then I can't help closing my eyes, or at least I think I do, and everything disappears in a flash of white just like earlier. When I'm able to see again, Liddick is standing in a field of fog with a bloody lip and one shoulder of his dive suit burned through.

"Liddick!" I say out loud, wondering if the NET is finally working.

"Rip! Are you *all right*? Are you really there? Is that... *Quinn*? And Liam! You're at the mountain!"

"Yes!" I laugh, relieved. "But you have to hurry! We're following Lyden and Arwyn to the bridge!"

"Rip, wait!" I hear his voice one more time before he fades into the fog, and everything in the port-carnate transfer room returns.

Quinn is unconscious on the floor next to me, and I catch Sarin moving toward us in the corner of my eye. I only have time to suck in a breath before Vox spins her around, then punches her in the face so hard that she drops to the ground. She's down long enough for Vox to hold a baton against her leg, making her whole body seize until she passes out. Liam grabs Sarin's baton as Jax helps me up.

"Do you *know* how long I've wanted to hit her right in that needle nose?" Vox asks as I get to my feet.

"Are you OK?" Jax looks me up and down, but I don't have time to answer before Liam is in front of me scanning my eyes. He nods.

"She's fine. Get her in the hub," he says to Vox, then turns abruptly to the back of the room where Azeris has returned to one of the pillar consoles, and Styx is waving a silver baton to keep my dad and Zoe from blocking his path to the door.

"Stay clear," my father says, holding his stomach with one arm and extending the other in front of Zoe. "You won't get back up if that baton touches you."

"Can't touch me if it's on the ground with his hand," she smirks, gripping her machete and advancing on Styx.

"They broke the seize code on the doors!" Azeris says. "And the preload sequence started—we need to go *now,* Jack!" he shouts to my dad, who shuffles behind a console and types something, then sighs in relief.

"All right—Lyden and Arwyn are across the bridge, come on, come on!" my father says after punching a final combination onto his screen. Jax rushes under his arm to help him down the stairs, and we're almost to the cubes when at least a dozen new guards in black start pouring through the door.

"Zoe—get in that box!" Azeris calls as his console is overwhelmed, but she runs to help him with the influx instead.

My father stops suddenly just before entering the cube enclosure with us, then pulls the door shut behind Jax and Liam. They both turn abruptly and pound the clear wall as Fraya and Myra hold onto each other behind them.

"I need to help Azeris shut down those clones—we'll get in the other hub!" my dad says, but Liam and Jax keep yelling and pushing at the door.

"Jazz!" Arco calls from inside the other cube, and when I turn to face him, Vox is nodding over my shoulder. By the time I follow her eyes to my father, he is already walking me into the enclosure.

"Get in this hub, Jazwyn. When you come out on the other side of the bridge, our contact will be there waiting for you. Her name is Calyx—she'll help you," he says in a rush, then looks over his shoulder before continuing. "When the light starts, try not to move, all right? Everything will be OK."

"Wait! You're coming with us—you're hurt! You have to get in with us!" I repeat.

"Omni-class Nanites…I'll be fine in a minute. Trust me, I designed them," he winks. "We'll follow you soon. I love you so much, Jazwyn," he adds, then kisses my forehead quickly before he starts back up the side aisle, and I know he must be trying to sneak behind one of the pillar consoles like Liam did earlier. I don't have time to protest before I nearly trip over my feet when Vox pulls me through the doorway.

"We have to help them! Vox, let me *go!*" I struggle against her until Arco grips my hand, and in the second I stop fighting, Vox reaches into the collar of my dive suit and pulls out the NET. "*No! We have to—!*" I start, but am cut off when we hear a loud whistle, then see Cal, Dell, and about twenty other people our age dressed in silver jumpsuits like Lyden and Arwyn pushing into the room.

"They came back!" Avis says, shoving Ellis. "I *told* you they would come back!" he adds as Dell makes his way to Styx. Within two steps, all the new guards in black seize and collapse like they've just been unplugged.

"Did you know these batons could fry the white ones?" Dell asks Mr. Styx as he flips a silver baton into the air, then swats it against his leg. "Wonder what else they can do." He raises his brows and pushes out his bottom lip in contemplation as two of the new boys grab Styx from behind and force him to drop his baton.

Ellis and Avis cheer loudly behind me as Cal runs down the steps to us, and Vox bolts out the enclosure door. She grips his shirt and kisses him hard on the mouth, surprising everyone, including him until he wraps his arms around her waist, then pulls back to talk.

"*Why* didn't you wait? I thought you'd be killed without—" he asks, but Vox stops his sentence with another kiss, then presses the NET to his chest.

"Waiting will kill you too…it just takes longer to die," she says as the floor starts vibrating.

"Dad!" I shout, pushing past Tieg and Dez on my way out of the cube enclosure, but Vox just pushes me back inside, and Arco closes his arms around me. I struggle until the buzzing in my ears starts again, and my breath stops in my chest as the doorway at the back of the room slides open.

*Riptide…*Liddick thinks, then stumbles down the stairs. Dez shouts his name too close to my ear and rushes out the enclosure door.

"Dezzie, stop!" Tieg yells, running after her and abruptly knocking the door closed behind him in his hurry. I flinch backward as it slams, tears flooding my eyes while everything inside me crashes into itself.

Liddick, come on! I call to him in my mind, relieved that he is finally here. I try to reopen the door, but it won't release. *No…*I think, my stomach sinking as I remember what Liam said about the code my father wrote to lock the doors. *Liddick, tell my dad to unlock the door! You all have to get in. Liam said no one would be able to follow us!* I shout in my head. He climbs halfway back up the stairs to help my father and Zoe with Azeris, who looks like he must have been grazed by a baton, then screams something when my father grips his shoulders. *Liddick! What's happening!?* I call in my mind. His brows dart in as he turns to me and shakes his head.

Rip, it's too late…but we'll figure it out, OK? Listen to me, you were right the whole time—I wouldn't leave. I heard you…I saw you. You're the reason I got out of the Woods. I wouldn't leave you, all right? I won't leave!

It's not too late! Liddick, my dad can open the door. It's not too late! I think as he starts to fade into a brightening light along with everyone else. *It can't be too late,* I plead in my thoughts with whatever code or wind it is that controls things down here. I try to yell through the cube wall, but my throat clamps down like a vice on the words.

We'll figure out a way to follow you—I'll find a way—I'll meet you on the other side of the bridge, all right? Just get to Admin City, Rip, and I promise I'll find a way!

The light surges again, swallowing him just as Dez throws her arms around his neck. I can barely make out Zoe shielding her eyes next to Azeris before I blink back another flood of tears, and the light takes her too. I won't let my eyes close again when I see my father standing on the other side of Azeris because I know if I do, when I open them again, he'll also vanish. He nods to me slowly, and I press my hands against the clear wall, which is alive with the same kind of current I felt from the Vishan's NET.

I drop to my knees. Suddenly, it's too hard to stand. Arco's arms fold me back into him, and my eyes start to burn. I won't blink, though, not even when the light engulfs my father, who was holding out a hand to me and probably still is. I look over at the other cube to find Jax, but only see the last of him fading into the light. *Breathe...* I think, hoping he'll hear me somehow.

Dell leans on one of the seated console stations closest to us and winks at me when I meet his eyes. He raises two fingers to his forehead in a salute when he starts to disappear into the light, and my breath hitches when two guards in white suddenly grab his arms. A mass of fiery hair appears at his side as red dragon lady nails tap the console where he was sitting, and in the second I blink, those, too, are gone.

Can't wait to see what happens on the other side? Join the Tracy Korn's VIP Reader Group below for exclusive bonuses and release updates:

www.bit.ly.com/ElementsReaders

Visit The Elements Series on social media!

https//www.facebook.com/TheElementsBookSeries

http://twitter.com/ElementsSeries

http://elementsseries.tumblr.com

http://instagram.com/elementsseries

Acknowledgments

This story would not have been possible without the support of my tribe. Countless thanks to my beta readers for their patience, keen eyes, and honest feedback: Katie Casavan, Deb Commons, Sami Hensely, Trevor Kehoe, Chloe Laubert, Olive Laurence, Jim McClain, Margarita McClain, Kathleen Merritt, Chris Nance, Katelynn Pittman, Dominic Porter, Lorelei Porter, Kathy Plank, Tracy Siri, Anna "Iron Chef" Swenson, Nico Valentijn, and Robert White. To Jim Emmons and the University Park Barnes & Noble staff, you guys are amazing! Thank you so much for being as excited about this book as I am. To my students, their parents, my administrators, and my colleagues, thank you for being such enthusiastic supporters, team players, and overall awesome people. To my writing partner Ryan Bachtel (who could probably recite the last three chapters of this book by now), you have my undying gratitude for not only being willing to review passages for the zillionth time, but also for being enthusiastic and resourceful to the end. Your support and encouragement, and most of all your friendship are invaluable to me. Of course, Mom, thank you for your unwavering support in this and all things. I can't imagine who I would be without you. To my children, thank you for letting these characters move in with us for a while. They seem to work their way into everything from car conversations to summer cookouts, and it would be impossible for me to dedicate any time to them without your acceptance, support, and inspiration. I love you guys! To my husband, who has not only been my sounding board for plot arcs, but also my art director, photographer, designer, and overall partner in the creation of this story (not to mention the one with significantly more plot twists), thank you for jumping with me and for believing that I can do anything. Last but not least, thank you to all the readers who have become as big a part of The Elements Series universe as the characters themselves. With each of you, a whole new story experience begins…and that might just be the coolest thing ever.

About the Author

Tracy Korn's years of teaching high school English have convinced her that young people superheroes. Their resiliency, drive, and passion in making the world a better place inspired her character driven, high action and adventure YA fiction. When she's not writing/reading/teaching, she coaches FTC robotics and tries to learn everything she can about filmmaking and virtual reality game design.

Tracy holds Master's degrees from Indiana University in Secondary Education, in Language, Culture, and Literacy Education, and in English. She lives in Indiana with her husband and their two very own superheroes. Stay in touch at **www.TracyKorn.com**.

Facebook: **http://www.facebook.com/AuthorTracyKorn**
Twitter: **http://twitter.com/ElementsSeries**
Instagram: **http://instagram.com/tracy_korn**